Best Friends

It was time to go.

The enormity of the step she was about to take made Rachel catch her breath. She was barely sixteen and a half, just becoming an adult and with nothing secure ahead of her. Had she taken leave of her senses? No, she was being cowardly and that was ridiculous after all her careful planning. Put it down to nerves and once she was on the train, turned her back on Dundee, she would be all right.

Silently she said goodbye to her bedroom that had been hers for all her life. Tonight she would lay her head on a strange pillow.

Also by Nora Kay

A Woman of Spirit

About the author

Nora Kay was born in Northumberland but she and her husband and son lived for many years in Dundee. They now live in Aberdeen.

She wrote more than forty short stories and a newspaper serial before her first novel, *A Woman of Spirit* was published in 1994. *Best Friends* is her second novel.

Best Friends

Nora Kay

CORONET BOOKS
Hodder and Stoughton

First published in Great Britain in 1995 by Hodder and Stoughton
A division of Hodder Headline PLC
First published in paperback in 1995 by Hodder and Stoughton
A Coronet Paperback

10 9 8 7 6 5 4 3 2 1

British Library Cataloguing in Publication Data

Kay, Nora
Best Friends
I. Title
823 [F]

ISBN 0 340 61338 6

Printed and bound in Great Britain by
Cox & Wyman Ltd, Reading, Berkshire

Hodder and Stoughton
A division of Hodder Headline PLC
338 Euston Road
London NW1 3BH

For Bill and Raymond

Chapter One

All day long fog had hung over Dundee but as darkness fell it had thickened and was like an icy-cold wet blanket. In the eerie light of the gas lamps the cobblestones glistened black as George Donaldson carefully picked his way to avoid the deep ruts caused by the cart wheels. A tram loomed out of the fog then with a clanking noise disappeared into the haze like a phantom monster. Fifteen minutes took George Donaldson to his tenement home at 23 Blackford Street in the west end. Here most of the houses consisted of a room and kitchen but as befitted a foreman of the Tayside Jute Mills, number 23 boasted a kitchen with a bed recess, a good-sized, square-shaped room that his wife, Amelia, referred to as the parlour, a small bedroom, a tiny scullery and an inside lavatory.

In his late thirties George Donaldson was a tall, well-built man with unruly black curly hair and regular features. Anxious to reach home he took the stairs two at a time to the second landing and opening the door let himself in. After hanging up his coat and cap on a peg he opened the kitchen door and immediately felt the familiar pity and despair.

She was huddled in a chair beside the blackleaded range where a fire burned and crackled. To him just in from the damp chill of the November night the heat was overpowering but Amelia had drawn the plaid tighter around her thin shoulders as though the opening of the door had lowered the temperature. She was always cold, had forgotten what it was like to be warm, yet Amelia was only thirty years of age.

'George!' Her blue eyes opened wide in welcome and the smile she gave him was the same smile that had captivated him from that moment when her pert little hat had blown away on a frisky wind and he'd caught it before it reached a puddle of dirty water.

'That's a filthy night out there, typical November,' he said stooping to plant a kiss on her forehead.

'Look, Papa, I'm making toast,' the child said unnecessarily. Nine-year-old Rachel, her black curls tied up in a ribbon and wearing a clean white pinafore, was sitting in front of the fire flushed with the heat and with a thickly cut slice of bread on the end of the toasting fork.

'So I see and if you're not careful it's a burnt offering I'll be getting.'

'Oh!' Hastily pulling back the fork she looked at it in dismay. 'It's gone all black.'

He laughed and rumpled her hair. 'No, just nearly black; it's all right, lass. I'll scrape it but see and make a better job of the other side.'

The child had her mother's small, neat features but in all else she resembled her handsome father. One day she would be beautiful.

'How was your day, dear?'

'Much as usual but I sense a bit of unease in the jute trade and I'm not the only one.'

'But not serious?' she said alarmed.

'Not yet, love, but India could become a real threat and I'm thinking the bosses had better take heed.'

'Why?' Amelia had always shown an intelligent interest in the jute trade and George, knowing how it pleased her, kept her up-to-date.

'Unlimited cheap labour, that's why. But never mind that just now, what did Mary say?'

'As I expected. She'll be happy to come in to see to the house and cook the meals but said there was no charge for being a good neighbour.'

'Even so it's too much to expect.'

'That's what I told her and I made it clear that I wouldn't be able to call on her if she didn't accept payment.'

'So it's all settled?'

'Yes, George, it's settled. She'll stay with me until Rachel gets home from school.' She paused and leaned back. The effort of speech tired her but she added. 'I think she enjoys being needed and the wee extra will be a help.'

After arranging the toast on a plate the child carried it over to the table. 'Papa, everything's ready,' Rachel said importantly before moving quickly to the range where the meal prepared by Mary Rodgers was simmering gently in the big black pots. She had just taken the pot holder from its hook when George was over, a constraining hand grasping her arm and making her wince with pain.

'Don't you ever do that again, do you hear?' he said sharply, more sharply than he intended but she had given him a fright. The pots were heavy, far too heavy for her skinny arms and wrists.

Amelia saw Rachel struggling to hold back the tears and with a reproachful look at her husband said soothingly, 'Papa didn't mean to shout at you, dear, but he is right; you're too little to do that.'

'Sorry, pet, but you gave me a fright,' George said hugging her to him and for a few moments she leant into him feeling his strength.

She was so precious to them both and they worried about her but in different ways. George worried because Rachel seemed to have no friends of her own age and the blame for that he placed firmly at her mother's door. Amelia had been determined that her daughter was to be brought up properly and that meant talking nicely and being well-mannered, not like the children round about. They had broad Dundee accents, wore ill-fitting hand-me-downs and spoke of their parents as Ma and Da whereas Rachel had been taught to address hers as Mama and Papa. George, remembering his own school days, could well imagine what Rachel had to put up with. Children could be so cruel and to be labelled as stuck-up was torture to a sensitive child.

Rachel had been bewildered and hurt to be singled out for ridicule and she had even tried to have a playground language but that had been greeted with hoots of laughter and she'd quickly abandoned it. Instead she'd concentrated on her lessons, getting praise from Miss Melville and earning herself yet another name – teacher's pet.

Earlier in the day Amelia had managed to take a little beef tea and now sat watching her husband and child tucking into their plates of potato soup followed by Irish stew. Mary was a good plain cook and she would have been hugely pleased to see each plate wiped clean with the last of the toast.

'Amelia, lass, tell Mary that was champion,' George said as he scraped back his chair. Rolling up his sleeves he went over for the black kettle and half emptied the hot water into an enamel basin. Rachel carried the dishes into the scullery and George washed them. The nightly ritual had gone on for a long time and both were accomplished at their tasks. George finished the job, emptied the basin, dried his hands and sat down with the newspaper. Rachel carefully dried the dishes and put them away in the dresser before returning to the table to cover it with the dark red chenille cloth with its edging of bobbles.

Amelia knew that death was near but she wasn't afraid, only saddened to be leaving George and Rachel, particularly Rachel. Her blue eyes clouded with distress as she wondered what would happen to her darling child when she was no longer here. George, after a decent interval would remarry. He was still young with a man's needs and though the woman might be good for George, would she be good to Rachel? A cold-water chill went through her at the thought of Rachel with a stepmother.

She was trembling, getting herself into a state and she knew that it was bad for her. What if she slipped away tonight before she had a chance – George wouldn't like what she was going to ask of him but he was a man of his word and if she got his promise then she could die with an easy mind.

She kept looking at the clock; would nine o'clock, Rachel's bedtime, never come? It wasn't quite that but Amelia was so dreadfully tired that even another five minutes seemed like an eternity.

'Rachel, dear, bedtime.'

'It isn't, Mama, it's not nine o'clock yet,' Rachel sounded aggrieved.

'By the time you drink your milk it will be,' Amelia said with unaccustomed firmness.

George sensed that there was something. 'Do as you're told, Rachel,' he said in a voice that brooked no argument and Rachel, with the smallest of sighs, closed her book and got up. The cup of milk was warming on the range and Rachel took as long over drinking it as she dared then said her goodnights.

Closing the kitchen door she went along to her bedroom. The gas mantle was lit and Rachel knew how to turn it up to give her enough light to read but it was forbidden. Other children got walloped if they misbehaved, she knew that, but no one had ever lifted a hand to her. Instead, if she was found out it would be a raging or the withholding of some treat.

When had she last had a treat? Feeling hard done by, Rachel sat on the bed and wished her mother would hurry up and get well. It had been so long since she had had any fun, not one picnic all summer, not even one. She sighed, remembering those lovely sunny afternoons and the dainty sandwiches her mama used to make and her papa saying there wasn't a decent bite in them. Later on they would play hide-and-seek and once she had come across her mama and papa kissing behind the bushes, and feeling strangely embarrassed, she'd pretended she hadn't seen them. Slowly Rachel undressed and put on her warm white nightie. Last night she had been too tired to say her prayers so God might be angry with her – but if she explained. Kneeling beside the bed Rachel put her hands together and closed her eyes.

'I'm very sorry about last night, not saying my prayers, I mean, but I was too tired. Bless Mama and Papa and please God make Mama well again as quickly as you can and make me a good girl. Amen.'

In the kitchen Amelia had moved from the chair to the couch which George had dragged nearer to the heat. He adjusted the cushions and tucked the blanket round her. 'Comfortable?'

'Yes, George, thank you, I'm fine.' It wouldn't do to let him see just how exhausted she was or else he'd be putting her to bed like a baby.

'You don't look fine to me and you'd be a lot more comfortable lying down in bed.'

'No.' She patted the place beside her. 'Dearest, we have to talk.'

He sat down suddenly apprehensive. 'Something is troubling you, isn't it?'

'Yes, George, something is.' She paused to push a strand of fair hair from her eyes and he took the fine-boned hand and folded it in his. 'I'm not going to get better, dear, and we have to stop pretending.'

'Oh, God, Amelia, don't, just don't! I can't bear it, can't bear to think—' George's voice was low and rough with pain.

'Sh, darling, don't upset yourself, I'm not afraid of death – just – just—' her voice wavered, 'leaving you both is so difficult.' Her blue eyes, too large in the small face, were filled with love and sadness as she saw his distress. Her mind went back as it so often did these days to the hardship that marriage to George had meant, but then she would remember their lovemaking and a tender smile touched her lips. Their love had been an unleashing of passion that had brought undreamed of ecstasy but there were other times when she had had to fight the loneliness, times when her body ached with weariness and it was then that she regretted her marriage. But those times were rare and George never knew of them.

She struggled a bit before beginning, wondering where to start, the words she had prepared already forgotten.

'George, I want you to promise me something.'

'Anything.'

She moistened her lips. 'Sitting here day after day I've done a lot of thinking and I know now that I want Rachel to be told about her grandparents.'

There was a silence, a tightening of the lips, then with difficulty the words came out. 'You always said you'd never – do you want me to get in touch, tell them—?'

'About me?' She shook her head. 'No, it's too late for that but Rachel has a right to know and neither of us should deny her that.'

'Then tell her.'

'No, George, she's too young to understand.' Amelia looked at him imploringly. 'Wait until she's twelve and old enough to understand.'

'Very well, I'll tell the bairn when she's twelve.'

'Your promise on it, George.'

She saw the hesitation then the rueful smile. 'I'm not so sure you're doing the right thing but you have my word.'

'Thank you, darling.' Amelia knew only too well what it cost him to give that promise. 'It was a very long time ago, dear, people change, we all do.'

George wasn't so sure. 'She's my child too,' he found himself saying. 'Don't you trust me to look after her?'

'George, that was unworthy of you and this is difficult enough for me. Of course I trust you but you could remarry.' She put up her hand as he started to speak. 'You're young and you have a right to happiness with someone else but Rachel's position could be awkward.' Her voice had grown weaker. 'One last thing, that box—'

'Your secret hoard,' he said trying to infuse some lightness.

She smiled. 'No secret hoard as you very well know. The key has always been in the vase on the mantelpiece. George, do you remember how angry you were when I took in sewing?'

'And rightly so, a man likes to see himself as the provider.'

'You were always that and not a penny of that money did I spend. All of it went into that box for Rachel. Not that my efforts brought in much but it is something for her and the brooch I got for my eighteenth birthday. It's valuable, dear,' she said anxiously, 'so do make sure that the child takes great care of it.'

'Look at you, you're absolutely exhausted!' Her face was completely grey and she made no demur when he began unbuttoning her blouse then undressing her. The nightgown had been warming beside the fire and he slipped it over her head, then taking the almost weightless body in his arms laid her on the bed in the recess. She moved herself nearer the wall hoping George wouldn't be long in retiring. Her only comfort now was the warmth of his body next to hers.

Chapter Two

The year was 1926 and the January night was bitterly cold. The wind was rattling the window frames when George fell into an uneasy sleep. Amelia, lying beside him, gave the smallest of sighs and quietly left this world.

Through the wall Rachel wakened at her usual time. Why hadn't her Papa knocked to make sure she was awake? Not that she was in any hurry to leave the warm bed but she was sure it must be morning. Throwing back the bedclothes she was about to get up when the door opened and Mrs Rodgers came in. That in itself showed that something was wrong. Mrs Rodgers never came before nine o'clock.

'Don't get up, lass, stay there the now.'

'I can't, I'll be late for school,' Rachel protested.

'There'll be no school for you the day.' Mary Rodgers looked at the bewildered face framed by a mop of springy curls, and wondered how she was going to break it to the poor wee lamb. But there was no one else. George, that big strapping lad, had gone to pieces and Mary's feelings were a mixture of pity, anger and something bordering on contempt. A man had no right to display his grief so openly, he should be able to control it by her way of thinking.

Sitting herself on the narrow bed, her weight a test on the springs, Mary took Rachel's hands in her own work-roughened ones and looked into the young face. 'Now, lass, you've got to be brave.'

Rachel's eyes widened and a terrible fear gripped her. 'It's Mama, she's worse?"

'She's gone, Rachel,' Mary forced the words out, 'but peacefully and God be thanked for that.'

'Gone!' Rachel whispered not understanding then suddenly she did and would have wrenched herself free had Mary not held on to her firmly. 'Mama! Mama! Mama!' she screamed shrilly. Then the tears came, painful gulping sobs that racked the small body. Mary rocked her in her arms until the shuddering stopped and she too wept but silently for that brave lass who had tried so hard to fit into a life so different from the one she had known.

At the table, her porridge untouched, Rachel stared at her father in acute embarrassment. Seeing him like that with his eyes all red and swollen and tears pouring down his face was awful. Mary saw the expression on the child's face and quickly moved over to the dresser. She knew where the drink was kept, never a great deal of it but enough for an emergency or for an unexpected guest. Taking it on herself she poured a good measure of whisky into a glass, added water from the tap and without a word put it beside George.

Rachel saw it all and that was when the nine-year-old first began to suspect that it had been her gentle mama who had been the strong one.

Wearing her darkest dress for the occasion, Rachel was taken through to the front room to say goodbye to her mother. The parlour, as her mother had always referred to it, looked different. The big sideboard with its large mirror was the same. The marble clock still sat in the centre of a crocheted cover with a charging horse on either side. The straight-backed chairs, the spindly-legged table and a footstool were just as always and now she saw that it was the couch that made the difference. It had been moved to the middle of the floor. Fearfully and reluctantly Rachel approached the couch and looked down on the still, white face. Her papa took her hand and squeezed it in reassurance. What had she expected? Something dreadful, something terrifying and it wasn't like that at all. Her mama looked pretty and she was wearing her best nightie.

'She looks pretty,' Rachel whispered to her father.

'She's beautiful,' George said hoarsely. His hand touched the cold brow. 'Goodbye, my darling Amelia,' then gently he pushed Rachel forward. 'Say goodbye to your mama, Rachel.'

'Goodbye, Mama.'

Mary Rodgers was at the door, a deep frown on her plump face. She'd advised George against it. Surely it was better for the child to remember her mother as she had been, but he'd been adamant and of course it was none of her business.

Neighbours came to pay their respects, to commiserate with George and to cast sympathetic glances at the motherless lass. They were completely natural with George as they had never been with his wife. She had been a strange one and no mistake but the woman was gone and it didn't do to speak ill of the dead.

Amelia's funeral took place in the early afternoon and when the men returned from the cemetery the womenfolk were already sitting in the parlour talking in hushed voices. Mary Rodgers had taken charge of arrangements and tea was handed round to the women. There was a murmur of 'Ta, lass' as Rachel dutifully followed with the sandwiches. George was kept busy pouring whisky for the men and very soon voices grew louder as the talk became general.

Rachel sat apart eating a sandwich and feeling appalled as someone laughed at a remark. How could anyone laugh when her mama was dead! Even her papa had smiled and she wondered what her mama was thinking. It was different for those in heaven, they could see and hear everything or so she had been told. She remembered her mama saying that God even knew what we were thinking. Rachel wasn't too happy about that, sometimes she thought naughty things but you couldn't help what you were thinking. Funny that she couldn't cry now; she'd tried to make the tears come but they wouldn't. Now why should that be when she was still sad? When would they go away? Would Papa be angry if she slipped away to the kitchen and read her book? Better not, she didn't want Papa to be cross with her.

'I think we'd better get on our way,' Mrs McDonald from the close wheezed as she got to her feet. Others followed, but reluctantly, they had just been beginning to enjoy themselves. Knowing this Mary Rodgers hastened their departure then shooed Rachel to her bed. Rachel needed no encouragement and she was asleep as soon as her head touched the pillow.

The day after the funeral at Balgay Cemetery a man, with his head bowed and a child by his side, stood before the loosened ground gazing down at the already wilting flowers. Rachel wore a navy pleated skirt and white school blouse and over it a navy nap coat. On her head was a velour hat held on by elastic under the chin. The two were hand-in-hand and after a few minutes they turned away to squelch through the sodden ground. George would have preferred to walk home, he was in no hurry to return to an empty house, but it was a fair step, too far for Rachel so they joined the others waiting at the tram stop.

'Papa, we can ride on the top?'

'Aye, if you want.'

★ ★ ★

The piercing scream shattered the silence bringing George instantly awake. The dying embers of the fire gave a little light but even so he swore as he stubbed his big toe on the leg of the chair. Thankfully he'd left the gas on at a peek and as soon as he went in he turned it up. Rachel was sitting bolt upright, her blue eyes huge and terrified in a white face.

'You've been dreaming, that's all,' George said soothingly as he went to her.

'It wasn't – it wasn't a dream. Papa, it wasn't,' she said wildly. Her arms went round his neck so tight that he had to force her to loosen her grip.

'Look about you, Rachel. Go on, have a good look. There's absolutely nothing to be afraid of.'

'Not here,' she whispered. 'It's Mama, I saw her waken up and she can't get out.'

George felt an icy chill go through his body and lifting the child on to his knee he cuddled her to him then spoke slowly and distinctly.

'Rachel, your mama is dead. You know that and you know she isn't going to waken up. Like I said you've just been having a bad dream.'

But Rachel wasn't satisfied, the horror had been very real and it had been in Balgay Cemetery where her mama was under the ground. What if she wasn't dead at all, just sleeping? Papa could be wrong, grown-ups did make mistakes.

'Mrs Rodgers said Mama was sleeping and when she wakened up she'd be in heaven but what if she wakened up before she got to heaven?' Rachel said fearfully.

George cursed Mary Rodgers. Rachel had always been one for questions, not giving up until she was satisfied. And now what in God's name was he going to say? Amelia had been religious, a believer, she would have known what to say but religion had never played a big part in his life. Just so long as a man led a decent life that was all that could be expected and if there was such a place as heaven he felt that he had a reasonable chance of getting there. Now he sought for the unfamiliar words.

'Death isn't like sleeping, people just use that expression. What happens is the body dies and the soul rises to heaven.' There, he'd done quite well, George congratulated himself.

'Will Mama be with the angels?'

'Sure to be and she'll be happy, but mind she wouldn't like you carrying on like this.'

'I'm sorry,' her lips quivered. 'I wish, I wish, I wish she'd come back.'

'So do I, pet, but we've got to be brave,' George said bleakly. In truth he wondered how they would manage. 'Snuggle down and you'll soon be asleep.'

'I'm still frightened,' she clung to his sleeve. 'Please, please, Papa,' she implored, 'let me sleep with you, just this once.'

George shook his head then relented. It was probably the only way to get any sleep and there was precious little of the night left. 'And it will be just this once,' he warned.

Slipping off his knee, Rachel hurried through to the kitchen before he changed his mind. Clambering into the bed she quickly got below the bedclothes and moved over to the place where until a short time ago Amelia had slept.

There were no more nightmares and though Rachel begged to be allowed to sleep in the big bed George was deaf to her pleas and she returned to her own bedroom.

During those early difficult days Mary Rodgers was a tower of strength and came in daily to prepare meals and tidy up the house. Once long ago she had felt sorry for George's young bride. The lassie had never cooked a meal in her life, that was clear enough, and she knew next to nothing about keeping a house. But she'd been very willing to learn and a lasting friendship had developed. Now it was Amelia's daughter she took in hand. Gradually, not pushing her too much, she showed the motherless lass how to prepare and cook a plain appetising meal. Later would come the harder work, the black-leading of the range, the scrubbing and the washing and ironing that were all a part of a woman's lot.

The pain of loss was an excruciating agony for George and he felt no shame at showing his grief. Why shouldn't he weep for the wife he had adored? He wasn't a coward, he could stand physical suffering as well as the next man but this was different, this was so much worse.

He had been surprised by Rachel's behaviour. After the early bouts of weeping there had been no more tears and she had become quiet and composed. He had remarked on it to Mary Rodgers.

'The poor lass hasn't faced up to it yet.'

'You mean she hasn't fully taken it in?' George said worriedly.

'She understands well enough that her mother is dead but it's the finality of it that hasn't registered.'

'What can we do?'

'Nothing, she'll cope in her own way.' She paused. 'Pity she wasn't back at school. I know she has a nasty cough—'

'I only did what Dr Maxwell advised and he thought she needed another week at home.'

'You couldn't do anything else.' She sniffed. 'Supposed to know best but being with other bairns would have helped.'

'She'll be back on Monday and that should keep her mind off things,' George answered, but he was none too happy. Rachel was in no hurry to return. She had no friends.

In those early days Rachel had clung to the hope that God, who could make anything happen if He wanted to, would let her mama come back. It could be the way it was in a dream when you wakened up. But with God showing no sign of changing His mind hope faded and she became listless just picking at her food. The very thought of returning to school was making her physically sick.

In the playground a group of girls surrounded Rachel who wore a black band round her sleeve to show that she was in mourning, but there was none of the taunting and jeering that had once made her life a misery. Instead, in their clumsy way they were trying to offer sympathy but unable to find the words. Agnes Boyd, auburn-haired and freckled, and who had once jeered the most, offered Rachel a sticky toffee.

Rachel had been about to refuse, to say no, thank you, but something in the girl's face stopped her. There was almost a pleading for forgiveness and Rachel, wise beyond her years, recognised it.

'Ta,' she said only just holding back the 'thank you' which so readily came to her lips.

That night Rachel waited in a fever of impatience for her papa to get home from work. She couldn't wait to tell him.

'Half a minute, lass, let me get my coat off.'

Rachel returned to the kitchen, keeping her eye on the bubbling pots.

'I'm ready to listen, so what is it all about?' he said as he stuck a fork in the potatoes to test them. 'A wee bit hard yet, we'll give them another minute or two.' She was dancing from one foot to the other.

'I know it's because of Mama but everybody is nice to me and Agnes

Boyd gave me a toffee and she's always been the nastiest.'

Poor lass, George thought, so touchingly grateful for that show of friendship and it was the best thing that could have happened. It would help her get over Amelia's death.

'And Agnes Boyd said I could be her chum. I've never had a chum.'

'Well, that's just grand. Over to the table with you and get this while it's hot.'

Rachel sat down obediently and picked up her knife and fork but couldn't help her lips curving into a smile.

'God!' George thought, 'it had to be that Boyd family, and shuddered to think what Amelia would have said. A hovel, that was the only way to describe the Boyd home. Big, fat, lazy and uncouth, Eddie Boyd was unable to hold down a job for more than a few weeks and most of what he got went on drink. Poor Jenny, he thought with a pang of genuine sympathy, she'd been a right bonny lass with her thick auburn hair and her laughing eyes and there had been a time when he'd fancied her himself but then he'd found Amelia and after that no other lass existed for him. Worn out with too many pregnancies Jenny had seemed to give up the struggle. Folk said the house was never cleaned and the bairns were allowed to run wild, but the more charitable admitted that the older ones were fiercely protective of the wee ones and heaven help anyone who laid a finger on them.

'Miss Melville said Agnes had—' Rachel searched for the word and came out with it triumphantly – 'ability but said she's too lazy to do any work.'

'Her mother was a clever lass.'

Rachel looked astounded. 'You know Agnes's mother?'

'She was in my class at school but it's years since I spoke to her.'

'Papa—'

This was something he could change, George thought, and it would make life easier for the lass. 'Rachel, how about calling me Da? It's no disrespect to your mother but I've never felt comfortable with this papa and mama business.'

Rachel nodded happily. 'Yes, all right – Da,' she said experimentally and liking the sound of it, then she added thoughtfully, 'Why did Mama like it?'

'It was the way she was brought up.' He smiled ruefully remembering his own difficult days. 'I had to watch my ps and qs I can tell you.'

'What are ps and qs?'

'Watching your ways, watching your manners. I had to watch mine but when you love someone the way I loved your mother,' he swallowed the lump in his throat and went on quickly, 'you'd do anything to please them. There were times I can tell you when I felt a bit of an ass but och I managed no' bad.'

Rachel smiled, her eyes dancing, she loved it when her papa – no, her da – spoke to her like this, it made her feel grown-up.

'In the mill was a different story; there I was as broad Dundee as the rest.'

'Why did Mama never speak about the time when she was a little girl?'

George was silent for a while and Rachel wondered if she had said something wrong, but she wanted to know so badly.

'Why, Papa? Why, Da?' she corrected herself.

'It made her unhappy.'

'Because they are dead?'

He frowned. 'Away and warm some milk for yourself.'

Rachel got up reluctantly. She knew that there was to be no answer to her question.

It all came crowding back to George, the unanswered questions. Had Amelia been unhappy? She had never complained but then she wouldn't, it hadn't been her way, but in the secrecy of her own heart had she sometimes admitted to regrets? There had been times when she had thought herself unobserved and he'd glimpsed a sadness in her eyes and been afraid to question it, too afraid of the answer. Had her love for him been enough to compensate for all she had given up? He would never know or perhaps she had given it away at the end. There was that promise, a promise she knew had been dragged from him and one he had to honour when the time came. The bitterness of being rejected without even a chance to speak for himself had never left him, the sour taste was still in his mouth. He had never met them, never set eyes on them but the hatred remained.

Chapter Three

The school bell had just gone and Miss Melville's class of boys and girls were impatiently waiting to escape from the confines of the classroom. Their behaviour had been worse than usual and she kept them waiting a few minutes, any longer and she would be punishing herself, she decided.

'You may go. Quietly!' she shouted as a desk banged and there was a scuffle to get to the door. 'Not you, Rachel Donaldson,' her eyes swivelled round. 'I want you to stay behind.'

'Yes, miss.'

Agnes Boyd slipped across the room to Rachel, her eyes anxious.

'What does she want you for? What've you done?' she whispered.

'Nothing that I know of.'

'I'll wait.'

'No, don't. Honest I don't think it's trouble,' she whispered back. Rachel knew that Agnes had to hurry home to look after the youngest Boyd who had only weeks ago put in her appearance. A puny infant, she was surviving against all the odds and taking up room in that already overcrowded house.

'Agnes Boyd, don't you have a home to go to?'

'Yes, miss.' At the door Agnes turned her freckled face and stuck out her tongue at Miss Melville's back giving Rachel a hard time trying to keep her face straight.

At twelve, Rachel was tall for her age. Miss Melville had watched this child grow, could see in her the promise of beauty and a natural grace that set her apart from the others. She, who prided herself on having no favourites, was drawn to Rachel Donaldson. Her good manners and pleasant speaking voice had served to alienate her from her peers, yet she had suffered it all with a quiet dignity and it had taken her mother's death to break down the barriers. Miss Melville had seen it all and the extraordinary friendship that had developed between Rachel and Agnes

Boyd. Yet was it so extraordinary? she asked herself. They were both intelligent, indeed Agnes Boyd was by far the brightest girl in the class but mostly she was inattentive and not prepared to work.

'Bring over a chair for yourself and sit down.'

Rachel obeyed and sat with her hands in her lap. All of a sudden she found that she was nervous and began to worry her lower lip, a habit she had developed.

'Don't do that!' Miss Melville said sharply, then more kindly, 'I'm not going to bite your head off.'

Rachel smiled weakly.

Miss Melville, Miss Charlotte Melville, was a tall, sallow-faced woman in her late forties with fine light brown hair drawn severely back from her face and fixed in a neat bun at the back. Her best feature, her eyes, were slate-grey and showed a sharp intelligence.

'It's early days yet, Rachel, but have you given any thought to what you'll do when you leave school?'

'No, miss.'

'You are quite intelligent and you work hard.' She paused. 'I think you would make a good teacher.'

Rachel blushed scarlet. 'I – I'd love to teach,' she stammered, 'and I would work ever so hard, Miss Melville.'

'You'd have to,' her teacher said dryly. 'Teaching calls for dedication and more than average patience – much more,' she added. Then she smiled. 'Nevertheless, I can assure you that it is a very worthwhile and rewarding profession.'

Rachel didn't know if a comment was expected so she merely nodded.

'Your friends will have left school to take up whatever jobs are available whilst you will be staying on and studying hard.'

'I shouldn't mind that at all.'

'And if you do well, Rachel, it means going on to college to get the necessary qualifications and this, of course, would depend upon your father's willingness or indeed his ability, to keep you on at school.'

'I'll ask my father tonight, Miss Melville.' It would be all right, Rachel thought, her da would be proud of her if she became a teacher.

'You do that, talk it over, and now run along.' She pointed to the chair. 'Put that back before you go.'

Rachel's stomach was churning with excitement but she forced herself not to run and make a noise in the corridor. Once in the playground, though, she ran nimble as a mountain goat, her curls flying, her cheeks rosy, until she reached home with a painful stitch in her side.

The key was under the mat and she let herself in. For about a year she had hated coming into an empty house and Mrs Rodgers had tried to be there when she got in from school. Now it didn't trouble Rachel at all. She was becoming independent. Cooking was something she enjoyed and if she didn't like black-leading the grate – who in their right mind would – she tackled it and those other jobs that Mrs Rodgers could no longer manage.

Mary had tried to deny it but was forced to accept that her rheumaticky joints were making it difficult to do as much as she would have liked. Still Rachel was getting on, she was twelve and a fine wee housewife and for that she could take the credit.

Rachel was bursting to tell her da the unbelievable news but she would have to be patient. Her da was never home before half past six.

There was an apple tart ready for the oven and Mrs Rodgers had put out the potatoes for peeling. Once she had taken half the potato away with the skin but Mrs Rodgers had shown her how to take a thin paring. The potatoes seen to she began on the vegetables. Cutting up the meat she browned it in the pot the way she had been taught, turning it around with a spoon. Satisfied that it was all nicely browned she added the vegetables, a little boiling water and put on the lid. It would be ready in plenty of time.

Half past six came and went. The apple pie was ready, the meat tender and the potatoes soft. If only he would come. Constantly her eyes went to the clock and it was on seven before she heard his heavy step on the stairs, the door opening and shutting and then the minute or two it took to hang up his jacket in the lobby.

'That smells good, lass,' he said, coming into the kitchen and sitting down at the table.

'It's stew and Mrs Rodgers made an apple tart.' Rachel wished that her da would remember to wash his hands before he sat down at the table. In her mama's time he wouldn't have forgotten – he'd even change out of his heavy serge trousers but his standards were slipping.

'You're late, Da,' she said as she spooned the meat and vegetables on to the plate added a good helping of potatoes and carried it over.

'You're going to turn into a right wee nark if you're not careful,' he said and she could see that he was annoyed.

She bit her lip wishing she hadn't said that, particularly tonight, and bent her head to concentrate on filling her own plate. He was already eating his before she sat down and taking huge mouthfuls as if he were starving. Rachel deplored his table manners then was immediately ashamed. Her da worked hard and he still got up in the morning to see to the fire before he left for work.

Rachel was on the point of blurting it out but stopped herself. Timing could be important and her da had never approved of talking at the table preferring to concentrate on the food and enjoy what he was eating. Far better to wait until the table was cleared, the dishes away and he was relaxed.

Everything was done and Rachel sat down in the chair that had once been her mother's. Her throat felt dry and she felt a kind of despair. What if he laughed at the idea of her becoming a teacher, getting above herself he might say and could he afford it? Would he want to afford it?

'Da, Miss Melville made me stay behind.'

The newspaper dropped to the floor. 'And why would she do that? What have you been up to?'

'Nothing – it wasn't like that. She wanted to know if I'd like to be a teacher, to train to be one.'

His eyes opened wide. 'A teacher! She thinks my Rachel could become a teacher!' He was shaking his head and looking absolutely delighted.

'You're pleased then?' All the tension had gone and she felt gloriously happy.

'Pleased? 'Course I'm pleased, what a daft thing to ask. I'm pleased as Punch.' Then his face clouded. 'Your mother should have been here, she would have been that proud. Not a job, a profession, aye she would have liked that fine.'

'Da, I'd be a trainee teacher then only if they are satisfied—'

'Of course they'll be satisfied.'

'It means going to college to get qualifications. I wouldn't be earning money for a long time.'

'Never you mind about that, I've a bit put by and we'll manage.'

Rachel got up to fling her arms round his neck. 'Thank you, Da, and one day when I'm earning money I'll pay you back.'

'That you won't,' he said frowning. 'It's my privilege to see to my daughter's education.' He was almost preening himself.

★ ★ ★

Agnes caught up with Rachel before she reached the school gate.

'What did old Melly want?'

'I'll tell you if you keep it to yourself.'

'Cross my heart.'

'You're not a Catholic.'

'I can still cross my heart. Honest, Rachel, I won't tell.'

'Miss Melville said I could be a teacher when I leave school.'

'She never!'

'She did.'

'You're lucky,' Agnes said wistfully. 'It's the mill for me or a shop assistant or mebbe I'll be a skivvy in a big house, only way I'll see the inside of one.' She laughed but it had a hollow sound.

'I wish, oh I really do wish that we could both be teachers,' Rachel said generously then honesty forced her to add, 'You're clever and you're quicker than me in learning things.'

'Mebbe.' Agnes saw no point in denying what she knew to be the truth.

'You could be top of the class if you wanted.'

Rachel saw a hint of tears in the brown eyes, then saw her give an impatient shake of her head. 'Reading and writing is all I need, what use is the rest to me? I'd like fine to learn and I ken I'm clever, my ma was too but like she says too much learnin' just makes you discontented. Your ma made you talk posh and that's why old Melly likes you.'

'You could talk like me and it's not posh just proper. If you want I'd teach you.'

'No, ta, I dinnae need your help.' She drew herself up the way Miss Melville did. 'If it was my wish to speak properly then I should do so.'

It was so like their teacher, Agnes was a good mimic, that Rachel took a fit of the giggles. Agnes joined in and the pair of them went into the playground falling about laughing.

Groups of girls were whispering and giggling among themselves and Rachel had a vague idea of what they were discussing but she had no wish to join them. Agnes did but not very often. It was Agnes who had prepared Rachel for her monthlies and a good thing too, Rachel thought, or she might well have panicked.

'You don't like talking about it, do you?' Agnes asked, jerking her head towards the group.

Rachel shrugged.

'Better to know what it's all about,' Agnes said matter-of-factly, 'you'll have to know one day.'

'Know what?'

'What happens.'

'What does?'

'You mean you don't know?' Agnes said incredulously.

Rachel looked shamefaced. 'I haven't got a ma to tell me.'

'It wasn't my ma, it was my sister telt me. If you want to know I'll tell you.'

Rachel wanted to say no but curiosity got the better of her. 'All right, tell me then.'

Agnes whispered into her ear.

Rachel looked shocked. 'I don't believe a word of that. My parents would never have—'

'You daft thing, they must have or you wouldn't have got born.'

Rachel felt sick. 'If it's true I'm never going to get married.'

'You won't be getting married anyway,' Agnes said scornfully. 'You'll be a teacher and become an old maid like your precious Miss Melville.'

'And you, Agnes Boyd, are just jealous.'

Agnes's eyes were bleak. 'I know I'm jealous, I can't help it.' She paused, gulped and looked down, scraping the loose stones with her boot. 'When you're a teacher you won't want anything to do with me.'

'That is just not true, Agnes Boyd,' Rachel said indignantly, 'you're my best chum and you always will be.'

Agnes cheered up but all she said was, 'Mebbe aye, mebbe no.'

'Lass, stop that and come and sit down,' her father said irritably.

'I'm almost finished cleaning the brasses.'

'Leave them I said.'

'What's wrong, Da?'

'Nothing is wrong. Your mother wanted me to have a little talk with you when you came twelve.'

He looked uncomfortable and Rachel felt herself go hot and cold with embarrassment. 'A little talk.' Surely that could only mean one thing, that he was going to talk to her about 'those things' and she didn't want to hear about them, not from her da. Dropping her eyes to the floor she tried to close her ears to the sound of his voice.

'Your grandparents, your mother's parents, are alive.'

Rachel's head shot up. 'What? What did you say?'

'You have grandparents living.'

She stared at him as though he had taken leave of his senses. 'But they are dead, Mama said . . .'

'They were dead to your mother from the time they disowned her.'

Rachel moistened her lips. 'Why did they disown Mama?'

'She married me, that's why,' George said bitterly. 'An ignorant millhand was no match for the daughter of a mill owner. Aye, Rachel, a mill owner. Your grandfather is Albert Craig of the Craig Mills in Lochee.'

Rachel knew of the Craig Mills. Who didn't? It was one of the biggest in Dundee. She was too stunned to say anything, her mouth hung open and she stared fixedly at her father.

'Mebbe I should begin at the beginning.'

She nodded.

'It started with a wee hat.' He gave a short laugh. 'I saw the thing and caught it before it landed in a puddle. And there was I feeling right stupid I can tell you when these two lasses came hurrying over.'

'One of them was Mama? That's right, isn't it?'

She saw his face soften and a faraway look come into his eyes. 'That was the first time I saw your ma. She was a bonny wee thing and I knew right then that she was the lass for me.'

'What happened?' Rachel asked eagerly.

'Well, I handed over the hat and your ma thanked me real prettily then they walked away.'

'Don't stop.'

'I was still standing when Amelia turned round and smiled and I took that as a wee sign of encouragement and began to haunt the Esplanade in the hope of seeing her and unknown to me she was doing the same thing. To this day I don't know how she managed it.'

'But you met and fell in love?' Rachel said, her face pink with excitement.

'Your mother was just looking for a bit of excitement before she became officially betrothed to one of her own kind.'

'Da,' she said impatiently.

'I was for doing the right thing, the honourable thing, and asking for her hand in marriage but Amelia had other ideas. She wanted to prepare them, make it easier for me when we did meet, but I never met them, Rachel, never got beyond the gate.'

'Oh, Da,' Rachel said feeling anguish for what he must have suffered. He was a proud man and she could imagine how dreadful it must have been for him.

'That's the way it was, lass,' he said heavily. 'Your mother was kept a virtual prisoner and told that if she had anything more to do with me she'd be disowned. They thought threatening her with an impoverished future would bring her to her senses but they didn't know their daughter.'

'Why didn't you just go up to the house?'

'And get my marching orders from some maid or their snooty housekeeper?'

'But it wasn't fair, Da, you couldn't help falling in love.'

'Love, real love is a very a powerful emotion, lass, one day you'll mebbe find that out for yourself. It makes slaves of us all.'

'How did Mama and you get married?'

'Amelia got one of the maids to act as a go-between and get notes to me. When she knew her parents were to be away on a social visit she packed a couple of suitcases and I was waiting.'

Rachel looked at her da with a new respect. It had taken a lot of courage but for her mother it had been a great deal more to give up all she had known.

'Where did you go?'

'Your Aunt Gwen and Uncle John had a house in Dundee at that time and Amelia stayed with them until I arranged things. The pity was that Gwen, John and the bairns were booked to go to America. Gwen would have been a great help and God knows your mother needed all the help she could get. Still, there is always a way and Mary Rodgers—'

'Mama always said that Mrs Rodgers was a godsend.'

'That she was and still is.'

'Why did Mama not tell me this herself?'

'I don't know, lass. She didn't mean you to know at all but she must have changed her mind. She asked me, saying you were too young at nine.'

'You didn't want me to know, did you?'

'No, lass, it was the last thing I wanted, but a promise to a dying woman is something that has to be honoured. Anyway, you know now and that is an end to it.'

'They sound horrible,' Rachel said close to tears, 'and I never want anything to do with them.'

George looked relieved. 'That's what I hoped you'd say.'

'Where do they live, Da?' George's relief vanished.

'At that time they had a big house on the Esplanade but the family home is somewhere in Perthshire. Your mother got snippets of information now and again. Your great-grandfather died and as the only son, your grandfather inherited the estate.'

Rachel was having difficulty taking it in. 'Does Mama's father still work in Lochee?' She couldn't bring herself to say Grandpa.

'His kind don't work, lass. A manager is put in charge to see to things.'

'Da, have I any cousins on mama's side?'

'Quite possibly. She had an older sister, Maud, but that's all I can tell you. One more thing – that box on the shelf.' They both looked at the wooden box out of reach on the shelf.

'That's where Mama kept her papers.'

'Is that what she told you? You've a fine memory. Mebbe there's papers too but there is a brooch, one your mother got for her eighteenth birthday. It's valuable, Rachel, so you'll need to take great care of it. Then there is a little money, what your mother earned from her sewing, that's yours too.'

'Da, that'll help with college when I go,' Rachel said eagerly.

'No, it won't. It doesn't amount to much but it'll buy you something nice to wear when you're older. Or when you go off to college.'

'May I see the brooch?'

'Not the now.'

Chapter Four

Amelia had been dead for four years and though Rachel often thought of her mother, still shed a few tears into her pillow, the pain of loss had gone leaving just an aching longing for what might have been.

At thirteen Rachel was a head taller than Agnes and both girls were still best friends though Rachel had gone on to the academy. They were together for their Sabbath day stroll. Leaving Blackness Road they approached Victoria Park then on to Balgay Hill and climbed the flight of steps known locally as Jacob's Ladder and on to the top of the hill. They looked at the clear, sparkling water which gurgled through an opening to trickle over stones, smooth and whitened over the years, then cupping their hands drank noisily until their thirst was quenched. Summer was nearly over and the first of the leaves had fluttered from the trees to make a soft carpet. Agnes flopped down.

'I'm tired, let's have a rest.'

Rachel dropped down beside her and watched as Agnes took off her boots and wiggled her toes. 'These are pinching,' she said as she adjusted the piece of newspaper inside.

Rachel looked away feeling uncomfortable. She was always well-dressed and her boots never worn through.

'Agnes?'

'What?' She turned to Rachel screwing up her face against the sun.

'There is only me and I've outgrown some things. I mean I have school boots that are too small and if you or one of your sisters—' she stopped. 'Agnes, I'm not trying to—' she stopped again.

'If you mean am I too proud to accept them the answer is no. Like you said, you haven't anyone coming behind you and there's plenty of us.'

Rachel was relieved that Agnes was anything but offended.

'What about coming to my house tomorrow after school and I'll have things looked out?'

'What about your da? Will he mind you giving me—'

'No, why should he?'

They sat in a companionable silence broken by the drone of a bee as it circled them, then as Agnes waved a boot at it, circled once more as if in defiance, then disappeared. Putting her boots back on Agnes stood up and Rachel, who had been lying with her hands behind her head, slowly got up. Instead of using Jacob's Ladder for the return journey they slithered down the grass to the path below.

'Folk are talking about your da and Peggy McKenzie.'

'That blonde woman with the awful laugh? Don't be daft, Agnes, he just blethers to her when he's in for his tobacco.'

'That's enough to set tongues wagging around here,' Agnes said knowingly. 'My ma says Peggy's no spring chicken and your da is a good catch.'

A vague disquiet touched Rachel then she shrugged it off. Her da would never replace her mama with the likes of Peggy McKenzie. The woman was common and vulgar.

Agnes touched her arm. 'Don't worry about it, you can bet it's only wishful thinking on Peggy's part.'

'I'm not worried, not in the least.'

But she was and Rachel worried about it long after she and Agnes parted company, Agnes to her home in Spinner's Lane off the Hawkhill and Rachel to her home. Little things, unimportant at the time, were coming back. Like how she had always gone for her da's tobacco until a month or so ago. And her da going out after his meal and not coming back until late. With a little shudder she recalled the time, the one and only time, that she'd waited up for him and unable to stay awake he'd found her curled up in his chair. She recalled too how he'd shaken her roughly.

'What's this? Why are you no' in your bed?' he'd demanded to know and leaning over her she'd got a whiff of his breath and knew that he had been drinking.

'I – I thought you might want something when you got in.'

'You thought wrong then.' Then his voice softened. 'There's no need for you to stay up for me. You just get to your bed at the usual time, at your age you need your sleep.'

After that she'd gone to bed and had no idea of the time he got in.

Agnes was greatly impressed with Rachel's home and that visit remained in her memory for a long time. The contrast to her own home could not have been greater. In her house the table was never without a clutter but in Rachel's it was cleared and a cover spread over. Her eyes settled on the range.

'Would you look at that grate, you can nearly see yoursel' in it.'

Rachel preened herself. 'My own work I'll have you know. Mrs Rodgers used to do it but she's not so able.'

'You mean you do everything?'

'Just about. Da sees to the fire and fills the coal bucket.'

'Proper little housewife.'

'I've Mrs Rodgers to thank; she said I would need to learn to look after my da. Want to see the rest?' she said carelessly not wanting to appear to be showing off.

'Wouldn't mind.'

Rachel opened the door into the front room, no longer called the parlour, and Agnes walked in.

'Gawd, it's like a blinkin' palace. Is it ever used?'

'Not very often. My mother used to sit and sew at the window. She liked the view.'

Agnes joined her at the window. 'Marvellous view of the Law hill. My ma would like this. When I was wee she used to take us up the Law hill and point out the pencil shape of the mill chimneys and make us count them. Maybe I should take the wee ones up, let them play there instead of the gutter. Listen to me. I'm full of good ideas but that is as far as it ever gets.' She grinned and followed Rachel out.

'This is my bedroom.'

'A room all to yourself?'

'Who else is there?' Rachel asked amused.

'Daft thing to say wasn't it? With us it's three in a bed and as for the house itself, it's a midden. Not my ma's fault,' she said loyally, 'it's a' they bairns, she never gets a chance.'

Rachel bent down and hauled the kist over. Under protective paper were the clothes that had belonged to her mother, all carefully folded. Mrs Rodgers had advised George to keep them, the material was good, she said, and they could be altered for Rachel.

'There,' she said, handing Agnes a navy blue serge skirt. 'It's too short for me and that's a blouse you can wear with it. One of the buttons is hanging off but you can sew it on, can't you?'

'No bother. But are you absolutely sure, Rachel?' Agnes said holding the skirt against herself then doing the same with the blouse.

'Of course I'm sure. They are no good to me and there is no one I'd rather give them to.' She looked over at Agnes. 'My mother kept some of the clothes I had when I was little and I thought they would do for your wee sisters.'

'Oh, ta, my ma will be over the moon.'

Rachel put out two pairs of boots, one pair well worn but the other pair had been a bad buy. She should have made sure that she had plenty of room to allow for growth but instead she had chosen a pair that just fitted. She added some underwear and left Agnes to wrap up the bundle in an old blanket.

'Rachel, did you notice Maggie Thomson was wearing shoes with a cross-over strap?'

Rachel nodded. 'I liked them and my da's going to let me buy a pair.'

'You're dead lucky, do you know that?'

'In some ways I am, Agnes, Rachel said quietly, 'but remember you have a mother and I don't.'

Agnes didn't answer. She loved her mother but even so, given the chance she knew she would willingly change places with Rachel.

'Look at the time,' Agnes shrieked, 'I'll better go.' At the door she stopped and said almost shyly. 'Ta, Rachel, ta very much, you're a good chum to have.'

Chapter Five

Jenny Boyd was leaning against the door post, the sleeping infant in her arms when Agnes arrived out of breath and clutching her precious bundle.

'About time too! Where do you think you've been?'

'Rachel's.' She followed her mother into the house and dumped the bundle. 'She's given me things she's outgrown.'

'Oh, aye, let's have a look.' There was a commotion at the door. 'Here, put the bairn in the cot and careful she doesnae waken.' The four-year-old twins, Daisy and Rose, came in, their faces filthy and Rose's nose was running.

'A piece,' Daisy demanded for them both. She was the dominant twin and Rose happily followed where she led.

Poor Rose squirmed as her mother, with a quick and none too gentle twist of the rag, cleaned the runny nose then cut two slices of bread and spread them with jam. 'Here,' she said handing one to each, 'and bide outside till you're telt to come in.'

Agnes had undone the bundle and her mother picked up the navy blue skirt. 'This'll be just grand for Meg; with her workin' she needs something decent to wear.' Meg, at fourteen and the eldest, had started work in the baker's shop just round the corner. To compensate for the meagre wage she was given a bag of stale buns and once a week a bag of broken biscuits.

'No, Ma,' Agnes said firmly, 'that's not for our Meg, it's mine.'

'What you have is good enough for school.'

'If Rachel doesn't see me wearing it she won't give me anything else,' Agnes said cunningly.

'Och, well, in that case—'

'I'm having the skirt, the blouse and the best pair of boots and one of the petticoats. Meg can have the others and Rachel put in some things for the wee ones.'

Jenny Boyd picked up the garments and shook her head. 'Poor lass, she must have wanted another bairn to keep a' this.' A tender smile crossed her face. 'Right bonny things, I heard tell she was good with the needle. Ta, Agnes, lass, this'll be a grand help.' She got up off her knees and took the blanket. 'It's a double; it'll do on oor bed.'

'I'm hungry.'

'It's herrin the day, I'll away and fry ours and we can have it in peace.'

For so long Agnes had lived with squalor that she took the untidiness and dirt for granted but coming from Rachel's spotless house she looked about her with disgust. The smell of herring was strong but not unpleasant and Agnes's stomach was rumbling with hunger. The house was a midden just as she'd told Rachel. The room was both kitchen and her parents' bedroom, the baby's cot was next to the bed which hadn't been made. The table was cluttered with dirty dishes, a loaf of bread, a jar of jam which without the lid was attracting flies as was the pot of congealed gravy and there were various other items that should have had no place beside food. With a grimace of distaste Agnes removed the pot to the floor and cleared a space.

'You never bring that lass, Rachel, here.'

'And I'm not going to either, you should see her house.'

'Huh! Easy for them – her da's a gaffer.'

'He was at school with you, wasn't he?'

'Aye. Geordie Donaldson was a fine lad, I fancied him for a bit.' For a moment her face lit up and showed something of the attractive girl she had once been, but her hair, her once beautiful hair, hung in straggles.

'But you married Da,' Agnes said accusingly as her mother dished up the herrings.

'Mebbe he's no' much now but your da was good-lookin' in them days and anyway Geordie wed that stuck-up piece.'

'Rachel's going to be a teacher, she'll be going on to college and it's not fair, I'm the cleverest.' Agnes hated herself for sounding resentful. She was glad for Rachel, she had to keep telling herself that but she felt a hatred of the system that deprived her of the opportunity to better herself. Surely it should be ability that counted and not the ability to pay.

'Nothin' is fair in this world, Agnes, I'm surprised it's taken you so long to find that oot. The likes of us are trapped in poverty from the day we were born.'

'If Da drank less and worked harder we wouldn't be.' Agnes said greatly daring.

A flush of anger settled on her mother's face. 'You watch that tongue of yours, my lass. A man needs a drink.'

'A drink mebbe but not a bucketful. Why should he need it anyway?'

Jenny Boyd gave an unpleasant laugh. 'Helps him forget he's a failure. And as for you, Agnes, take my advice and get yoursel' a job in one o' they big hooses.' She paused to cut herself a slice of bread to clean her plate. 'Keep on the right side o' them that can dae ye a favour and mebbe you'll end up a cook or a hoosekeeper.'

Agnes, her good humour restored, grinned across at her mother. 'Mebbe I'll wed someone with money.'

'Be an auld man's darlin'?'

'Or better still a young ane's.'

'Dinnae expect him to put a ring on your finger or you'll be dafter than I thought.'

Just then the twins trailed in dirtier than ever. Eddie and Bobby, a year between them, were fighting as usual and eight-year-old Peter, in trousers several sizes too big for him, was yelling encouragement.

'In the lot of you,' Jenny Boyd bawled, separating the fighters and cuffing Peter's ear. 'Gawd, who would hae bairns?'

Agnes picked up the infant now known as Ruby, and cuddled her in her arms.

'You can't complain about this one, Ma, she's always good.'

'More's the pity, times I'd welcome a bit of temper.'

'Why?'

'I'm not sure, just a feeling.'

Jenny had noticed right away that this one was different and she was proved right. The youngest Boyd was a mongol and would need to be looked after all of her life.

Chapter Six

Swirls of sea mist chilled the very bones and there was the moist feel of snow in the air. On Hogmanay morning an overnight sprinkling, like a dusting of icing sugar, appeared on the distant Sidlaw Hills.

Dundee housewives were up early that morning cleaning the house from top to bottom and polishing the brasses until they shone. Carrying unfinished handwork into the New Year was said to be unlucky and the more superstitious had been known to unravel knitting that could not be completed in time rather than risk misfortune.

Rachel had been up since six and she was flushed and happy as she looked over to the table. Cooling on it were cakes of shortbread, scones and a light fruit cake. Mary Rodgers had baked a black bun and this, too, was on the table. Rachel didn't care for it, it was much too heavy for her taste, but to Mary the New Year was just not the New Year without a piece of black bun to go with a dram.

George had disappeared to the Tally-Ho to collect some bottles to add to those already in the cupboard. And that was his step she heard in the lobby.

'By, there's a right nip in the air,' he said putting down his purchases and blowing on his hands.

'Da, look at that!' Rachel said indicating the table.

'Looks grand, lass, a fair treat and I'm thinking you're going to make some man a fine wife one day. And now you can give me a hand by opening that dresser and I'll pack away this lot.'

'Who is coming anyway?' Rachel asked as she began handing him the bottles.

'Never know who might cross the door and I'd think shame if I was caught out.'

Now was the moment when he was in a good mood.

'Da, Agnes is getting to go into the town to see the New Year in and she's asked me if I'll be allowed.'

George stopped what he was doing. 'What, just the pair of you?'

'No. Davie Burnside and Tommy Allardyce are going.' She played her trump card. 'Davie said to tell you he'd see me right to the close. Please, Da, I'd like to go,' she pleaded.

George Donaldson looked into the young face pleading with him and sighed inwardly. His lass was growing up and he didn't know how much freedom she should be allowed. He knew that he would prefer to err by being overcautious, no doubt about that, but the lass had the right to some enjoyment. She worked hard at school and in the house and she was sensible.

'By all accounts Alex Burnside's son is a nice lad and I think I could trust him to look after you but that doesn't mean to say I'm entirely happy. To my way of thinking you are all too young to be gallivanting in the town.'

Rachel let out her breath in relief. 'Then I can go?'

'On one condition,' George said sternly. 'The four of you keep close together all the time. I know what I'm talking about, Rachel, I've been often enough in the High Street to bring in the year. It'll be crowded and a lot of them far gone on drink and it could get rough.'

'We'll keep together, Da.' She would have promised anything.

'Mind you do then and what time is this lad coming?'

'Half past ten, we've to meet Agnes and Tommy at the Pillars about eleven.'

George nodded. 'That's all right then but you're not to stay out too long.' He knew he was beginning to sound like an anxious mother hen but the responsibility for her safety was all his.

Rachel chose to ignore that. If they were to stay together she could hardly dictate and she didn't want to anyway. She felt the thrill of approaching independence, of what it was going to be like when she was grown-up and this, her first experience, she was going to enjoy.

'What about you, Da? What are you doing?'

'Oh, a few neighbours will drop in I wouldn't wonder. Don't worry about me, lass.' There was a small, satisfied smile on his face but Rachel was too busy thinking of the evening ahead to notice.

Davie Burnside looked a little self-conscious as he was shown into the kitchen. Just short of fourteen and a few months older than Rachel, Davie was tall and painfully thin. He had a pleasant, open face and a surprisingly firm chin for one so young. His hair was the colour of sand and thick and his eyes were blue-grey. He would likely broaden out and end up like his father, a tall, broad-shouldered man with thinning fair hair and a good, friendly manner for the grocer's shop which he owned. With three daughters and one son the shop would one day belong to Davie.

After school Davie served in the shop to relieve his mother and she saw to it that her son had smart clothes and coppers in his pocket. In a year or two the lasses would be looking hopefully in his direction for Davie Burnside would be a fine catch.

They were on their feet and George put his hand on Davie's shoulder.

'She's in your keeping, lad.'

'Don't worry, Mr Donaldson, I'll look after Rachel and bring her safely home.'

Rachel was beginning to feel distinctly annoyed. Agnes wouldn't have to put up with this, she thought resentfully.

At last they were outside and she could begin to enjoy herself.

She was wearing a warm skirt and a high-buttoned thick blouse and over it a lovely rose pink cloak that had belonged to her mother. Amelia had been small and some of her clothes already fitted Rachel.

'That's bonny and you look nice in it,' Davie said shyly as he touched the cloak.

'It was my mother's,' Rachel answered then wished she hadn't said it. All that was called for was 'thank you', she would have to learn how to accept a compliment.

With matching steps they walked smartly down Blackness Road, not saying a great deal but comfortable with each other. Once they reached the West Port Davie tucked her arm in his.

'Better hang on to me.'

Rachel thought that she'd better as they were swept along and into the Overgate where stalls were doing a roaring trade in gifts for first footing. All afternoon the city centre had been throbbing with excitement which intensified with the hour. For the revellers Dundee had much to offer, so many places of attraction.

Leaving the stalls Rachel and Davie wound their way to the Town House affectionately known as the Pillars. The impressive stone building was designed by William Adam in 1731 and consisted of a vaulted ground-floor arcade with shops and a bank. Above those were the council chambers, courts and jail. Enjoying a good position in the town centre made it a popular meeting place for Dundonians. It was somewhere to shelter from the rain and pass the time by looking at the various window displays. Rumours were about that the Pillars was to be demolished but few believed that it would actually happen.

Straining their eyes they soon picked out Agnes and Tommy from the noisy crowd congregated there.

'Look that's them yonder,' Davie said pulling Rachel with him just as Agnes waved and screamed their names across the length of the Pillars. There were shouts and laughter as the four friends got together. Tommy Allardyce cast an admiring glance at Rachel.

'You look like a princess in that pink thing.'

Rachel blushed. 'Don't be so daft.'

'When does it come to me?' Agnes whispered with a hopeful grin.

'Never. This is something I keep for ever, it was my mama's favourite.'

Agnes was always decently dressed and if she took it for granted that Rachel's outgrown clothes would continue to come her way, Rachel didn't mind. She knew that they eventually reached the younger Boyds and made things a little easier in that household. The three of them were warmly clad and Rachel just wished that the same could be said for Tommy Allardyce. The threadbare coat he wore would do little to keep out the cold but he was always clean and tidy. Like Agnes, Tommy knew poverty but unlike Jenny Boyd his widowed mother kept a clean house and took in other people's washing to help earn enough to feed and clothe her family.

The old year was slowly but steadily drawing to a close and a magical air of expectation was all around. Time seemed to stand still as silence fell for the last few moments. In the hush that was almost eerie, Rachel felt a lump in her throat and she could see that others were affected too, some were openly weeping. Amidst the joy of welcoming in the New Year there was sadness at seeing the old year slipping away and the feeling of anxiety of what the New Year might bring. Then cares were forgotten as the awaited signal, the firing of the time-gun, shattered the silence and was followed by the pealing of the bells from the Steeple and St Paul's.

As the sky filled with the coloured lights of rockets lighting up the heavens the crowd screamed its delight. Friends and strangers alike shook hands wishing one another a guid new year and four young people were unusually subdued as they gripped each other's hands in friendship. A year from now would they be together or would fate have sent them in other directions?

By one o'clock a tired but happy foursome was heading for home and in the early morning frost the boys' heavy boots rang hollowly as they left the crowds. At the West Port they parted company, Agnes and Tommy to go along the Hawkhill and Rachel and Davie into Brook Street and Blackness Road.

Rachel gave a deep sigh and yawned.

'Tired are you?'

'Just a bit but I wouldn't have missed it for the world.'

'My da said it's always a marvellous occasion when people are just happy to be together.'

'It was, it was very special but sad too. Did you think that, Davie?'

'Everybody gets emotional at the New Year and those with a good drink in them are the worst.'

They laughed as they saw two men trying to hold each other up as they struggled to keep their balance.

'Happy New Year,' Davie shouted across the road.

'An' you as weel and your bonny lass,' came the reply.

For one awful moment Rachel thought they were going to stagger across the road and she gripped Davie's arm.

'That was daft.'

'A harmless pair, Rachel.'

'How can you possibly know that?'

'Through the shop and watching my da. He knows the type itching for a fight and gets them out before it develops. That pair are just at the happy stage when everybody is a friend.'

'And the world a lovely place,' Rachel added softly.

'It is an' all, wouldn't you say?'

'Pretty good,' she agreed.

'Doesn't all that swotting—'

She stopped him. 'Davie, I'm happy to work hard and I'm grateful to my da for giving me the chance to stay on at school.' She paused. 'You could easily stay on for your certificate. Why don't you?'

'Waste of time, I'm going into the shop with my da.' He grinned. 'And he says as long as I can coont he's no' bothered by the rest.'

They had now reached her close and she was taken completely by surprise when he bent his head to touch his lips to hers in a feather-light kiss. Pushing him away she voiced her indignation.

'What did you have to go and do that for?'

'Just wanted to and anyway you're supposed to like it.'

'Well, I did not, Davie Burnside,' but Rachel wasn't telling the truth. That touch had sent a strange, tingling sensation through her body that both alarmed and delighted her.

'Never mind,' Davie said not in the least put out. 'I'll get better at it.'

She tried to hold back the giggle and put her hand over her mouth but it came out and Davie laughed with her. 'He's really nice,' Rachel thought as she moved inside the close.

'I'll wait until I hear the door shutting.'

Each landing had its own gaslight between the two doors but more often than not the gas wasn't lit or the mantle was broken but this was the New Year and negotiating the stairs in darkness after a few drams could be a risky business. No one wanted to be held responsible for a broken limb or worse, so tonight the close and stairs were well lit.

Even before she reached and opened the door Rachel could hear voices and laughter and was glad that her da had company. No one heard her until she opened the door of the front room and she immediately saw that they were neighbours from round about. Her da had seen her and was getting up from the horsehair sofa, his faced flushed with too much celebrating and then she saw with a sinking heart who was still on the horsehair sofa.

'Happy New Year, my own wee lass,' George Donaldson said, his whisky-warm breath on her face as he kissed her.

'Happy New Year, Da.'

'You enjoyed yoursel' and the lad brought you home?'

'It was great, really great, Da.'

With a hand not quite steady George was pouring out some ginger cordial.

'My Gawd, Geordie, you're no' on that stuff!'

'No, Bella, this is for the young lass.'

'Rachel, that's surely no' you wi' a lad already and you not turned fourteen?' Lizzie Skinner said as she helped herself to a piece of black bun. Her own two plain, ungainly daughters were eighteen and nineteen with no lad showing an interest in either.

'Of course not, Mrs Skinner,' Rachel said furious with herself for blushing, 'it was only Davie Burnside and – some of my friends.'

'Take my tip and hang in there,' Bob Skinner nodded knowingly, 'that shop is a wee gold mine and it'll go to the lad one day.'

'No wonder it's a gold mine,' Bella McDonald added her twopence worth, 'with the prices Alex Burnside charges. Fair disgrace that he gets away with it.'

'My lass has more to do than bother her head wi' lads. She's going to be a teacher,' George said proudly.

There was a moment's silence then a few mutterings. 'Would you credit that?' followed by words of congratulations.

'Only if I pass the examinations,' Rachel said desperately and wishing her father hadn't told them. It was so unlike him but then drink was loosening his tongue.

'Wouldn't you say that calls for drinks all round?' Bill Webster shouted after draining his glass. 'A toast to the lass.'

'If your hand is steadier than mine you can pour.'

'Steady as a rock,' Bill Webster declared as he lurched forward and earning himself a warning from his grim-faced wife. One small sherry hadn't sweetened the night for her.

Rachel did the round of the room shaking hands and suffering a kiss if there was no escape.

'You've missed Peggy,' her da said pushing her towards the horsehair sofa, 'I want my two lasses to be friends.'

Rachel didn't miss the look that passed between her da and Peggy McKenzie and as the implications of that look took shape she knew with a dreadful certainty that the relationship had gone far beyond friendship. If only she didn't dislike the woman so much, Rachel thought wretchedly, it wasn't just the loud, coarse laugh, it was more than that. She didn't trust her. To be fair, Rachel accepted that there would be some who found Peggy attractive – her da for one obviously – though how he could admire someone so different from her mama was hard to understand. Her mother had been small and dainty whereas Peggy was the big blousy type. She looked well in her black skirt and red blouse, though to the women present, the plunging neckline showed too much of the heavy bosom. George was called away and Peggy settled her hard eyes on Rachel.

'A happy New Year.'

'And to you,' Rachel answered as their hands touched briefly.

'Fancy you wantin' to be a teacher! Wonder Geordie didn't mention it afore now.'

'Why should he? If my father hadn't been drinking it wouldn't have come out at all. Incidentally, Peggy, my father's name is George, my mother wouldn't have dreamt of calling him Geordie.' They were speaking quietly but the others were too busy among themselves to pay attention.

'I'm sure your ma wouldn't.' The bold eyes flashed with anger mixed with amusement. 'Your ma thought herself a cut above the rest of us and tried to mould her man to her ways and Geordie being the big, soft lump he is did his best to please her.'

'That's a lie. How dare you say such a thing.'

Her father was back, his face wreathed in smiles. 'Now isn't that just grand, my two lasses getting acquainted,' he said drawing Rachel down with him on the sofa and putting an arm round each of them.

How much longer were they going to stay? Rachel wondered. It had gone three o'clock and still no sign of a move. Sheer determination to see Peggy off the premises kept her awake. And then just as she thought she would have to give in Bella McDonald heaved herself out of the chair.

'Would you folk take a look at the time?'

'My, it's fair flown but we'll hae to be like the beggars,' someone said.

'That was a rare night, Geordie.' Bella gave him a resounding kiss before he helped her on with her coat.

They were all on their feet, all except Peggy.

'Where is your coat, Peggy?'

'It's all right, Rachel, it's in the lobby with mine,' George answered for her.

Anxious to be given her rightful place, Rachel stood with her father at the door while the departing guests made their slow way down the stairs.

'Is Peggy waiting for you to take her home?'

'She won't be going for a while yet,' he said shutting the door and walking back to the front room. Peggy lived about ten minutes away in Ure Street where she shared two rooms with her invalid mother and Aunt Kate, her mother's unmarried sister.

'Geordie, I could murder a cup of tea.'

'I'll make it,' Rachel said.

They both turned almost as though they had forgotten her existence.

'It's bed for you, my lass.'

'Don't I get a cup of tea?'

'No, you do not. I said bed and I meant it.' If only he hadn't winked to Peggy, Rachel thought miserably. Perhaps it had been the look on her face but George added, 'I'll escort Peggy home just as soon as—'

'We have that cuppie,' Peggy finished for him. 'And I'll see your da hurries back home, Rachel, if it's staying in the house on your own that is worrying you.'

'It doesn't, not in the least,' Rachel said as she marched from the room still smarting from being treated like a little girl. She undressed, put on her nightgown, pulled the bedclothes over her head and slept the sleep of the dead.

At a quarter past eleven Rachel got up, opened the curtains and went through to the kitchen. Only when she was in there did the events of the previous night come crowding in. A little apprehensively she looked over to the recess. Surely she hadn't expected to see them in bed together? Of course not, she blushed at the very idea. Her da would never do anything like that, shame on her even to have considered it. But then drink did strange things to people, she mused, and her da had had a skinful. For a moment she looked at him lying in the middle of the big bed, his mouth slightly open and giving out an occasional snort. She had always thought of her da as handsome but he didn't look it now. His skin had coarsened and the black curly hair was peppered with grey. Would he still have aged if her mama had been alive or would love have kept him young-looking?

Suddenly she shivered, the fire hadn't been backed up and only the cold ashes remained. Quickly she returned to her room to dress in an old skirt and warm jumper. She would get the fire going, her da would be pleased to get up to a warm room and his breakfast all ready for him. He would see that she could look after him and that Peggy McKenzie wasn't necessary in his life.

Chapter Seven

The shrill sound of the hooter brought sighs of relief from the mill workers as they hastened to leave their looms. Soon they were a laughing, noisy crowd bursting through the gates to join shop assistants and others all homeward bound. Propping herself against the newsagent's window, Agnes Boyd watched them and bitterness rose like nausea in her throat.

With her brains she should be at the academy with Rachel and studying for a worthwhile career instead of being forced to leave school when she was still short of her fourteenth birthday. Agnes hated herself for being jealous and resentful of a friend, particularly a good friend like Rachel, but she couldn't help it. And each time she saw Rachel in the distinctive uniform of the academy it was like adding salt to the wound.

Standing there waiting for the crush of workers to pass, Agnes began to think about the unfairness of life. Why, she wondered, didn't God see to it that everyone got an equal chance? And that brought to mind the earnest, bespectacled minister who came twice in term-time to address the pupils in the school hall. Droning on in that ministerial voice that always made her want to laugh, he had stressed the importance of being good and obedient and showing fitting gratitude for all His loving kindness.

Yet how could He expect her to be grateful for being born into a family like the Boyds? She had even begun to have secret doubts about His existence but thoughts like that scared her too. Even if He hadn't been fair to her, and some others she could name, it was comforting to think of a God in heaven.

Something else was troubling her, the gulf between them was growing wider though Rachel strongly denied it. She needed Rachel, needed her chum's quiet good humour and her kindness to help forget the poverty and squalor of her own home.

Over and over again a slightly impatient Rachel had assured her that attending different schools would make no difference to that friendship but they were both aware of the lengthening silences when they were together. If she detected a change in their relationship Rachel put the blame on Agnes. More often than not she was short-tempered and forever moaning as though only she had problems.

Officially it was spring but hard to believe. The east wind was bitingly cold and the drawn faces of the passers-by were pinched and blue. Rachel reached the corner of Tay Street, the arranged meeting place, hoping to find Agnes already there but of course she wasn't, Agnes wasn't strong on punctuality. Stamping her feet to keep the circulation going Rachel waited almost ten minutes before Agnes put in an appearance.

'Come on, Agnes, this isn't good enough,' Rachel fumed, 'you're late as usual and it's perishing standing on this corner.'

'Sorry.'

'What's wrong? You've got a face on you like a wet Sunday.'

'So would you in my shoes. I start work on Monday.'

'How can you when you're not fourteen?'

'Easy enough. My ma went up to the school and told them I had a job if I could start straight away. Laying it on thick about needing the money and jobs being hard to come by.'

'That's true enough, Agnes, my da says the mill isn't taking on any weavers meantime.' Then seeing the misery on her friend's face she said gently, 'What kind of job?'

'Our Meg's got a living-in job as a maid in one of the big houses in the Broughty Ferry Road and I've to take over hers in that bloody baker's.'

Rachel was shocked. 'Agnes, you shouldn't swear, not that terrible word.'

'Why not? It's the way I feel and bloody is tame to what you'd hear in our house.' She gave a cheeky grin. 'Finish your education it would if you heard what my da and ma yell at each other.'

Rachel had no desire to further her education that way.

'You don't have to stick it for long, you can look for something better.'

'That's exactly what I mean to do. I'll do the same as Meg.'

'You don't like housework, Agnes.'

'Neither does Meg. Mind you, come to think about it how do we know— neither of us has had any experience. Only the minimum gets done in our house.'

Rachel had no answer to that.

'She's to share a room with another maid but she'll have her own bed and that must be bliss.'

Rachel nodded. She knew that Agnes had the twins, Daisy and Rose, sleeping beside her and that a damp bed was nothing unusual. Poor Agnes, she did have a lot to put up with and if she moaned who could blame her?

'Mind telling me where we're heading?'

'The Wellgate. We could have a look round Hunter's unless you have a better suggestion,' Agnes said.

'No, that's fine by me provided you behave yourself.'

'What do you mean by that?'

'As if you didn't know! And, Agnes,' Rachel said severely, 'it isn't fair to pretend you're going to buy something, have the assistant go to the trouble of bringing things out, then tell her it isn't quite what you were looking for.'

'No harm in it and it gives her something to do. I don't do it when they are busy.'

'Wait until someone does that to you when you're behind the counter.'

'In a baker's?' Agnes said scornfully.

'Yes, even in a baker's. I could come in, ask for half a dozen pancakes, four scones, four morning rolls, a loaf of bread and when you'd got them in bags ready to hand over, I'd tell you I've changed my mind.'

'Gawd! I'd murder you.'

'Then behave yourself in Hunter's and just by way of a change, Agnes Boyd, you can listen to my troubles.'

'Heavens! What have you got to moan about?'

'Plenty, as it happens. Honestly, Agnes, I'm sick of the sight of Peggy McKenzie, she's never away from our house.'

'Your da must invite her?'

'Her kind don't need an invitation.'

'Could be you are about to get a stepmama.'

'Don't joke about it, Agnes.'

Agnes wasn't but she kept silent and Rachel took a deep breath, relieved to be able to unburden herself even though Agnes was unlikely to be very sympathetic.

'That awful laugh of hers makes studying impossible.'

'Tell her to shut up.'

'Wish I could.'

'Well if you can't bring yourself to do that take your books elsewhere. No great problem I would have thought.'

'And freeze? The bedroom is like an ice box I'll have you know, and the front room fire is only on when we have visitors.'

'Not counting Peggy?'

'That one considers herself family.'

'My heart bleeds for you.'

'Thanks,' Rachel said huffily, 'I should have known better than expect sympathy from you.'

'What good is sympathy, but I'll give you some advice.'

Rachel shrugged but looked at her friend questioningly.

'Better learn to stick up for yourself because once Peggy gets the ring on her finger—'

'*If* she gets the ring on her finger.'

'Have it your own way, but Peggy knows you dislike her and she'll do her best to blacken you in your da's eyes.'

'What rubbish! What utter trash you do talk, Agnes Boyd. My da wouldn't believe any bad of me.' She stormed ahead with Agnes hurrying to keep up.

'I hope it does turn out to be rubbish, Rachel,' Agnes said in an unusually quiet voice.

Rachel slowed down and smiled. 'Sorry, Agnes, I know you mean well and I didn't mean to bite your head off. It's looking after the house and keeping up with a mountain of homework.'

'Not finding it too difficult are you?' Wasn't that her secret hope?

'No, not really but it's frustrating when you can't get a bit of peace and quiet. Stop here,' she said taking Agnes's arm. 'I want some barley sugar or something that lasts.'

Agnes made to stay outside. 'For goodness sake, Agnes, come on, Da gave me money for both of us.'

'Ta, tell him ta from me.'

The table was cluttered with books and Rachel was scribbling furiously.

'Rachel, take a break from that.'

'I can't, Da, I have to get this done before Peggy comes.'

'Why?'

'Why? You ask me why? Because, Da, I need peace and quiet and there is precious little of that when Peggy is around.'

'No need to be sarcastic.'

'It happens to be the truth and if it wasn't so cold I'd study in my bedroom.'

She saw his face harden. 'You'd better get used to Peggy being about the house.'

Rachel put down her pencil and stared at him. 'Da, are you trying to tell me something?' She could feel a sudden tension emanating from him as though he were steeling himself to get something off his chest.

'Yes, Rachel,' he said sitting forward in his chair, 'I do have something to tell you.'

'And I know what it is. You are going to marry her, aren't you? That is what you're trying to tell me.' She was almost shouting and sobbing at the same time.

'Yes, Rachel, I have asked Peggy to be my wife and she—'

'Accepted like a shot.' She saw his colour rise, saw the anger but she was uncaring. 'Oh, I heard the rumours but I wouldn't believe them and I almost quarrelled with Agnes.'

'I'm not bothered about rumours but I would have thought that my happiness would have meant something to you.'

'Da,' she was over and sitting in the chair the other side of the fire, 'of course it does. Of course I want your happiness.'

'Then give Peggy a chance, she's willing enough to be friends.'

What was the using of saying any more, Rachel thought dully.

'Your mother has been dead over four years, Rachel, and it is a lonely life.'

'You have me.'

He smiled and bent forward to pat her knee. 'You're a good lass and you've done wonders but in a few years you'll want to get married yourself.'

'Maybe, but, Da, it's just that – just that Mama was so different. I remember her you know,' she added.

'I know you do, lass, and I agree that Amelia and Peggy are very different.' He turned away so that she couldn't study his face. 'Let me tell you something, Rachel, and it is no disrespect to your mother. I'm comfortable with Peggy, we talk the same language, laugh at the same things, I can be myself.' Then turning back to her she saw the pleading in his face. 'Amelia will always have a place in my heart, nothing is going to change that, but remember this, only the deep love I had for your mother made me change into the person she wanted me to be. And trying to be something you're not can be a big strain.'

'More difficult for Mama though, wasn't it?' she said accusingly.

'Yes,' he said slowly, 'I was only too well aware of what Amelia had given up and trying to please her and keep her happy was what I was determined to do.'

They were both silent, both staring into the fire and thinking their own thoughts. George sighed and was the first to speak.

'Give Peggy a chance, Rachel, do that and I'll guarantee that the three of us will get along just fine.'

'I'll do my best,' Rachel promised but she had to steel herself when Peggy, a triumphant look on her face, went over to kiss her da on the mouth.

'Told Rachel our news, have you?'

'Yes, Peggy, Da told me,' Rachel said forcing a smile, 'Congratulations and just you be sure to make my da happy.'

'Och, I'll make him happy, never fear. Made for each other, aren't we, Geordie?' She winked and he laughed and something about that exchange sickened Rachel.

Peggy proved to be a reasonably good cook but admitted that she was hopeless at baking and Rachel was happy enough to see that the cake tins were filled. All-in-all the marriage that Rachel had dreaded made little difference to her. True there was that first embarrassment of going through to the kitchen and seeing them in bed together but mostly she managed to avoid the kitchen until they were both up.

Afterwards, Rachel was to remember it as the calm before the storm as Peggy, tiring of housework, pushed more and more of it on to a resentful and hostile stepdaughter.

Rachel had grown a lot in the last year and was already an inch taller than Peggy. Standing straight she faced up to her stepmother. Her dark curls reached to her shoulder and she had her hair tied back with a black, velvet ribbon that was almost invisible. Her skin was clear and healthy with a faint blush of colour and though her body was unformed and flat she carried herself well.

'Peggy, I am not going to black-lead that grate, I do enough already and you are supposed to be the housewife.' She almost added that she had tried hard enough for the position but stopped herself in time.

'Listen, you,' Peggy said in her roughest voice, 'don't you dare take that attitude with me. You'll do as I say, my lass, or your da's goin' to hear of it.'

'Your version of it anyway,' Rachel flung back. 'I know you're trying to turn my father against me but you won't succeed.'

'No? Want to bet on it?'

Rachel turned her back and went through to her bedroom. The cold, damp weather had seeped into the room but Rachel's anger kept her warm. For weeks now she had been irritated at the treatment she was receiving from Peggy when her da was absent and then the smiling show of friendship when the three of them were together. Collecting her books she put them beside the bed and pulled down the bedclothes. Then fully dressed apart from her shoes, she went into bed to do her studying.

Rachel stuck to her guns about the housework and continued to tidy her own bedroom, clear the breakfast table and wash the dishes before she left for school. The wash house was out at the back and shared by all the tenants. The Donaldsons were allocated Tuesdays and George had the boiler fire going before he left for work ready for Peggy to do the washing. If the weather was good the clothes were hung out to dry and Rachel got all the ironing done in the evening but if it rained the wet clothes were draped over the 'horse' and put in front of the fire and the ironing completed sometime the following day. The grate had long since lost its shine.

As part of her homework Rachel had three chapters of David Copperfield to read and putting up her feet she settled on the couch looking forward to an hour or two of uninterrupted reading. Peggy was visiting friends. Her da had just gone into the scullery to add water to the drink he had poured himself. When he came out he drank some of the whisky but instead of returning to his chair towered over her. Startled, Rachel looked up then got to her feet.

'Rachel, I want to talk to you.' He had never used that tone of voice to her before and she knew that it spelt trouble.

Though shaking inwardly Rachel faced him bravely. 'What has Peggy been saying? No, let me guess. I'm lazy and rude and never lift a finger to help. And, of course, you believe every word she says.'

'I do as it happens and get that defiant look off your face.' He stabbed his finger towards her. 'Peggy has bent over backwards to gain your friendship, I've heard her myself, and you've gone out of your way to be nasty.'

'That is simply not true, I have never been nasty but what you don't understand because you don't want to, is that Peggy is only pleasant to me when you are about.'

'She called you a spoilt brat.'

'She what?'

'A spoilt brat and that is exactly what you are. Since you've gone to that academy you've become impossible and I'm warning you, Rachel, I won't stand for Peggy being upset.'

Rachel could say nothing, only stare at her father. She felt choked but tears were the last thing she would allow herself.

As if regretting his harshness George's voice softened. 'I'm not asking much, lass, just for you to give Peggy her place and give her a hand with the housework.'

'I already do,' she managed to get out.

'A wee bit more wouldn't hurt.' His eyes went to the clock. 'I'll away and meet her and that'll give you time to think on what I've said.'

After he'd gone Rachel sat for a long time and wondered how she was going to stand it. But, of course, she had to while she was at school. And then it would be college and eventually independence. But those years between still had to be lived through.

Chapter Eight

The kitchen door was shut. Rachel had just come into the lobby but she could hear Peggy.

'Geordie, I tell you it's a monstrosity and I want rid of it and a fireplace put in.'

'But, Peggy—'

'Don't Peggy me, it's got to go. It's a devil to clean and that little madam doesn't like to get her hands dirty.'

'She used to—'

'Well, she doesn't now. And a lot of folk are getting rid of them. Jeannie Forbes for a start, Her man wasn't in favour at the beginning but now he's highly delighted.'

'It's kind of homely, Peggy, I'd miss it,' George said wistfully. 'And come to think about it how to you propose to do the cooking?' He brightened thinking he'd found a flaw in her argument.

'A gas stove or a cooker as Jeannie calls it.' Peggy was now in full flow. 'Their house is similar to this and they have a cooker in the scullery. Yon shelf would have to go but that's no problem.'

Rachel had come into the kitchen but they seemed unaware of her presence.

'Cost a tidy bit,' George said worriedly.

'Don't start that, Geordie, we can afford it and Jeannie says not having that fiend to clean has given her a new lease of life.'

Rachel bit her lip. She felt guilty, for in a way it was her fault. Before Peggy came she'd black-leaded the range and, filthy job though it was, she could have gone on doing it. And her da wanted to keep it that was clear enough. She wanted to please him.

'I like it too, Da, and I'd hate to see it go. Tell you what, if Peggy does the ironing I'll black-lead the grate.'

'You keep out of this,' Peggy said furiously, 'this is between Geordie and me and none of your business.'

George looked from his wife to his daughter and for a moment she saw approval, was sure of it, and believed that she had won a small victory until he turned away.

'Mebbe Peggy's right, lass, and we should move with the times.'

A glance at her stepmother and Rachel saw the satisfied smile on her face. Defeated, she bowed her head and closed her eyelids tightly and, as the tears welled up, she turned abruptly and went into the scullery. The dirty dishes were piled high, and keeping her face averted she went to pick up the black kettle, carried it through, filled the basin with the hot water then topped the kettle up with cold. They were still talking when she returned with the kettle but her ears were closed to them.

Washing the dishes wasn't a favourite occupation of Rachel's but she found the simple task therapeutic and her hands in the hot, soapy water was calming her. It was obvious that her opinion counted for nothing, she wasn't allowed any say and come to that her da's wishes didn't count for much either. It was easy to see that he was completely under Peggy's thumb and the worst part of all, Rachel thought, was the certain knowledge that he didn't mind. Her one time hero, her big, strong father was a weak man, a man who allowed a woman to rule his life. If she ever married she wouldn't want her husband giving in to her every whim. Maybe there was a lot to be said for being a teacher, staying single and keeping her independence.

At Peggy's insistence, George accompanied her to the Forbes's house to see how it looked with its modern fireplace and how the gas cooker fitted into the scullery. Jeannie and Danny Forbes spoke through each other in their eagerness to explain the working of this wonderful invention and George nodded dutifully but was far from convinced that it was a worthy successor to the old-fashioned range.

'Cannae go wrong with it, Geordie,' Danny said as he slapped George on the back. 'Mebbe takes a wee bit getting used to but once you get the hang of it you'd never go back to the auld way.'

'That's right, Geordie,' his wife nodded vigorously.

'What about baking?' Peggy asked in a subdued tone. She wouldn't admit it for the world but seeing the gas flames and hearing that peculiar hiss was terrifying her and she wondered how she was going to cope on her own.

'You'll get an instruction book and it tells you everything including the oven.' Then Jeannie admitted shamefacedly that she'd never used theirs. 'I just use the top for cooking and, well, that's what bakers' shops are for after all. Didn't know you baked, Peggy.' She made it sound like a fault.

'She doesn't,' George said, 'Rachel's a good wee hand with the baking though.'

'Och, she'll manage then,' Danny said as he turned away to get them seated round the fire with its tiled front instead of a fender. 'Rachel's a bright lass, she'll understand the instructions though I'll admit I couldnae mak' head nor tail of them but then that's them with their fancy words. Call a spade a spade I always say.'

Peggy was unusually silent as they walked home.

The men arrived with the gas cooker, carefully protected by cardboard and settled it in it position in the scullery. One of them seeing the worried look on Peggy's face tore a bit of the cardboard away and fished inside until he found the instruction book.

'They'll be up the morn to fit it in so I'd suggest you studied the book the night. My missus managed the cooking a treat but took a long time to get her baking to rise the way it did with the range oven, but then the daft besom never bothered reading the instructions.' He went away chortling to himself. Rachel, who had witnessed it all went to her bedroom to hide her amusement but Peggy followed.

'You'd better read that book, Rachel.'

'Why?'

'You're still goin' to do the bakin', aren't you?'

'I didn't think I would be allowed to touch the cooker.'

'Don't be so daft. Come on, I'll make us a cup of tea and you study the instructions so we can tell Geordie we've mastered it.'

Only too happy to encourage this show of friendship though well aware of the reason, Rachel read the instruction book from cover to cover and found it easy to follow.

'Seems simple enough, Peggy.'

'Still we'd better make the meals together for the first while.'

'When are they coming to take out the range?'

'Tuesday.'

'Then we've the range to fall back on – until Tuesday that is.'

'You're goin' to rub it in, aren't you?' Peggy said fiercely, 'Just because I want to improve things.'

For the first time Rachel felt a prick of sympathy for her stepmother.

'No, I'm not going to rub it in, in fact, I'm quite looking forward to using the oven.'

'You are?'

'Yes, I am. I'll have to adjust some of the timings so maybe we'll have a few flops to begin with.'

'Never mind,' Peggy said hastily as she filled up Rachel's cup, 'we can have something in reserve from the baker's.'

George, coming in at six thirty, saw the change, the absence of hostility and smiled. His two girls were getting on at last.

The fitter arrived in the early morning and by the time Rachel arrived home from school the cooker was in place, the scullery tidied and an excited Peggy going back and forward for yet another look at the brand new cooker.

'You know something, Peggy?'

'Oh, God, what now?'

'The pots, we'll have to buy lightweight ones.'

'Won't what we have do?' she said anxiously.

'For the time being, but getting through that thickness is a waste of heat. It's all in the instructions, didn't you read them.'

'No, I did not, I'm not much good at understanding—' she flushed, 'we weren't all at the academy, you know.'

Rachel felt like saying that it didn't need more than an elementary education to understand it but she was suddenly sorry for this flustered and worried woman.

'Don't worry, we'll manage.'

'That'll mean new pots and a new kettle. Gawd, Geordie's goin' tae go his dinger about that.'

'You don't have to splash out all at once.'

'No, that's right, we don't, do we?'

By the time the workmen arrived with their hammers and chisels, Peggy had mastered the top of the cooker and bought a lightweight kettle and two pots. Rachel had done her first batch of baking and declared herself well satisfied.

Then it began. The neighbours were up in arms about the noise as the dreadful hammering went on and on and the once pride and joy was dragged out and broken up. The dust was everywhere, on table and furniture and even finding its way into the other rooms. Peggy's blonde hair looked grey, her nostrils were filled with the fine dust making breathing difficult and her eyes felt gritty.

Rachel came home to find the close and stairs under a thick film of dust and wondered just what to expect. What met her eyes was so awful that her mouth hung open. Where the range had been wrenched out, bits of the wall had gone too and loose plaster covered the linoleum. Then she looked at Peggy, grey from head to foot and she began to giggle, the giggle gave way to laughter and soon she was helpless with mirth. After an indignant outburst, Peggy's laughter, that loud laughter that had once grated on Rachel, joined her own.

'Gawd, Rachel, what am I goin' to do? There's goin' to be murder done this night.'

Rachel was beginning to recover. 'Peggy, make a cup of tea, please, and I'd like a scone or something that isn't covered in dust.'

'Och, the food's all right, everything in the scullery is covered and I kept that door shut.'

'Good, I'll get out of my school uniform and get dug in here.'

'Thanks, lass.'

'We'd better set the table in the front room and have the meal there.'

'Just what I was thinkin'.'

Refreshed after the tea and the dust now reasonably settled, Rachel and Peggy set to with a will and sooner than they could have expected, they had the worst of the rubbish away. Old dusters made out of worn-out clothes took care of the dirt and dust and gradually the kitchen became ship-shape, all except the wall and that looked even uglier now that the furniture was back in place.

'Time we were gettin' somethin' ready for your da.'

'Yes, you're right.' Rachel lifted an exhausted face streaked with dirt. 'I feel absolutely filthy.'

'You look it and I'm an even bigger mess.'

'Any hot water?' Rachel asked.

'Oh, Gawd no, I'll have to fill the kettle and it takes a while to heat up.'

'Not if you turn it up full, the gas I mean.' She gave a sly look at her stepmother. 'One thing about the old range, there was always hot water.'

'Well, what is done is done and I'm not one to cry over spilt milk.'

'Neither am I,' Rachel smiled, 'We'll get used to it.'

'We'll have to,' Peggy said grimly.

George, forbidden the kitchen, had eaten his meal in the front room and was now in the kitchen and looking with horror and disbelief at the broken wall.

'God's truth, what have you done, Peggy?'

'Da, it isn't all that bad. The plasterers are coming tomorrow to even up the wall and then you'll get your nice new fire.'

'Nice new fire,' he said bitterly, 'I'm goin' out for a drink and don't expect me back this side of bedtime.'

'Peggy?' Rachel said uncertainly once the door banged after George.

'What?'

'May I make a suggestion?'

'If you think it'll help.'

'The coal bunker's about empty, isn't it?'

'Aye.'

'Get it filled and all the dirty jobs over at one time.'

'That's sensible. Wait till I mind,' she puckered her brow, 'I mind now, Jock comes this way tomorrow late afternoon. I'll get him to bring up four bags.'

The plasterers had filled the holes and evened the wall where it was bumpy. They arrived as George departed with his 'piece' to see him through the day. Rachel had her dinner 'piece' too and promised to come home smartly.

'Peggy, that's the coal cart turning the corner.'

'Go on then, catch him and tell him to bring up four bags and I'll get the bunker ready.' Raising the lid she reached down and brought to the surface a number of flue brushes and a shovel and placed them on the floor in front of the bunker. In a little while heavy footsteps sounded on the stairs. Rachel opened the door and it was pushed wider as Jock, a bag of coal on his back came into the kitchen, crossed to the bunker then let the bag slither from the leather protector which eased the pressure on his back. Then picking up the corners of the bag emptied it out to send coal dust flying in all directions.

'Think it'll take four, Jock?'

'Nae bother.'

A young lad, his face streaked with coal dust arrived with the second bag passing Jock as he went down for another. With the last bag in the lid would only half close. Peggy, not noticing, got out her purse.

After taking the money Jock began shaking his head. 'You've made a big mistake there, lass.'

'What are you talkin' about?'

'Getting' rid of your range. Best friend a man could have.'

She shot him a look that would have warned another to drop the subject. 'I'll have you know that Jeannie Forbes told me it was the best thing she ever did.'

He raised his eyebrows. 'What would you expect her to say? She's not goin' to admit her mistake and I'll tell you this, lass, and mind I see it first hand, many a wife thought it would make life easier and mebbe it has in one way but they wee fireplaces don't send out the same heat and a man feels at home with his old-fashioned range and a place to put up his feet.'

'Quite finished have you, Jock Thomson?'

'Aye, Peggy, I've had my say and now I'll be gettin' on my way, but mark my words this'll no' endear ye tae Geordie.'

She banged the door behind him and with a great show of energy and a few muttered oaths, arranged the coal so that eventually the lid went down properly. Wisely Rachel kept silent but was ready with a duster to clean the top and replace the wilting plant.

Peggy was smiling. A fire burned brightly and if the heat was less than that given out by the range it was enough to heat the small room. Geordie had done the redecorating and everything looked fresh and clean. The coal bucket had been replaced by a brass scuttle that shone with newness and the upheaval was now a distant memory as was the old range.

In the last few weeks the atmosphere in the house had improved but Peggy's swift changes of mood kept Rachel wary. What did concern her, though she said nothing, was the worry she saw in her da's face. Once she would have demanded to know what was wrong but now she held back. No longer did she feel close enough to her father to expect him to confide in her.

She was to find out very shortly and he arranged it for a time when they were alone.

'Come over here, Rachel, lass, and take Peggy's chair.'

Rachel welcomed the prospect of a comfortable chair and went over to sit on the chair that had once been hers. The kitchen had two easy chairs, sagging a bit, but comfortable nonetheless and four wooden, straight-backed chairs. These were pushed under the table and in the evenings one was brought out for Rachel to sit on. She would have welcomed a cushion but none was provided.

'You like it then?' her father said indicating the room.

'Yes, I do, you made a good job of the papering.'

'Aye, I think I could take some credit there.'

She could see he was pleased with what she had said. 'You don't miss the range after all?'

'For the first week or two mebbe I did, but I think Peggy was right and it gives her a bit less to do.'

He was working up to something and Rachel wondered what it could be.

'Cost a good bit more than I expected.'

'Is that why you've been looking worried?'

'Oh, I've been worried all right.' He was looking more uncomfortable than she had ever seen him. 'Worried, lass, because of what it will mean for you.'

'For me?' Rachel felt the blood drain from her face. 'I don't understand what has it got to do with me?'

'Obvious I would have thought.'

'You can't,' she whispered, 'you can't mean what I think you mean.'

He nodded. 'I'm sorry it's come to this.' He lifted the poker and poked away at the coal though it didn't need it, 'but the truth is it's goin' to cost too much to put you through college. I'm right sorry, lass, but that is the way it is.'

She was on her feet her eyes blazing with anger. 'You've a short, convenient memory, Da, haven't you? Who was to be so proud to have his daughter a teacher? And the money,' she said bitterly, 'not to worry my little head about it, was I, the bit you had put by would take care of that.'

'And so it would but—'

'But Peggy wanted a whole new kitchen, to be able to show off to her friends and that was more important than the promise you made to your daughter.' She shook her head in disbelief. 'At one time I thought you were the most marvellous da on earth and now,' he heard the cold contempt in her voice, 'I think you are just pathetic.' For a moment she thought that he was going to hit her with the poker, his hand was clenched round it, but he put it down.

'You watch that tongue of yours or you'll be shown the door. And I'm thinkin' the sooner you leave that academy and get yourself a job the better it will be for everybody.'

'That is just what I intend to do and don't worry I won't be a burden to you a moment longer than necessary.'

'You're not a burden, lass, and I'll forget those harsh words of yours.' The anger had left him and he looked at her with the beginning of a smile but Rachel stared back with eyes which were hard and unforgiving. Without another word she left him, got her coat and slammed the door after her.

Slipping her arms into it, Rachel walked the whole length of the road without noticing, registering nothing but the fact that she had teaching no longer as her goal. All her hard work had been for nothing, her dreams trampled upon, finished. The sour taste of bile rose in her throat and she thought she was to be physically sick. With some surprise she found herself in the Hawkhill and not far from the baker's shop where Agnes worked. It was Thursday, Agnes worked until eight, she would still be there. The shop was on the corner of the lane where the Boyd family lived. Rachel had never been in Winter's the baker's, there was no reason why she should shop in the Hawkhill. The Blackness Road shops were almost on the doorstep and most of them had well-maintained premises and windows that in the early part of the day showed an attractive selection of home-baking together with bought-in bread and fancy teabread. In contrast, this part of the Hawkhill was run down with peeling paint work and shabby doors too often kicked open. Rachel turned the knob and went in. There were no customers and if not bright and welcoming the inside of the shop was clean enough.

The woman had been staring out of the window but she turned to smile. Not much was left to sell but it was nice to get rid of what wouldn't keep until the next day.

'Yes?'

'Is Agnes in, please?'

The smile turned to a frown as she went into the back shop and reappeared with Agnes showing her surprise.

'Rachel, you look awful, is something wrong?'

She couldn't speak, just nodded.

'This is my friend, Rachel Donaldson,' Agnes said to her employer. The woman was small and stout and could be difficult at times but she'd come to rely on the Boyd family. In time the younger ones would take over from Agnes and rough though they were they had been brought up to be honest.

'Looks like your friend is upset so you can go but mind be here tomorrow mornin' on time,' she warned.

'Ta, Mrs Winter and I'll mebbe even manage to be early.'

'Cheeky devil,' she said, but she was smiling as Agnes took off her overall and collected her coat. Then she stopped them at the door with two dough-rings hastily picked up from a plate in the window. 'Nobody's goin' to come in now and the sugar will be gone afore long.'

'She's a besom but no' bad at times, like now,' Agnes said as she bit into a dough-ring. 'Come on, eat that up then tell me what's the matter.'

Rachel could have done without the dough-ring. It was heavy, not to her liking, but she managed to eat it.

The day had been warm but a coolish breeze had got up and both girls were glad of their coats. They walked to the Sinderins then sat down on the wooden bench that, during the day, was occupied by old men with nothing better to do than pass the time.

'Peggy's doing, of course?' Agnes said when Rachel had poured out her misery, hating herself for the leap of joy she felt. Rachel wasn't going to be a teacher after all, she would have to get an ordinary job and be no better than herself.

'No, my da's more at fault than Peggy.' A great sob burst from Rachel's throat. 'How could he, Agnes? How could he break his promise?'

'Maybe he'll change his mind.'

'No, absolutely not,' she choked. 'I gather it's going to take every penny he has to meet the bills and our Peggy has extravagant tastes.'

'In that case you've got to accept it, Rachel, and working yourself into a state won't help. Things'll go from bad to worse if you carry on like that.'

Rachel dried her eyes, swallowed and looked over at Agnes. 'I suppose you're right,' she said at last. 'And thanks for listening.'

'That's what chums are for. And if I sit here much longer I'll be frozen to the seat.' They both got up and parted in the Hawkhill, Rachel to walk up Peddie Street. She wasn't ready to go home yet.

Mary Rodgers was baking when the knock came and after wiping the flour from her hands went to see who her caller was.

'Rachel!' she exclaimed in surprise, 'Come away in, lass.'

Rachel was breathing hard and trying to get a grip on herself.

'Sit yoursel' down and not a word till you get a cup of tea into you.'

Rachel sat down and watched Mary Rodgers make the tea then rush to the oven to take out a sponge. It had risen beautifully and Mrs Rodgers sighed with relief.

'Just in time,' she said as she put it on the wire tray to cool then buttering two scones she put them on a plate beside Rachel and poured tea into both cups.

Rachel lifted the cup and took a sip. 'Thank you, Mrs Rodgers, but nothing to eat. The woman in Agnes's shop gave us a dough-ring.'

'Then you'll need that to put the taste away. I'm never that sure what goes on in the back o' they shops. Mebbe better not to know,' she added with a smile as Rachel bit into a scone.

'I've a nerve, haven't I? I haven't been near you in weeks and when I come it's to load you with my troubles.'

'Och, lass, I was young mysel' once and I'm only too happy that you come to see me. It's nice to be needed, you know,' she said wistfully.

Rachel took a deep breath. She'd done her crying and she wasn't going to do any more. 'I'm not getting to go to college. My da says he can't afford it.'

Mary nodded, her face showed nothing but there was a seething anger in her. Those two had a lot to answer for, she thought grimly, making the bairn suffer for their own extravagances. It wasn't just the money spent on the house, it was what went on drink. George Donaldson, to give him his due, had never been a heavy drinker but Peggy liked a drink and as George couldn't take her into the rougher public houses, it meant paying out more for a better class bar. She knew all this, it was common knowledge.

'And now you've to leave school and get a job?'

Rachel nodded miserably. 'I'm not going into the mill.'

'I thought they were payin' off?'

'So they are but Da would find a place for me but he can't force me to work there and I won't.'

'What do you have in mind, lass?' she said gently.

'Nothing, Mrs Rodgers, but I suppose it will have to be a shop, that's to say if I can even manage that,' she said bitterly.

Mary was silent for along time, her head bowed and Rachel wondered if she'd nodded off. Then the head went up.

'Mebbe this'll help and mebbe it won't.' She reached for a scone and nibbled at it. 'Lizzie Reid, you know, the dressmaker?'

'Yes, I know of her.'

'She's very busy and I hear tell that she is thinkin' of takin' on a lass to help. Needs to be good with a needle.' Her eyes held Rachel's. 'Your ma was neat with the stitches, did some fine work and I'm wonderin' if her daughter could mebbe learn to be a dressmaker.'

A genuine look of interest crossed Rachel's face. 'I'm quite good at sewing. We get one period a week and my teacher complimented me on my small even stitches.' Her face dropped as she remembered that there would be no more classes of any kind.

'Can't promise anythin', lass, but Lizzie's been a friend of mine for years and if she has no one in mind I'm thinkin' I could persuade her to take you.'

'You've been very good to me, Mrs Rodgers,' Rachel said with a catch in her voice, 'and I hope some day that I can repay you in some way.'

Mrs Rodgers looked embarrassed. 'Och, lass, your happiness is all I want, but mind if you do land the job it won't be all roses. Lizzie has a sharp tongue and she'll expect plenty for the pittance you'll get. But look at it this way, you'll be learnin' a trade and able to make your own clothes one day.' She smiled. 'If she shouts at you dinnae heed, Lizzie's bark is worse than her bite.'

'When will you ask her?'

'I'll take mysel' along there first thing the morn.'

Rachel was dry-eyed as she said goodbye to her teachers and the friends she had made. They were all sorry to see her go. The school had a shop where outgrown uniforms were sold to the more needy. Rachel handed hers in and pocketed the money. Saving had suddenly become important and the first seeds of a plan were taking root. Fifteen was too young but when she was sixteen she would make her move. Had her mother foreseen this when she left her daughter an address in Perthshire?

Chapter Nine

Before taking up her position as helper to Miss Lizzie Reid, Rachel had expected to be interviewed, but apparently Mrs Rodgers' recommendation had been enough. The house was in Ainslie Park, off the Perth Road, a respectable cul-de-sac of cottages with their doors giving directly on to the pavement. That it was a dressmaker's establishment no one would have guessed from the outside and only the number told Rachel that she had come to the right place.

Swallowing nervously, she knocked and it was immediately opened by a small, sharp-featured woman.

'Good morning, Miss Reid, I'm—'

'I know fine who you are, come in.'

Shutting the door she led Rachel through a narrow lobby and into a cluttered room. There was a fireplace against one wall and being September and still warm the black iron grate was filled with pink crêpe paper. Against another wall were a few bales of material and a box of odds and ends. The centre was taken up with a table on which was a large pair of scissors and tweed cloth in the process of being cut to a pattern. Nearby was a Singer sewing machine. Fine net curtains adorned the window and gave privacy without noticeably darkening the room.

Rachel stood awaiting instructions. For her first day she wore a dark blue skirt with box pleats and a pink-striped cotton blouse and over it a short beige jacket. The packet clutched in her hand held a cheese sandwich and an apple.

'Take your jacket off, you'll be bidin' I take it,' Miss Reid said with an attempt at humour.

Rachel smiled and some of her earlier nervousness disappeared. 'Where shall I put it?'

'Ben there,' she said pointing to a door that led directly into another. 'You'll find a nag on the back of the door.' Rachel went through to what was obviously the living quarters. She hung up her jacket and took a quick look round. The room was of similar size to its neighbour but there was a door off it which Rachel took to be a scullery. A tall dresser had a row of plates in the Willow pattern and on the table was a teapot hidden under a knitted cosy. After a brief hesitation Rachel put her 'piece' beside it.

'Now, lass,' her employer said as Rachel reappeared, 'you bring that chair over and we'll have a wee chat.' She was sitting at the sewing machine but turned to face Rachel. 'I'm particular, very particular, and with a reputation for good work I have to be.'

'I'm very neat, Miss Reid,' Rachel said quietly.

'I'm glad to hear it but I'll be the judge of that when I see your work.'

'Yes, of course,' Rachel murmured. She had been sitting on the edge of the chair but moved to a more comfortable position. The seat was cushioned and Rachel was relieved that she wouldn't have to sit on a hard chair all day. Its comfort was more than she was accustomed to at home.

'Most nights you'll be away at six but occasionally I have a rush order and I'd expect you to stay on and help.' She looked over at Rachel with her eyebrows raised.

'Yes, I'd be prepared to do that.'

'Good and for that there'd be a wee extra at the end of the week.' She paused. 'Did Mary Rodgers tell you to bring something to eat?'

'Yes, I left it through on the table, was that all right?'

She nodded. 'I supply the tea and I'm partial to a cuppie in the morning, mebbe in the afternoon too. Take it as I'm workin' so don't feel guilty. You'll see to that, Rachel, and if I need a bit of shoppin', you'll not mind goin' for a few messages, will you?'

'I'll be happy to.' Rachel was warming to this woman, who though she had a sharp voice didn't order but rather asked. She couldn't imagine Peggy saying 'you'll not mind'.

'Ever worked a sewing machine?'

'No.'

'Nothin' to it, I'll teach you when I've the time. Only use it for straight seams, the rest is done by hand, time-consuming but the result makes it well worthwhile. 'Here,' she said handing Rachel a piece of material. 'Let's see what you can do. Take up a half inch hem on that.'

This was work Rachel could do easily. After pinning then tacking, she threaded a needle with matching thread and began to sew. Meantime

Miss Reid had risen to pick up the scissors and finish the cutting out she had begun. They worked in silence until Rachel finished her task.

'Give it here.'

With growing confidence Rachel handed it over.

'Mmmm. Quite good but why rush the last bit? See,' she said putting the material in front of Rachel, 'compare your stitching at the beginning then at the end. Would you call that regular?'

Rachel bit her lip. 'No, it isn't. I'm sorry, shall I unpick it?'

'No, but I saw by your face that you thought you'd done a good job and I'm just showin' you that it doesn't meet my high standards. But don't look so worried, lass, I'm sure I'll make a dressmaker of you given time.' She smiled. 'Am I right in thinking that Mary Rodgers told you I'd be a tartar to work for?'

'No, Mrs Rodgers didn't, really she didn't.'

'What did she say?'

Rachel blushed and stayed silent.

'Come on tell me, I'm not easily offended.'

'All she said was that your bark is worse than your bite.'

'Oh, she did, did she? Well, mebbe she's right and mebbe she's wrong but you'll find out in time and now this won't do. I can't be talkin' here and me with all the work I've to get through.'

'What shall I do?'

'Put the kettle on. Through in the scullery, you'll find everythin' there if you use your eyes. Then I'll show you how to take up a skirt hem without the stitches showin' through.'

At ten past six, her first day's work over, Rachel felt contented as she walked home. The awful disappointment at having to leave school was easing and thanks to Mrs Rodgers she'd be learning something useful. That didn't mean she had forgiven her da, no, it would be a long time before she forgave him for breaking his promise.

Whenever possible Rachel and Agnes would spend part of Sunday together and if the weather turned out to be good they would often take a walk to Luigi's in Lochee High Street and treat themselves to an ice cream. Today it was warm with a pleasantly cool breeze and Agnes immediately suggested Luigi's.

'Fine by me,' Rachel said looking curiously at her friend and wondering what had brought the colour to her cheeks. Her eyes were dancing the way they did when she was bursting to tell something. But she wouldn't ask, she'd let Agnes come out with it in her own time.

They had reached Glenagnes Road and gone beyond the dairy before Agnes spoke of what was uppermost in her mind.

'I'm going into service, I'm getting Meg's job.'

'Meg's job? But where is she going?'

'Nowhere, just back home.'

'Back home?'

'Do you have to repeat everything I say? Yes, back home. For goodness sake, Rachel, think girl, why would she be sent home?'

'Oh, no! You don't mean—'

'Yes, I mean that my stupid sister has got herself into trouble or if you prefer someone has had his wicked way with her.'

'But that is awful and you shouldn't be joking about a thing like that.'

'I'm not joking but being miserable about it isn't going to help anyone.'

'What about whoever he is, isn't he going to marry her?'

'No chance of that and anyway she won't say who it is. Just stood there like a dummy with my ma and da yelling at her and my da threatening to throw her out if she wouldn't tell.'

'Would he do that?'

'No, he wouldn't.' She shook her head vigorously. 'Not that he has been much of a da to us but to give him his due he wouldn't throw any of us out no matter what we'd done.'

For all their rough ways, Rachel thought, the Boyds were a united family and for the first time in her life she felt the faintest touch of envy. Not having brothers or sisters hadn't troubled her before but now she wished that she had someone of her own, someone who cared what happened to her. Peggy didn't, she'd be only too happy to see the back of her stepdaughter and as for her da – Rachel pondered on that. Then she sighed, her da's life was bound up with Peggy, she was his wife after all and would always come first. His love for his daughter hadn't changed but she would have to learn to take a back seat.

'Sorry, Agnes, what were you saying/'

'Shows how much attention you've been paying; however, I shall repeat it. My ma thought she would get it out of Meg when they were alone but she's stopped asking now.'

'Maybe your sister just wants to protect whoever it is.'

'That would be like her.'

They walked in silence for a little while. 'What will happen to Meg's baby? Will she stay at home to look after it?'

'Good heavens, of course not. What's another bairn in our house,' Agnes said airily. 'My ma will look after it and like as not Meg will go back to the baker's shop. Mrs Winter wouldn't survive very well without the Boyds.'

They were in Lochee High Street and in sight of Luigi's café which being open on a Sunday did a brisk trade with hikers glad of a short break and a refreshment, and young children who pestered their parents for an ice-cream cone.

'Agnes, would you marry for money and security?'

'Like a shot and don't look so blooming superior and disapproving. If you'd known want you'd do the same.'

'I hope I wouldn't, Agnes. A marriage needs love if it is to be happy.'

'Granted a perfect marriage has both but how many perfect marriages are there?'

'I'm sure lots of people do marry for love and I know I'd rather stay single then enter into a loveless marriage.'

'Oh, I'd have to like the person but that's a far cry from being in love and a little pretence would keep everybody happy.'

'You are absolutely hopeless, Agnes Boyd.'

They were both laughing as they went into Luigi's and over to sit in one of the cubicles. The elderly Italian after finishing tying his blue striped apron came over for their order.

Agnes leaned her elbows on the mock-marble top. 'Two ice creams with raspberry sauce,' then added with a beaming smile, 'don't be sparing with the sauce.'

He turned away mumbling something they didn't hear.

'Any more news?' Rachel asked.

'Yes, nearly forgot to tell you, Tommy Allardyce is starting work in the Caledon Shipyard.'

'What to be doing?'

'Office work.'

'I am glad, he deserves to get on.'

'Apparently he is over the moon. The wage isn't much but he doesn't mind since the prospects are good.'

'Next time you see him tell him how delighted I am.'

'Can't say when that will be.'

'I forgot, I wasn't thinking, but we'll still be able to see each other, won't we?'

'I won't be a prisoner. Meg says I get one Sunday off in three and so many hours other days.'

'Broughty Ferry Road isn't that far. I can take a tram out to see you once in a while.'

'Certainly you may visit me in my mansion.'

'Servants' entrance, of course.'

Agnes gave her a strange smile. 'One day it's going to be different.'

In those moments Rachel believed it too.

The son of the proprietor placed the dishes in front of them. A liberal amount of raspberry sauce ran down the ice cream.

'That enough for you?' he asked with a cheeky grin.

'Lovely, thank you,' Rachel smiled.

'Just about,' Agnes grinned back as she lifted her spoon.

Conversation all but dried up as they let the ice cream linger in their mouths.

'That was delicious, you've got to hand it to Luigi, he knows how to make good ice cream,' Agnes said as she put down her spoon on the empty dish.

'Looks as though he agrees with you,' Rachel laughed as she pointed to a notice pinned on the wall behind Agnes. Agnes turned round. In bold print Luigi's customers were informed that the ice cream they were about to enjoy was the best in Dundee.

'Nothing like blowing your own trumpet,' Agnes laughed. With no one waiting for their seats they sat on and talked. 'You haven't said much about your job?'

'You haven't asked but now that you have I can tell you that I'm really enjoying it.'

'Told my ma about you landing the job. She'd heard it said that your Miss Reid is a pernickety wee besom.'

'If by that you mean particular, yes she is and it's because of that that people keep coming back to her. I can't complain; she's nice to me and I've learnt a lot in the short time I've been there.'

'Making your own clothes before long?'

Rachel laughed. 'Not for a very long time I'm afraid. I have to perfect each stage before I'm allowed to move on to the next.'

Agnes nodded her head but Rachel knew that she had been barely listening. It was a habit she'd developed of late that irritated Rachel.

'You'll let me know if I'm boring you,' she said sarcastically.

'What? Oh, you weren't, I heard all you said but I was thinking—' She looked apologetic and was immediately forgiven.

'Thinking about what?'

'About what I'm going to do with my life. Being a maid in Kerne House is just a beginning, the first rung of the ladder. And you can laugh if you like but I know, I just know that one day I'm going to be someone—'

'Who gives orders rather than takes them?'

'You don't believe me, do you?'

'On the contrary, Agnes, I can very easily picture you giving the orders.'

'Want to know how I'm going to go about it?'

'I'm all ears, I might get some tips.'

'You're in the wrong job for that. You see, Rachel, every chance I get I'm going to watch this family, study how the toffs behave, how they talk, their table manners, everything. I'll pick it up in no time. Mind you the Taylors are not gentry, the real gentry I mean, but it's a start.'

One moment Rachel wanted to laugh and then the next to cry. How improbable it all was but what would life be without our dreams, she thought.

'You're laughing inside, Rachel Donaldson, I can always tell with you.'

'No, I'm not. Maybe I think you're being a bit over ambitious but I know that if anyone can do it you can.'

'I've a long way to go before I'm a lady but you're halfway there already.'

'Flattery will get you nowhere.'

Agnes wasn't listening. 'It will mean going well away from Dundee and making a completely new start.'

'You'd drop me?'

'No, not you. I'd keep in touch but you would be the only one.'

'What about your family?'

'I'd have to drop them, be ruthless and cut myself free. Sounds awful I know but I'm intelligent enough to realise that they would always bring me down.'

'You wouldn't, Agnes. You couldn't.'

'I could, but I'm not all bad. Once I make a bit of money I'd send some home and I bet that would be more welcome than a visit from me.'

They got up, paid for their ices and left.

'Got over your disappointment?'

'About going to college? Had to.'

For a little while they walked in silence, the air was pleasantly warm for early spring and a lot of families were enjoying a Sunday stroll and stopping to talk to friends.

'Surely you've got some ambition, Rachel? I can't see you spending the rest of your life making clothes for other people.'

'Neither can I.'

'What do you want to do with your life?'

'I don't know, Agnes, but I've a feeling I'll be leaving Dundee too.'

Chapter Ten

The spring day was soft, with puffballs of cloud against a blue sky. It was the fourteenth day of April 1933 and the sixteenth birthday of Rachel Donaldson. She should have been happy, she had expected to be happy but instead she was choked with disappointment and a deep, deep hurt. How could he have forgotten? How could her father have forgotten her sixteenth birthday?

Getting up in the morning she had gone through to the kitchen, so sure that there would be something at her place on the table but there had been nothing and her da had already left for work. Peggy, never at her best in the morning, had grunted that there was porridge keeping hot but to go easy on the milk.

By evening Rachel was still not without hope. Maybe her da had wanted to wait and hand over whatever it was himself. She gave Peggy a hand with the meal and when her da came in looked at him expectantly. He smiled. It was an evening no different from any other, just the usual routine before the three of them sat down to eat.

'You'll mind we're goin' to the Club Rooms, Geordie, so don't you be sittin' yoursel' down with the paper.'

'Five minutes, surely?'

'Not even five minutes. There's to be some good turns tonight and I want a seat near the front. If I'm stuck at the back I won't hear or see what is goin' on.'

'All right! All right! I'll get mysel' ready in good time.'

Rachel watched with distaste as Peggy gobbled her food then pushed back the plate. 'I'll get mysel' washed and changed first then you can get in.' She went into the scullery and shut the door.

'Had a good day, lass?' George looked across the table.

'Yes.'

'You're likin' the job?'

'It's all right.' She wasn't going to give him the satisfaction of saying that she liked it. Anyway it came a poor second to what she had expected to be doing.

'Geordie!' She was towelling herself as she popped her head out. 'That's me finished.'

'I'll be there in a minute. If I bolted food the way you do I'd suffer for it all night.' He smiled to Rachel and shook his head. But in a few minutes he was obeying instructions and taking his turn in the scullery.

They were gone. The house was silent. Tight-lipped Rachel went about the tasks left to her. She cleared the table, washed and dried the dishes and put them away in the dresser. To think she could have been out tonight enjoying herself. David Burnside had been a bit put out when she'd declined his invitation.

'There's a good picture on at La Scala.'

'I know and I'd love to see it, Davie, but I can't, not tonight.'

'Why not?' he'd asked suspiciously.

'I'm sorry, Davie, I just can't that's all.'

'Or don't want to?'

'That's not true but if you want to think it then you do just that.'

They had almost quarrelled and now she wondered why she hadn't told him the truth. That it was her birthday and she thought her da might have a surprise evening ahead. Instead of which he had gone off to the Club Rooms with Peggy. Not so long ago her da wouldn't have gone near the Club, not his kind of entertainment, he used to say. Changed days.

Plans that had been little more than dreams began to take shape. She was sixteen, a time to put childhood behind her and take her place in an adult world. Her secret hoard as she termed it, was on the floor of her wardrobe in her bedroom. Going there she took out the rosewood box that had once belonged to her mother. Until Peggy had started coming about the house the box had been on a shelf and out of reach, but Rachel had removed it to her bedroom. She couldn't bear the thought of Peggy touching anything that had belonged to her mother. If her da had noticed he'd kept quiet about it.

The key was in the drawer below her underwear and she went to get it. Once it had been stiff to turn but not now that it was opened regularly for the little she managed to save each week. Peggy frequently complained of the pittance she got from Rachel for her keep but in this her da had been firm. It was enough, he said, with the work the lass did about the house.

Inside the rosewood box was a small velvet jewel case and nestling in the white satin the brooch that had once belonged to her mother, a gift for her eighteenth birthday. Gently she lifted it out and held it up to the light as she always did. She loved the way the stones sparkled and she'd asked her da what they were but he couldn't tell her. All he said was that the brooch was valuable. Next she touched the heavy brown envelope addressed to 'Rachel'. The familiar lump was in her throat as she thought of her darling mama taking in sewing not to make life easier for herself but to have something to leave to her daughter. That money had never been touched, only added to. The knowledge that she had something of her very own was comforting.

Finally the folded sheet of notepaper, no need to look at it. Rachel knew it by heart. In her mother's neat script was a name and address. Two names. Albert and Katherine Craig, Duncairn House, Hillend, Perthshire. Her grandparents. Were they still alive? And if so did they know that their daughter, Amelia, was dead? Would they care? After all, she had been dead to them since that day so long ago when she had left her comfortable home to marry the man she loved. The man she loved. Rachel thought of her da as he was today. Would Amelia still love the man George was today? But that was unkind, unfair. Her da had made himself into the man her mama had wanted him to be – and was there greater love than that?

Her da wouldn't like it but it wouldn't stop her. One day, she promised herself, she would go to Duncairn House, announce herself as Amelia's daughter and see how she was received.

It was a full week later and possibly something in the paper had brought it to mind. Whatever it was, George dropped the paper and all but yelled at Rachel.

'You let me forget your birthday, you deliberately didn't remind me. Your sixteenth birthday.' He looked shattered and angry.

'It doesn't matter, Da,' Rachel said quietly.

'Of course it matters. You could have reminded me, you knew that I'd forgotten. If you wanted me to feel rotten then you've succeeded.'

'For Gawd's sake, what's all the fuss about? I'm only too happy to forget mine.'

But for once George was ignoring his wife.

'Of course I was disappointed, but as Peggy says it's only a birthday.'

'A very special one it should have been and now it's belated birthday greetings.' His anger never lasted long and he was taking the money out of his trouser pocket and counting it. 'Peggy, you got half a crown you could lend me?'

'No, I haven't.'

'Come on, woman, you'll get it back.'

'I'd better,' she muttered as she went for her handbag and threw half a crown on to the table.'

'There you are, lass, ten shillings should buy you something?'

'Thanks, Da.'

'Don't I get a kiss?'

She dropped a kiss on his brow and his hands went out to grip hers.

'Forgiven, am I?'

'Of course.'

'Don't you dare let me forget the next.'

'There'll be a few changes by then,' Peggy said looking pointedly at Rachel. 'Could be that lad of yours will have popped the question.'

'There's nothing like that between David Burnside and me,' Rachel said hotly.

'Then have the decency to tell the lad instead of stringing him along.'

Rachel's mouth tightened. 'Peggy, will you kindly mind your own business.'

'As long as you're under this roof you are my business.'

'Then the sooner I'm away the better.'

'That is enough, you two,' George thundered. 'It's my house and what I say goes, so you can both think on that.'

Rachel added the ten shillings to her savings, glad now that her da had given her money rather than bought her a gift. Every little was needed and ten shillings was a big help.

Was Peggy right? Was she being unfair to David Burnside? The trouble with childhood sweethearts, she thought, was that you grew away from them or one of you did. A few short weeks ago Davie had seemed all she had ever wanted. Compared to the other boys, she saw him as better looking and always polite and she'd been proud to be seen with him. Holding hands and the goodnight kiss had been pleasant, more than pleasant, enjoyable, but the boy was no longer a boy. Suddenly he was a grown man and when he had pressed himself against her she hadn't liked it and wriggled free. His face had darkened and he'd muttered something she hadn't caught before leaving her abruptly at her close.

So much for David Burnside. Her thoughts flitted to Miss Reid. Was the woman unwell? That something was wrong was obvious to Rachel. A few weeks ago she had kept the finer work for her own nimble fingers telling Rachel that it would be a long while yet before that kind of work came her way. Yet here she was getting it to do and having to stop that delicate work to thread a needle for Miss Reid.

'Sorry, lass, you'll need to thread that for me, these specs of mine are leavin' me and I'll have to see about getting another pair.'

She had come back from the optician's strangely quiet and withdrawn and had snapped at Rachel when she enquired as to how she had got on.

'Well enough,' then regretting her abruptness. 'I'm just in a bad humour, all those tests just a waste of time when all I need is a stronger pair of glasses.'

A month later Miss Reid seemed ill-at-ease as Rachel prepared to start work.

'Rachel, sit down, lass, I've something to tell you and it's not easy.'

'I thought you didn't look very well, Miss Reid.'

'Oh, my general health is fine. It's my eyes, Rachel, I've tried to deny the truth making out that stronger specs was the answer and knowing fine that it was more than that. No, no, lass,' she hastened on when she saw Rachel's expression, 'there is little danger of me goin' blind but my eyesight is deteriorating and I won't see well enough for this kind of work.'

'Miss Reid, let me do the fine work, I promise I'll be very careful.'

She shook her head sadly. 'You're a good lass and it was a lucky day for me when Mary Rodgers recommended you but I'm afraid my days as a dressmaker are all but over. In fact I've stopped taking orders and we'll just finish what is on hand.'

Rachel couldn't hide her dismay. 'That means—'

'The end of the business. My sister in Edinburgh, she's widowed and on her own, wants me to share her home and that's what I've decided to do. Mind you, we haven't always got on but we're older now and I'll say this for mysel', I've a sharp tongue but I never carry grievances.'

'I'll miss you, you've been good to me.'

'I'll miss it all, it's been a way of life to me and I'll have many a quiet greet I've no doubt, but you are young, Rachel, your whole life stretches before you. I won't be finishing off here for six or seven weeks but I wanted you to be the first to know. Needless to say I'll be glad, very, very glad to have you stay on but you must feel free to go whenever you want. You'll get a good reference, the best, and now, lass, that's been quite an ordeal and I think we both need a cuppie.'

For the remainder of the day Rachel worked steadily, taking care to keep her stitches even though she doubted that Miss Reid would notice the occasional stitch larger than its neighbour. All the time her mind was working. What good would a reference be if there were no jobs? And jobs like hers would be difficult to come by. Perhaps she should have done a commercial course and gone into an office. Too late now to be taken on as an office junior. Employers wanted cheap labour and a fourteen-year-old could be trained to do the job.

'You are worryin', Rachel,' Miss Reid said as she looked up from the sleeve she was pinning into a blouse.

'Just thinking.'

'When you come to my age you begin to see that all things in life have a meaning. What looks bleak just now, Rachel, may just be the turning point in your life. Added to which you are a bonny lass and I have no doubt more than one lad has his eye on you.' She got up as a customer arrived but something she had said stayed with Rachel. A turning point in her life – perhaps it was.

Miss Reid didn't ask but she showed her relief when Rachel offered to stay on to help finish an evening gown and an afternoon dress for Mrs Mildred Lyall-Black who was fussing about the garments not being ready on the promised day.

'Never liked that one, Rachel, but she's been a good customer and one who paid her bills promptly. It's that haughty manner of hers I can't be doin' with. Not the top drawer you know. The real gentry don't carry on like that.'

'They are just like the rest of us?'

'Oh, dear me, no. The proper gentry can dress in rags but still look right. Something to do with breeding and our Mrs Mildred Lyall-Black hasn't had that advantage.'

Well behind her usual time for getting home Rachel heard the voices as she let herself in. Peggy and her da must be sitting down to their meal. She wasn't deliberately quiet, it was just her way of coming in – no doubt when she was little her mother had discouraged a noisy entrance. Peggy banged doors and accused Rachel of creeping in and taking them unawares. She was on the point of opening the kitchen door and announcing her arrival when she heard her own name. Eavesdropping was something she deplored but there is something about hearing one's own name, a need to know what is being said. She stayed where she was, the voices carried clearly.

'Stop sticking up for Rachel, Geordie, you're just as sick as I am.'

'I'm not denyin' it would be fine just the two of us, but this is her home for as long as she needs it.'

'And that could be long enough. From what I hear she's coolin' off with that Burnside lad. Pity she didn't fancy goin' into service like that chum of hers.'

'Rachel is cut out for something better than that. Mebbe I should have tried to get her into the mill office.'

'It was the looms she thought you had in mind and turned up her nose.'

'The looms – I never suggested that.'

'Doesn't matter whether it's the mill or that Miss Reid, she'd still be livin' here.'

'Wheesht, that's the door, that's her comin' in.'

Rachel deliberately opened and shut the door with enough noise for them to hear. Anger was boiling up inside her but she forced herself to act normally, even to managing a smile.

'Sorry I'm late, we had a rush order to finish.'

'That's all right, lass,' her da said, 'nice to hear that some folk are doing well in these hard times.'

'She's not dependent on the workin' classes,' Peggy sniffed. 'Help yoursel' to what's left and don't complain if it's dried up.'

'Do I ever complain, Peggy?'

'Not in so many words, but it's there in your face.'

Going into the scullery Rachel looked into the pot. Most of the gravy had dried up but she spooned the meat on to her plate, added potatoes, mashed carrot and turnip and carried it to the table. The meat was tender, Rachel was hungry and she ate it all. For a pudding Peggy had tried her hand at an apple sponge but without much success. Rachel avoided the soggy sponge but scraped out as much of the apple as she could. Her da looked up.

'Peggy can't make an apple sponge like you, Rachel, you'll need to give her a lesson.'

In spite of her misery Rachel wanted to laugh. If looks could have killed her da was stone dead but with his head once again in the paper he didn't notice. Peggy had already started on the dishes when Rachel collected hers and took them through. Picking up the tea towel she began to dry them and marvelled that more weren't chipped with the rough treatment they received.

After drying her hands Peggy flounced out and sat down opposite her husband. Her knitting, a jumper for herself in royal blue wool, had been on the go for some time and was grubby. The back and front were complete and the stitches cast on for the sleeve. She picked it up and soon the clicking of the needles was the only sound in the room.

Should she go out? No, why should she? It had rained off and on all day and the evening didn't look much better. In any case where would she go? Agnes was no longer at home. She wondered how she was getting on. Davie would be preparing orders in the back shop. She'd helped him on occasions and enjoyed it. Mr Burnside had been pleased enough for her to be there and Davie's mother had brought through tea and biscuits. A wave of longing for those days to return gripped Rachel but she knew that it was impossible to recapture what had been. Davie and she were no longer comfortable with one another.

Taking out the hard wooden chair from below the table Rachel brought it nearer to the fire. Then she saw that it needed attention and making use of the paper bag added coal and a log without dirtying her hands. That done she settled on the chair and opened the magazine she'd got from Miss Reid that day. She made no sense of the written word but it gave her a chance to think. The plans that had once been but an idle dream were about to become reality. This could be the turning point in her life but only if she were brave enough to turn her back on all she knew for an unknown future. Turning her back on unhappiness was all it was she told herself. She was nearly sixteen and a half, old enough to make a fresh start but she would have to do it secretly. No one, least of all her father, must know what she was contemplating. It needed careful planning to get away from Dundee and if it should happen that she was not made welcome at Duncairn House then she would get a job. Perth was the nearest town to Hillend and if she was willing to turn her hand to anything, there would be something for her before her savings ran out. In an effort to boost her morale she began to number those jobs she could perform. Sewing, she could do that and she had a reference. Shop assistant shouldn't be beyond her capabilities and if all else failed she could copy Agnes and go into service. Feeling happier, Rachel went back to the beginning of the magazine and this time the words made sense.

Chapter Eleven

The outside of the house was a big disappointment. She had never got around to seeing it when Meg worked there but from her description she had expected something better. Kerne House was a large dwelling made of stone blocks and not a patch on the beautiful houses out on the Perth Road. Agnes stood with her battered suitcase and looked up at the house at the end of the long drive then moved herself hastily as a motor car came speeding down before swinging out on to the road. Shaken at her narrow escape she had just time to see a red-faced man shake his fist at her and without taking time to think she stuck her tongue out at him.

Kerne House was set far back on a rise and had a panoramic view across to the Fife border. The present owners, Edwin and Margaret Taylor, had returned from Bengal four years previously with rather less money than they had expected and been forced to lower their sights and settle for the rather drab-looking Kerne House. Years in India with servants to see to their every need had made Edwin Taylor expect far too much from the small domestic staff who ran Kerne House. Used to shouting at the natives he had continued the practice and scared away more than one maid. Girls, as his wife kept reminding him, were less willing to go into domestic service these days and the point had been reached when new staff of reasonable intelligence was difficult to find.

Margaret Taylor was very different to her husband. She was a head taller and a quietly spoken woman with a gentle manner who accepted that servants, black or white, were human beings and should be treated properly. By that she meant that they should know their place, treat their employers with respect, and work diligently and uncomplainingly. Believing that a wife's duty was to be by her husband's side she had suffered the heat and boredom of India without complaint but had counted the days when she would be back in Scotland. Her one passion was the garden and her interference, as the gardeners saw it, infuriated them until they realised that she was knowledgeable. Now she was an accepted and familiar figure kneeling on her rubber mat, tending the plants and flowers. Deploring the perfect borders and manicured lawns of their neighbours she delighted in a glorious, tangled growth. It wasn't until one got nearer that it was realised that the natural almost wild look was the result of a great deal of work and planning. Agnes went round to the back of the house and here the gardens were surrounded by high hedges. The stables, now empty, were a reminder of the elegant age of the horse and carriage. Motor cars did come into the poorer streets of Dundee but it was still a rarity and an object of interest. Gradually and to the regret of the older generation the horse-drawn vehicles were themselves becoming a rarity as vans and lorries took to the road.

Agnes felt hot and sticky as she knocked at the back door.

'Come in, my hands are all flour,' came the shouted command.

The door scraped the flagstone floor as Agnes got herself and her case inside. 'I'm Agnes Boyd,' she announced.

'So you are and Meg's sister, I see the resemblance. I'm Mrs Robertson as you'll know.'

'Yes,' said Agnes putting down her case.

'Bring a chair and sit yoursel' down, it's a fair walk from the tram.'

'It is lugging this thing,' Agnes smiled as she sat down.

The cook, Mrs Robertson, was a big woman with a face that could fold into laughter lines one minute then scowl the next. She was exacting and demanding but warm in her praise when she felt it was merited. In her fifties, she had never married but wore her mother's gold wedding ring on the third finger of her left hand and when addressed as a married woman by her first employers had seen no point in a correction. To her way of thinking that gave her the advantages of the married status without the demands of a husband. No one at Kerne House ever asked about Mr Robertson, no doubt believing him to be deceased and of course she never referred to her 'husband'.

She wore a voluminous white apron tied round her ample waist and her sleeves were rolled up as her hands worked the scone dough in the wide brown bowl. Flour was scattered on the table and a scone cutter ready for the dough once it was rolled out.

Agnes settled back in her chair. Only one had arms and was for the cook. As she viewed the kitchen, Agnes thought it was a bit of all right. She had never seen anything like this big room with its long table down the middle, its ovens that looked huge to Agnes, it array of pots and pans and shelves of jars all labelled and containing the essential ingredients for the preparing and cooking of food. Until she sat down Agnes hadn't noticed the girl, the kitchen maid, at the far end of the room. She was straining vegetables through a sieve into the deep sink. Briefly she turned her head to study the newcomer then got on with her work.

Agnes hadn't eaten since breakfast and even then had only half finished her plate of porridge. It was unusual and her mother had remarked upon it.

'Nerves, didn't think you suffered from them?'

'I'm not nervous,' lied Agnes, 'just wondering how I'm going to get on. Housekeeping skills are in short measure around here and they'll expect me to know something at sixteen years of age.'

There was an angry flush on her mother's face or was it that she was ashamed?

'Housekeeping skills indeed! You can keep that high falutin' talk for someone else. Meg managed without the benefit of household skills,' she said with heavy emphasis on the words, 'and you'll just have to swallow your pride and ask what you don't know.'

'Meg was younger, it was easier for her.'

'Not much, but she's a sight more humble and while I'm about it don't you dare come back here in the state she's in.'

'No fear, I'm not so bloody stupid.'

'Stupidity has little to do with it as you'll find out, my lass.'

'You don't like me, do you?' Agnes surprised herself by saying as she pushed her plate away and got up. 'Meg and the twins and the boys, of course, you like them better.'

'You've a brain so I won't insult you. I love all my bairns and that includes you but you're a bit of a cuckoo in the nest and there are times, I confess, when I don't much like you.'

'That's plain enough,' Agnes replied and finding that she wasn't deeply hurt.

'Rachel Donaldson's fault I would say; that lass has class and you're always trying to emulate her, big mistake that.'

'Oh, Ma, emulate, such words from Spinner's Lane.'

'Like you, Agnes, I have brains and like you no class. I've the sense to accept it and for your benefit it isn't something you pick up, it can't be learned. You have it or you don't.'

'Rachel's da is working class and so is Peggy.'

'True but her ma had whatever it is. That one was a lady married out of her class and I'll warrant she often went to bed with a sore heart.'

Agnes was starving, her stomach was rumbling with emptiness and Mrs Robertson could hardly fail to hear. Rachel would have come out with a quiet 'pardon me' but she didn't see why she should. It wasn't her fault, it was the mouth-watering smell of beef roasting in the oven and of freshly baked scones and cakes.

'You'd like a cup of tea?'

'I wouldn't mind, thanks.'

'Then I'll get Gloria here,' she jerked her head towards the sink, 'to show you to the room you'll be sharing with Polly. Nice lass, you'll get on fine with her. Gloria, dry your hands and make a fresh pot of tea then butter a couple of scones for – for—'

'Agnes.'

'I've a poor memory for names and I was about to call you Meg, and speaking of the lass, how is she?'

'All right.'

'Your folk standin' by her?'

'Yes.'

'Least said about it the better, but I was real vexed just the same,' then she turned with an irritated expression. 'Gloria, you'll have to stop that sniffin', it's gettin' on my nerves. I take it you do have a handkerchief?'

The thin mousey-brown-haired girl with a face the colour of a suet pudding finished infusing the tea then took out a greyish-white handkerchief, blew noisily into it them promptly gave another sniff. Speaking through her nose she said, 'Blowing makes no difference, Mrs Robertson, my ma says it's just a stuffed head and it'll go away in its own good time.'

'Then let's hope that it won't take too long,' the cook said with a wink to Agnes. 'Gloria comes in daily to do the vegetables and other odd jobs. We're a small staff here with only two live-in maids, that's Molly and yourself. Our last tablemaid left in a hurry about the same time as your sister and we were lucky to get Molly so quickly.' She looked at Agnes picking up the last of the crumbs from the scone. 'Take another but don't be spoiling your appetite.'

'Thanks,' Agnes smiled as she reached for another.

'The master and mistress dine at seven, no visitors tonight for a change, then the staff eat here in the kitchen and if Kerne House has its faults it isn't with the quality or quantity of the food. Mrs Taylor entrusts all that to me,' she said proudly. 'I'm never wasteful, hate to see good food left on the plate, but then there very seldom is.'

The official day for the closing of Miss Reid's dressmaking business was 30 June 1933 and it was just ten days short of that. Miss Reid was looking relaxed and almost happy.

'Rachel, that's us well on with everything and now I think we should spend a little time on you.'

'On me?' Rachel looked up from her sewing.

'Yes, my dear,' she got up to bring over two lengths of material. 'Plenty here of the paler blue to make you a blouse.'

'No, no, really, you've been good to me and I couldn't.'

'This is goin' to give me pleasure, Rachel, so don't spoil it.' She smiled. 'You're getting shapely—'

Rachel blushed scarlet under the close scrutiny. She knew that her body was changing. In the privacy of her bedroom she had looked at herself in the full-length mirror on the wardrobe door and felt the wonder of the changes from girl to woman. Her hips were swelling gently below her small waist, her bosom was rounded and even her face had altered. It was now a perfect oval.

'Blue is your colour, Rachel.' Miss Reid sighed. 'What I would have given to look as you do. That wonderful thick black curly hair is a gift from heaven and those dark-lashed eyes—' She stopped suddenly. 'Yes, I'm goin' to say it, you've no mother and a steppy doesn't count. My father inflicted one of those on us and I don't imagine you think any more kindly of yours than we did of ours. Mind you, it is a difficult relationship for all concerned but I'm digressin'.' She paused. 'Don't throw yoursel' away, lass. You've good appearance and more than that, a natural grace. There'll be a fine young man for you, so don't promise yoursel' before he comes on the scene.'

Rachel threw back her head and laughed but deep down wasn't that what she hoped? That she would meet someone very special who would sweep her off her feet – a fairytale romance.

'Now as I was sayin',' Miss Reid continued as she picked up the material and felt its texture. 'You'll choose a pattern for a blouse and this darker blue tweed made into a skirt will be perfect with it. I'll cut them out but you've enough expertise now to make up a skirt and blouse yoursel'.'

Rachel felt close to tears. 'Thank you very, very much, Miss Reid, and I'll tell you this, I'll never forget you.' She hesitated just for a moment, then made up her mind. Miss Reid was going to Edinburgh and it would be nice to tell someone, someone she could trust to keep it to herself.

'My mother's family live just outside Perth and I'm going to see them but I don't want anyone to know. You see my mother's people were fairly well-off and didn't approve of my father and he would hate to think of me going there.'

'I see, my dear, and you've thought it all out very carefully?' she said with her eyebrows arched.

'Yes, I have. Peggy and my father would be much happier on their own but Da feels responsible for me and I want that to end. I'm over sixteen and I should be able to look after myself.'

'Have you been in touch with these relatives of yours?'

'No.'

'Then I should make some enquiries before you decide to leave home. But, of course, you're sensible, you'll do that?' She looked worried and Rachel wanted to put her mind at rest.

'Yes, I'll do that.' But she had no intention of getting in touch and the reason for that, she could be honest with herself, was the fear that the letter would be ignored. Much better to go there and find out the position for herself.

The skirt and blouse were beautiful. Miss Reid complimented her on the neatness of the finished garments but Rachel knew that the cutting out was what really counted. As Miss Reid had so rightly pointed out, clothes had to hang right to have any appearance and that's where a good pair of scissors in the right hands made all the difference.

'Is this true, Rachel, that Miss Reid is giving up and you'll soon be out of a job?' Peggy said accusingly from the chair at the fire, and her da looked up from filling his pipe.

Peggy hated darning. George's big toe had come through his hand-knitted sock and Rachel was searching for matching grey wool to mend it. Finding a suitable match, she cut off a length, threaded it into the needle and began to darn. Then she answered.

'Yes, it's quite true,' she said quietly.

'And it didn't occur to you to tell us?' Peggy had got to her feet and stood with her hands on her hips looking from her husband to her stepdaughter.

'Miss Reid didn't want it common knowledge before—'

'Meaning I'd spread it?' Peggy said dangerously quiet.

'Yes, Peggy, if you want the truth. You wouldn't have been able to keep it to yourself, now would you?'

'The lass is right, Peggy love, you wouldn't have been able to resist that piece of gossip.' He turned from his wife's furious face to Rachel. 'Now that we do know have you anything in mind – a job I mean?'

'Nothing definite, Da.'

'So we've to keep you until you find somethin' that's suitable to your ladyship?'

Rachel stopped weaving the needle in and out and let the sock rest in her lap while she looked at her stepmother. 'Sit down, Peggy, you look menacing standing like that and now to put your mind at rest let me promise you this. My father will not have to keep me.'

'Then you do have the promise of a job?' Peggy said, sitting down.

'I didn't say that. What I did say was that I would not be a burden.'

'You are not a burden, Rachel.'

'Yes, she is, and be man enough to tell her that to her face instead of trying to keep in with both of us.'

George flushed with anger or embarrassment or perhaps both and Rachel had to admit that Peggy had scored there.

'Why is it, can anyone tell me, that two grown women can't be civil to each other?'

'That's the way it is, Geordie, in circumstances like this.'

In silence Rachel darned the sock and another two pairs needing attention. The job done she put the workbox away and handed the socks to Peggy.

'Ta.'

'You'll miss me for that,' Rachel smiled as she got up.

'Oh, I'll no' deny you've got your uses.'

'Da's hard on his socks and if I were you I'd reinforce the thin bits before they become a hole.'

'Proper wee housewife, aren't you?'

'Not so wee. And now if you'll excuse me I'm going out for a breath of fresh air.'

Tomorrow would be her last day. Miss Reid had insisted that she take an extra week's pay saying that she had more than earned it. They were both dreading the last day. A working relationship to the surprise of them both had developed into friendship and both knew that their paths were unlikely to cross. In the event the day passed off like any other, only the firm handshake that turned into a hug at the end making it different. Returning home, Rachel went over her plans and wondered anew why she hadn't told Agnes. She could have made a point of seeing her. Agnes was her best friend yet she didn't want her to know, not at present anyhow. Perhaps it was because she'd never talked about her mother with Agnes and Agnes knew nothing about her mother's background. Once out of curiosity she'd asked about Rachel's other relations. Her da's folk, her aunt and uncle and cousins in America, she knew of them but what of her other grandparents? At the time Rachel had believed them to be dead and after her da had spoken to her about his in-laws she had wanted to keep it to herself. There were some things one didn't discuss, not even with one's best friend.

And now the time had come to think seriously about her departure from Dundee and how she should go about it. For her plan to work she did need someone and Mrs Rodgers was really the only one she could approach. So far so good, she would go there this evening.

'Rachel, lass, come away in. I was fair wearied wonderin' what to do with mysel'. My knitting's finished and I've nothin' on the pins.' Rachel followed her in and closed the door. 'And what brings you?' Mary Rodgers said as she shuffled ahead in her carpet slippers.

'Oh, dear, does there have to be a reason?' Rachel smiled.

'Young folk comin' to visit the old, more than likely there's a reason, but that's as it should be.'

'Any tea in the pot?'

'There is and it'll be fresh enough. My, but it must be bad if you're askin' a cup of tea. No,' she said when Rachel made to speak, 'let's get ourselves comfortable first. Bring two cups and matching saucers out of that press and save my legs.'

Rachel opened the cupboard door. Some home-made jam was on the top shelf and a few empty jars ready for the next jam-making session. On the second shelf Mary Rodgers had what she called her stock. There were bags of sugar, packets of tea and packets of cornflour, semolina and sago all neatly arranged. The shelf under that had china and Rachel picked up two cups in a faded rose pattern and saucers to match.

'That's fine, lass,' as Rachel set them on the corner of the table where Mrs Rodgers had just covered it with an embroidered cloth. She brought over the cosy-covered teapot and poured the tea. 'Help yoursel' to milk and sugar, I forget what you take.'

Rachel put one teaspoonful into her cup and added milk.

'Bit late to be askin' if you're one of those that needs the milk in first.'

'No, it makes no difference to me.'

'Rich Tea biscuits, it's all I have,' she said offering the plate.

'Thanks.' Rachel stirred her tea, bit off a bit of biscuit, ate it, drank some tea then took a deep breath.

'You must know about Miss Reid?'

'I do, and this'll be about a new job you have in mind?'

Rachel shook her head. 'I haven't been looking for one. I'm going to see my mother's people, they live just outside Perth but I don't want my father to know.'

'You think he'd try to stop you?'

Rachel's voice hardened. 'Like Peggy, he'd be happy enough to see me go but he'd hate to think of me going there.'

'Your da doesn't want rid of you, it's just your imagination.'

'No, Mrs Rodgers, it isn't my imagination. They didn't hear me coming in and I heard with my own ears what my da said.'

'And what was that?' Mary Rodgers said gently, 'and drink that tea before it gets cold.'

Rachel drank some and put the cup down. 'He said,' she swallowed the lump in her throat, the hurtful words were still fresh with her, 'said that, like Peggy, he wished it was just the two of them and words to the effect that he couldn't do anything about it, that he was responsible for me and for a roof over my head.'

Mary sighed. She could imagine the scene. Peggy goin' on about life bein' better if it was just the two of them and George, no doubt to get peace, agreeing with her. But a sensitive lass hearing those words and believing herself unwanted, would take them to heart. Some folk should have been drowned at birth, she thought savagely. She leaned forward and patted Rachel's knee.

'The way I see it your da loves you both but he'll agree with Peggy because it's from her he gets his comforts and you can take what you like out of that.' She looked at the lovely young girl, no not a girl, a young woman. 'The days of bein' a bairn are over, Rachel, and though you're no threat to Peggy she's jealous of your youth and beauty now that she's lost whatever she had.'

'It's not that and I don't think I'm—'

'That's your great attraction, lass, but you'll need to be careful you don't know the effect youth and beauty can have on some men and I'd be a sight happier if I knew you were to be welcomed into your mother's family. Have you been in touch?'

This wasn't going the way Rachel wanted at all. 'No, I haven't been in touch,' she said sharply, 'and I don't intend to.'

'A letter would prepare the way. How do you know that your grandparents are still alive?'

'I don't, but I must have cousins, some relatives and my mother must have wanted to me to get in touch or she wouldn't have left me their address.'

'And if things don't work out, what then?'

'I have a little money my mother left me and I've saved some. Honestly, Mrs Rodgers, I'm not stupid. I've thought of all those things and the job position may well be better in Perth than Dundee.' She smiled. 'I can keep myself until a job turns up and I do have a good reference from Miss Reid.'

'That I would have expected, she was well pleased with you.' They were both silent. Mary drained her cup, set it on the saucer and sat back. 'You could be right with your ma leaving the address. Amelia was a happy enough soul before the illness took her but I always thought there was a sadness too. She was bound to have missed her own folk but being Amelia she would hide it from your da. Likely she wanted you to be accepted, wanted them to see their granddaughter.'

'Don't blame my da, Mrs Rodgers, it must have been very hurtful when they refused even to see him.'

'It would be their way of protecting their daughter. She was such a fine lass and I'm sure she would have been a much loved daughter and their bitterness all the worse for that.'

Rachel felt a burst of happiness. 'I love to hear you talk about my mama. Da never does, not now, and sometimes I think he's forgotten her.'

'No fear of that. He has his memories and you have yours, but life goes on and a second wife doesn't want to be reminded of a first, particularly a well-loved one.'

'You always make me feel better.'

'That's nice to know and perhaps it's time I knew where I come in to these plans of yours.'

'Only if you are agreeable.'

'And I'll know that when I hear them.'

'Like I said I don't want my father to know and if I could leave my suitcase with you I could collect it on my way to the station.'

'He'd be worried out of his mind. Mebbe he hasn't played fair with you, not letting you go on to college was a terrible disappointment and I doubt if you're really over that, but even so, disappearing without a word is cruel and I'm surprised and disappointed in you, Rachel Donaldson.'

Rachel hardened herself. 'He would do everything in his power to stop me. He hates them.'

'Hatred like that is unhealthy but after all this time it's more likely to be resentment caused by hurt pride.'

'It's more than that, I know it is, but once I'm away I don't mind them knowing.'

'You'll leave a note?'

'No, I won't. I'll leave at a time when I know they are both to be out. If you wish, you can tell them I've gone to Perth – my father will know what that means.'

'You're a stubborn soul I'll say that for you.'

'May I leave my case?' she wheedled.

'I suppose so.'

'Thank you,' Rachel said getting up and thankful that she'd got her way.

'And now you promise me one thing, Rachel. I'm not one for interfering but I'm dealing with Amelia's daughter and I think I'd have her blessin' in this.'

Rachel waited.

'Writin' is not for me so there'll be no reply but you send me a wee note to put my mind at rest and you won't insult me with anythin' less than the truth.'

'No, I won't insult you with anything less than the truth.'

Chapter Twelve

Peggy wasn't one for the house and got out of it most afternoons. The highlight was going into town to do a little shopping with her married sister then having afternoon tea in one of the big stores and listening to the orchestra. Customers were encouraged to request a favourite tune and Peggy, along with some other matrons, was not slow to take up the offer.

The only suitcase was on top of the wardrobe. Rachel stood on a chair to bring it down then proceeded to give it a good dust. A cheap cardboard case would not have survived the passage of time but this was a leather case, darkened almost to black, and it still looked good. Rachel wondered if it was the same case that had transported her mother's possessions on the night she fled her parents' home.

She was alone when Mary Rodgers came round and for a heart-stopping moment Rachel thought the woman had had second thoughts about becoming involved. But it was only to say that she had been called away to a sick bed and that the key would be under the mat and to leave her case in the lobby.

The open suitcase was on the floor and her clothes on the bed. She had taken some tissue paper with Miss Reid's permission. First she wrapped her shoes in old newspaper and put them at the bottom of the case with toiletries and other items to fill in the spaces. Then carefully she folded the new skirt and blouse as she had been taught and slipped the tissue paper between the folds. The rest of the clothes went on top. Her mother's rosewood box would take up too much room and very reluctantly she decided to leave it behind. The velvet case with its precious brooch she put between the layers of clothes then she shut the suitcase. Into her handbag that she had bought herself when she started to work she put her purse with her money. Then a comb, a pale pink lipstick that both she and Agnes had bought for themselves in Woolworth's, and a lace-edged handkerchief that had been her mother's. Some of her oldest clothes still hung in the wardrobe and Rachel had no doubt that Peggy would soon get rid of them. She took a last long look at her mother's rosewood box, empty now and with its key in the lock. Should she give it to Mrs Rodgers, the woman who had been her mother's friend, or should she leave it in the bottom of the wardrobe? In the end she left it. Peggy would very likely use it for her cheap jewellery but her da might like to think that something belonging to his first wife still remained in the house.

Lifting the suitcase, heavier than she had expected it to be, Rachel hurried as fast as she could to Mrs Rodgers' house. She was both surprised and relieved to have met no one she knew. Flushed with nervous excitement and the effort of carrying the case, she picked up the key from under the mat, opened the door and put the case in the narrow lobby. Then making sure that the door was securely locked she replaced the key under the mat and had a quiet smile. Most of the folk round about were particular about locking up yet left an open invitation under the mat. Outside the close she lifted her face to the sunshine and gave a little shiver of excitement. So far so good.

Everything had gone to plan and it had been so easy. Her father had left for work and she'd helped Peggy with the housework.

'You doin' anythin' about a job?'

'No.'

'It won't come to you, you'll have to look.'

'I know.'

'You've somethin' in mind then?' she said suspiciously.

Rachel hung up the tea towel on its hook. 'Yes, Peggy, I've something in mind and I have paid you for this week.'

'Doesn't keep you.'

'I don't agree.'

'You wouldn't.'

'One day you may realise just how much work I do in the house, not forgetting the darning and mending which you profess to hate so much.'

'What am I supposed to do, go down on my knees and thank you?'

'A word of appreciation wouldn't have gone amiss.'

'Gawd! Is that the time? I'll have to get my skates on.'

Ten minutes later her face thick in pancake make-up and her mouth a red slash, she appeared in the kitchen.

'You're off then?' Rachel said.

'Aye. If you've a mind you can peel some tatties, save me when I come in.'

'I'll do them. Cheerio, Peggy.'

'Cheerio.'

It was time to go. Her stomach was behaving strangely, making her feel slightly sick as she gazed about her for the last time. The day was warm and she wore a print dress with a three-quarter-length oatmeal coat over it. She checked her appearance in the mirror then stood stock still. The enormity of the step she was about to take made her catch her breath. She was barely sixteen and a half, just becoming an adult and with nothing secure ahead of her. Had she taken leave of her senses? No, no, she was being cowardly and that was ridiculous after all her careful planning. Put it down to nerves and once she was on the train, turned her back on Dundee, she would be all right.

Silently she said goodbye to her bedroom that had been hers for all of her life. Tonight she would lay her head on a strange pillow. Not that she would be at Duncairn House, she liked the sound of Duncairn House, her grandparents' home and wondered how it had got its name. Arriving at the door clutching a suitcase would make her appear like a little lost orphan. Far better to put up the first night at a lodging house or perhaps she would make that two nights. Free of her suitcase and freshened up and in a more suitable outfit she would set out to make herself known to her relatives.

Mary Rodgers embraced her in a motherly hug then all but pushed Rachel and her case out of the door.

'Just go, lass, I cannae be doin' with partin's, no' at my time of life.'

'Thank you, dear, dear Mrs Rodgers,' Rachel called to her from the door, biting back her own tears. She had only a few minutes to wait for a tram. Someone helped her on with her case and in a short time she was walking down Union Street towards the station. Her new life had begun.

George Donaldson and his wife had finished their meal.

'Where on earth can she be?'

'I'm clearin' the table. She's not even workin' so there's no excuse.'

George grunted as Peggy began carrying the dishes to the scullery then removing the tablecloth.

It was half past seven before Peggy went through to Rachel's bedroom and her startled shout had George leaping from his chair as a ripple of fear went through him.

'What is it? What in God's name is the matter?'

'She's gone.'

'Gone!'

'Look,' she said and with a dramatic movement held the wardrobe door open. 'She's scarpered with all her stuff, the sly besom, and not a word of her intention.'

'Shut up, Peggy.' George was a sickly white as he stared about the room. Peggy was still holding the wardrobe door and his eyes moved to the rosewood box. 'No, she wouldn't,' he whispered.

'Wouldn't what?'

He ignored her and picked up the rosewood box then he lifted the lid. Peggy stood on tiptoe to peer in. 'It's empty.'

'I know where she's gone.'

'And where would that be?'

'It doesn't matter,' he said wearily.

'She'll come back in her own good time, just you wait and see.'

'No, Rachel won't be back. She knew you wanted rid of her and this is her way of going.'

'Don't start blaming me, George Donaldson.' Peggy shouted. 'You were just as anxious to be rid of her.'

'That's a lie, Peggy.'

'You said so yoursel'.'

'To shut you up, that's all.' He stopped suddenly. 'That time, Peggy, we were talking, I thought I heard the door earlier. Maybe she heard us, you have a loud enough voice.'

'Listeners never hear any good of themselves.'

'I remember what I said and I hope to God she didn't hear. Even if she did, she would know I didn't mean it.'

'No use upsettin' yoursel', that won't bring her back.'

'You've never got on with her but she's my daughter, Peggy, and I love her – perhaps I didn't realise how much until—' his voice broke and Peggy watched in appalled silence as the tears rolled down his cheeks. Almost motherly in her actions, Peggy led him through to the kitchen and into his chair, then she went to the sideboard poured a stiff whisky and handed it to him. Then she went back and poured an equally stiff drink for herself. She wasn't heartbroken, how could she be when she'd wanted rid of her stepdaughter, but she wasn't happy either. The lass was too stuck-up for her liking but she'd been good about the house and as for the mending and darning, those dreary jobs, she'd never complained. She had always done a baking at the weekend too and it was a lot better than bought stuff.

She didn't know what was wrong with her and George in the midst of his own grief didn't know either. Not someone to do anything by halves, Peggy broke into noisy sobs and all but collapsed into the chair.

Rachel Donaldson's disappearance was the main topic of conversation as groups of housewives gathered at the mouth of the closes to discuss it.

'That Peggy gave her a hard life, I hear. No wonder the lass up and went, only hope no harm's come to the lamb. She was a right nice lass, never let you pass without a smile.'

'From what I hear Peggy is real upset.'

'Puttin' it on more like.'

A stout woman dropped her voice. 'Got it from Bella McDonald, she bides beside them, and she says that her da knows where she's gone and so does Mary Rodgers but they're no' lettin' on to Peggy.'

'What about the laddie Burnside, they were goin' steady?'

'No, that had cooled a while ago and I've seen him mysel' with the lassie from the chemist but for all that he's in a bit of a state and cannae throw any light on it.'

'I'm real sorry for Geordie but I'm away for my half-loaf before the shop closes.'

Agnes had come home intending to see Rachel.

'Your chum's gone and done a bunk,' Meg said as she greeted her sister.

Agnes wasn't paying much attention, she was studying the strained skirtband. 'You're showing and what you're wearing makes it worse. That skirt was always too tight for you.'

'What am I supposed to do, buy maternity clothes?' she said sarcastically, but there was a trace of tears in her voice.

'My pink dress, it's loose enough and it looks awful on me, you can have it if you want.'

'Ta,' she said cheering up a bit. 'Kerne House, you gettin' on all right there?' she asked with studied indifference.

'So far, but you're a hard act to follow,' Agnes said generously. 'Seems you were a good worker and Mrs Robertson for one misses you.'

The tears began to flow and Agnes put her arms round the heaving shoulders.

'Want to tell me about it?'

'It was good, Agnes, everythin' was great. Good food, a bed to mysel' then I have to be a bloody fool and – and – it's too late now but I wish to God I'd got rid of it.'

'Why didn't you?'

'I don't know. In a funny sort of way I suppose I wanted it, even now – oh, I just don't know,' she ended wretchedly.

'Were you in love with him?'

She didn't answer, just wiped her eyes with the back of her hand and looked at Agnes with a tear-streaked face. 'Back here after Kerne House I'll go mad I think. It didn't seem so awful before but—'

'But you'll just get used to it.'

'Have to, won't I? And you didn't hear what I said about your chum.'

'What about Rachel?'

'She's cleared off.'

'Cleared off where?'

'That's what nobody knows.'

'Rachel wouldn't do that. I just don't believe it.'

'It's true,' Meg said, enjoying giving the sensational news, 'and you should just hear some of the rumours goin' about.'

'But where would she go?' Agnes said, her hands raking through her hair and a bewildered look on her face. 'She must have told somebody?'

'Mebbe she would have told you but when were you here last?'

'You didn't come home very often either did you, not to stay overnight, so don't start on me. And when I did try to see Rachel she was working – that's it,' she said excitedly, 'I'll go and see—'

'You can save yoursel' a journey, her da and Peggy are not sayin' anythin'.'

'Not them, but Miss Whats-her-name – Reid. They were pretty close and she'll know Rachel would want me to know her whereabouts. I bet she knows.'

'Mebbe she does but it's too late to find out. The business closed and she's gone to Glasgow or Edinburgh or some place.'

'Maybe Rachel's gone with her. Yes, that could be it.'

'Why would she leave a good home?'

'Peggy, that's your answer. Rachel felt she was only there on sufferance and yes, wait I'm remembering something – something she said but I didn't think anything of it at the time.' She puckered her brow. 'We were in Luigi's, it was when I was blethering about—' Agnes stopped, she had almost given herself away, she'd been about to say 'leaving Dundee to better myself.' Quickly she corrected herself, 'blethering about Kerne House and me starting in your job.'

'Go on then, what did she say?'

'She said,' Agnes spoke slowly, 'I have a feeling that I'll be leaving Dundee.'

'There you are then, mystery solved and you'll just have to wait until she writes to you.'

'Seems like it,' Agnes said quietly. She was hurt, deeply hurt, but she wasn't going to show that hurt to anybody.

Those first days at Kerne House had been bewildering but Agnes was coping. So far she had been kept to the kitchen and the back quarters and had seen nothing of the master and mistress. With unfamiliar work taking up all her attention she had all but forgotten the incident with the car and her unthinking and unfortunate response to the fist shaken at her. Visitors, as she was discovering, came frequently to Kerne House and more than likely it had been one of them.

The Taylors were childless, in their case from choice. India was not the best place to bring up children and Margaret Taylor had no intention of remaining in Scotland while her husband was free to take up with someone else in her absence. Since she didn't much care for children she didn't consider it a sacrifice. The owners of Kerne House enjoyed giving hospitality to former friends home for a holiday after a spell of four years in India. In many cases the novelty of staying with relatives quickly lost its appeal for all concerned and they were only too happy to descend on the Taylors for a few days or longer if they could manage it. Margaret Taylor was a gracious hostess though less enthusiastic than her husband about overnight guests. It meant being away from her beloved garden and engaging in conversation about the 'old days' and in her husband's hearing having to pretend a longing for them which she didn't feel. Edwin Taylor's heart and his interests were still in India and he enjoyed nothing better than to hear what was going on in the East. Wistfully he wished himself back there.

The steady breathing from the other narrow, iron bed showed Molly to be asleep. Usually she liked to chat but tonight she'd gone to sleep almost the minute her head touched the pillow. Agnes grinned into the darkness. The heady excitement of going on the back of a motor-bike must have been too much for her. In Agnes's opinion Molly was a bit of a dumb cluck but she was nice and she'd been helpful and shown Agnes how things were done that both the cook and housekeeper took for granted that she knew.

The letter was the cause of it all. It was from Tommy, her new boyfriend, to say that he was getting a loan of his brother's motor-bike, that he had mastered it without any trouble, and was coming to Kerne House to take Molly for a spin on her day off and that he could change his time off to suit hers provided it wasn't a Saturday when he worked all God's hours.

'What does he do?' Agnes had asked.

'Learnin' to be a butcher in his uncle's shop and he's keepin' in with him because he'll mebbe get the business one day.'

'This uncle has no children then?'

'None that counts. They do have a son but he's soft in the head.' She smiled happily. 'Tommy says he doesn't get it any easier because it is his uncle and that he can be a real, I won't say the word, but I told him he can't afford to cheek back else he'll lose out.' She suddenly switched to talk about the motor-bike. 'What if I fall off?' she asked anxiously.

'You won't if you keep your arms tight round his waist and hang on for dear life.'

'He wouldn't like it if I fell off.'

'I don't imagine you would be too happy about it yourself.'

'Not if I hurt mysel', 'course I wouldn't.' She paused. 'There's something else, Agnes.'

'What?'

'When he turns corners do I bend the same way as Tommy or the other way to help balance the bike?'

Agnes was stumped, she'd never been on the back of a motor-bike, didn't know anyone lucky enough to have one. 'You've got me there. Bend the same way he does I think but you'd better ask him.'

'I will.' She smiled dreamily. 'He's ever so nice, Agnes, and he's awfully good-lookin' just like a film star.'

'Sounds a bit of all right to me.'

'You'd like him I know you would.'

'Better watch out then, hadn't you?'

Molly was blessed with a good figure though perhaps a little on the heavy side and she was pretty. Her expression was almost smug as she looked at Agnes and shook her head.

'I'm not in the least worried.' She touched her dark blonde hair and twisted a strand of it round her finger. 'Tommy told me he didn't like girls with ginger hair.'

'Auburn if you please.'

'Same thing.'

'What has this Tommy of yours got against auburn-haired girls?' Agnes was just the teeniest bit annoyed. 'Come on he must have given a reason.'

'Well, if you must know he says they are – they are – I don't remember what he said.'

'Yes, you do and I'm waiting.'

'He didn't mean you, Agnes, how could he? He hasn't even met you.'

'What did he say?' Agnes almost shouted.

'That you are a fast lot and lead a fellow on.'

'What rubbish, what absolute tripe and you can tell him that from me.'

'I will not and I wouldn't have told you if you hadn't made me.'

Agnes lay with her hands behind her head and smiled at the memory of that exchange. She'd heard it said that red-haired girls were generally more passionate than their black, brown or fair-haired sisters but that didn't apply to her. She didn't believe it was in her nature to be passionate about any man but that didn't mean that she wouldn't like someone being that way about her. In any marriage, she'd heard it said, there was always one partner more in love than the other. And as for giving herself before marriage, there was no danger of that. Meg, silly girl that she was, had fallen for promises but she wouldn't. She would get that ring on her finger. She accepted that she might have to feign love but provided he was a person of means and intelligence that shouldn't be too difficult. Of course, he wouldn't have to be hideous or anything like that.

And what kind of bargain was he getting? Agnes asked herself and found the question easily answered. Admiring glances had only confirmed what the mirror told her. She was an attractive young woman of medium height with a good figure, a face that wasn't beautiful but passably pretty. Her thick, auburn hair she had always considered to be her crowning glory and if Molly's boyfriend didn't admire the colour then he was in the minority. It was silly of her to let a remark like that bother her but it had. One important quality she had omitted. She was intelligent and able to hold a conversation, not like some she could mention.

She stretched herself in the bed enjoying the still novel experience of having a bed to herself instead of sharing it with her sisters. In fact, the only fly in the ointment at Kerne House was the housekeeper, a proper tartar that one, and a frustrated old maid, Agnes decided, who delighted in taking out her frustration on the staff. She was a tall, thin, sharp-featured, middle-aged woman with iron-grey hair scraped back from her temples and secured in a tight little bun held in place by a large number of hair pins. Irene Templeton was the kind of woman who looked for faults and invariably found them.

In her presence poor Molly was a nervous wreck, the girl was highly strung at the best of times and was in fact extremely efficient in all tasks bar the one for which she had been primarily engaged. She knew how to set a table, how to place the cutlery, how to stand at the side of each guest, not too near, to serve the various courses. Left alone she was fine but a wrong word or a raised eyebrow from the mistress at some tiny omission was enough to throw her completely. It made her clumsy and had resulted in more than one unfortunate accident.

Agnes was well aware that Miss Templeton regretted giving in to cook and engaging Meg's sister without an interview. Nevertheless, Miss Templeton had to accept that the domestic position regarding new staff was difficult, very difficult indeed and the bold piece was intelligent. Too clever by half was her personal opinion. Molly was her biggest worry, the girl was a disaster at table and the Taylors (she thought of them as the Taylors but spoke of them as the master and mistress) were holding her responsible since it was she who had engaged the girl.

It left a sour taste in her mouth but the Boyd girl would have to be trained as a tablemaid and Molly demoted to housemaid.

Chapter Thirteen

The train puffed into the tiny Hillend station and two passengers got off. One was Rachel. The other, a middle-aged woman carrying her shopping, walked briskly along the platform to be met by a man of similar age who relieved her of her packages and together they went out. Rachel followed more slowly and wondered which way to go. She stopped and put down her suitcase. The couple had turned right into a quiet country road. Rachel decided that their home was a secluded cottage or perhaps a farmhouse. She would walk the other way. Picking up her case she set off to where a few people were about and after a few minutes she was in a street of small houses with a corner shop – the sort of shop that appeared to sell anything and everything and the thought struck Rachel that here she might get information about a lodging house.

She went in and waited her turn.

'Yes, miss, what can I get you?' The woman was a cheery soul, her face wreathed in smiles at something her last customer had said.

'I'm looking for accommodation and I wondered if you could recommend someone.'

'How long for?'

'Two nights.'

She pursed her lips and seemed to be considering. 'Mrs McGregor, two doors down takes boarders but if it is just for a couple of nights you'd be better with Mrs Shepherd, her laddie's just gone to work out of town, and she'll have his room. She's a nice soul and you'll be all right with her.' She was pointing along the road.

'Which house?'

'Can't say the number but halfway along, the green door with the bonny shiny brasses, can't miss it. Tell her Mrs Mackay from the shop sent you.'

'Thank you, I'm very grateful.'

'You're not much more than a bairn to be lookin' for a room,' she said suspiciously as Rachel turned to go.

'I'm nearly seventeen,' Rachel said with as much dignity as she could muster. Sixteen years and seven months was near enough to seventeen she told herself.

The green door with the well-polished brasses stood out from the others. Rachel put down her suitcase and knocked. In a few moments it was answered by a woman who looked questioningly at the girl then at the case as if she were sure the caller was at the wrong house.

Rachel smiled to hide her nervousness – making plans and the reality were very different she was just finding out. The woman in the shop didn't seem to be sure of her. Perhaps a young girl with a suitcase and looking for accommodation did appear suspicious, like someone running away from home. She really must try to sound more confident, act like a mature person who knew what she was about.

She held her head high. 'I'm looking for accommodation for two nights and Mrs Mackay in the shop suggested I try you first.'

'I've a spare room right enough. Come away in and you can see if it'll be suitable.' She was a sturdy, pleasant-faced woman with short light brown fly-away hair and a complexion that many a young girl would have envied. Rachel's protests were swept aside as she leaned over the step and picked up the case. 'Straight ahead, the door to the left,' she instructed as she shut the outside door. It was a nice, homely, shabby room with photographs, probably of family, covering the surface of the sideboard. 'My but there is some weight in that, did you carry it from the station?'

'Yes, I did.' She smiled. 'I'm Rachel Donaldson, Mrs Shepherd.'

'You'd like to see the room now?'

'Yes, please.'

'Come along then. It was my son Eric's room but he's workin' out of town and he's been lucky enough to find a room with a nice old lady who seems glad of his company.' She laughed, a pleasant little tinkle of a laugh. 'Always falls on his feet, our Eric.' They went up a stairway covered in maroon and brown carpeting with brass rods to keep it in place. The door to the bedroom was wide open. 'Like to keep it well-aired. Well, what do you think? Will it do you?'

'It's perfect, Mrs Shepherd.' The room was similar in size to the one she had been used to. It had a single bed covered by a deep blue bedspread. There was no mirror on the wall but Mrs Shepherd opened the wardrobe and on the inside of the door was a full-length mirror. A basket chair was beside it and alongside that a table with a glass ornament in the centre.

'Looks empty without all the rubbish Eric used to accumulate. I used to go on at him complaining about the untidiness but I'll tell you this, lass, I'd willingly have the mess back if I could have my laddie.'

'You must miss him very much?'

'I do but I'm glad too that he's away. It was high time the lad learned to stand on his own two feet instead of expecting everything to be done for him. You like it then?'

'Yes, and of course I'll pay you in advance.'

'You've an honest face but if you'd prefer it that way?'

'Yes, I would.'

'We'll go downstairs and have a cup of tea and don't worry I won't be taking much from you, and that,' she pointed to a closed door and lowered her voice, 'that is the convenience if you want to make yoursel' comfortable. I'll away down and put the kettle on. Oh, by the way, I'd better know now about breakfast if you'll want something cooked. I take a plate of porridge and toast myself but the young people are mebbe not so keen on that.'

'Porridge and toast is what I'm used to, Mrs Shepherd.'

The woman looked relieved. 'That'll save me goin' to the shop for I don't keep a lot of food in the house, well you don't when you're on your own.'

Before Rachel could do more than open her case the call came that the tea was infused and just to leave everything and come down.

Feeling happier now Rachel ran down the stairs and into the living-room. A small table was set at the fire with two cups and saucers of fine china and there was a plate with slices of fruit loaf.

'Come late afternoon I usually put a match to the fire, it can get a bit chilly and it's cheerier than looking at an empty grate. Eat up, lass, don't be shy and I won't be charging you for this.'

Rachel took a piece of the fruit loaf and bit into it. 'It's lovely, did you make it?'

'Yes, I make two when I'm about it and send one in a tin box to Eric. There's mice in those sorting offices, you know, but they won't nibble through tin. Eric was always partial to fruit loaf and his landlady gets her share.'

She was such a friendly person, Rachel thought, and showing no curiosity in her unexpected lodger. All the same, she must tell her something.

'I'm from Dundee and before I visit my relatives I wanted to see Hillend. You see, someone I loved very dearly knew this village and spoke so well of it that I simply had to come and see it for myself.'

The woman smiled and nodded. That wasn't the whole truth, there was something the lass was keeping back and she had a perfect right to do that. Some folk around here, Mabel Mackay among them, wouldn't let it rest there, awful to be bothered with your nose. She was glad she wasn't like that and she'd put the lass at her ease. Nice lass, bonny too, she hoped Eric would choose well and not one of those silly, giggly types.

'Hillend is a bonny wee place and there's some fine walks. You've a sturdy pair of shoes with you, I hope?'

'Yes, I have, in the case,' Rachel said with a glance at her thin-soled shoes.

'There's the walk along the side of the burn and up to the auld kirk and then the village itsel' is worth a look at. Then you'll need to take the Glen Road, it's a fair climb and I've to stop halfway to get my puff back but it's an excuse to look over at Duncairn House.'

Rachel was tired and the strain of the last few hours was beginning to tell but at the mention of Duncairn House she was fully alert and wanting every scrap of information she could get without appearing to be curious.

'Is it a very grand house?'

'It's an estate, lass. The Craigs of Duncairn House are Hillend, if you see what I mean. The family has been here for generations but like others of their kind they hit hard times and jute has been their saviour.'

Rachel feigned surprise. 'Not the Craig Mills in Dundee, by any chance?'

'One and the same. The old master, gossip would have it, was quite a character and put the fear of death into his staff, yet he could be kindly too. He lived to a ripe old age and not many changes were made in his day. But when the son and family took over they spent a power of money bringing Duncairn House back to its former glory. That I may say was the time I got married to a Perth lad and went to live there.' She was silent for a little then gave a deep sigh. 'Bidin' with in-laws isn't the ideal way to start married life, so be warned. We had three years of it before we got our own wee place and Eric already a toddler. What on earth made me tell you that?'

'You had left Hillend to live in Perth?'

'That's it. Eric was twelve when I lost my man and I came back to Hillend with my laddie and hopefully I'll spend the rest of my days here.'

'Thank you for making it all sound so interesting, Mrs Shepherd,' Rachel said as she declined another cup of tea. 'Tell me, though, is the family still in residence?'

'The old lady is and she must be quite an age. It's a long while since she lost her man, I lose track of time, but it's some years. There's a married daughter living with her and a granddaughter I'd put to be ages with yourself.' She stopped, smiled and shook her head. 'Dear me, here I am goin' on about the folks at Duncairn House as if it was of any interest to you.'

Rachel smiled and got to her feet. She had learnt all she needed. 'May I wash these up for you?'

'And you a payin' boarder? No, thank you, lass, but it shows you've been well brought up.'

'I'll go up now and empty my case.'

'Do that and there should be a few spare coat-hangers. I'll be up shortly to put sheets on the bed.'

Tired though she was, sleep would not come. Maybe it was the silence, a country stillness different from the nights in Dundee to which she was accustomed. Even after the last tram had trundled by on its way to the depot, the silence was never complete.

Suddenly her face was wet with tears and Rachel was wishing with all her heart that she was back in her own bed at 23 Blackford Street with the dear familiarity of everything. She tried reasoning with herself that her tiredness was to blame, bringing to the front of her mind all the hurtful things that had driven her from home, but even Peggy at this distance didn't seem so bad. And her da, what would he think of her leaving in that manner?

She dried her eyes, put the sodden handkerchief under her pillow and closed her eyes. It was too late for regrets was her last unhappy thought before sleep overtook her.

Light filtered through the curtains and Rachel could hear movement downstairs. On first awakening in the strange bedroom she had wondered where she was or indeed if she was still sleeping and this was a dream.

As the previous day's events caught up with her she got out of bed and padded over to the window. The bedroom was to the front of the house and drawing back the curtains Rachel looked down onto the street. Not much activity, just a few people leaving their homes probably for their place of employment. Looking up she saw that the sky was overcast with the threat of rain. It decided her against wearing her best outfit. If it did rain, her new skirt would get wet under her short coat and she couldn't risk that. Instead, she would wear her workaday clothes and walking shoes. In any case she didn't want to approach her relatives today but there was nothing to stop her looking at Duncairn House. Tomorrow, dressed in her new blouse and skirt, she would know that her appearance would not let her down.

After breakfast and porridge that would have put Peggy's to shame she made her own bed and tidied up before setting out. How fortunate she had been with her accommodation – Mrs Shepherd was certainly not overcharging her. Most of those she met greeted her with a 'good morning' and a smile. Dundonians were friendly folk but they had to know a person by sight before passing the time of day.

Mrs Shepherd had been right. The dullness was no more than early morning mist and already the slight breeze was dispelling it. Rachel walked by the side of the burn enjoying hearing the sound of the water lapping against the stones but she didn't linger to admire her surroundings. She was too anxious to get on to the Glen Road and have her first look at Duncairn House.

She stopped halfway up the hill and drank in the soft beauty of the Perthshire hills and the lovely countryside.

Her first glimpse of Duncairn House was through a gap in the hedge and she caught her breath. It was so much more than she had expected. So beautiful was this majestic stone-built house with its well-proportioned windows and its wide, impressive entrance. Tearing herself away, Rachel left the Glen Road for a narrow path, not noticing the PRIVATE sign partly hidden by the overhanging branches of an oak tree. She walked on until she had Duncairn House in full view. The gates with their intricate pattern were open and two cars sat in front of the entrance. From that distance she could make out the figures of a man and a woman leaving the car and walking up the steps closely followed by a girl in a summery dress that ballooned out as she ran ahead of the other two and disappeared inside.

Rachel's throat was a tight knot. Was the girl her cousin and the woman her Aunt Maud? She stopped where she was and looked about her. Such a commanding position must have an unspoiled view of the gentle rolling hills of this lovely part of Perthshire. And this was where her mother must have spent many holidays with her grandparents before returning to the more modest residence in Dundee.

The gardeners were busy, gardens such as these must need a great deal of attention, Rachel thought. She was walking on when she heard the voice and stopped. It was one of the gardeners and he was shaking his head at her.

'Not this way, lass,' he shouted. 'Take the other fork and you'll find your way round to the back.'

'Thank you,' she called back and struck out in the other direction. She fell to wondering what he would say if she had told him that she was family and not trespassing as he had indicated she was doing. Probably would not have believed her.

For an instant, a single instant, she had felt as though her mother were there urging her on and she felt guilt at her lack of courage. Tomorrow and it couldn't be delayed, she had to bring herself to walk up that drive, ring the bell and announce to whoever answered it that she was Rachel Donaldson, Amelia's daughter, and that she wished to see her grandmother.

Deep in thought she was at the back of the house and a girl was hurrying towards the open door. The figure at the entrance hurried the girl inside then catching sight of Rachel signalled for her to get a move on. Not quite sure what to do she found herself hurrying forward.

'Follow that girl and take a seat.'

'But—'

The woman had gone and Rachel walked into a small room, like an anteroom was her first thought. The girl was already seated with her legs crossed and very much at her ease. She looked Rachel up and down with unfriendly eyes and the smile died on Rachel's face. The door leading into another room opened and a head popped out. 'I'll see you now.'

Less than ten minutes later the girl came out, glanced briefly across at Rachel and said. 'You've to go in.'

She really must apologise for the mistake. Rachel got up, gave a small tap at the door and went in. It was a sparsely furnished room she entered with a table not unlike the one at 23 Blackford Street, and behind it sat a woman her head bowed as she wrote on a pad. She didn't look up only indicating with a wave of a hand that Rachel should be seated at the other side of the table. In another minute the head went up and grey-blue eyes regarded her coolly. Difficult to determine her age but Rachel put the woman to be in her late forties or early fifties. Her brown hair, peppered with grey, was bobbed in the fashion that was becoming popular and her long face was sallow. She kept the pen in her hand.

'Name?'

'I—' began Rachel.

'You do have a name?'

'Rachel Donaldson.'

'And how old are you?'

'Sixteen.'

'Are you in employment?'

'No.'

'You will address me as Mrs Anderson,' she said coldly.

'I do beg your pardon, Mrs Anderson, I'm not – I mean—' she floundered and stopped.

The woman spoke irritably. 'That other girl ahead of you was sullen and disrespectful. You appear to be unable to answer a simple question when it is put to you. What is the matter with the younger generation? I take it that you are interested in the vacancy for housemaid or why else would you be here?'

Suddenly it dawned on Rachel that she was being interviewed for a job, a maid's job, in her grandmother's house. About to explain the true position she stopped herself. This was perfect. The ideal way to find out about her relatives and the woman who had disowned her own daughter. The housekeeper, or whoever she was, must think her an idiot the way she was acting and if she wanted this job, and suddenly she wanted it very much, then she had better start making a better impression.

Deliberately she moved to sit on the edge of the chair, a sign she knew that was associated with nervousness and being ill-at-ease.

'Mrs Anderson, please excuse me, I'm just nervous because I have so little experience but I am very willing.'

'Let me hear about the little you do have,' she said unbending a little.

'After my mother died I kept house for my father and did the cooking and baking.'

'That is rather different to working in a large house like this,' she said looking amused. 'May I ask when this stopped and for what reason?'

'My father married again.'

She nodded. 'I see and now you are seeking a position, preferably a live-in position?'

'Yes, Mrs Anderson.'

'Do you live locally?'

Rachel hesitated then decided to keep as close to the truth as possible.

'Until very recently my home was in Dundee,' she said quietly and as she said it a picture of her father and Peggy came into her mind. Had her disappearance upset them? She thought not.

'Where are you staying at present?'

'I have accommodation in the village.' Rachel had a thought. 'Perhaps I should mention that I can sew.' She opened her handbag thankful that she had Miss Reid's reference with her, and handed it over. Mrs Anderson read it then handed it back.

'Very satisfactory,' she said as Rachel put the envelope back into her bag. 'It doesn't say but obviously you can use a sewing machine.'

'Yes.'

This seemed to please her and she kept nodding her head. 'We do have a woman who comes in to attend to the mending of the bed linen but she is far from satisfactory. Now if you could take on this task as part of your job I could see my way to offering you the position.'

Rachel almost laughed with relief but she kept her face straight. 'I would be happy to work in whatever capacity you feel I am best suited,' then wished she hadn't phrased it just like that.

'You don't talk like a maid.'

Rachel could think of no answer to that and remained silent.

'But then you weren't, you were keeping house for your father.'

Rachel smiled.

'How soon can you start? We are short-staffed at present.'

'Thursday,' Rachel answered promptly. She would stay at Mrs Shepherd's tonight, after all she had paid for it and she could have the whole day to explore.

'That would be very suitable. Usually the servant girls share a bedroom but there is a room available, much smaller of course, which you could have and it is next to the sewing-room.'

'I'd like that, thank you.'

'Very well,' she said getting up to show the interview was at an end, 'report to me on Thursday at nine a.m. Oh, we haven't discussed wages or your hours of work.' She proceeded to do so but remained standing no doubt expecting it to be satisfactory to the new maid, which it was.

After Rachel had gone Mrs Anderson smiled to herself, well pleased. Whatever the circumstances it was easy to see by the girl's appearance, manners and speech that she came from a good home. She could congratulate herself that the girl could sew. The old lady wasn't mean but she was of that dying breed that threw nothing away as long as there was wear in it. The sheets were badly in need of rehemming and there was plenty of work to be done in the linen cupboard. The old lady would be pleased, she was not above checking on the condition of the linen and voicing her disapproval of the frayed hems.

Rachel was outside and barely able to contain her excitement. How different it all was to what she had expected.

The ordeal of walking up that long drive, knocking at the door or ringing the bell, whichever it was, was no longer ahead of her. It was cowardly that she should feel such relief but she didn't care and in the fullness of time she could either announce to a startled household that she was Amelia's daughter or if she found that she disliked or wanted nothing to do with her mother's people then she could leave without anyone being the wiser.

The air was pleasantly cool as she walked away from the back door of Duncairn House. Like the front the gardens at the back of the house were well-kept and the borders were a blend of carefully chosen perennials their soft colours making Rachel think of peace and tranquillity. As that thought came into her head she wondered how her grandparents could ever have known real peace of mind. Had they ever tried to find out about their daughter? She thought not. After all, it shouldn't have been too difficult for people with money and authority to discover the couple's whereabouts. Her mother by all accounts had told them that her beloved worked in the Tayside Jute Mills. In the end was it just pride that kept them apart? Would she ever know?

Chapter Fourteen

It was the deafening sound of a motor-bike arriving in the yard that sent Agnes flying out of the kitchen. What she had expected to see was an excited pillion-seat passenger, instead of which she saw a distressed Molly all but stumble in her effort to be free of the bike. Her face was almost green and Agnes hurried forward to help.

'Leave me, I'm goin' to be sick,' she said in an agonised voice and Agnes had her arm roughly shaken off.

'I'll come—'

'No,' she said wildly and with her hand pressed over her mouth ran behind a nearby clump of bushes.

'She'll be all right in a few minutes,' a voice said when the retching had stopped.

Agnes barely glanced at the young man.' No thanks to you,' she said curtly.

'And what exactly do you mean by that?' The voice was dangerously quiet and he'd moved away from the bike to tower above her.

'Showing off, that's what you'd be doing and driving like a maniac I bet.'

His eyes narrowed. 'Nothin' of the kind. For one thing I've more respect for other people's property.' He patted the bike with affection. 'Belongs to my brother.'

'You could still have been speeding,' but she was less aggressive now.

'Well, I wasn't. I've enough sense to know my own limitations.'

They were glaring at each other when a sheepish-looking Molly reappeared. The greenish tinge had gone from her face but she was still very white.

'Feelin' better?' Tommy asked as he put an arm round her shoulder.

'A bit, but I think I'll go to my room and lie down for a while,' she said beginning to move away, then stopped. 'Oh, sorry, I was goin' to introduce you. Tommy, this is Agnes Boyd and Agnes,' her voice softened, 'this is Tommy Kingsley.'

There was no way they could get out of shaking hands. Agnes saw the hesitation, or was it reluctance, as Tommy extended a lean brown hand and she met it with the tips of her fingers. For a moment she looked up into a pair of startlingly blue eyes and was shocked at her own feelings as he abruptly turned away to give Molly a hug.

'No bike next time, I promise,' he said as he mounted the machine and in a few minutes he was just a speck in the distance.

Molly had gone ahead to lie down and Agnes tried to make sense of her own feelings. Molly hadn't exaggerated, Tommy Kingsley was quite the most handsome young man she had ever met. He was quite tall with dark good looks and long lashes over those incredibly blue eyes. Duty called and for once she was thankful for something to do. She wanted to forget that arrogant, disturbing young man.

The kitchen at Kerne House was old-fashioned and a lot of work but Mr and Mrs Edwin Taylor saw no reason to spend money on something that had worked well in the past and continued to do so. There were faint mutterings of complaint from the cook but they never reached the master and mistress. In truth Mrs Robertson had no wish for change, indeed she would have fought it tooth and nail. It would be time enough for that when her days at Kerne House were over.

With just the three maids, Molly, Agnes and Gloria, the work had to be shared though Molly as tablemaid did fewer menial tasks. Gloria came in daily but she was never in a hurry to go home where more work awaited her and willingly tackled far more than her share of the work. A simple lad came when he felt like it and chopped wood and filled the buckets with coal.

Gloria and Agnes cleaned and black-leaded the grates once a week and each morning Agnes had to lay the fires and sweep and dust. She thought they were trying to make a fool of her when she was told to sprinkle tea leaves on the carpets before sweeping them.

'What for?'

'Doesn't your mother do that?' Molly asked her.

'Tea leaves on the mat,' Agnes said scornfully, 'no, she damn well doesn't, they go into the teapot.'

Molly giggled. 'Old tea leaves, silly. Mrs Robertson said you were a caution and so you are. It's to give a sweet smell to the rooms.' Agnes half smiled, she was unsure whether to believe it or not.

The one job Agnes really enjoyed and the other two didn't, especially on a cold and frosty morning, was taking the rugs out to the back-yard then throwing them over the clothes line to be punished with a carpet beater. If she was in a good mood she enjoyed it and if she was in a bad temper the exercise got it out of her system. The dust had long since gone but Agnes raised the beater for one last good wallop.

'God! I wouldn't like to be at the other end of that.'

Agnes lowered the carpet beater then turned to the voice. He wasn't very tall, quite broad-shouldered and with sandy-coloured hair. He smiled and it was a nice friendly smile.

'I'm looking for Meg Boyd, do you think you could get her for me?'

'She isn't here,' Agnes said carefully.

He looked disappointed. 'Know when she'll be back?'

'Why do you want her?'

A shadow of annoyance crossed his face and she came in quickly with, 'I'm her sister.'

'You're Meg's sister?' He came right up to her. 'Mebbe she's spoken of me? I'm Sam Robson.'

Agnes shook her head. 'Hang on here a minute, I'll shove these in.'

'I'll help you.' He gathered up the carpets and she opened the back door to let him put them inside. At the disturbance Gloria turned round.

'If anyone asks for me, Gloria, I'll be back in a few minutes.'

Gloria nodded and winked.

Sam Robson was looking puzzled as they walked away from the house. 'Is there something wrong?'

'You could say that.'

'Where is Meg?'

'She's left here and gone home.'

'But she liked it here, why would she go and do that?'

'Why, indeed?'

He stopped and gripped her shoulders and Agnes almost expected to be shaken. 'Just tell me what all this is about and stop monkeying around.'

'Were you her boyfriend?'

'You could say.'

'She left here because she's pregnant and if you don't know that word it means having a baby.'

'Cut that out,' he said angrily but she could see that he was shaken. 'I did odd jobs about here workin' on the cars, anythin' really and that's how I met Meg.'

Agnes waited, she wanted him to go on talking so she repeated – 'that's how you met Meg.'

He nodded. 'When I got this other temporary job it was only to be for a month to six weeks, I was coming back. I mean she knew I would.' He looked at her helplessly.

'A letter, it's not all that difficult to write one.'

'Shouldn't be but it is. I mean mebbe it's all right for you but I couldn't write on paper what I wanted to say, anyway I thought she would understand.'

From where she was Agnes could see Gloria waving frantically.

'I'll have to get back or I'll be like my sister and out of a job.'

'But about Meg, I've got to—'

'Tomorrow about half past six – can you make that?'

'No bother. I'll have the van.' But Agnes was already out of earshot.

Punctually the next evening at half past six Agnes was out of her uniform and into her own clothes and hurrying along the path. The day's work was over and she was free until nine thirty or ten at the very latest. She barely glanced at the van parked half on the path and half on the grass verge. He wasn't at the appointed place that was what registered. Typical, Agnes thought bitterly, Sam Robson was more than likely the father of Meg's unborn baby but no doubt after a night's sleep he'd wakened up to the cold reality that he could be trapped if he didn't put a few miles between them. Agnes was just about to turn round and go back to Kerne House when the van door opened and Sam Robson came to meet her.

'You're here,' she said stupidly.

'Did you think I wouldn't come?'

'There's some who would have taken to their heels.'

He smiled. 'You're Agnes, aren't you?'

'Yes.'

'Meg often spoke of you.'

'Did she?'

'Brains of the family, she said.'

Agnes laughed. She felt at ease with this young man and could almost envy Meg. No, that wasn't true, the shameful truth was that she had only to think of that arrogant Tommy Kingsley to feel – she couldn't put a name to what she felt but it was disturbing.

'I would have expected you to do more with your brains than—'

'Be a skivvy here. You're right, I do have plans but I have a lot to learn and this is a start. And now to the reason for us being here. Do you want to see Meg?'

'Of course I want to see Meg.'

'Well seeing as you have a van and I don't have to be back until half past nine we could go and see her.'

'Fine by me.' He paused. 'I'm no coward,' then he grinned. 'Yes, I am and I'd like to see Meg on her own.'

'Scared of my ma and da are you?'

'Should I be?'

She just smiled. 'Ever spoken to you, has she, about her family?'

'Only you.'

He had the passenger door open. 'Hop in.'

She got in and before she sat down he hastily removed a spanner. It was a very old van and it rattled along the road but Agnes wasn't troubled, her stomach wasn't easily upset.

'Learnin' to be a mechanic and I get the use of this to take me to jobs. Not much to look at but the engine's good. Which way, left or right?'

'Left here. You know Dundee?'

'Bits of it. Where are we headin'?'

'Spinner's Lane.'

'Never heard of it.'

'You haven't missed much but it's off the Hawkhill.'

'Should have said. I know the Hawkie, know most of the main roads.'

'Where is your home?'

'Barnhill. My mother has a wee shop there, took it over when my da died.'

Sam was a good careful driver who took no chances and they arrived safely at Spinner's Lane. The twins' eyes nearly popped out of their head when they saw Agnes getting out of the van. Sam remained inside.

'Listen, you two, is Meg in?'

'Yes.'

'Then go and tell her someone wants to see her but don't tell anyone else. Got that?'

'What's it worth?'

'Nothing but a thick ear if you don't do it.'

Agnes was all right but it was safer to do what she asked.

Meg appeared with a grey cardigan over the awful pink dress and

Agnes was glad to see that the miserable look had gone from her face. Now it was just resigned. She was smaller than Agnes with light brown wavy hair. Until now she had worn it to her shoulders but got a bit cut off since that way it would be easier to keep clean and she was particular about her hair. The sink was always cluttered with dishes and they had to be cleared away before there was any hair washing.

'Hello, Agnes, it's just you,' she said surprised. 'I'll kill those two, they said it was someone to see me.'

'So it is, look!'

Sam leaned forward so that she could see him but he kept within the van.

Agnes watched her sister's face go deathly white then flush a lovely pink.

'Sam?' she breathed.

'In you go, Meg,' Agnes said helping her sister into the van, 'and, Sam, you go slowly, she can't afford to be joggled about in her condition.' Then she winked to Meg who seemed to be undecided as to whether she should laugh or cry.

The van moved away, the twins were at the door as Agnes tried to push past. 'Move,' she said forcing her way in.

'Who was that?' Daisy demanded.

'Yes, who was that?' Rose asked.

'A friend of Meg's, that's all.'

Her mother had been at a neighbour's house and just come in. She gave an exaggerated start of surprise at seeing Agnes.

'My! My! We're honoured, two visits this month. What brings you?'

'I got the chance of a lift and just took it that's all. Where's Da?'

'The pub. No, here he is and before closing time, wonders will never cease.'

Her da nodded to her as if she were a stranger and without a word to anyone slumped into his chair which had long since lost its springs. After a few minutes the occasional snore showed that he was asleep.

'Is he still working?' Agnes jerked her head at the sleeping form.

'Still workin', Agnes, that's six weeks, must be a record.' She looked at him with some affection. 'Mind you it's back-breakin' work and it's takin' it out of him.'

Agnes looked about her and knew that she could never come back to Spinner's Lane to live. It was all so dreary. She felt a spurt of anger,

anger directed at her mother. Her da was working, so was Eddie, the laddies did messages after school and Meg was back in the baker's shop. She, herself, gave a little every month. Money couldn't be in such short supply and surely her mother could make some effort to tidy herself and the house. What on earth did she do with herself all day? Then she looked down at her youngest sister, the mongol child and largely ignored. She was sitting on the floor picking up a spoon and letting it fall with monotonous regularity. Her chin was wet and sore-looking, she slavered non-stop, her tongue was too big for her mouth, yet when given just the smallest bit of attention the reward was the sweetest of smiles. On an impulse Agnes picked her up and cuddled her. Chubby arms went round her neck and a wet face touched her own.

Agnes knew that her mother worried about her poor damaged babe and that she hoped the good Lord would see His way to take back the wee lamb before she, herself, departed this earth. For who else but a mother would look after the child? Agnes felt shame but she knew that none of them would be willing to shoulder the burden.

'Cup of tea?'

'Wouldn't mind.'

'Where's Meg?'

The twins didn't answer, just looked at Agnes.

'She's with a friend.'

'And who might that be?'

'She'll tell you herself.'

She shrugged and got on with infusing the tea. Agnes could be the limit but she wasn't going to quarrel with her.

It was nearly half past eight when Meg appeared. She was alone. Her eyes were bright and there was a flush of happiness on her face.

'Thanks, Agnes, thanks very, very much.'

'That's all right,' she said awkwardly.

'You've to go when you're ready, the van's at the corner.'

'Did you not ask him in or did he not want to come?'

'He wanted to but I said I would rather tell—'

'Tell what?' Mrs Boyd demanded. 'Will someone kindly tell me what this is all about?'

'I'm goin' to be married.'

'You're what?' The yell of surprise brought the sleeping figure to life.

'Can't a man sleep? What the hell's the racket?' he said as he tried to raise himself in the sagging chair then gave up and settled further into it.

'Your daughter is gettin' hersel' married.'

He looked at Agnes.

'No, not Agnes. It's Meg.'

'So she should and be quick about it by the looks of her.'

'Come on, lass, tell us about it,' her mother said kindly.

'Wait until I go,' Agnes said draining her cup and getting to her feet. 'I can't keep Sam waiting any longer.'

'So it's Sam is it – and, oh, afore you go, Agnes, cast your eyes over that.' She handed Agnes an official-looking letter.

Agnes opened it, read the letter and looked at her mother. 'That's great and not before time. It's taken them long enough to realise we're living in condemned property.'

'A corporation house,' her mother beamed, 'there's even a bathroom.'

'That's for keepin' the coal in,' Daisy said with a cheeky grin.

'So it is,' Rose agreed.

'That's enough, Daisy, you and your shadow are gettin' far too cheeky.'

'You'll be real toffs,' Agnes said as she took her departure.

Promotion was to come to Agnes quicker than she had dared hope. She was only too happy to be trained as tablemaid but she was upset that it meant Molly being downgraded to housemaid and general dogsbody.

'You're absolutely sure you don't mind, Molly?'

'I've just said so, haven't I?' She smiled. 'In fact it is a big relief.'

'In that case I'll stop worrying.'

'Mind you, Agnes, I was a bit bothered about the drop in wages but Miss Templeton isn't goin' to reduce them. She isn't so bad after all.'

So that's it, Agnes thought grimly. The rotten bitch isn't going to increase mine if she can help it. Fair enough until I'm competent at the job then just you wait, Madam Templeton. I'll get my rightful increase, you just see if I don't.

Agnes threw a bucket of water over the back steps then used a hard brush. She ought to have been on her knees to scrub it properly but there was no one about and she'd got away with it before. A little breather, she could do with it before going back in, and it was such an invitingly lovely, fresh morning.

'Hello, Carrot Nob.'

Agnes turned quickly, she was furious. She hated being called Carrot, Rusty or Ginger but most of all Carrot Nob. Heaven help him. It was Tommy Kingsley but a smiling Tommy Kingsley.

'We got off on the wrong foot and I want to apologise for my part in that.'

Agnes was taken aback, an apology was the last thing she expected from this arrogant friend of Molly's.

'You're still off on the wrong foot. I cannot stand being called Carrot Nob,' but a smile played around her mouth.

'Sorry. You've gorgeous hair, Agnes, I love the colour.'

'Liar.'

'What did you say?'

'You heard me or clean your ears if you didn't. Molly told me exactly what you said about auburn-haired girls.'

'And it nettled you?'

She shrugged and wondered why she didn't just walk away. She didn't even need an excuse, it was more than time she was back and inside Kerne House polishing the brasses. But still she stood.

'Now I remember the occasion. I'd taken Molly to the dancin' and there was this carrot – sorry, auburn-haired girl—'

'Giving you the glad eye?'

'How did you guess?'

'The conceit of some folk.'

'No, honestly, the girl comes into the shop, her folk are good customers, and I felt forced to give her a dance.'

'Keeping in with the customers?'

'Of course. Knew you'd understand, but Molly went in the huff and that's why I told her that load of rubbish.'

'I'll take that with a pinch of salt but what is a workin' man doing out at this time of day?'

'The benefit of bein' family means I don't have to work regular hours just as long as I'm at my uncle's beck and call.'

'You're here to see Molly?'

'I suppose so.'

'What do you mean you suppose so?'

'Could be I'm more attracted to someone else.'

The way he looked at her made the colour rush to her face and she turned as if to go.

'Don't, Agnes,' he pleaded. 'Don't go, not just yet.'

'I'm in trouble if I don't get back.'

He laughed. 'I'll bet you're seldom out of hot water and if it's Molly you're thinkin' of then don't. Her feelin's aren't involved any more than mine.'

'But you came to see her?'

'To tell her Friday is off, she knows it was a possibility. Will you tell her that from me? And I bet you anythin' she won't be upset.'

'I don't believe you but I'll tell her just the same.' With a determined effort she made herself walk away towards the back door of Kerne House but he was beside her.

'My brother's goin' to Canada.'

'What has that got to do with me?'

'He won't need his motor-bike.'

'You're buying it?'

'Yes.'

'Lucky you to have that kind of money.'

'I don't, but my uncle's goin' to lend me the money, take it off my wages every week I mean.'

'Very obliging uncle you have.'

The smile left his face. 'I'm no scrounger, Agnes, I work hard in that shop and at night I'm in the back making up orders. In a way I'm doin' two jobs for one wage and my uncle is shrewd enough to recognise that. He doesn't want to lose me.' He paused and touched her arm. 'Come out on the bike, you'd love it, I just know you would.'

Agnes was tempted, very tempted. She didn't know which was the bigger attraction, the bike or Tommy Kingsley. Together she was finding them irresistible.

'The last thing I want is to hurt Molly and I don't want any unpleasantness. I get enough of that from that sour-faced housekeeper.'

'Listen, Agnes, I wouldn't want to hurt Molly either but if I'm not very much mistaken I'm about to get the shove.'

'I'm going in.'

'Got a spare evening this week?'

'Wednesday,' she said, then could have bitten out her tongue.

'Great, I'll be at the end of the road sevenish.'

She was shaking and at the door she couldn't resist turning round and for a few moments she watched him walk away with his long swinging stride. What was she letting herself in for? This wasn't part of her plans. I'm letting myself in for nothing, she told herself, and that Tommy Kingsley can go and take a running jump. Too full of himself by far. Still just the once wouldn't do any harm and it was probably the only time she'd get the chance of being on the back of a motor-bike.

Chapter Fifteen

It was just on eight forty-five on a close and clammy morning when Rachel arrived at Duncairn House and knocked at the door of the servants' entrance. The door was slightly ajar and the voices carried to Rachel standing on the step with her suitcase by her side. Her fingers ached, it had been a long way to carry a case that got heavier by the minute and she had had to keep switching it from hand to hand. The only transport she was informed was a bus service to the neighbouring villages and that didn't go near the Glen Road.

'See who that is.'

There was a clatter of feet and then the door was flung wide and a girl in a light green overall beamed at her.

'Don't tell me! You're the new maid, Rachel something-or-other?'

'Rachel Donaldson.' Some of the nervous tension left Rachel and in that first exchange she felt that she had found a friend.

'Come on in. Shove that case in the corner there, it won't be in the way and we'll get it up to your room later.' Another girl had dried her hands and was walking over. 'This is Janet. Janet Harris and I'm Hetty Porter, awful name I hate it.'

'Shut up, Hetty and stop moaning.' Janet shook hands with Rachel. The pale grey eyes were cool and assessing but not unfriendly. Hetty followed Janet's lead and shook hands too. The girls were very different in appearance but of a similar age, Rachel thought. She put that to be seventeen or eighteen. Hetty was small and plump with a round cheerful, face and mischievous brown eyes. Janet was almost as tall as Rachel. She was big-busted and with her slim figure it made her look slightly top-heavy but for all that she was an attractive young woman with short, thick, fairish hair and a pretty face.

'I've to see Mrs Anderson at nine o'clock.'

'That's a whole quarter of an hour yet,' Hetty said touching the teapot.

'Sit yourself down and have a cup of tea and I'll join you. What about you, Janet?'

'No, thanks. These things have to be put away and I can't do that until I clean the press out. Your fault, Hetty, you should be doing it. Honestly if you would just do what you were told.'

'How was I to know there was a tear in the bag?'

'That's not the point. The bag of lentils should have been emptied into the jar.'

'I know, I know, I know and I've said I'm sorry.' She grinned over to Rachel not in the least put out. 'I don't know why but I always seem to be in hot water with somebody.'

Rachel smiled and looked around her.

'If you are wondering where cook is she always has forty winks after breakfast.'

'A mighty long forty winks if you ask me,' Janet muttered as she wiped out the shelves and collected the stray lentils.

'She is getting on a bit,' Hetty said with just a touch of censure in her voice. 'Sugar?' She held up the sugar bowl to Rachel.

'Yes, please, and a spot of milk.'

'While she's snoozing we get it all our own way so who is grumbling? And don't look so worried, Rachel, she's nice you'll get on with her.'

'I hope to get on with everybody,' Rachel said as she took her cup.

'That's a tall order.' Janet stopped her cleaning for a moment.

'Pay no attention to her, we're a friendly bunch and you'll soon get used to Janet and her funny ways.'

'That's enough from you, fatty.' Rachel looked from one to the other but it was just friendly banter.

Janet came over to the table and sat down. 'I think I will have that cup after all. Pour me one will you, Hetty?'

'She always does this, Rachel,' Hetty grumbled, 'just when I was about to tell you something about Duncairn House but madam, here, thinks she can do it better.'

'At least I don't take so long about it.'

'Get a move on then before I take her to see Bluebell.'

Rachel looked from one to the other, she didn't know what to make of them.

'Bluebell is our housekeeper, Mrs Anderson.'

'Oh.'

'Bella Anderson by name but as you'll find out she's almost always dressed in blue. Someone, can't remember who, called her Bluebell, not to her face of course, and it stuck.' Janet stirred her tea slowly. 'The old lady, the mistress, doesn't keep very well.'

'Nothing wrong with her mind, she's right on the ball,' Hetty added, determined to be in on the telling. 'Janet has the job of looking after her.'

'I take her breakfast to her and if she doesn't feel like getting up for her other meals I serve them to her in her room.' She paused. 'Let me tell you this, Rachel, it is a properly set table if you please with all the niceties.'

'She is old-fashioned, so what, it is her home after all.' Hetty smiled to Rachel. 'Sometimes I see her crossing the hall and muttering to herself about things going from bad to worse.'

'Once she's gone there'll be changes.'

'And not for the better,' Hetty said darkly. Her face took on a gloomy expression. 'With your looks, both of you, you'll get married and it's only fatty here who'll be left.'

'Nonsense, Hetty, that new red-haired lad can't take his eyes off you.'

'The one come to help in the gardens? That one?'

'That one.'

'I haven't noticed. You're having me on, Janet Harris.'

'I'm not. Next time you see him give him a big smile and see what happens.'

Rachel was loving it all but worried about the time.

'It's almost nine,' she ventured.

'Lord, save us so it is,' Hetty said getting up. 'Come along, Rachel, Bluebell doesn't like to be kept waiting.' Rachel followed the broad figure hurrying out of the kitchen and along a passage that led into the hall, a beautiful hall with dark panelling, but there was no time to admire it. Hetty had turned into a narrow corridor and stopping halfway along she opened the door.

'That's Rachel for you, Mrs Anderson.'

'Come in, Rachel. Thank you, Hetty.'

'Sorry if we are a few minutes late, Rachel was early enough, it was us that kept her talking.'

'That I can well believe,' the housekeeper said dryly, but Rachel saw her mouth quirk. 'Sit down, Rachel, yes, there,' she said and Rachel sat down. Mrs Anderson was sitting in a comfortable armchair and a newspaper was neatly folded on a footstool. There was a spirit stove and a kettle beside it. She waited until Hetty had shut the door then shook her head. 'Hetty can be a problem at times and not at all dependable, I'm afraid, but she is such a sweet-natured girl that we tend to overlook her faults.'

'She is nice.' Looking about her Rachel could see that the name Bluebell was very apt. It wasn't just what she wore and that was a plain dark blue dress with a white lace collar and cuffs, the colour had been carried into her sitting-room. The fire was set but not lit and in front of it was a fireside rug in shades of blue and with fringes at each end. The blue scheme stretched to the wallpaper and curtains and the cushions were of a deep blue velvet. A collection of glass animals sat on a polished side table. There was a plant at the window.

'Have you been to see your room?'

'Not yet, Mrs Anderson.'

'It's rather bare at present and I apologise for that.' She frowned with remembered annoyance. 'The previous occupant was rather careless and the chest of drawers was damaged. It has been mended but is still in the attic. I had meant to get Benny, our handyman, to bring it down but it escaped my memory. Still it will allow you to choose one or two other pieces for which the family has no further use. Nothing big, there isn't the space.' She smiled as she said this.

'Thank you.'

'Hetty will show you and once you've selected what you want get Benny to bring it down.' She paused. 'That deals with that, now as regards your duties I have been giving some thought to them and I've decided that you should spend two hours each afternoon in the sewing-room. Once you get through the bulk of the work we can reduce your time there and you'll take on other duties.'

'Yes, Mrs Anderson.'

'I do like my staff to be flexible where possible but when it comes to looking after the mistress, Janet sees to most of her needs. When she is not available I see to Mrs Craig's requirements myself. Janet knows what is required and is very understanding. Like all elderly people who do not enjoy good health, Mrs Craig can be difficult. Nevertheless,' she said severely, 'she is mistress of this house and our employer and it is our duty to carry out her wishes.'

'I do understand.'

'Not for a moment am I suggesting that you would be guilty of it but I warn my staff that I will not tolerate gossip about any member of the household.'

'I do not gossip,' Rachel said feeling annoyed at the turn in the conversation.

Mrs Anderson smiled. 'Nevertheless, you do require to know something about the family you are about to serve. There is, as I have said, the mistress who is a widow. Her daughter, Mrs Maud Meldrum and her granddaughter, Miss Betsy, reside here. Mrs Meldrum's husband is frequently in London on business, and his son,' she laid emphasis on 'his', is away at business college. Until now Mr Brian has spent only holidays here but I believe he has now completed his studies and will be spending more time at Duncairn House.'

Rachel decided to risk a question. 'You did say Mr Meldrum's son, does that mean—'

'You are quick. Yes, it is a second marriage. Mrs Meldrum's first husband, Colonel Wood, was killed abroad before their daughter was school age. That is all you require to know about the family,' she said briskly.

'Thank you, and about my other duties, Mrs Anderson?'

'All in good time.' She looked over at the clock on the mantelshelf and registered surprise. 'Dear me, is that the time? Let me just say hurriedly, I'll go into details later, what your other duties are. You will assist Hetty with the washing-up and the making of the beds. There is a special way in which it should be done but Hetty has at least mastered that and it is Hetty's job to clean out the fires and set them. Benny brings in the coal and logs and Janet does the dusting and polishing of the downstairs rooms. You can take a share of that.' She was still talking as she got up and Rachel got up too. 'We have help from women in the village who come in for an hour or two as and when it is required. Have you taken in most of that?'

'Yes, thank you, Mrs Anderson.'

Hetty was flicking a feather duster over the ornaments on the hall table but stopped when she saw Rachel.

'How did it go?'

'All right.'

'We got Benny to take up your case.'

'I need to find him. Apparently I'm getting to choose some pieces of furniture from the attic.'

'Harriet, the girl before you, was a wrecker, she didn't last long, thank goodness. I get on with most people but I couldn't stand her.'

'Why was she engaged?'

'Good references and of course she was on her best behaviour at the interview.'

'If she was as bad as all that how did she manage to get a reference?'

'Good question.' She grinned. 'It's one way of getting rid of unsatisfactory staff without having to sack them.' She gave a final flick of the feather duster. 'Better let you see your room.' She went ahead to the end of the hall and along a corridor to a flight of uncarpeted stairs leading to the servants' quarters. Taste and elegance were left behind, what Rachel saw was gloomy brown paint work and badly scuffed linoleum underfoot. The door Hetty was opening would have been much improved with a lick of paint. It angered Rachel. Servants were entitled to something better than this. At little cost that dreary brown could have been replaced with something lighter and prettier. She followed Hetty inside and the room was as bare as Mrs Anderson had warned her it would be. There was a small washstand and on it a chipped china bowl with a jug inside, a narrow wardrobe and a single bed. On it was a lemon-coloured, freshly laundered top cover. A mirror, mercifully uncracked, hung on a nail beside the window. Linoleum covered the floor with a half-moon rug beside the bed. There was one hard wooden chair. The story of my life, Rachel thought and decided there and then that her first purchase would be a cushion. Faded curtains hung at the window and the light was a single ceiling bulb with a torn shade.

'You don't think much of it, do you?'

'Frankly I'm appalled but it has possibilities.'

'If it had been nice you wouldn't have got it. Janet would have taken it for herself. She'd rather be on her own; me now, I like someone to chat to.'

'I'm used to my own bedroom,' Rachel said as she tried but failed to improve the hanging of the curtains. 'I'm an only child.'

'You must have been lonely.'

'Not when you've known nothing else.'

'Suppose so. Where do you come from?'

'Dundee.'

'What brought you to Hillend if I'm not being too nosey?'

'My father married again.'

'And you wanted to put a few miles between you and your step-mother?'

'Something like that.'

'You'll get an overall for the mornings like this awful thing I'm wearing and for the rest of the day you'll wear a black dress. Mrs Anderson sees to all that. You'll get two dresses from a shop in Perth that specialises in that sort of thing.' She looked wistful. 'Janet looks lovely in black and when she puts on the white pinny, honest I'm not kiddin', it's the size of a postage stamp, she looks great. So will you. Me, now,' she patted her ample frame, tried to grin and failed, 'can you see a wee white pinny on this fatty?'

'Hetty, don't think of yourself as fat; my da would call you nicely rounded.' Thinking of her father she felt tears at the back of her eyes and blinked rapidly.

'You all right?'

'Yes, just got thinking.'

'Regretting leaving home?'

'No.' She smiled brightly. 'You're very kind going to all this trouble for me.'

'A pleasure and Mrs Anderson did tell me to take you under my wing until you find your way about.'

'Mrs Anderson is very nice.'

'Most of the time she is but Mrs Morton, that's the cook, is a real pet. Maybe she does take more time off than she should,' she began to giggle. 'Janet is convinced she doesn't go to her room for a rest but for a tipple. Don't be shocked, my ma told me most cooks do, it's one of the perks of the job.'

Rachel smiled. 'I'm not so easily shocked as I used to be.'

'Mrs Morton looks after us like a mother and if we have problems hers is a sympathetic ear and she doesn't gossip.'

Rachel pointed to the jug and basin. 'Where do I get the water?'

'Benny, this place would collapse without that man, gets it for you. Put your jug out at night and he'll fill it with hot water in the morning. Speaking of which, better show you the bathroom.'

They went out and further along the corridor, Hetty threw open the bathroom door letting it hit the wall. 'We are allowed one bath a week but no one would be any the wiser if you had an extra.'

The use of the bathroom even once a week pleased Rachel. All her life she had had to use the scullery, shutting the door to strip off and have a good wash all over. She went right inside for a better look. The walls were green and the bath had cast-iron feet. All around was a tide mark. There was also a brown stain caused by the small but steady drip of the cold-water tap which was in need of a new washer. A cake of Lifebuoy soap was on the window ledge and there was a cork mat in front of the bath.

'Don't forget to take your own towel along and believe me it's no joke if you forget it and no one around to get it for you.'

Rachel grinned. 'I get the picture. What's this wonderful Benny like?'

'Benny? He's old,' she said dismissively. 'After his wife died he didn't like to be alone in the cottage and spends most of his time here. Tomorrow do for your furniture?'

'Yes, fine.'

'I'll take you up in the morning and you can have a good nosey round.'

'Thanks for everything, Hetty, I'll go and hang up my clothes.'

Hetty took Rachel along to the kitchen which was warm and inviting. it wasn't quite time for the midday meal and no one was seated at the table.

'Brought our new maid to meet you, Mrs Morton. This is Rachel Donaldson.'

'Sit down, lass, it's all the same price,' she said continuing to beat the cake mixture. 'This is me all behind but a few more minutes and I'll have it in the oven. Test the potatoes, one of you,' she turned briefly to a woman and a girl. The woman went over to the pot and stabbed the potatoes with a fork.

'Ready for straining I would say.'

'Then do it.'

Mrs Morton was small and stout with a motherly face. She had a large white overall tied round her middle and judging by the effort going into the beating she had unlimited energy. Satisfied with the mixture she emptied it into a cake tin, evened off the top and placed it on the middle shelf of the oven. A rush of hot air came out and she shut the door hastily then put up a plump hand to tuck away a stray wisp of hair which hung damply to her forehead. A leg of pork sizzled on a spit and was being turned by a young boy, a relative of the cook's Rachel was to discover, who had not yet found suitable employment. It kept him out of mischief and gave him a few coppers for his pocket.

'No, Hetty, lass, keep your eyes averted. The pork is for THEM but like as not there'll be enough to make a good meal for us tomorrow.'

Rachel was to remember that first meal in the warm kitchen. They were like a big family. The long scrubbed table had a bench down each side. Mrs Morton at the head of the table occupied a chair with arms and it was she who dished out the food which was then handed down the table. The hourly workers had departed but the two gardeners came in. The younger one had light ginger hair and Rachel saw Hetty colouring prettily as the youth gave a shy smile in their direction. Mrs Anderson was served her meals in her own room. Janet, who had been attending to the mistress, was the last to arrive.

For the servants and workmen this was the main meal of the day. It was good and substantial. Oxtail soup was followed by a rich stew thick with vegetables. The kind that sticks to your ribs was how her da used to describe it. She wished that she didn't keep remembering things. A huge tureen of potatoes was put in the centre of the table for everyone to help themselves. Apple tart with pouring custard followed and judging by the comments was a firm favourite. Hetty got up to bring the big brown teapot to the table but the two gardeners got up, mumbled something that could have been appreciation of the meal and went out. They preferred to make their own brew and take it in the shed that held their tools.

Forty-five minutes was the time allowed and as soon as it was up Mrs Morton pushed back her chair, got to her feet, and that was the signal for the kitchen to be cleared. Hetty rolled up her sleeves and began to pile up the dirty dishes and Rachel went to give her a hand. The cake was not yet ready to come out of the oven and Mrs Morton sat herself down beside the fire with her swollen feet on the wooden stool.

Her first day at Duncairn House was all but over. She lay in the creaking iron bed with sleep far away. Her brain was too active and in her mind she was going over all that had happened. On the whole she supposed it had been a satisfying day and she had learned something about life in her grandmother's house.

An alarm clock supplied to the servants gave them no excuse for sleeping in. It went off and Rachel groped over to silence it. A weak sunlight streaked in through the inadequate curtains and fleetingly changed the brown of the linoleum to a warm treacle. She got out of bed and opened the curtains then opened the door and brought in the jug of hot water. She poured it into the basin and washed as best she could. In a dark skirt and fresh blouse she went quietly through the sleeping household to the kitchen. The cook and Janet were already there. Good mornings were said but little else. It was too early for talking and time was precious with breakfast trays to be prepared for those who did not go down to the breakfast room. Rachel was getting it easy for the first day or two and after the breakfast dishes were washed and put away Hetty took her up to the attic. It was cold and cobwebby but with sufficient light from the small windows to see around.

'I'll leave you to it and get on with my chores. See and choose something decent.'

'I intend to. Thanks, Hetty.'

Dust was everywhere and Rachel was glad of her overall to protect her clothes. It was thick on some of the forlorn-looking articles of furniture that, along with boxes and wicker hampers, littered the floor area. Before long she found a small chest of drawers that would suit her and taking Mrs Anderson at her word put a tapestry stool in poor condition beside the drawers. Next she hunted for a chair and found one, small and comfortable-looking and in need of repair which she thought she could manage. No harm in having a look around to see what else was kept up here. As she moved along the head space grew less and there were more cobwebs, some getting into her hair. Her face broke into a smile when she saw the doll's house complete with furniture. There were games and grubby soft toys. It was over at the window and she had almost missed it – a large rocking-horse and she went over to touch it letting her hand glide over the smooth wood. Had her mother and her Aunt Maud played with these toys, she wondered? She pictured two small girls arranging and rearranging the tiny furniture. So engrossed was she that she didn't hear the light footsteps, only the sound of a voice that brought her quickly upright to bang her head against a rafter.

'Ouch! You didn't half startle me,' Rachel said as her fingers gingerly touched the top of her head.

'Obviously,' the voice said haughtily, 'and may I ask what you are doing sneaking about up here?'

'I was not sneaking,' Rachel said matching her tone for haughtiness and she noticed a flicker of surprise in the eyes looking at her. 'I happen to have Mrs Anderson's permission to choose furniture for my room.'

'And have you?'

'Yes.'

'Does that include the rocking-horse you seem to have taken a fancy to?'

Rachel coloured. 'I apologise for that, I'm afraid I couldn't resist touching it.'

'Very well, I shan't mention this to my grandmother but if she were to hear about it your days at Duncairn House would be numbered.'

She is my grandmother too, she wanted to say, but the time was not right. Perhaps it never would be.

'You had better get down and I'll follow.'

This could only be her cousin Betsy, Rachel thought. The girl wasn't very tall with straight fair hair cut in a fringe which suited her small face. Rachel thought her very attractive but could have wished to meet her cousin under happier circumstances. She sighed. It wasn't a very good start.

Chapter Sixteen

Agnes was emptying the teapot when Molly joined her.

'You making fresh?'

'I am but it's not for us. Where have you been, I've been looking for you?' she said as she spooned in the tea.

'Well, I'm here.'

'Your boyfriend can't make it for Friday.'

'Where did you see him?'

'Out the back. Said he was in a hurry and to tell you.'

Molly sucked her lip and puckered her brow. 'I wanted to see him.'

'Why?'

'To tell him to his face that I wouldn't be goin' out with him again.'

'Thought he was the light of your life?'

'So he was for a while but I've gone off him. Anyway I hate that bike and he's mad about it.'

'He's buying it from his brother, he told me.'

'Not in much of a hurry when he took time to tell you that,' she said suspiciously.

'Just mentioned it as he was walking away,' Agnes said carelessly. 'You got your eye on someone else?'

'What's it to you?'

'Nothing.'

'I know better. You're keen on Tommy.' She smiled knowingly.

'No, I'm not.'

'Bet if you got the chance you would go on the back of his bike.'

'Quite like to go on the back of his bike and I've got a stronger stomach than you.'

Molly smirked. 'You're welcome to Tommy Kingsley and his bike. Geoffrey's lovely and he's a marvellous dancer,' she said dreamily.

'Sounds a bit of all right.'

Molly laughed. 'That tea is goin' to be stewed.'

'God! I forget all about it.' She hurried away.

Such hilarity had seldom been heard in the kitchen of Kerne House and it was obvious that Miss Templeton was out of earshot. The staff were seated at the long table and Mrs Robertson supervising the proceedings.

Agnes was doing her training and a dress rehearsal was the reason for the hilarity. Over her dark dress she had on a white frilly apron, the lace cap was all but lost in the thick auburn hair and only a wisp of it showed. She was unsmiling, she was concentrating hard for very soon now she would be serving the master and mistress in the dining-room.

Miss Templeton had thrust at her the book entitled DUTIES OF A TABLEMAID with instructions to read it and read it again until every word of it was understood. Agnes glanced at it then went back to read it properly. Most of it, she decided, was just plain common sense apart from the setting of the table and that she admitted had taken longer to master. The rest was straightforward enough and she wondered what all the fuss was about.

Now that she was actually handling plates filled with soup she was finding it rather more difficult. In theory she knew it all, in practice it was a different story.

'Keep your hand steady, Agnes, the soup shouldn't move in the plate.'

It was moving all right, it was splashing on her hand.

'Don't slouch, straighten your back and you'll find it easier,' Molly said. She was secretly pleased that Agnes, the know-all, was not finding the duties of tablemaid as easy as she had expected.

By the time she put down the last soup plate she was beginning to get the hang of it. Her trouble, she realised, was that she was too slow and careful. Quicker movements and she was getting better results.

'Not too bad, Agnes,' Mrs Robertson said kindly, 'and don't look so smug, Molly, everybody has to learn and you've had a few accidents in your day.'

Molly sulked through the main course. The others were full of praise though one or two had expected the soup to go down their necks.

'Hope there is plenty left for me,' Agnes said seating herself at the table.

'There's plenty since you refused second helpings,' someone muttered.

There was nothing wrong with Agnes's hearing. 'Demanding extra helpings is not done in the best of circles and you lot were supposed to be acting ladies and gentlemen for once in your life.'

'Mrs Robertson, I got ever such a little helping of rice pudding,' Gloria said.

'As much as we got,' the gardeners spoke together, 'and we are two growin' laddies.'

'Wheesht the lot of you,' the cook scolded but she was happy. The rice pudding would just have to be thrown out and with all those starving people in the world, she read all about it in the papers, it was a sin to waste good food. Plates were quickly handed up the table and after checking that the helpings were much the same for quantity, they were handed down again and the pudding disappeared in record time.

They left leaving just the cook and Agnes.

'I made a right mess of it, didn't I?'

'Och, not as bad as all that, you're needin' a bit more practice that's all. Better just practise on me. Serving one is no different from serving half a dozen so you just remember that and don't get flustered. You've one pair of hands and folk just have to be patient and wait.'

'Thanks, Mrs Robertson, you're a gem and you really think I'll make it?'

'Agnes, lass, I've no fear of you failin'.'

'You quite happy there?'

'Yes, fine,' Agnes said as she settled herself on the seat and put her arms around Tommy's waist.'

'I won't go fast.'

'I don't mind. I'm not Molly.'

'All the same, I'll go slow until you get used to it. It's a cold night and it's colder on the bike. Did you put something warm on?'

Agnes giggled. 'My da's drawers. No, honestly I'll be all right. I've a warm jumper under this jacket.'

'Right then, we're off.'

They weren't going fast but there was a wind and Agnes's hair was whipped round her face. Tommy had given her a pair of goggles that had belonged to his brother and Agnes longed to see herself in a mirror to see how they suited her. The wind sang, the countryside sped by and she wanted to burst out in song herself. She was so happy, she'd never been happier in her life.

'Mind if I go a bit faster?'

'Fast as you like,' she said throwing caution to the wind. Faster and faster they went and she clung to the figure in front and wished that she had worn gloves. Agnes seldom felt cold except for her hands. She could be warm all over and her hands go numb and they were going numb now. Her hands were slipping, she had no grip.

'Stop, Tommy.' But the wind blew away her voice and if anything he increased the speed.

'Stop! For God's sake stop, you idiot,' she screamed as her arms began to slip away from the leather jacket.

This time he did hear and brought the bike to a slithering stop at the side of the road. Agnes was almost in tears and Tommy's face was thunderous.

'Yelling like that could have caused a bloody accident. God, I thought Molly was bad but you're a damned sight worse, at least she suffered in silence.'

'I tried to get you to stop before,' Agnes whimpered. 'I couldn't hang on much longer.'

'I'm sorry.' Suddenly he was all concern as she raised a face pale with fright. 'What was it, Agnes? What frightened you?'

She started to speak but she was still reliving the moments when her hands, her useless hands, were slipping and she was going to be thrown off. She shivered and strong arms went round her, holding her close. She clung to him on that quiet country road and felt his comforting warmth. When her face came up from his jacket his mouth came down on hers. Agnes had been kissed before, light kisses that meant nothing but this was different. The first gentle butterfly kisses had given way to fierceness, an urgency, that both alarmed and thrilled her. This was different, this was exciting and all kinds of peculiar sensations were flowing through her body.

Then just as suddenly the old Agnes was back and she was pulling herself away ashamed and appalled at her show of weakness.

'Agnes! Oh, God, Agnes! That was wonderful.' His voice was rough with emotion. 'You felt it too, I know you did. You must have.'

'No, I did not,' she said furiously, 'and don't you ever do that to me again.' He was too angry and surprised to hear the tears in her voice.

'You asked for it,' he said brutally.

'That's a lie.'

'Is it, Agnes? Is it?' he demanded gripping her arms and bringing her close to him but she fought him off pounding at his chest.

'I'd got a fright, I was scared and you took advantage of me.'

'Wrong, I've never forced myself on any girl, I don't need to. For me it has to be a two-way thing. Your trouble, Agnes, is you're afraid of your own feelings.'

She shook her head and looked at him. She'd taken off the goggles as soon as the bike stopped and made as though to put them on.

'No, keep them off. Let me see the expression on your face.'

'I've got plans for my life, Tommy Kingsley, and they don't include you.'

'I've got plans too,' Tommy said quietly, 'and they could include you. Come on, sit down and let us talk it over.'

'There's nothing to talk about,' but she allowed herself to be led away and they sat down together on the grass verge.

'For a start I want to know what happened to scare you. I thought you were all right on the bike.'

'So I was, I was loving it but it was my hands,' she said shamefacedly, 'they go dead with the cold and I have no feeling at all in them. Stupid of me not to bring gloves but I didn't think.'

'You can have mine going back.' He took off the leather gauntlet gloves and she slipped her hands into them. They were deliciously warm and she began working her fingers inside the roomy gloves until a painful tingling returned them to life.

'Won't your hands get cold?'

'I'll manage.' She smiled. 'Those cosy enough for you?'

'Lovely.'

'Want to hear what my plans are for the future?'

'If you want to tell me.'

'I do. I'm a lad with ambition, Agnes, and I go after what I want. It doesn't depend on getting my uncle's shop though I expect it will come to me.'

'That could be ages, he can't be that old.'

'Getting on a bit, he is the eldest of the family and I see him wanting to take life a bit easier. Probably got quite a bit by him to see him through. He needs me, Agnes, more than I need him and that is nice to know.';

'You want your own business?'

'More than that. I want a shop and a fleet of vans on the road.' He laughed a little self-consciously. 'Can you see it, Agnes, KINGSLEY,

SUPPLIER OF PRIME BEEF in huge letters on the van?'

'Delivering orders you mean?'

'No, I do not. Folk out in the country, anybody away from the shops, would appreciate the shop coming to them. In the back of the van I'd have a slab to cut the meat to requirements, a scale to weigh, in short, the same as the shop. Must charge a wee bit more for the service but I don't see that a problem.'

'Neither do I, they would be saving the fare to the shops.'

'Exactly. What do you think of the idea?'

'Has merit. I'm impressed.' She was.

'More to being a butcher than people think,' he said importantly, 'have to know the cuts of beef for a start and just where to put the knife.' He watched the changing expressions on her face. 'I don't go after the impossible, Agnes, I'm a realist and I don't waste time dreaming. I don't expect to be wealthy but a comfortable living will do me fine.'

It sounded like a good life, Agnes told herself, much, much better than she'd known in Spinner's Lane but she knew it wasn't enough. It fell far short of her own ambitions. It wasn't only the money though that came into it. She wanted to be with educated people who would talk intelligently and effortlessly about things that mattered, not the awful trivia that was about all she ever heard. All the same, she conceded, for a working lad, Tommy spoke reasonably well but not good enough and his manners, hers were nothing to boast about, but there lay the difference, she would learn because she wanted to. Tommy would change as he became successful but his working roots would always show because he would have no wish to change that part of himself.

'Not saying much are you? But then it's money and position you're after isn't it?' he said heavily.

'Maybe it is. I'm certainly not going to throw myself away.'

'Is that what you would be doing if you ended up with me?'

'I didn't say that, you did. In any case there is no possibility of us ending up together.'

'You are afraid to admit it but you are just as attracted to me as I am to you. We belong together but you'd marry any ugly sod just so long as he had the means—'

'You go too far, Tommy Kingsley, how dare you say such a thing.' Her eyes were flashing fire as she got to her feet. 'When I marry it will be to someone who knows how to behave, not to an ignoramus like you.'

He got up but taking his time and she saw the contempt on his face. 'I'm sorry for you, Agnes,' he said quietly, 'there's no happiness in the road you're taking. A lady is born a lady. You'll aim high but like me you'll always be working class and those with breeding will make use of you for as long as it suits them.' He gave a cruel smile. 'Gold-diggers end up in the gutter where they belong.'

'Have you quite finished?' she said icily.

'I have.'

Going over to his bike, he swung himself into position and waited until her arms stole round his waist, then they were off. For the short journey he kept up a reasonable speed then stopped in front of Kerne House. Wordlessly she handed him his gloves and the goggles. He took them without looking at her then he was lost in a storm of dust and small stones.

Agnes was more shaken then she cared to admit. He had the measure of her as her mother would say, only she didn't believe it not for a single moment. She would be somebody and no one would look down on her.

Two weeks later Agnes had forgotten Tommy Kingsley or so she told herself. Her mind was concentrating hard on the ordeal ahead. Mostly she had been kept to the back of the house and rarely saw the mistress except as a hunched-up figure tending to her plants. As to the master, she had never laid eyes on him.

That was about to change. Miss Templeton had decided the time had come for Molly to step aside and Agnes take over the duties of tablemaid. To get to that stage had been nerve-wracking for all concerned. Twice or three times Agnes had only just stopped herself from emptying the plates into Miss Templeton's lap.

The housekeeper was to remain in the background to see that all went well. Agnes was dressed in the regulation dark dress with a small white apron and a frilly cap which Agnes had managed to secure at a jaunty angle. Her hands and nails had been inspected for cleanliness and now she stood against the far wall of the dining-room to await the arrival of Mr and Mrs Edwin Taylor.

The dining-room had two large windows that looked out onto the garden. The dining-table could be extended at either end to suit the number of guests but since it was to be only Edwin Taylor and his wife who were to be eating it was reduced to its smallest. Even so there was a good length of table between the master and his good lady. The straight-backed cushioned chairs were in the Regency pattern and had come from a sale in one of the big houses which had been bought over for a hotel. On the handsome sideboard were two heaters to keep the food warm.

The door opened and Margaret Taylor, in a burgundy dress that did nothing for her complexion, preceded her husband to take her place at the foot of the table. Agnes had glanced away from the door but now she turned back to it. A smallish, stout, red-faced man came in, shut the door, and Agnes nearly fainted. There was no question in her mind that this was the man who would have run her over had she not stepped smartly aside and at whom she had stuck out her tongue. Dear God! she thought in agony, would he remember her? But of course he wouldn't, not after all this time. Her eyes followed him until he sat down, took the white, stiffly starched napkin from its silver ring—'

'What are you waiting for, girl?' Miss Templeton hissed.

Agnes gathered her wits together. 'Do I start now?'

'Of course.'

Soup needed a steady hand but after a number of mishaps she had finally mastered the technique. A little less in the plate would have made it a bit easier, Agnes thought as she carefully placed the soup before the mistress. Mrs Taylor smiled and Agnes's confidence grew. When she lowered the plate before the master she would have sworn with her last breath that he moved and jerked her arm. For one nightmarish moment she expected the plate to empty over the table. The liquid swung from side to side and some of it went over the top and on to her hand. She bore with the pain, thankful that only a small amount had gone on the cloth.

'Sorry, sir, but you jerked my hand.'

'I did nothing of the kind,' he thundered, his face almost purple.

'You are new,' the quiet voice came from the foot of the table.

'Yes, ma'am.'

'First day nerves and don't worry, no great damage has been done.'

Agnes returned to her position at the sideboard. Miss Templeton's eyes were closed as if it was all getting too much for her. When she did open them Agnes was over collecting the empty plates. She dealt with the remainder of the meal with reasonable efficiency and Miss Templeton left after the sweet course. It was as she was going over with the cheese board that Agnes felt eyes watching her, and when she forced herself to look up and into his, she saw his puzzled frown.

★ ★ ★

The master and mistress were back in their sitting-room. Edwin with his cigar and brandy and Margaret with idle hands in her lap.

'Clumsy girl, bad as the other, maybe worse.'

'No, dear, I thought she did rather well particularly in the circumstances. You did knock her arm, accidentally, but you were to blame and you must have known it.'

His hand came down with a large smack on his knee. 'By God! I've got it. Never forget a face and that hair clinched it.'

'What are you talking about, dear?'

'That girl, how long has she worked here?'

'Let me think, it was just after – oh, I should think two months.'

'That fits.'

'What does?'

'That's her all right. Impudent madam put her tongue out at me.'

'Put her tongue out at you?'

'That is what I said.'

'Must have been a reason, and where did this take place?'

'Outside the gate, the fool girl was standing right plonk in the middle waiting to be knocked down.'

'You were in that car coming down the drive and into the roadway as if no one but you had the right to be there.'

'Nonsense, woman, the fool was standing there with no intention of moving.'

'What did you do?'

'Shook my fist at her and mouthed a few oaths which she couldn't hear, so don't upset yourself.'

'The truth is you nearly knocked her down – no wonder she stuck her tongue out at you. It's precisely what I would have done if I hadn't been so well brought up.'

'She's got to go, Margaret, I won't have that girl under my roof.'

'I refuse to dismiss her.'

'I insist that you do.'

'Insist all you like but the girl remains. You, Edwin, have no idea just how difficult it is to get honest and reliable staff these days. I can see it coming when we shall have to do a great deal more for ourselves.'

Edwin Taylor looked alarmed as well he might. He was a man who liked his creature comforts and someone at hand to see to his every need.

'Not as bad as that surely, you exaggerate, Margaret?'

'I assure you I am not exaggerating. All you need do is take a look in the paper for domestic help and you'll get some idea of what the position is.'

'I see,' he said tersely.

'The girl stays?'

'I suppose so.'

'Your chances of remaining at Kerne House are very slim after that exhibition.' Miss Templeton had sent for Agnes.

Agnes shuffled from one foot to the other. She was of the same opinion, it was just a question of how long it would take for Mr Taylor to remember the incident at the gate.

'He knocked my elbow,' Agnes said stubbornly, 'and I'd like to see you doing any better if someone knocked yours just as you were putting down a plate of soup.'

'That is not the point. I would have had the good manners to blame myself for the mishap. Really, to more or less tell your employer that it was his fault – words fail me they do, Agnes, they fail me.' She gave a deep, deep sigh. 'Just go away.'

'Thank you, Miss Templeton.'

For a whole week Agnes awaited her fate, certain that she was to lose her job but when it didn't happen she just assumed that Edwin Taylor had as yet not connected her with the incident. Life at Kerne House went on as usual and Agnes was quite happy. She had been too busy with unfamiliar tasks to give more than a passing thought to Rachel, but now she began thinking about her and wondering why she'd heard nothing. Surely she was sufficiently settled by now to let her best friend know where she was working and if she was staying with Miss Reid. There was a niggling worry, something wasn't right and she longed for a letter to clear up the mystery.

Chapter Seventeen

Two extra bedrooms would be required for that night and Rachel was on her way down after preparing them. As she saw the solitary figure move away from the foot of the stairway Rachel felt her mouth go dry. This could only be her grandmother. A chill had confined the old lady to her room and this was the first day she had ventured downstairs.

Unaware of the watching eyes the woman moved on supported by her rubber-tipped stick and gazed out of the long, narrow windows that gave light to the hall. From where she stood she could see the sloping fresh green lawns and beyond that the soft rolling hills that seemed to merge with the blue-grey sky. Katherine Craig loved Duncairn House and the view from it. Was heaven to be compared to this? she wondered and how many years or months before the good Lord claimed her for that so-called Paradise in the skies? A small sigh escaped her. How lucky were those people with their faith and their absolute certainty that a better life lay beyond the grave. She could never be sure how much she believed and on the great Day of Judgment how would she fare? She closed her eyes. As God was her witness she had always done what she thought best. But best for whom? She gave another sigh. Useless to keep going over the past but it was becoming clearer than the present. Her thoughts these days were all for Amelia, that pretty child, that wicked young woman. No, wicked was too strong a word though Albert had used it. Thoughtless and silly more like, but, oh, the heartbreak she had caused.

Why? Why? Why? Life was full of questions that couldn't be answered. Why did she keep thinking of Amelia, feel her nearness? Amelia was dead, had been these long years. Perhaps it was of the child she was thinking. The girl child she knew existed, fathered by a rough, working-class nobody but still Amelia's child, the Craig blood in her. Her granddaughter.

How long was she going to stand there? Rachel asked herself. She made polishing the woodwork her excuse for remaining where she was. The woman moved at last but only to one of the chairs placed on either side of the hall table. Gingerly, and with a grimace of pain, she lowered herself into one and hung her stick on the edge of the hall table.

There was no way Rachel could avoid passing her grandmother and she couldn't linger any longer. A pile of sewing awaited her. Swiftly and holding the dusters in her hand, she went down the remaining stairs, made to pass the woman staring into space but the voice stopped her, a surprisingly strong voice.

'I don't recall seeing you before,' she rasped.

'I've only been here a few weeks, ma'am.'

Old and slightly stooped though she was, Katherine Craig had retained her haughty look. She had faded, watery blue eyes that must once have been beautiful. A myriad tiny lines criss-crossed the colourless face and the white hair was thinning to show patches of pink scalp. All this Rachel took in in those first moments.

'Don't rush away, girl,' she said irritably as Rachel made to go. 'What is your name?'

'Rachel Donaldson, ma'am.'

She pursed her lips and nodded. 'The seamstress.'

The description displeased Rachel. It made her sound like a hundred, she thought resentfully.

'I was a dressmaker's assistant, ma'am.'

'Is there a difference?'

'I would think so.'

'Sharp tongue you have, miss, doesn't become a maid.'

Rachel bit her lip and kept quiet. She wasn't going to apologise.

'Get on with your work then,' she said, fixing Rachel with a fierce look from those faded blue eyes.

Rachel needed no second bidding. Her grandmother had not endeared herself. She hadn't much liked her cousin either. Perhaps she would just stay long enough to get another job, perhaps as a dressmaker's assistant in Perth.

Nothing much was missed by Katherine Craig and this girl interested her. She was well-spoken and with a certain something she couldn't quite put her finger on. Perhaps it was pride though what a maid had to be proud about was hard to imagine unless it was in her work. Janet served her well and knew her likes and dislikes but this girl might be interesting to study, relieve the boredom too. She'd get Mrs Anderson to arrange it. A small groan escaped her as she saw the hurrying figure and from that distance could almost hear her tut-tutting.

'Mother, really, what are you doing sitting in the hall, you know how draughty it is and you just getting over that chill.'

Maud Meldrum had retained her slim figure but she had the face of a woman ten years older with pronounced bags under her eyes. She dressed well and suited what she wore. Her skirt was rough Harris tweed in a heather mixture and the cashmere twin-set picked out the palest shade of pink.

'Don't fuss, Maud, just help me up,' Mrs Craig said irritably, 'and if I want to sit here I'll sit here and if I get another chill then I get another chill and that'll maybe be the one that sees me off.'

'I do wish you wouldn't speak like that, Mother, it distresses me and it's childish.'

'Second childhood,' the woman said with a wicked grin, she liked to torment her daughter. She got her stick and with Maud's help started the slow painful process of walking.

'Is your arthritis playing up?' her daughter asked sympathetically.

'Arthritis doesn't play up, Maud, it is like bad toothache, the hell of all diseases, and it's in the family so you are not likely to escape.' She smiled grimly. 'That husband of yours, when is he expected?'

'Between six and six thirty, he's meeting Brian's train. Mother, I told you this before and I also told you that Mr and Mrs McGregor have been invited to dinner tomorrow evening and Peter too if he can manage.'

'Yes, I daresay you did.' They had reached the sitting-room where a fire was burning and a guard up to stop the sparks from flying. 'Take that thing away, keeps the heat from getting out and old bones need the heat.'

The guard was removed. The easy chair was refused and one with wooden arms replaced it.

'Are you quite comfortable now, Mother?'

'Yes, I'm fine, just fine,' but the tiredness was etched on her face. 'Leave me a while then come back and help me up to my room. I'll need a rest if I have to share a meal with that good-for-nothing husband of yours. You were a fool to marry him, Maud, you weren't the attraction,' she said brutally. 'All he's interested in is getting his hands on Duncairn House but that'll be over my dead body.' She gave a peal of laughter like someone demented and Maud looked at her with concern. 'I'm not mad just amused at my own remark "over my dead body" and that's exactly what he wants. He wants me dead and out of the way. You, he can twist round his fingers and Betsy is too young to be a problem but I'm a match for him and he knows it.'

'Henry is my husband and I refuse to listen to any more of this.'

'Your husband in name only, that is right isn't it, Maud?' her mother said with a new gentleness.

Maud's mouth quivered. 'That is our own affair, nothing to do with you.'

'It's none of my business I know that but I doubt if these trips are all business. You are too trusting, my dear.'

'Don't underestimate me, Mother, I may surprise everyone yet.' She paused. 'You are fond of Brian so don't make it difficult for him. Just try to be pleasant to Henry and particularly tomorrow when we have guests.'

'Hoping for a match between Betsy and Peter?'

'What if I am, it would be a good match.'

'I'd welcome it too but I'm afraid the spark isn't there, not with Peter, if I'm any judge of that sort of thing.'

The sewing-room next to Rachel's bedroom was a cold room and the uncurtained window made it feel even colder. The empty grate didn't help either and Rachel hoped that come winter, and some of the October days were cold enough for winter, she would be allowed a fire. The Singer sewing machine was similar to the one to which she had been accustomed and with her foot on the treadle the sheet was racing through her fingers. Two more and that would do for today. Hetty gave a light tap at the door and came in.

'Got the two bedrooms done, did you?'

Rachel raised her head. 'Yes. Who else is coming apart from Mr Meldrum and his son?'

'No one.' She nodded as if understanding. 'The extra bedroom is for Mr Henry. Separate rooms,' she giggled. 'Isn't it awful but maids know what is going on better than anyone.'

Rachel whipped out the sheet and tied the loose threads. 'What is he like, this Henry Meldrum?'

'Depends on your type I suppose,' Hetty said closing the door and ready for a gossip. 'Tall and broad with a moustache and thinks no end of himself.' She lowered her voice. 'Janet's smitten, I happen to know that.'

'Surely not, I mean, a married man,' Rachel said shocked and not really believing it. Janet didn't seem the type somehow.

'For some that makes it all the more interesting and I'm not saying this about Janet but he has plenty of money and a car and can give a girl a good time.'

'What about Brian Meldrum?' Rachel asked more to get off the subject of Henry Meldrum than genuine interest.

'As different to his old man as could be. Must take after his mother. He's not very tall, skinny, hardly any flesh on him. You know the half-starved-looking arty type, but he's nice.'

'Thought he was doing a business course?'

'Janet says he didn't make university and his father insisted he got some qualifications so that he can use his business connections and get him a job in the City. That's London.'

'I know that.'

'Brian would hate it, he's a real country lad at heart.'

'You know him?'

'I'd be so lucky. No, but he isn't in the least standoffish and talks to anyone. Tell you something else for good measure.'

'Go on then,' Rachel smiled as she began on the next sheet then decided it was so thin in places that it wasn't worth the trouble and tossed it aside.

'Mrs Craig has a soft spot for him and encourages him to make use of his artistic talents.,'

Rachel doubted if the woman she knew to be her grandmother would have a soft spot for anyone.'

'I'd better move my body.'

It was just as well she did for a minute later Mrs Anderson came into the sewing-room and Rachel took her foot off the treadle.

'You are doing very well, Rachel, but I think you can give the sewing a rest for a few days. Janet could do with some help in the dining-room. You could assist with the setting of the table and also help to serve the food.'

'The setting of the table, of course, Mrs Anderson, but I'd be a bit nervous about serving the meal, I've never done it before.'

'Neither you have but it is time you started. In any case, Janet will keep you right and she'll show you where to get a fresh white apron and cap.' She smiled. 'Just keep calm.'

She left and Rachel sat with idle hands thinking of the evening ahead. What worried her was having those faded blue eyes watching her and she had a sinking feeling they would be.

Rachel failed to hide her amusement. Janet was treating her as though she were a halfwit.

'What's so funny?'

'You! I have set a table before, you know.'

'Not in a proper dining-room.'

Rachel's thoughts went back over the years. She had been no more than eight or nine but her mother had been firm. To use the correct cutlery, to know how it should be placed, were so important to her and she had made sure that her small daughter would be no stranger to a properly set table. Sunday was the day everything was done just so and she could recall her father looking at the table and asking if royalty was expected. Looking back she wondered where all the cutlery had come from then supposed her mother must have bought six of everything when she could afford to.

Janet was waiting for an answer as she folded the white damask napkins.

'Perhaps not a proper dining-room but my mother set high standards.'

Janet's sharp look made Rachel think she had made her first mistake, she would have to be more careful. 'She was trained in a big house like this,' she added as a quick afterthought.

Janet nodded seemingly satisfied. 'I'm only following instructions from Mrs Anderson. She said I was in charge and you are to do as I say.'

'Yes, Janet, or should I say yes, m'am.'

'Cut it out.'

'Sorry.'

They worked in silence until Janet declared herself satisfied with everything.

Dinner was to be served at seven thirty and it was nearly that now. Dressed identically both maids were standing well back and near to the huge mahogany sideboard. It had a mirror along the back and Rachel took a hurried look at herself, the lace-trimmed cap was making her feel self-conscious, such a silly little thing. Watching her Janet felt irritation and jealousy and jealousy was a new experience. Aware of her attractive appearance, her power to attract men, she had always been full of confidence. Now here was Rachel and eyes that had followed her were showing an interest in the new maid.

'Done admiring yourself?'

'I wasn't.'

'I saw you.'

'You saw me looking at this stupid thing on my head that's all. I wish I could take it off.'

'Well, you can't.' Janet wished that she could take it off. The touch of white lace was barely noticed in her own fair hair but nestling in Rachel's black curls it was very eye-catching.

With time to spare Rachel took the opportunity to look around her and liked what she saw. Both windows were pelmeted and had floor-length curtains in rich green velvet. Matching material upholstered the dining chairs which were high-backed and cream embossed wall-paper made a fitting background for several large oil paintings and a few small watercolours which she thought could be of the gardens at Duncairn House.

There were no guests, the five for dinner were family. The seating arrangements surprised Rachel. As was expected, her grandmother was at the head of the table but it was her daughter, Maud, who sat at the other end. Rachel had expected it to be Aunt Maud's husband though maybe she was wrong there. Henry Meldrum had a side to himself and Betsy and Brian were opposite him.

A murmur of conversation prepared the two maids. Mrs Craig came in on the arm of her daughter. She was wearing a silver-grey dress with a black beaded top. Maud had on a cream silk dress with a red chiffon scarf at the neck. The old lady fussed until she was comfortably seated and the napkin spread over her knees. Henry Meldrum had advanced quickly to assist but a frosty look from his mother-in-law made him step aside. Before sitting down himself he waited until his wife was seated. The two young ones came in slowly, they were still talking but stopped when they reached the table. Like his father, Brian wore a dark suit, white shirt and tie. Henry Meldrum was a fine figure of a man and the touch of grey at the temples only enhanced his good looks. Brian's suit hung on him and he looked as though he could do with a few good meals inside him but in fact he had a hearty appetite and enjoyed good health. He was the type who would remain thin all through life.

Mrs Craig looked across at Janet and Rachel. 'You may serve now, Janet.'

'Thank you, m'am.'

Mrs Craig was served first with the tomato soup. Rachel carefully lowered it in front of her then hurried to serve the others. A warmed roll was on each side plate and little curls of butter decorated two dishes. Janet busied herself with the next course and having her offer of assistance refused, Rachel studied those around the table. Brian Meldrum was much as Hetty had described him though the description didn't do him justice. He had a thin, clever face and eyes that could be serious or fun-filled. Rachel liked him on sight.

Remembering Hetty's bit of gossip about Brian's father and Janet, she looked for signs but all she noticed was Janet's heightened colour and that could have been due to the heat of the room.

Janet's arm nudged her. 'Pay attention.'

'Sorry, what do you want me to do?'

'Be quite sure that everyone has finished before collecting the plates.'

Rachel stood back from the table until the old lady had put down her spoon.

'If you have finished, m'am, may I take your plate?'

'Yes, girl, take it away.'

Girl indeed, Rachel thought fuming inwardly. If she's forgotten my name surely she could ask. She carried the plates over to the sideboard. Until now conversation at the table had been subdued but with the main course served it all but dried up.

Under the eagle eye of her grandmother Rachel had expected to be nervous but the old lady had shown little interest and seemed tired. Instead it was Henry Meldrum who disturbed her, there was nothing obvious just moving to brush her when she served him. More disturbing was having those bold eyes follow her across the room.

'Not too bad,' Janet said condescendingly. 'You can get Hetty to help you clear the table and carry the dishes through to the kitchen.'

'What about coffee?'

'I prefer to see to that myself.'

Rachel smiled and nodded.

'You will remember that tomorrow evening will be more demanding. Three guests are expected.'

★ ★ ★

The table was fully out and three glasses were at each setting. There was to be a choice of starter followed by leg of lamb with fresh mint sauce, garden vegetables and even-sized small potatoes also from the gardens. The dessert was fresh fruit salad and cream or a light apricot sponge. By seven thirty the table looked very attractive with candles at either end. The only other light came from the corner lamps which together with the candles gave a soft glow to the room and added a sparkle to the silver and crystal.

Janet was fidgetting with the serving spoons. 'Dr McGregor hasn't turned up yet,' she said with a frown of annoyance. 'We've to hold back the meal for another fifteen minutes then serve it whether or not he has arrived. You could go and have a look out the hall window and see if his car is in sight.'

Rachel had just reached the hall when a loud ring proclaimed someone at the door. It was Hetty's duty to answer it but she wasn't in sight and Rachel opened the door herself. Standing there was a tall man with rugged good looks and an apologetic smile.

'Have they started?' he whispered as he stepped in.

This must be Dr McGregor. 'No, sir, they were giving you another fifteen minutes.' She found that she was whispering too. He wore a dinner jacket with the bow tie slightly crooked as though he had been in a rush to dress. Her fingers itched to straighten it but of course she couldn't.

From the drawing-room came the sound of animated conversation as they got up from their comfortable chairs.

'I'm so sorry to be late, my apologies, Mrs Craig,' he said lifting her hand and kissing it.

'No need to apologise, Peter, a busy doctor can never call his time his own. We are just delighted to see you here and now, young man, you can take my arm and escort me through to the dining-room.'

'My pleasure.'

There was more than a hint of the flirt in the old lady's manner and Rachel wondered if long ago her grandmother had flirted with handsome young men before settling down to marriage and raising a family.

With Janet, Rachel watched the company take their seats at the table. All the gentlemen wore dinner jackets and between John McGregor and his son, Peter, there was a strong resemblance. They were both about six feet tall, with the same straight, strong nose and the small cleft in the firm chin. What remained of John McGregor's hair was dark brown sprinkled with grey but Peter had inherited his mother's thick, dark blond hair. On his arrival mother and son had exchanged a warm smile. Waiting to begin her duties Rachel saw the pride in the motherly face as she watched her son and his gentleness with their hostess.

'No nine-to-five with the medical profession,' John McGregor said with a look along the table to Henry Meldrum.

'Nor in the City,' Henry answered a little too sharply and as if regretting his words, John McGregor nodded his head in agreement.

'I'm sure you're right. Like lawyers one can be working hard with precious little to show for it.'

'Not like Peter. He'll have bandaged limbs to show for his trouble,' Betsy said and flushed scarlet. She did so want to say something witty. There was a faint titter, then Mrs Craig gave the signal for the meal to be served.

The hostess looked regal in a deep purple velvet gown with a brooch at the neckline. Maud wore a café-au-lait lace dress which suited her slim figure but not her sallow skin. Peter's mother had favoured a black skirt with a white silk blouse. Her only make-up was a touch of pale pink lipstick, she needed nothing more. Betsy, occasionally bothered by spots, envied the woman her pink-and-white complexion. She had been so looking forward to this evening. Seated between Peter and Brian she had seen herself being gracious to both but letting Peter see where her heart lay. She knew too that she was looking fresh and pretty in her navy blue princess-style dress with its wide white collar and piping round sleeves and imitation pockets. It just wasn't fair that the new maid could look marvellous in that cheap uniform but worst of all was that special smile Peter had given her and the tell-tale flush on the servant's face.

There was an attraction there and some way would have to be found to get rid of that girl. The beginning of a plan was forming in her mind. Her stepfather, fool that he was, thought his affair with Janet had gone unnoticed and it suited her mother to let him think that. What if he switched his affections from Janet to Rachel. Janet would be out for revenge and a word to her grandmother about finding the girl snooping about the attic should seal her fate.

Rachel went round to Henry Meldrum with the basket of rolls. Before lifting one the thick fingers touched hers, pressing into them and Rachel felt her flesh crawl.

'He's a bit of all right, isn't he?' Janet whispered as they worked together at the sideboard.

'Who?'

'The doctor of course, you like him, don't you?'

'Don't be silly I've only just set eyes on him.'

'Waste of time if you are interested, he's Miss Betsy's property.'

'Not Brian?'

'He's keen enough but it's the doctor she wants and means to have and she usually manages to get her own way.'

Sleep was a confusion of dreams that night. Peter McGregor's face would slip away and then it would be her da and Peggy and her father's accusing eyes. Her thoughts went back to what she had done. Running away as she had was unforgivable, she could see that now when it was too late. She was trapped in her own stupidity, cut off from everyone she knew. At least Mrs Rodgers would have put her da's mind at rest. He would expect her to be comfortably settled at Duncairn House, accepted as Amelia's daughter. She moved restlessly. What would he have to say if he knew the true state of affairs, that she was a maid in her grandmother's house?

What remained of her money was in her purse in the drawer with the brooch. It wasn't a question of not trusting anyone but the money would be better in the bank. Hillend had its own post office and one day Rachel walked in, deposited her money and became the proud owner of a post office savings book with her signature inside the cover.

Her bedroom – what a difference there and at little cost she thought with justifiable pride. Approaching Mrs Anderson about old curtains a pair had been unearthed. They were maroon-and-cream-striped curtains that had once graced the dining-room. They were still good but faded with the sun. Being very long the faded material had been cut away and enough left to give a fullness at the window. With the remainder she made a cushion cover and recovered the stool. Earlier on, she had removed the ugly nail and replaced it with a hook for the mirror.

At long last Rachel sat down with pen and paper and wrote to Agnes. It took her an age, she had to be careful what she said. Agnes was quick to pick up something if it didn't sound right. She read it over again before putting it in the envelope and decided it would do. Much of it was about Agnes's job, how she was getting on and about family and friends. Only when she started on the envelope did Rachel discover that she couldn't remember the name of the house or the number in Broughty Ferry Road and it was a very long road. She would address it to Spinner's Lane.

Sadly it was all wasted effort. The houses in Spinner's Lane had been demolished and the Boyd family were in their new corporation house.

'Come in.'

'Oh, it's you, Janet,' Rachel said putting down the magazine she had been reading. 'You look very smart in that tweed costume. Where are you off to?'

'The village. I want a lipstick if the chemist has the shade. Fancy a walk?'

Rachel was surprised. Janet was a bit overdressed for a walk to the village and she had more make-up on than usual. She didn't remark on it, of course, Janet didn't have much of a sense of humour.

'Yes, I'll come. Sit down with that magazine and I'll get ready.'

'This is nice,' Janet said taking a look around her. 'Wish I'd taken it when I had the chance.'

'It was a mess then, that's why you didn't,' Rachel reminded her as she slipped off her uniform dress and stepped into a brown pleated skirt. Opening the drawer she took out a cream and brown jumper and pulled it over her head. Her lovely skirt and blouse, Miss Reid's gift, were still in the wardrobe awaiting a special occasion. She wondered when that would be.

'That's true,' Janet agreed looking up from the fashion page. 'When you are so good at sewing, what on earth made you take a job as a maid? I know for a fact that there is a shirt factory in Perth crying out for machinists.'

'A live-in job was what I required, Janet, and I don't imagine a machinist's wage, a beginner's anyway, would cover digs,' Rachel said shortly.

'I don't know, others must do it, everybody doesn't stay at home.'

'Most do.'

Rachel powdered her nose, drew a lipstick over her mouth and combed her hair. Her oatmeal jacket was hanging on the back of the door, she took it down and put it on. It was shabby and she was tired of it. Apart from money for the cinema and the fare to Perth she had few expenses and her wage, small though it was, was found money. She would save up for a coat withdrawing a pound or maybe two from her post office account so that she wouldn't have to wait so long. The helpful assistant had explained the procedure for withdrawing money but warned her always to leave in a little to save having to start all over again with a new book.

'I'm ready.'

They walked smartly down the drive and along the country road. It was the end of October and the countryside had already felt the sharpness of frost. Summer was reluctantly giving way to a short autumn then would follow a long bleak spell when roaring fires were the greatest comfort. Neither had much to say, and after a few desultory attempts at conversation, they gave up and walked in silence. Their feet crunched through the crisp, dry leaves lying thick on the ground. A few still clung determinedly to the trees flaunting their lovely scarlet and gold.

The village was one street of shops and housewives seemingly reluctant to return home, gossiped at shop doors. Hemmed between the butcher's and the grocer's was the chemist's shop. Two women, one with an irritating cough, were awaiting prescriptions; both looked miserable. Janet made for the selection of lipsticks and other make-up on display. The shade she wanted wasn't there but after uncapping some and testing the colour on the back of her hand, she decided on one. She paid for her purchase and they left.

'We'll go back by the station road,' Janet announced.

Rachel didn't mind but noticed that Janet was suddenly ill-at-ease. The road was vaguely familiar and Rachel realised then that this was the road she had taken when she had arrived in Hillend. She remembered the shop too.

'Hang on, I'm going in here for a tube of pastilles.'

'I'll wait outside.'

Three months was a long time but even so Rachel moved away from the window, only turning when she heard the door and Janet come out. Mrs Mackay was behind her to take in a bundle of newspapers dropped off by a passing van. A look of puzzlement crossed her face then she was smiling broadly.

'Took a wee while to place you but I have you now. You're the lass who asked about accommodation and I sent you to Mrs Shepherd?'

Rachel smiled and nodded but was aware of Janet's interest as she looked from one to the other.

'You were quite comfortable?'

'Yes, thank you.'

'You're from Duncairn House aren't you?' she asked, turning to Janet.

'We both are.'

'Well isn't that nice.' Her eye caught a customer going in. 'No patience some of them so I'll get back.' She hastened away.

'A bit of a dark horse, aren't you?' Janet said as they began walking.

'Why do you say that?'

'Just a feeling there is a mystery about you.'

'Nonsense, I could say the same about you.'

'No, you couldn't, but right away I wondered about you. I mean Mrs Anderson had three girls to interview for the vacancy and one wrote later to apologise for not turning up.'

'What conclusion did you draw from that?' Rachel was playing for time.

'None really. Mrs Anderson decided you must have heard about the vacancy and come along on chance.'

'Which is exactly what happened,' Rachel said, relieved that it sounded so plausible.

'Being able to sew clinched it for you.'

'It helped.'

'I'm going to ask a favour of you,' she said abruptly. 'Would you go back to Duncairn House on your own?' She paused. 'I'm meeting someone, you see.'

'Someone you don't want me to know about?'

'Someone I don't want anyone to know about. Look, Rachel, it isn't much to ask and I'd willingly do the same for you.'

'I don't mind, away you go and I'll go back the way we came.'

'Thanks, you're a pal.'

'Before you go tell me why you bothered to ask for my company, you didn't need to.'

'Oh, but I did. The two of us going out together wouldn't raise an eyebrow but on my own and dressed like this,' she touched her costume jacket, 'they would wonder—'

'You should just let them wonder.'

'Could you go now, please,' she was getting agitated. 'I'll be late and he'll think I'm not coming and not a word to Hetty or anyone.'

'You have my word.' Rachel walked quickly away only turning back once to look, but Janet was out of sight.

Janet was an adult, what she did was her own business but even so she was uneasy. Was Hetty right? Was she seeing Henry Meldrum? If it were true, poor Aunt Maud. She thought of the woman as her aunt, had come to like her which was more than could be said for her grandmother and her cousin. Even if it were a marriage in name only her aunt would feel humiliated if she were to find out about her husband and a servant girl.

So engrossed was she in her own thoughts that she was unaware of the car drawing up alongside.

'May I offer you a lift to Duncairn House if that is where you are heading?'

'It is and thank you.' Rachel found herself looking into the smiling face of Dr Peter McGregor. He leaned over to open the passenger door.

She got in and pulled the door; it didn't shut properly but it wouldn't open either. She felt a fool.

'Needs a good tug,' he said, leaning over her to secure it.

'Sorry.'

'Don't be, my mother never manages it. Were you in the village?'

'Yes.' She wasn't usually tongue-tied but she couldn't think of a thing to say and she felt breathless and excited.

'Where do you come from?' he asked as he changed gear.

'I was brought up in Dundee.'

'Know this part well?'

'No, but I hope to see a little of it before the winter sets in.'

'By bus?'

'Or train, whichever is more convenient.'

Peter McGregor knew that he was very, very attracted to this dark-eyed lovely girl. That she was a servant in a friend's house was of no importance. No maid he had ever seen had that quiet, ladylike grace nor spoke in such a beautifully modulated voice. He sensed there was a mystery here and he meant to solve it.

'When have you to be back on duty, if that is the correct term?'

'Not until half past six.'

'And I'm free until evening surgery. I could show you a little of our lovely countryside if the idea appeals to you.'

'Are you sure? I mean it is very kind of you.'

'My pleasure.'

She couldn't stop smiling and her eyes were shining, it was all so unexpected, so wonderful. It wouldn't do to show just how thrilled she was and Rachel was glad he was concentrating on his driving.

'My afternoon was to be a dreary session with medical journals which I'll gladly put off to another day.'

They were both smiling and happiness surged through her. She had never felt like this before. Only one thing was spoiling it for her, if only she had been wearing something smarter. Taking a sidelong look she was relieved that he had on an ancient tweed jacket with worn leather patches on the elbows and trousers that had lost their crease. Dr McGregor, she could see, was a man who put comfort before appearance and she liked that.

Very soon they were in Perth and in the busy centre. Peter concentrated on his driving until they were clear of the congested streets and out onto the quiet country roads. He kept his speed down while he pointed out places of interest.

'Where are we now?'

'Coming into Dunkeld. Pretty little place to stop in and the cathedral is worth a look. Pitlochry was where I was heading but I think we'll leave that for another time.'

Another time! Peter had said another time. She hugged the words to her then suddenly she was remembering about Betsy and her heart plummeted. Peter and Betsy, names linked, a union to delight both families. She had better stop her impossible dreams and come down to earth. Peter was being kind, a spur-of-the-moment invitation, but Pitlochry, that sounded as though he wanted to see her again. Safer, though, if she said nothing about Pitlochry.

'Have you always lived in Perthshire?'

'Born and bred. I share my time between my parents' home in Hillend and Perth.'

'Is that where your surgery is?'

'Yes, on the Crieff Road. Dr Smart, the senior doctor, is a widower with an absolutely marvellous housekeeper. I have a room in his house and can come and go as I please.' He paused at a junction. 'How do you like working at Duncairn House?'

'Quite pleasant. Much of my time is spent sewing and I'm glad of that. I find Mrs Craig rather terrifying.'

'Do you? To someone who doesn't know her well she could be, I imagine. I like her, she's quite a character with a lot of spirit and if she's difficult at times who could blame her. She suffers a lot of pain but tries to hide it.'

'Now that I know I'll make allowances,' she smiled. It was nice to hear her grandmother being praised.

'Peter was slowing down and looking about him. The frown changed into a broad grin as he pointed to a sign. 'Martha's Tearoom'. 'For one awful moment I thought the place had closed down.' He parked the car down a side road and they walked side by side.

'This is very kind of you, Dr McGregor.'

'Peter is the name and I don't knows yours. We should have introduced ourselves in the car.'

'I'm Rachel Donaldson.'

'Then Rachel Donaldson come and taste scones like you've never tasted before.' He took her arm and they went into the tearoom. A few elderly ladies having afternoon tea broke off their conversation for a moment to watch the good-looking young couple being shown a window table.

'Is it the set afternoon tea, sir?'

'If that includes scones?'

'It does,' she smiled. 'Afternoon tea for two.' She went away.

The teapot and hot-water jug were placed before Rachel. Then followed a tray with home-baking to replenish the cake stand. Last to arrive were the scones, hot from the oven.

'Do you like the milk in first, Peter?'

'Yes, please, and two of sugar, heaped ones.'

'Tut tut that's not what the doctor ordered! All that sweetness isn't good for you,' she said as their met across the table.

'I'm of the school that thinks a little of what you fancy does you good.'

She didn't know why but she blushed and he laughed as he cut open a scone buttered both sides and topped them with jam. 'Delicious,' he said.

She did likewise with her scone.

'Go easy if you're troubled with indigestion.'

'I'm not and I take it you aren't either?'

'No, but I'll probably pay the price in years to come.'

'Live for today and let tomorrow take care of itself.' It was what she was doing she told herself.

She's lovely, she's delightful, Peter was thinking to himself, and I want to go on seeing her. They were on their second cup of tea.

'Tell me about yourself, Rachel. I'm not curious but I am interested.'

An expression of sadness crossed her face then she shrugged. 'Nothing much to tell, Peter. As I said I was brought up in Dundee and I'm now working at Duncairn House.'

'Risking speaking out of turn I would say there is a great deal to tell, but it can wait.' His hand closed over hers and it was like a current of electricity. She tried to withdraw it but his hand remained firmly on hers. 'I'm very attracted to you, Rachel, and I hope we can go on seeing each other.' He let her hand go and she drank some of the tea then put down her cup.

'My story isn't all that unusual, Peter.' She liked the sound of his name on her lips. 'My mother died when I was nine years of age and there was just my father and I and a neighbour who came in to help.'

'Then your father decided to take a new wife?'

'How did you guess?'

'To me it seemed very obvious. The child and her father had been everything to one another then suddenly there was this stranger, this woman, and you felt yourself pushed out, unwanted.'

She smiled sadly. 'For as far as it goes that is more or less right and I'm certainly not blameless.'

'Do you feel like telling me the rest?' he said gently when she fell silent.

'Might as well finish what I've begun. I didn't get on particularly well with my stepmother, probably because she is so different from my real mother. It was an accumulation of things that drove me away from home but mostly it was because my father broke his promise to me.' She swallowed, painfully. 'I wanted to train to be a teacher, Peter, and my father was to be more than delighted to see me through college. Peggy, that's my stepmother, is very extravagant, the money put aside for me got spent and I had to leave school and get a job.'

'Even so, Rachel, with your intelligence and appearance you could have done a lot better for yourself than become a maid.'

'A roof over my head was a consideration,' she said shortly, 'and a live-in maid seemed like a good idea. And another thing, I rather resent your remarks suggesting a maid is a nobody.'

'Oh, dear, now I've put my foot in it and you couldn't be more wrong. All I meant and I think you deliberately took that the wrong way,' he said frowning at her, 'was that you are very obviously a superior girl who could have done a lot better for herself.'

'I did work for a dressmaker and it was when she was forced to give up the business that I decided to leave home.'

'Why Hillend?'

Twice she had been asked that. 'Why not? I just thought it would be a pleasant place to live.'

'Which it is.' He looked at his watch. 'Rachel, I could go on sitting here with you but unfortunately duties lie ahead for both of us.' He called for the waitress, settled the bill adding a good tip for the length of time they had occupied a table. Then they walked out to where the car was parked.

'We'll have to give the cathedral a miss, we spent rather longer in Martha's then I intended.' Peter knew that he had cut it fine and was forced to put his foot down though not to endanger life. The silence was comfortable with Peter turning occasionally to give her a smile.

Too soon for Rachel they were drawing up before the gates of Duncairn House. Peter got out to open the door for her just as a figure came flying down the drive.

'Peter, darling, how lovely to see you.'

'Hello, Betsy.'

She took his arm. 'Come along in.'

'Can't, I have a waiting-room full of patients.'

'A few minutes won't make much difference.'

Peter turned only to see Rachel's figure hurrying round to the back of the house. Drat Betsy, he thought uncharitably, he'd wanted to make arrangements with Rachel, now he would have to make it a letter.

'Two minutes to say hello to your grandmother,' he said, 'and not a moment longer.'

She linked him up the drive. 'Peter, dear, you are much too kind-hearted, you shouldn't be giving a lift to the maids, they can perfectly well walk from the village.'

Peter thought it best to say nothing.

Rachel turned the corner and almost bumped into Benny, the handyman.

'Steady there, knock an old man down, would you?'

'Sorry, Benny, my fault, I was rushing.'

'Mrs Anderson's been askin' for you.'

'For me?'

'Aye, for you. Better change into your workin' togs.'

Rachel smiled. 'I'll take your advice.'

There was no answer when she knocked at the housekeeper's door but just as she made to turn away Mrs Anderson arrived and unlocked the door.

'Come in, Rachel.'

Rachel stood in the centre of the room, she wasn't asked to sit.

'It has been decided, Rachel, that Janet and you are to take turns at seeing to Mrs Craig. This will relieve me and Janet's day off will cease to be a problem. Monday, Tuesday and Wednesday for you and Janet will do the rest of the week.'

This was what she wanted, a chance to get to know her grandmother but now that it was about to happen, Rachel could only feel panic. It must have shown.

'Good gracious! I wouldn't have expected you to be nervous,' Mrs Anderson said, showing annoyance. 'Your duties will be perfectly straightforward. At eight o'clock you will take a tray prepared by Mrs Morton to Mrs Craig's bedroom. She may want her breakfast in bed or she may prefer it at the small table. This will be properly set as if in the breakfast-room but Janet will keep you right there.'

Rachel nodded. It sounded easy enough.

'Some days she is in a lot of pain and won't leave her room all day. On those days you will attend to her every need. By that I mean her meals and seeing her comfortably seated with cushions for her back.'

Chapter Eighteen

As each day went by Agnes was becoming increasingly uneasy. The darkening of Edwin Taylor's face whenever he saw her made Agnes believe that he was struggling with a memory, and she thought it just a question of time before he connected her with the incident at the gate and she got her marching orders.

At Kerne House, newspapers read by and cast aside by the master and mistress, were collected and used to light the fires. Before this happened, Agnes made a point of getting hold of them to tear out the pages headed SITUATIONS VACANT then studied them when she was alone. She could not have said rightly what she was looking for, only that she would know it when she saw it. The weeks went by and with them her seventeenth birthday without her having applied for a single vacancy. Then just as she was beginning to lose heart she saw it. Set apart from the others it had caught her eye immediately. Her eyes flew over it.

> Domestic help urgently required for large country house on outskirts of Kirriemuir. Must be prepared to live in. Own room. Preferred age 17-19 years. Only girls of good character need apply. Applications in own handwriting to:
>
> Mrs Harrison, housekeeper, Drumoaks,
> near Kirriemuir, Angus.

This was it, Agnes thought with a flutter of excitement. She was meant to get this job, she was sure of it.

Pen, ink and cheap lined notepaper were provided, it being expected that even servant girls would occasionally wish to write home or to friends. Agnes disliked writing on lined paper, it reminded her of school. She was perfectly capable of writing in a straight line.

Fortunately for Agnes, Mrs Margaret Taylor was an enthusiastic correspondent and wrote regularly to her friends. For this purpose she kept a good supply of writing paper, some headed, some plain, and envelopes in the bureau which was usually kept open. The headed paper Agnes decided to ignore but the continuation sheets were of good quality. At the first opportunity, and that would have to be sometime today, she would help herself to a couple of sheets and an envelope. The stamp she would buy herself. Agnes saw nothing wrong in taking stationery but drew the line at stamps though her employer had a good supply to hand.

Mistakes were something she couldn't afford so on a page of cheap notepaper and in pencil Agnes scribbled down what she was going to say. Satisfied at last with the wording she copied it out in ink. Agnes could write well when she took the trouble and she was pleased with her effort. With the same care she addressed the envelope, sealed it then threw on her coat and took herself down to the corner shop. Though not permitted to sell stamps to the public, the elderly shopkeeper saw no harm in having a small supply for her own use and being able to oblige folk reluctant to walk the extra distance to the post office. It was good for business too.

'A letter for you, Agnes.'

Too soon to expect a reply to her advertisement; it could only be from Rachel.

'Thanks, Gloria.' She took the letter and her heart skipped a beat. It wasn't from Rachel, she knew her friend's handwriting. That could only mean it was from Drumoaks and to reply so promptly must be good news.

Gloria had disappeared but Mrs Robertson was there. 'Now that you've examined it aren't you goin' to open it?' She was trying unsuccessfully to hide her curiosity.

'No hurry, Mrs Robertson,' Agnes said carelessly, 'friend of mine getting round to writing at last.'

'Nice envelope,' Cook said suspiciously.

'Probably pinched it from her employer,' Agnes grinned.

Mrs Robertson nodded. 'Goes on I daresay.' She paused to take a handful of flour and scatter it liberally before rolling out the pastry. 'Gloria's got the sniffles again and I'm going to send her home in a wee while. No use spreading germs but it means you'll need to scrape those carrots, I've only one pair of hands.'

'All right.' Agnes scraped furiously at the carrots hoping the rest was already prepared. She was desperate to get away. 'That do?'

'For the now.'

Agnes made her escape and flew up the stairs and into her room. Shutting the door she went over and sat on the bed. Her hand was shaking as she took the envelope out of her overall pocket and opened it. She brought out a neatly folded single sheet of paper with an embossed heading and Agnes nearly died of excitement.

Dear Miss Boyd, (She'd never been called that and it gave her quite a thrill.)

Thank you for your application. Please attend for interview on the afternoon of Tuesday 24th. Drumoaks is about a mile and a half from Kirriemuir but there is a local bus to bring you the rest of the way.

Information regarding transport can be obtained from the newsagent in the square. Travelling expenses will be refunded. On arrival go round to the side door and ask for Mrs Harrison. It is essential that you bring this letter with you.

Lavinia Harrison.

Agnes was hugging her knees and rocking herself. She was jubilant and refused to entertain the possibility that she could be unsuccessful. This was her future, her destiny. She looked again at the date. Tuesday, the twenty-fourth, that was a week tomorrow. Bad luck that it was Molly's day off and not hers but she didn't see it as too much of a problem. The big romance with Geoffrey was off, she was sure of it. Why did that immediately make her think of Tommy Kingsley? It maddened Agnes that she couldn't forget him.

'Why do you want my Tuesday? Where are you going'?'

'To Kirriemuir to see a friend I haven't seen for ages and this is the only chance we'll have.' Agnes thought it safer to keep as close to the truth as possible. There was always the outside chance that someone who knew her might see her stepping on the Kirriemuir bus.

'Male or female? Daft question,' Molly grinned, 'I don't see you goin' to all that trouble for a female.'

'Actually it is a girl.'

Molly looked her disbelief.

'Honestly, Molly, she's someone I was at school with, my best friend, as a matter of fact.' As she said the words Agnes asked herself if it was true. Would she have gone to all this trouble for Rachel and she believed the answer to be yes.

Molly took her time, not wanting to give in too easily.

'I'll think about it.'

'That won't do, I have to know now.'

She gave a big sigh. 'I suppose so, all right I'll change.'

'Thanks, Molly, you're a pal.'

'Seen anything of Tommy Kingsley?'

'No, I haven't, but there is no reason why I should, he's nothing to me,' Agnes said shortly.

'No need to snap, I was just askin'.'

'Sorry, didn't mean to.'

'In a way I'm sorry I gave Tommy up for Geoffrey.'

'All over with lover boy, is it?'

'Agnes, he had the nerve to stand me up,' she said indignantly, 'and no one does that to me,' she continued, forgetting that someone just had.

'Better without him if he's that type.'

She nodded. 'Mebbe I should try to get Tommy back – after all it was just that bike of his that caused the trouble.'

Agnes was shocked at just how much she disliked the thought of Tommy and Molly getting together again. Stupid, since she didn't want him herself.

'You are on a loser there, he worships that bike.'

Molly shrugged. 'You could be right.' She picked up the dusters and the Brasso and made to go, then stopped. 'How about comin' with me to the dancin' on Saturday, see what the talent is like?'

'Sorry, can't, I have to go home. I'm in trouble. They've been in their corporation house for over three weeks and I haven't seen it.'

'Some other Saturday?'

'Sure.'

Molly departed to polish up the brass candlesticks and Agnes returned to the kitchen to do more of Gloria's duties. As she opened the door Mrs Robertson stopped talking to Mrs Fairlie, the woman who came in to scrub the floors. They both looked at Agnes.

'You throw any light on it, Agnes?'

'On what?'

'Someone's been tearing pages out of the old newspapers, the "jobs vacant" ones and after me promising Mrs Fairlie here that she could take them home to her laddie.'

Mrs Fairlie got off her knees to give an explanation. She dried her hands on her coarse apron, tucked her hair behind her ears and began, 'When Mrs Robertson is kind enough, there's no need for me wasting money buying a paper that'll no' get read. You see, lass, it's just the job page I want.'

'Can't help you, I'm afraid,' Agnes said looking genuinely sorry, 'but I tell you what, I'll collect the papers myself before anyone else gets at them and bring them to the kitchen. How's that?'

'That's real good of you, lass, many thanks.' Mrs Fairlie smiled showing ill-fitting false teeth then dropped to her knees and set to with a will to scrub the floor.

It was warm and clammy the afternoon Agnes left Kerne House to catch two trams to take her to the West Port. Before making her way to the Boyds' new corporation house, Agnes decided to have a look at Spinner's Lane then wished she hadn't. Rubble was everywhere and it had become a playground for youngsters from the Hawkhill. The bigger boys were a menace as they threw bricks to break them up and generally make a nuisance of themselves.

Agnes hadn't meant to linger but watched with amusement as three little girls no more than five years of age played happily amongst the rubbish, their clothes and their faces filthy. Choosing the larger bricks and bowed down under their weight they began to build their own little house. The walls to their satisfaction they then went in search of linoleum and dragged back a torn piece which they managed to lay on the floor.

'I'll be the ma and I'll cook the dinner,' one said as she stirred an imaginary pot.

'And I'll be the da and do nothin',' another piped in.

The third child, hands on hips, looked belligerent. 'I am not bein' the bairn again and gettin' hitted, it isn't fair.'

Seeing it about to develop into a noisy quarrel, Agnes had a final look round then took herself away. She couldn't imagine anyone sorry to see the vermin-infested houses reduced to rubble. Ten minutes' smart walking took her to Brady Street, a short street with corporation houses down each side. Some had bright clean curtains at the windows and a few of the front gardens were being turned over. The houses were in blocks of four with a garden to the front and drying green to the back. Four poles had been hammered into the ground with jutting arms for the rope to be wound round. The washing was then pegged out and on a dry, windy day it dried in no time at all.

Opening the gates Agnes walked up the path to find her mother and Ruby sitting on the door-step. It was late afternoon and there was still some warmth in the sun.

'Hello, Ma,' Agnes said brightly and tickled her little sister under the chin.

'Took your time about comin'?'

'Better late than never.'

Only her hair was different, Agnes thought, as she looked at her mother. Was there to be an improvement now that she was better housed? It was shorter, looked clean and appeared thicker. She wore shabby carpet slippers showing a little of her big toe, her legs were bare and marbled through sitting too close to the fire. Her thin overall-style dress would have been acceptable had it been washed and ironed but it was stained and the material badly crushed.

'Do we go in or do I have to sit on the step?'

'We'll go in.' She got up and Agnes made to help Ruby.

'Leave her, she'll manage, she's just bone idle.'

'What do you mean she's just bone idle?'

'Had a visit from the nurse no' long after we came. Seems we've been doin' too much for her and if everything is done for her there's no need for her to do anything for herself if you get my drift.'

'Makes sense I suppose.' Agnes paused to watch Ruby lumber into the living-room then plonk herself down on her bottom. 'There should be a place for bairns like Ruby with trained people who understand them. Some could be taught to do something.'

'That depends on the severity of their handicap,' Jenny Boyd said wearily and repeating the nurse. 'Our Ruby is at the lower end of the scale.'

Agnes nodded. She'd seen other mongol children coping reasonably well but recognised that her sister was incapable of learning very much. To change the conversation she said, 'I like your hair short, makes you look younger.'

'Ta. Your da didn't even notice and what do you think of our new abode?'

'Nice what I've seen of it.'

'That brown linoleum goes all round the house, keep to one colour and you get it cheaper.'

Apart from the linoleum Agnes thought that Spinner's Lane might have been transferred to Brady Street. In fact there was a minus point in Brady Street. There was no recess for the bed, it wasn't intended to hold one, and the double bed took up a large part of the room. Her da's old, sagging chair was at one side of the fireplace and its neighbour in slightly better condition, at the other end. The dresser was cluttered, the table was cluttered, and the curtains removed from Spinner's Lane were six inches too short. The kitchenette referred to by her mother as the scullery was well fitted with cupboards and had a gas cooker. Agnes examined the wall cupboards and found most of them to be empty.

'Ma, that stuff on the table should be in here, there's plenty of room for everything and the dirty dishes go on the draining board until you get round to washing them.'

'The fire heats the water and it is only on at night.'

'Boil a kettle then.'

'And who is to pay the gas bill I'd like to know,' she shot back. 'Anyway I like things the way they are and it's my house. I've told that to Meg and I'm tellin' it to you,' she said with dangerous calm.

'Fair enough,' Agnes said carelessly, 'you must find a difference having a bathroom, though.'

'Your da still washes at the sink, he cannae be doin' with that wee wash-hand basin.'

'I meant the bath.'

'Friday night, the same water does the lot of them.'

'You don't look very happy, don't you like it here?'

She shrugged and walked into the kitchenette, Agnes followed. Her mother began filling the kettle and spoke through the rush of water. 'To tell you the truth I miss Spinner's Lane and so does your da. We miss the folk.'

'But you didn't even like them, you were always at loggerheads.'

'Mebbe we were but we understood each other and a good yelling match cleared the air.' She lit the gas and put the kettle on the ring then jerked her thumb upwards. 'That one up there had the nerve to say that this was a respectable district and sitting on the front step was common.'

'She didn't!'

'She did that and a bit more. Seems my bairns are out of control and more or less suggested that Ruby should be kept indoors.'

'What a cheek, what an absolute bloody cheek,' Agnes stormed. 'I hope you—'

'Don't worry she got a lot more than she bargained for and if anyone leaves here it'll be her I'm thinkin',' she said with a satisfied nod of her head. 'Meg'll be in any minute, I'll infuse the tea and you take a look round.'

Agnes went out to the narrow lobby and opened the first door. Again it was Spinner's Lane brought to Brady Street but the beds were made, the room quite tidy. The curtains like the others were well above the sill. The girls' room had an extra single mattress on the floor and this Agnes surmised would be where Ruby slept.

The outside door opened. 'It's me, Ma.'

'Tea's infused and see what the cat's brought in.'

'By that I suppose she means me,' Agnes said, following her sister to where she was emptying the bag of groceries.

Meg smiled her welcome. 'Thought we would have seen you last week.'

'Couldn't manage. You look great, positively blooming,' Agnes said and it was true. The loose coat covered her expanding waistline and there was a healthy look about her skin and a shine to her hair. Best of all she looked happy.

'Feel good now,' she smiled. 'Ma, better check that I've remembered everythin'.'

'Miracle if you have but let's get them away before that lot gets in from school.'

'Bit further for them to go,' Agnes said as she opened the cupboards and Meg put the groceries away.

'The bread is still hot, Ma, I'll leave it out.'

'Put it on the table.'

'No, I'll leave it here, make less crumbs when you come to cut it.'

Jenny Boyd, with a thunderous expression on her face, marched forward, grabbed the bread and banged it down on the table.

Agnes raised her eyes and Meg whispered. 'She's been like this since we came here, just wants to carry on the way she used to.'

'Better leave her, she'll come round in her own time,' Agnes said. She thought she could understand something of her mother's frustration. Those know-alls on the council should have had the good sense to keep the Spinner's Lane folk together instead of scattering them about Dundee.

'What are you two whisperin' about?'

'Nothin', Ma, and are we gettin' that tea before it's stewed?'

'It's poured and I'm puttin' jam on three pancakes.'

They sat down together at the table and ate in silence for a few moments.

'Well, tell her the news,' Mrs Boyd said impatiently.

'I'm just about to.' Meg swallowed the last of the pancake. 'Me and Sam are gettin' wed. Just the Registry Office of course,' she said, patting her stomach. 'We need two witnesses. Sam is askin' his cousin, John, and I want you.'

'Should think so too, I'd be furious if you hadn't asked me. When is it?'

'Tuesday, the twenty-fourth.'

Agnes's face fell. Oh, God, it had to be that day. 'I can't, Meg, any day but that day.'

'Tell them I'm gettin' married and you'll get off.'

'It isn't as easy as that,' Agnes said wretchedly.

'Me gettin' married isn't important enough, is that it?'

'Of course it isn't and I'd give anything to be there.'

'Then what's stoppin' you?'

'I'm askin' it too, what's stoppin' you?' Jenny Boyd added.

'I have an interview for a job that day.'

'Explain and say you'll attend another time.'

'There won't be another time.'

'Plenty of other jobs you can apply for later.'

'Not like this one, Meg,' Agnes said quietly.

'What's so special about this one and where is it?' Meg was looking hurt and angry and her mother grim.

'It's special, Meg, Ma,' Agnes said desperately, 'because it is the kind of job I've been looking for. It's in Kirriemuir, a mile or two out actually, but I get my expenses and it's all arranged.' She ignored her mother and looked pleadingly at Meg.

'Is it your day off?'

'No, I've got Molly to change. Honestly, Meg, if it were possible—' she broke off at the look on Meg's face and felt a spurt of anger. 'And just for the record, Meg, I doubt if there would be a wedding at all if it hadn't been for me. Give that some thought, will you?'

Meg crossed to the window and spoke with her back turned. 'It's something I hadn't forgotten, never will and it's all right, you go for your interview and I'll get another witness.'

'I'll come and haul your da with me.'

'No, Ma, that would mean askin' Sam's mother and her gettin' someone to look after the shop.' She turned back from the window and smiled. 'I'll get someone no trouble and as Agnes says there might not have been a weddin' and another bairn about your feet.'

'I wouldn't have minded that, you would have been company for me.'

Meg put her arms round her mother. 'Give this place a chance, Ma, everybody isn't like that besom upstairs and it could be that the other folk hereabout are waitin' for you to make the first move.'

'Wait a long time then, won't they?' She broke off and rushed to the window. 'Oh, God, here they come, and Bobby's been fighin' again by the look of him. Give me strength, I'll murder him.'

Bobby was first in, his brother just behind. Bobby had a black eye and an ugly bruise on one cheek and his mother gave him a sharp slap on the other.

'What was that for?' he yelled but backed away in case it was to be followed by another.

'Fine you know what for. I told you what you would get if there was any more fightin'.'

'That's not fair, Ma,' Eddie came to the defence of his brother. 'He was only sticking up for our Ruby.'

'What's this about Ruby?'

'Jimmy Cochrane said I had a daft sister.'

Jenny Boyd bridled. 'Don't tell me you let him get away with that?'

''Course I didn't. Told him she wasn't half as daft as his sister and that his da is a wee shrimp and my da would make mincemeat of him.'

Agnes and Meg were laughing helplessly and Bobby preened himself.

'He would have got a lot more than he did if old Matthews hadn't seen us.'

'The headmaster.' Mrs Boyd closed her eyes. 'What did he have to say?'

'We've to report to him in the mornin' for a beltin'.'

'You tell him what Jimmy Cochrane said about your sister.'

'No, Ma, that's like tellin' tales.'

'You big softie, he'll blame you.'

'No, he won't, we're pals most of the time.'

There was a further commotion as Peter, closely followed by the twins, Daisy and Rose, came in. Peter demanded a piece an' jam, and totally ignored Agnes. The twins were growing, she thought, both had long thin legs and though not identical there was a strong resemblance.

'What are you doin' here?' Daisy demanded.

'You don't live here any more,' Rose added.

'Thanks for the welcome, I came to see how you liked your new house.'

'We like it,' Rose said timidly.

'You do, I don't,' Daisy said firmly, 'Spinner's Lane was better.' She turned to her mother. 'Nobody likes us here, do they, Ma?'

'If you behaved yourselves they might.'

'When does Da get in?' Agnes asked.

'Your guess is as good as mine. Said he'd likely be workin' late and took a piece with him.'

'Can't wait very long.' Agnes was ashamed at how much she wanted to get away. She no longer felt part of the family and suspected that she wasn't greatly missed by any of them except perhaps by Meg.

'I'll come a bit of the way with you,' Meg said picking up her coat.

'No further than the tram stop,' her mother warned, 'you've done enough walkin' for one day.'

'I'll go then, Ma, tell Da I was asking for him.'

'When are we likely to see you again?'

'Not sure.'

'You'll not hurry yoursel' that's for sure.'

Outside there was a coolish breeze and it was very welcome. Meg linked her arm in Agnes's.

'How can you stand it, Meg?'

'After Kerne House you mean? Thought I'd go mad but you just get used to it again.'

Agnes smiled. 'Easier when you know it won't be for long.'

She nodded. 'Silly I know, but I worry in case somethin' goes wrong.'

'What could possibly go wrong?'

'That's what I don't know.'

'You'll get married to your Sam and make a good life for yourself.'

'I'll work at it. I'm determined we won't end up like Ma and Da.'

'You won't.'

'I don't think so either. I'm very lucky, Agnes, Sam is good and considerate and his ma couldn't be nicer. She's happy too about us stayin' with her until we get our own house.'

'Knowing you you'll be helping in the shop.'

'Because I want to, Agnes. She'll be a lot easier to get on with than Ma and there's been no sly remarks about me expectin' before the ring is on my finger.'

'His blame as much as yours I would say.'

'You're clever in some ways, Agnes, but you don't know everything. It's always the girl's fault. Lads can't control themselves but girls are supposed to.' She paused. 'What is so special about this job?'

'Probably nothing but I have a feeling I'm meant to get it. It's difficult to explain but believe me it had to be something very important when I put it before your wedding.'

'Don't worry about that. I would have liked you there but I do understand and I hope you get it and it proves to be all you wish.'

Agnes looked at her sister in surprise. 'Thanks, Meg, that means a lot to me.'

'Is it a bigger place than Kerne House?'

'Much bigger, it's an estate, a country estate.'

'Sounds posh. Fancy your chances there?'

'Stranger things have happened. Why shouldn't I fancy my chances?'

'No reason at all. You've got brains and you're not bad-lookin'.' She sounded worried. 'I always feel closer to you than the rest and I wouldn't like to think of you gettin' hurt.'

'In what way would I get hurt?'

'Aimin' too high.'

'Further to fall you mean?'

'I'm not sure what I mean,' Meg said slowly, 'only that happiness is bein' with someone you love even if it is a struggle to make ends meet.'

'You're wrong there, Meg. When poverty strikes love flies out the window.'

'You're sayin' that because our two are always at each other's throat.'

'Perhaps I am.'

'Stayed together though.'

'Out of habit or laziness.'

'No, Agnes, deep down they care about each other but have forgotten how to show it.'

'You'll better get back now.' They stopped and looked at one another. The Boyds were not given to an outward show of affection but the sisters were hugging each other.

'You know that I wish you and Sam all the happiness and luck in the world and when I save up some money I'll get you a decent gift.'

'Thanks, Agnes, and no hurry for the gift. Time enough when we get our own place.' She paused and brushed a tear away. 'I hope one day that you'll be as happy as I am.'

'Ma will blame me if you don't get back now.'

'In a minute. I didn't want to ask in front of her but do you ever hear anything about Rachel Donaldson?'

'No, and I can't understand it.'

'Mebbe wanted to make a clean break.'

'Looks that way but somehow I think she'll get in touch with me.'

Chapter Nineteen

Rachel was watching the breakfast tray being prepared in the kitchen. The tray itself was of polished wood with a brass handle either end and on it Mrs Morton placed a snowy white embroidered tray cloth taking care that all the wood was hidden. Then she brought over cup, saucer and plate in delicate china followed by matching sugar bowl and cream jug.

'Rachel, lass,' Mrs Morton pointed to a large dish of prunes, 'choose four and put them in the wee plate.'

Very carefully, Rachel selected four fat, juicy prunes and using a big spoon added a little of the dark brown liquid.

'Will that do, Mrs Morton?'

'Lovely.' She put it on the tray. The toast browned to perfection was already cut into fingers, the butter into curls and there was a tiny amount of marmalade in a dish. A rolled-up napkin was secured in a silver holder and placed beside the cutlery.

'That the lot?'

'Dear me, no,' she said pouring boiling water into the silver teapot and picking up the tea strainer, set both in the centre of the tray. 'That way it'll help to keep it balanced. Don't want to spill, do you?'

Rachel tried lifting it. 'Goodness, it's heavy!'

'Surprising what the tray itself weighs but don't you worry you'll soon get used to it,' she said as she sat down to give her swollen legs a much needed rest.

Rachel was suddenly unsure as to how she would cope then ridiculed herself. Heavens! she was only carrying a tray to her grandmother's bedroom.

'Be as quick as you can, she doesn't like her toast cold. Janet would tell you the quick way to get there?'

'No, she didn't.'

'Must have forgotten. Difficult to explain, just muddle you. Just go the way you know but hurry.'

Inwardly fuming at Janet and not so sure that it had been a slip of memory, Rachel set off. More likely to be deliberate. Janet was proud to be the one to look after the mistress and sharing duties wouldn't be at all to her liking.

The tray was heavier by the minute, her arms were beginning to ache not so much from the weight but from trying to keep the tray steady. At last she reached the thickly carpeted stairs leading to the room she knew to be her grandmother's. Breathless she put down the tray and knocked at the door.

'Come in.'

Rachel turned the knob of the door then bending down picked up the tray, heard china knocking against china and pushed her way in.

'Close that door, there's a draught.' The voice was sharp and irritable.

'Sorry, m'am.'

She pressed it with her back until it clicked shut. Janet had told her to put the tray on the table at the window until Mrs Craig decided if she wanted her breakfast in bed or at the table. She put it down. Daylight was filtering into the room and Rachel went to draw back the curtains. It was a lovely morning and sunshine flooded the room.

'Half close them.'

Rachel did so. 'Good morning, m'am,' she said quietly, 'do you wish your breakfast in bed?'

'You're late.'

'I'm sorry, I came as quickly as I could.'

'Not good enough, need to smarten up. Janet has no difficulty getting here at the proper time.'

'No, m'am.'

Rachel felt a rush of compassion, she looked so old and frail and lost in the big bed. Going over she adjusted one of the pillows that had slipped. 'If you would raise yourself a little, m'am, I could make you more comfortable.' Putting her arm round the thin shoulders she kept it there until she had all three pillows in position.

'Thank you, but it was wasted effort since I intend getting up for my breakfast. Fetch my bed-jacket, no leave it, I'll have my dressing-gown.'

Rachel expected it to be on the chair nearest the bed in case the old lady required to get up during the night.

'On the back of the door, are you blind?'

Rachel swallowed her resentment and went over for the warm pink, fluffy dressing-gown. By now Mrs Craig had manoeuvred herself to the edge of the bed and Rachel bent down to put slippers on her feet. She helped her on with the dressing-gown.

'Tie the belt, my hands are useless at this time of the morning.'

She did as requested and the old lady sat down at the table.

'You should have had this set.'

'I haven't had time.' Quickly she spread the cloth over and from the tray collected the prunes and a spoon.

'A napkin if you please.'

'Sorry.' Rachel took it out of its holder, shook out the folds and placed it across her knees. While removing the dessert plate Rachel had noticed milk spilt on the tray cloth but that was a minor disaster. What horrified her was the sight of the soggy toast. If only she'd had the sense to turn the spout of the teapot the other way it wouldn't have happened.

'Do you think I could perhaps have a cup of tea?'

Swallowing nervously, Rachel went to remove the dessert plate. Four stones remained and she breathed a sigh of relief, at least she had something in her stomach. With a shaking hand she poured the tea then groaned when she remembered the milk.

'Do you take milk, m'am?'

'A little which I prefer in first but since it is too late for that you may add some.'

Rachel put the cup down in front of her and gave a silent prayer of thanks that none had gone in the saucer. She took a deep breath. It had always been her way to confess to failures rather than wait to have them pointed out.

'Mrs Craig, m'am, I'm very, very sorry but I'm afraid the toast is soggy, the tea must have – must have spilt when I was carrying the tray. I'll go back to the kitchen and make fresh.' She lowered her eyes waiting for the storm and when it didn't come she risked looking up.

Her grandmother was smiling, then chortling. 'You know, girl – what is your name?'

'Rachel.'

'You know, Rachel, I thought I'd like a change from Janet's super efficiency and I think you'll agree I'm getting it.'

Rachel dimpled. 'From one extreme to the other but I do assure you, m'am, that I am not usually so clumsy.'

'I should hope not or you wouldn't last long.'

'May I see to the fire?'

'Yes.' The old eyes were twinkling, 'better remove that toast to the fire and you can tell Mrs Morton that everything was satisfactory.'

'That is very good of you, m'am.'

There was a knock. 'Answer that, it'll be the morning papers.'

They had been left at the door and Rachel brought them in.

Mrs Craig had removed her own dressing-gown to reveal a flannelette nightdress with a trimming of lace at the neckline. Without bothering to ask, strong young arms clumsy with a tray were gentle as she assisted the frail old lady into bed. She helped her on with her bed-jacket and adjusted the pillows.

'Is that comfortable, m'am?'

'Yes, thank you, you would have made a good nurse.'

'It was a teacher I wanted to be.'

'Indeed! That's a far cry from a maid.'

Rachel smiled. 'Circumstances, m'am. May I remove the tray?'

'You may but I'll have the newspapers first and my spectacles.'

Rachel did as requested. She then threw the toast into the fire and collected the dishes together. Once all was tidied she made for the door.

'Either this print is getting smaller or my eyes weaker,' Mrs Craig said peevishly, then looked at Rachel. 'Get rid of that tray then come back.'

'Yes, m'am.'

Why had she to go back? Rachel pondered on that on her way to the kitchen.

'You've been a while.'

'I know, Mrs Morton, Mrs Craig required assistance to get back into bed and I had the fire to see to.'

'I'm not complainin',' Cook said as she uncovered the tray. 'My! My! the old dear must have been hungry, she's finished the toast.' Then she frowned. 'Dry toast, no butter or marmalade, mebbe the poor soul's stomach isn't right.'

Rachel started a giggle which she quickly managed to change into a cough. 'I've to go back.'

'What for?'

'Don't know. Will you tell Mrs Anderson if she comes looking for me?'

'I'll do that and hadn't you better get a move on, patience isn't your employer's strong point.'

Rachel almost ran across the hall but had to stop.

'Where do you think you're going?' It was Janet at her haughtiest.

'Mrs Craig wants me.'

'What for?'

'I don't know.

'Or aren't saying. How did you manage?'

'Not very well you'll be pleased to learn.'

Janet's eyes narrowed. 'What's that supposed to mean?'

'You didn't bother to tell me—'

'The shorter way – you could have worked that out for yourself, you've been here long enough.' She smirked as she walked away.

Part of the newspaper had been marked with a pencil.

'Bring over a chair for yourself and push the table back. That's it.'

Rachel sat down.

'Reading aloud should hold no problems for you since it was a teacher you wanted to be.'

'No problems at all,' Rachel smiled.

'Straining my eyes with the small print gives me a headache.'

Rachel missed reading the newspaper. There was usually one in the kitchen but Mrs Morton, though she didn't pay for it, considered it her property and woe betide anyone who dared remove it before she was finished reading it and she was a slow reader.

The room Rachel was in was large with a high ceiling. It had to be large to take the four-poster bed, a double wardrobe, a dressing-table, two small tables and a number of chairs. The dressing-table had a glass top and on it were a hand mirror, a brush and comb set and crystal ornaments that sparkled.

She was enjoying this, it wasn't work it was a pleasure. Occasionally her grandmother would make a remark berating some political figure for shortsightedness or more often plain stupidity.

'That'll do, girl.' She saw Rachel frown as she folded the paper and put it down. 'I'm sorry, Rachel, isn't it? I can see by your face that you object to being called girl.' She gave one of her chortles. 'If the years would roll away I wouldn't mind being addressed as girl.'

Rachel smiled as she took back her chair and thought that her grandmother was really rather nice once you got to understand her.

'You have a lovely clear voice and now if you don't mind an old lady's curiosity, what happened that you didn't take up teaching?'

'Lack of money. There would have been enough to see me through if my father hadn't remarried.'

'An extravagant stepmother?'

'Yes,' Rachel said shortly.

'Would you read to me when required?'

'I would be happy to, m'am.'

Her eyes were closing, she was beginning to nod and Rachel moved away.

'Thank you, my dear,' the words were little more than a murmur and Rachel wondered if she'd imagined them.

Had the time come to reveal her true identity? And if she did what kind of shock would it be for her grandmother?

'Leave those letters, Mrs Anderson, and I'll sort them.'

'Thank you, Miss Betsy,' the housekeeper said handing them over. Letters for the family went on a silver tray and those for the staff were distributed by Mrs Anderson.

'I'll leave those for the staff on the table and you can see to them later.'

Betsy was bored, glad even of this small task. The only pastime that gave her pleasure was playing the piano and that didn't give her the satisfaction it used to. Once her dreams had been of becoming a concert pianist but her teacher, though loud in his praise for his talented pupil, quickly brought her down to earth. Only a very, very few attained those heights and she was not in that class. Teaching music she might have settled for, but her mother hadn't wished such a lowly occupation for her daughter. Marriage to Dr Peter McGregor was what she had in mind.

She flicked through the bundle hoping there might be a letter from Joanna. Perhaps she should have gone to that school in Switzerland but she had expected it to be a disciplined life and she'd had enough of that. Joanna had written to tell her of the marvellous time she was having and hardly any discipline. Lucky Joanna.

Turning her attention back to the letters Betsy began to study them. Three for her grandmother, one of them highly scented. One for her mother. So far none for her. One, two, three, four for her stepfather. Her lips curled. More debts which her mother would feel obliged to meet. Why didn't she divorce him? Come to that why had she married him in the first place? All that charm, of course, that would have done it and he wasn't bad-looking. Pity her mother wasn't a strong character like her grandmother. Betsy smiled. She made it all too plain what she thought of her son-in-law but even so she was careful. If she threw him out of Duncairn House she couldn't be sure that his wife wouldn't go with him. Betsy shuddered. If that happened she might be dragged away too.

If only Peter were a bit more ardent. He was always charming and had partnered her on many an occasion but it only ended with a peck on the cheek. Her mother had pointed out that this was quite proper since she was a lot younger and he wouldn't want to rush things.

She gave a deep sigh. Oh, well, she'd have to do something about it herself – but what? She could hardly throw herself at him. She gave her attention back to the letters. That seemed to be all the letters for the family. The one for Mrs Morton made her smile, what atrocious writing, pity the poor postman or whoever sorted them. The letter under it, and she'd almost missed it, made her go pale. A local postmark and addressed to Miss Rachel Donaldson. Staring at it and willing it not to be what she suspected, Betsy kept looking at the writing. No two people could have that distinctive scrawl. It was Peter's writing but what would he be doing writing to a maid. Surely sensible Peter wouldn't be foolish enough to get involved with a girl of that class. Jealousy such as she had never experienced gripped her and the humiliation was almost more than she could bear. She wanted to scratch that girl's eyes out.

Bad enough that he had given her a lift from the village – or was that all it had been? Betsy had a desperate need to know, she had to know what was in that letter. What she was contemplating was dreadful, it was wicked, but she couldn't help herself. She wouldn't know a moment's peace until she knew for certain what Peter had written. Checking to make sure that no one saw her Betsy put the letter in the deep pocket of her skirt. Not a moment too soon either, here was her mother with the usual worried expression on her face.

'Any letters for me, dear?'

'Just one.'

She took it and examined the small, neat writing. 'I don't recognise the writing, I wonder whom it is from?'

'Open it and you'll find out,' Betsy said rudely.

'No, I'll wait and I'll take those for your grandmother.'

'What about his? Four, probably bills, do you want them?'

'I do not. Leave them and where are you off to?' she asked as Betsy tried to make her escape.

'Change out of this old skirt and spend a while at the piano.'

'That would be nice, dear, we miss hearing you play and it would be a pity to lose your touch. You know, Betsy, I'm far from convinced that being a concert pianist is beyond you.'

'Mother,' Betsy said wearily, 'we have been through all this before. I am not good enough. Like Brian with his painting we both lack that extra something and if we can accept that, isn't it time you did too?'

Maud smiled a little sadly. 'Perhaps you're right, dear, I won't mention the matter again.'

Some hope, thought Betsy as she hurried away. Once inside her bedroom she stood with her back against the door. Was it worth making a thief of herself for that's what it was? It was a struggle but one she wasn't going to win.

It was a young girl's room and after the austere school dormitories it had been her pride and joy. Allowed to make her own choice she had selected a pink bedcover with fringes, pink-and-white-striped wallpaper and white had been her choice of carpeting. She'd lost out there though and the carpet was pale grey. At fifteen she had loved it, at eighteen she hated it.

She fingered the envelope, bending the corners, putting off the moment, then tore it open. Two pages she drew out, one headed with Peter's home address. Her eyes blurred as she began to read: 'My dear Rachel,—'

Not a love letter just a sincere wish that they should meet again. Her hand clenched, her fingers screwed up the paper and she hurled it across the room. They had been together, had visited Dunkeld together, had had tea together, there was mention of a tearoom. How dare he? If he'd wanted company she was available but instead he had invited that maid. Throwing herself on the bed Betsy sobbed as though her heart would break. After a while she sat up and dried her tears. She had just had a thought that she could accept. Servant girls were easy, look at Janet and her stepfather. Not that Peter was a bit like him but all men had needs she had heard it whispered and the girl was nice-looking no use denying that. Yes, she could forgive Peter but it must not be allowed to continue, it would have to be nipped in the bud.

Getting no reply to his letter, Peter would begin to wonder. The post office wasn't guilty of losing letters but it couldn't be ruled out and Peter would no doubt give Rachel the benefit of the doubt. He would maybe write again so she would have to be on the look-out for the postman. Another thought struck her, she could use her stepfather. The fool thought himself the answer to a maiden's prayer and if she could just drop a hint to him that he had an admirer in the dark-haired maid then perhaps—

Feeling more like herself again. Betsy picked up the letter, smoothed out the pages and returned them in the envelope to her pocket. Burning it was the answer but there was only a fire in the drawing-room and sitting-room and there was a risk attached, admittedly small, but she wasn't willing to take it. Before flames devoured it someone might have come in and asked questions she didn't want to answer.

Putting a cardigan on, Betsy left the house, glad that the weather was warmish and dry. The leaves were well trodden into the path giving it a patterned appearance. Onwards through the gardens she went to where the burn, higher than usual after more than average rainfall, gurgled merrily. The wind, playfully boisterous, whipped at her skirt as she tore up the letter and envelope. She held her hand in the water fearful of some pieces escaping to land near the house. Opening her fingers she let the paper free and watched the tiny paper boats being swept away and out of sight. Only then did she dry her hands on her skirt and return to the house.

Working in the sewing-room Rachel could afford to let her mind wander to the family at Duncairn House. Her grandmother was a proud and difficult woman, a demanding one too but there was a kindliness that showed itself in different ways. The toast, the soggy toast was one example. Vague Aunt Maud she already liked but Betsy was the problem. Her cousin disliked her, made no secret of it, and Rachel was at a loss to understand. Certainly there had been the incident in the attic when Betsy had accused her of snooping around but nothing further had been said and Rachel had dismissed it from her mind. More than likely it was to do with Peter. Seeing a servant girl getting out of his car she must have wondered. Perhaps Betsy was in love with Peter, perhaps there was an understanding between them and Peter had merely been amusing himself. A spare afternoon, and she had been on hand. Rachel's face burned at the thought.

Work, what was needed was plenty of that to keep her from thinking of Dr Peter McGregor. Fortunately there was enough to keep her fingers busy. The linen was in good order and Rachel had expected her sessions in the sewing-room to be cut instead of which other work of another nature began to come her way. Shorter skirts had become the fashion and Mrs Anderson, moving with the times, made use of Rachel's expertise. Seeing an opportunity to improve her own lot, Rachel had requested curtains for the window and a fire in the room. The former she got without difficulty but a fire was not permitted until the last day of October though the temperature could have dropped before that.

How her Aunt Maud came to hear about her dressmaking skills Rachel never did find out but skirts and dresses requiring to be shortened or in need of minor repair such as the tightening of buttons, began to arrive. She was doing fewer and fewer household tasks.

Earlier on, Mrs Anderson had tried to be tactful. 'Do you mind, Rachel, if Janet goes back to being in charge of Mrs Craig's breakfast tray?'

'Not in the least, Mrs Anderson, in fact I'd be delighted.'

'Needs quick feet and a steady hand and we can't all be good at the same things.'

'Very true.'

Nights were the worst. Rachel tossed and turned unable to get to sleep and sometimes it was well into the small hours before she got over. Stupidly she had allowed herself to dream impossible dreams while Peter was no doubt regretting his impulsiveness, if not, surely he would have made some attempt to get in touch with her. All the time she had been at Duncairn House she had never had a letter. Only one person could have written and that was Agnes and she hadn't.

At times she was so unhappy that she thought seriously of applying for other jobs and leaving Duncairn House, yet she couldn't bear the thought of leaving it either. She had come to love the old house and this quiet part of Perthshire. Then there was the bond with her grandmother, it was getting stronger. With each passing week she wished for the courage to tell her grandmother that she was Amelia's daughter but something always held her back.

The waiting-room was empty, Dr Peter McGregor had seen the last patient off the premises himself then gone back to sit behind his desk. Some paperwork needed to be done and he saw to it then he put down his pen and sat looking at the blank wall. His thoughts were of Rachel. As a doctor he knew all about hope. One had it and one kept going, his had died slowly as October gave way to November and still no reply to his letters. One could have gone astray but not two. Peter was hurt, surprised, angry and unexpectedly depressed. At twenty-eight years of age he had had a few girlfriends, been quite keen on one or two, but when the romance ended he'd felt no real regret, no sense of loss.

Rachel had seemed to him to be so different. He had enjoyed talking to her and happy that there had been no need for non-stop chatter. The silences were comfortable, two people completely at ease with one another or so he had thought. He was wrong, he must be. The attraction had been all on his side or she would have replied to his letters. Twice at Dr Smart's request, he had visited Duncairn House to see Mrs Craig but though he'd lingered, there had been no sign of Rachel. No sign of Betsy either and he'd been glad of that. Just lately he'd got the impression that she was becoming possessive expecting him to escort her to this, that and the other. Being friendly with the family made it difficult to refuse but that was what he was going to do. Brian Meldrum would be more than happy to oblige, it was easy to see where his heart lay.

That other maid, Janet, had come to the door with him and he could have asked about Rachel, but he hesitated and the moment was lost.

Reading helped but it didn't throw off her depression and reading aloud to her grandmother was very much part of her daily routine. They had moved on from newspapers.

'Perhaps you could read a chapter or two of a book, Rachel, there isn't a great deal of interest in the papers these days.'

Rachel was touched. 'Of course, m'am, I'd be delighted.'

'You will have been into the library?'

'No, I haven't.'

'My husband used to collect books and I read them. He didn't have a great deal of time to do so himself but expected to do a lot of reading in later life. Sadly it was not to be.' She frowned as if she had said more than she intended. 'What I wanted to say was that you have my permission to choose a book for your own pleasure. I've watched you handle them and feel sure I can trust you to be careful.'

'That is very kind of you, m'am, and you have my word that I would take the greatest care.'

'Less of your time will be spent in the sewing room since the linen is now in good repair.'

'Not really, I'm there quite a lot.'

'Doing what?'

Rachel hoped she wasn't getting anybody into trouble. 'With the change in fashion I am getting a lot of skirts and dresses to shorten.'

'Is there a change? I hadn't noticed.' She smiled. 'Once upon a time I took a great interest in clothes but at my age one puts comfort first.'

She closed her eyes, an indication that she was tired talking and wished to be alone. Rachel left quietly.

Another day and she was with her grandmother. Outside a thin, grey November mist shrouded the countryside but there was a roaring fire in the bedroom. The old lady sat up very straight in her high-winged chair, her slippered feet on a pouffe.

'I've had enough of the papers today and all that talk of poverty. One gets heartily sick of it. Folk would be able to manage if they used a little common sense.'

'They would if they got enough to cover their basic needs.'

'Nonsense, that kind take things on credit without thought as to how they are going to keep up the payments. If they would just realise that they are paying a lot more for goods which I believe in many cases are repossessed if the payments fall behind. Save up then buy is what they should be taught.'

Rachel hadn't expected her grandmother to know about hire-purchase but she was going to put her right on a few things.

'M'am, those people you speak of are well aware that they are paying about half again for the goods but that is better than not having the basic essentials for living such as a bed, table and chairs.'

'Don't enter into marriage until you have something behind you.'

Rachel wanted to laugh. 'Precious few would get married if that were the case and don't lump them together. Many do manage to keep up payments, they budget for it and once the debt is nearly cleared they buy another article of furniture or clothes for the family.'

'And never get out of the bit,' came the sharp reply.

'They don't see it that way and incidentally that is why it is called the never-never.'

'Well named, I would say. Surely you don't approve of it?'

'My father saved before he bought but then he was in the fortunate position of being in a reasonably well-paid job.'

'Exactly, he was working not like those others just looking for handouts.'

Rachel was getting angrier by the minute but her grandmother hadn't finished. 'In this day and age all children receive an education to the age of fourteen and all but the most stupid should be able to read, write and count.'

'And all that is available for the majority of them are poorly paid jobs with no prospects. Indeed, m'am, many at sixteen find themselves unemployed through no fault of their own, merely that the job can be done more cheaply by a fourteen-year-old.'

'Go on.'

Rachel wasn't sure if it was sarcasm or not. She hesitated then decided as she'd gone this far she might as well continue. 'Walking the streets looking for a job with boots lined with newspaper or cardboard because they are beyond being repaired then returning to a cold house with no money to buy coal, not enough to eat and knowing that the next day and the next again will likely be the same,' she paused to take a breath, 'twenty or more after the same job, what chance, m'am, what chance have they?'

'You seem to be very knowledgeable on the subject,' her grandmother said tartly, 'yet I don't imagine you've known want.'

'No, it's true I haven't, but I've seen at first hand what poverty and hopelessness can do to people. My father has been reduced to tears by men coming to him pleading for work, prepared to do anything, and having to turn them away. Seeing in their faces the bitterness, the hopelessness, the guilt that goes with being unable to provide for a wife and family.'

'Where does your father work?'

'In the jute mill.'

'Yes,' she nodded her white head, 'times are difficult in the jute trade, I do know about that, my family has suffered too.'

Rachel felt like screaming that she knew nothing about it. How could she, brought up in luxury, wanting for nothing? The plight of those people was beyond her understanding. Rachel bit back the words waiting to be said, she had probably said too much already. Leaning over she picked up a leather-bound copy of *Jane Eyre* and opened it at the place.

'M'am, would you like me to begin reading?'

'If you've come down from that soap box.'

'I'm sorry, I shouldn't have said all that.'

She inclined her head as if to agree. 'Don't let that fire go down,' she said irritably, 'and get me my shawl, there is quite a drop in temperature.'

Rachel rose to see to the fire. It was stifling in the room but she added a few more lumps of coal then went for the shawl and draped it over the narrow shoulders. Already she was regretting her earlier impatience, a woman of her grandmother's age would have set ideas and newspaper accounts could be very misleading. The one way to understand real poverty and wretchedness was to experience it.

As Rachel began to read, the beautiful words soothed her. The story, familiar though it was, never failed to move her and she saw the glint of tears in the faded eyes. After two chapters Rachel closed the book.

'Thank you, I'll rest now.' Her head went back, her eyes closed and Rachel went quietly closing the door behind her. Hoping for a cup of tea she ran down the stairs, across the hall and through to the kitchen. She was thinking of nothing in particular when the name Kerne House was released from her memory. For long she had racked her brains trying to remember the name of the house where Agnes was employed. This very evening she would write to Agnes at Kerne House and if that brought no reply then she would just have to accept it that Agnes had no desire to keep up the friendship.

Mrs Morton produced a welcome cup of tea.

'Thanks, Mrs Morton, you've saved a life, I needed that.'

'Are you all right, lass, you've been lookin' a bit peeky this while back?'

'I'm fine, touch of the cold that's all.'

Mrs Morton nodded but she wasn't satisfied. The lass didn't have a cold but something was making her unhappy.

Hetty, too, was concerned about Rachel and voiced it to the cook.

'What is the matter with her, Mrs Morton. I've asked but she just says nothin' is the matter?'

'Noticed it mysel'. Lost all her sparkle, mebbe it's a lad and she's had a disappointment.'

'Can't be that. She's never been out with a lad or I would have known.'

'Mebbe it is something she doesn't want to talk about.'

Hetty nodded. 'Never mentions her home and that's strange, isn't it?

All she's ever said is that she belongs to Dundee.'

Mrs Morton pursed her lips. 'I'd say there is something far wrong when a lass doesn't mention her home.'

'No letters, she never gets any.'

'A mystery, Hetty, but it's none of our business.'

Hetty wasn't ready to go yet and Mrs Morton was in a chatty mood.

'Janet and Rachel hardly speak.'

'Nothin' more than jealousy on Janet's part.'

'Jealous of Rachel's appearance you mean? But Janet is good-lookin' hersel'.'

'Not in the same class, Hetty, and that to my mind is where the mystery comes in.'

Hetty was slightly offended. 'You think she's above us?'

'I think you'd better get those hands workin' and get those brasses shining.'

'Bloomin' awful brasses,' Hetty grumbled. 'I'm tellin' you this, Mrs Morton, when *I* get married there won't be a blinkin' piece of brass in my house or for that matter anything that needs polishin'.'

'Away with you and let me get on.'

'I'm just goin',' Hetty said heaving her body up and collecting the Brasso tin, a dirty rag and some clean dusters. 'What a life!'

Two hours off in the afternoon was a waste. A little longer and she could have taken the bus into Perth and done some window-shopping. The weather was mild for the beginning of December and Rachel decided on a stroll in the gardens to get some fresh air into her lungs. With it being so mild Brian Meldrum might be there. He called the scenery an artist's paradise and could well be busy painting. If he was around she would have a chat with him.

She liked Brian, liked his open friendliness and disarming smile. Absolutely no side with him, he spoke to everyone and being of the same generation he and Rachel found much to talk about. It was nothing more than friendship they shared and because of it there was no awkwardness. He told her a lot about Duncairn House knowing his disclosures would go no further.

'The old lady's been marvellous to me,' he'd said on one occasion, 'encourages me with my painting even to giving me a room—'

'Your own studio,' Rachel smiled.

'As good as. It has plenty of light and room for all my paraphernalia.' His face hardened. 'Or rubbish as my father would call it. Not likely to make my fortune and I accept that, but I know I'm reasonably good. Get better too if I get the chance to work at it.'

'What I've seen of your work I'd say you were very good.'

'Sweet of you, Rachel, but I know my limitations. Betsy is a very good pianist, did you know that? and we console each other that we just fail to be in the genius class.' He laughed but without mirth. 'A job in the City is what my father wants for me and for the present I am going along with it.'

'Then you'll please yourself?'

'When I'm twenty-one I'll make my own decisions and that won't be long. It's when I come into a little money from my mother. Enough to keep the wolf from the door until I make up my mind what to do with my life. The rest comes to me when I'm twenty-five.' He paused. 'I lost my mother when I was twelve and I didn't think I would ever get over it.'

'I can understand, Brian. I lost my mother when I was nine.'

'Did your father remarry?'

'Yes, my stepmother was the reason I left home.'

'Tough. My stepmother is very good to me and Betsy. I don't have a chance there, Betsy only has eyes for that doctor chap. Nice bloke but I could see him far enough at times.'

There was no sign of Brian today and Rachel decided to turn back. Suddenly and without warning it got colder, the daylight seemed to vanish and the grey bleakness of December take its place. What had seemed friendly countryside had taken on a menacing look and a rustle in the bushes made her start. An animal, nothing to be afraid of, then out of the greyness loomed a figure and she saw that it was a smiling Henry Meldrum. Her stomach muscles tensed.

'What a pleasant surprise, my dear, but I didn't mean to startle you.'

'It's all right but if you'll excuse me I'm in a hurry. Please let me through.'

'Oh, Rachel, my dear girl, I don't think you are in all that much of a hurry.' He gave her a knowing little smile. 'You see, a little bird whispered to me that my advances would not be unwelcome.'

Chapter Twenty

It was Tuesday the twenty-fourth and Agnes who prided herself on never getting into a state was a bundle of nerves from the moment she put her bare feet to the cold linoleum floor and padded over to the window. Holding back the curtains she checked on the weather. There were puddles on the uneven ground after the heavy overnight rain but the clouds were breaking up with the promise of a good day. A good day for Meg's wedding. She couldn't help feeling guilty about it but Meg was a decent sort, she wouldn't hold it against her. Anything but this she would gladly have given up to be with her sister on this day of all days. Put it out of your mind, Agnes, and concentrate on what lies ahead.

Though the interview wasn't until the afternoon she was up early unable to stay in bed any longer. The other bed was empty, Molly would have started her chores by now. After enquiring at the bus station Agnes found the most suitable bus to be the one o'clock which would mean leaving Kerne House shortly after twelve to catch a tram into town.

First impressions were lasting impressions or so she had been told and with that in mind Agnes had the previous day made one of her rare visits to the hairdresser.

'Could you give me a Marcel wave or something? It's important I look nice so what style do you suggest?'

The hairdresser, young and stylish herself, played around with the auburn hair pulling it through her fingers. 'It's in good condition and you have a hint of a natural wave so I'd say all you need for a neat, fashionable look is a bit off the length then the ends turned in.'

'Just turned in, is that all?'

'Up to you, of course, but that is my professional opinion,' she said haughtily.

Careful, Agnes, she warned herself. 'Right! You're the expert and I'm in your hands.'

The girl knew her job. The new pageboy look was perfect with her small features.

'Happy with it?' the stylist asked as she held the mirror to let Agnes get a good view of the back.

'You're a genius so you are,' Agnes beamed, hugely delighted with the result and only wished as she handed over the money that she was in a position to add a tip. One day she would be but not quite yet.

'Good luck,' the girl said as Agnes went out.

'Thanks.'

An end-of-season sale had produced a bargain of a navy trench coat, perfect for fit. Tightly belted and with the collar turned up at the back Agnes felt attractive and well-dressed. She was less happy about what she wore under it, the grey skirt had seen better days and the pink blouse with its frilly neckline was too fussy and had been a poor buy. Still the likelihood of being asked to remove her coat was slim and even if she were it would be in the kitchen where she hoped to be offered something to eat before travelling back to Kerne House.

She looked down at her feet, the shoes, flat-heeled, brown and scuffed at the toes, were a let-down but there was no way her funds would stretch even to the cheapest pair. Agnes felt the familiar irritation at still being expected to contribute to her mother's household expenses. Without that she would be able to save a little.

Molly came in. 'You look quite smart,' she said, then frowned, 'except about the feet. I know you don't have big feet but those shoes make you look as though you did.'

'Thanks a lot, any more encouraging remarks like that and keep them to yourself.'

'You suit your hair like that, I may think about having that style myself.' She fingered her blonde tresses. 'My hairdresser says I have marvellous hair and she can do anything with it.'

'Lucky old you.'

'Molly, if you promise to keep it to yourself I'll tell you something.'

'Tell me what?'

Agnes remained silent.

'All right I promise and anyway I'm not a gossip.'

'I've got an interview for a job.'

Molly's mouth fell open. 'You haven't! But why, Agnes, why do you want to leave here? I thought you liked Kerne House.'

'I do, it's not that but I want to better myself and this could be just what I'm looking for.'

Molly looked put out. 'Where is this job?'

'Kirriemuir.'

Molly was silent, her fingers playing with her hair, then she said slowly, 'In one way, Agnes, I hope you get the job but in another I hope you don't.'

'Care to explain that.'

'I'll miss you and then you know yourself the bother it is trainin' someone new.'

'Don't worry about it yet, there's no guarantee I'll get the job.'

'I've a feelin' you will,' Molly said glumly then added. 'Not a very good service to Kirrie so you'd better check on the buses back unless you want to be stranded.'

'If I had a watch I'd know the time. What about giving me a loan of yours?' she asked hopefully.

'That's askin' a lot and I don't like folk borrowin' my things.'

'I hope I'm not just folk and honestly I would take great care of it.'

'I don't know, Agnes,' Molly said doubtfully.

'Please.'

Molly swithered and then decided to be generous. Going over to the set of drawers she took the watch out of its box. 'I wound it up last night and it keeps good time so don't you dare touch it.'

'Wouldn't dream of it.' Agnes took the silver watch with its black moiré ribbon band and slipped it on her wrist then secured the catch.

Molly looked as though she were already regretting her generosity. The timepiece had come to her through her uncle who had a pawnbroker's shop. Goods unclaimed after a specified time were frequently sold at a fraction of their worth and being family Molly's mother got the watch for next to nothing to give to her daughter for her eighteenth birthday.

Agnes was the first to board the Kirriemuir bus and sat near the front. By the time they left, two minutes late by Molly's watch, the bus was slightly more than half filled. There were a number of stops where passengers got off and others got on. Bush with her own thoughts Agnes hardly noticed the passing countryside as they sped through the small villages. only when they approached Kirriemuir did she begin to pay attention to her surroundings.

Kirriemuir was a quaint, attractive little town on the Braes of Angus with sandstone cottages lining the narrow streets. Agnes knew a little about it but this was her first visit. She did know that its most famous son was born at 9 Brechin Road and that Kirriemuir had been immortalised as Thrums in the tales of J.M. Barrie who also wrote *Peter Pan*.

The bus stopped in the square and after collecting their belongings the passengers stood waiting until it was their time to get off. Agnes had no belongings other than her handbag which she opened yet again to check that she had the all-important letter. Touching it she shut her handbag and looked about her. Sunshine flooded the square and a group of men she took to be farmers shouted greetings to those who passed.

The newsagent's shop was two-windowed and was on the corner. The floor was cluttered with cardboard boxes and bundles of newspapers and Agnes had to pick her way to get to the counter. A head turned from arranging packets of cigarettes on the shelf.

'Yes, lass?'

'I'm waiting for the local bus. When is it due?'

'Anytime now. Where would you be going?'

'Drumoaks.'

'Some parcels for them so he'll be stopping right at the gate. Don't be wandering far, Willie is his own timetable and that means he leaves when he's ready.'

Agnes smiled. 'Thanks very much.'

In less than five minutes a small, shabby vehicle with wooden benches for the passengers trundled into the square. Agnes had been alone but suddenly others arrived, cracked a joke to Willie who grunted a reply before his face creased into a smile. Fares were taken as they got on and the money dropped into a large brown pouch. Agnes climbed in. Since her expenses were to be refunded the cost didn't worry her.

'Drumoaks, please.'

'Tuppence.'

Agnes handed over two pennies. 'Will you tell me when I get there?'

'I'll give you a shout.'

Shopping baskets took up about as much space as the passengers and as Agnes sat down a stout woman in a woolly hat drew her shopping closer to her.

'Move up, lass, there's plenty of room.'

'I'm fine here,' Agnes said from her seat at the far end. The woman looked ready to talk but Agnes wasn't and she was relieved when she turned to someone else and drew her into conversation.

Some time later a voice from the back shouted. 'Let me off at the corner, Willie.'

'Take you all the way – save your legs.'

'No, it means you turnin' and I don't mind the wee walk.'

'Just as you say, Annie, and mebbe it's the exercise that keeps you looking so trim.'

Her ample frame shuddered with laughter as she heaved herself up. 'That's enough from you, you saucy old devil.' She got off and stood still to give a cheery wave.

Drumoaks was the next stop. 'This is you, lass.'

'Thank you,' she said getting up quickly.

'Biding there are you?' He jerked his thumb.

'No.'

'If you need a lift back I pass here between five and five thirty.'

'I'll keep it in mind, thanks for telling me.'

A lad in heavy working togs and big boots climbed on to get the parcels for Drumoaks. He nodded to Willie then got off and walked away smartly not giving Agnes a chance to speak to him. She began walking in the same direction. The drive had wide grass borders leading up to the house and the sun glinted on the stone walls washing them to a pale gold. Drumoaks was a lovely old house with no harsh lines about it, just a grace and gentleness in tune with the surrounding countryside. Agnes experienced a sense of awe that people could live in such a magnificent dwelling. There was an archway and stone steps led up to a door that could have belonged to a castle. Ivy clung to the wall above the archway and continued along the line of windows.

Remembering her instructions, Agnes looked for and found the narrow path which led to the side of the house. There was a short flight of steps much worn by the weather. She went down them and on to a short path to a door. On it was a heavy black knocker and Agnes gave it two sharp raps. Hurrying footsteps could be heard, a bolt was drawn back then the door opened. A small, thin girl and rosy cheeks and light-brown straight hair looked at Agnes and smiled showing white even teeth.

'I have an appointment with Mrs Harrison. I'm Agnes Boyd.'

'Come in, Mrs Harrison is expecting you.' The girl had a clear, pleasant voice with a lilt. 'Wait here till I get this door bolted.'

There was an inner door. Agnes shivered though she'd been quite warm until then. The stone floor and the stone steps leading from it gave it the chill of a cell.

'Don't worry, it isn't all like this,' the girl said noticing the shiver. 'Did you come with Willie's bus?'

'Yes.'

'He's very obliging and even in the worst weather he tries to keep the bus running.' Agnes followed her up a half-flight of stairs and through a door similar to the other but minus the knocker. Here a waft of welcome warmth greeted them and a bewildering number of passages. Out of one came a tall, bespectacled girl. She looked Agnes up and down and Agnes did the same to her.

'Where do you think you are going, Madge?'

Madge flushed. 'This is the girl from Dundee, Beatrice. Miss—' she floundered and Agnes came to her assistance having taken an instant dislike to Beatrice.

'Agnes Boyd.'

'I'm taking Agnes to Mrs Harrison,' she said nervously. 'Is she in the office or her own room?'

'In the office. You should know that she is always in the office at this time of day.' Then to Agnes. 'You'll be after the job of housemaid?'

'Yes,' Agnes said shortly.

'Get back to your duties, Madge,' she ordered.

'Are you going to take—'

She gave Madge a withering look. 'Follow me, Miss Boyd,' then not waiting to see whether Agnes was following or not went quickly through a passageway then down a particularly narrow stairway. 'Watch your head,' she called back carelessly and too late for Agnes to avoid the unexpectedly low ceiling at the foot of the stairs. Fortunately it wasn't a hard bang but it hurt. The oath died in her throat when Agnes remembered where she was.

'Sorry, did you bang your head?' Beatrice said sweetly.

'No,' Agnes lied.

The door they came to was slightly ajar and Beatrice knocked before putting her head in.

'The last applicant has arrived, Mrs Harrison.'

'Show Miss Boyd in, Beatrice.'

Agnes was annoyed that Beatrice hadn't bothered with her name. She walked in totally ignoring the other girl and Beatrice shut the door with unnecessary force.

Mrs Harrison frowned. 'Beatrice in one of her moods. Do sit down, Miss Boyd.' She indicated a chair and Agnes sat down knees and feet neatly together. She opened her bag and put the letter on the desk.

'Thank you. You had no difficulty getting here?'

'None at all.'

The housekeeper looked fortyish. She was of average height, thin and with a narrow face, brown hair parted down the middle and plaited into a neat bun. She had a sweet smile and Agnes began to relax.

'Your letter told me a little but I'd like you to go into more detail.'

Agnes proceeded to do so. She had it off by heart.

'You do realise that the vacancy is for a housemaid and not a tablemaid?'

'Yes, I understood that.'

'You would accept that drop in status?' Her eyebrows rose.

'Yes.'

'Did you bring a reference with you?'

Agnes's face dropped. 'I'm afraid not, Mrs Harrison, and may I tell you the reason for that?'

'I think you had better.' She looked amused, unaware that Agnes was playing for time, deciding what best to say.

'My employers returned to this country after many years in India and have had difficulty in getting and keeping domestic staff.'

'Why should that be?'

Agnes wanted to laugh out loud, it was all going to be so easy. She didn't have to make it up, she could tell the truth. 'My employer forgets that he is no longer in India and being used to shouting at the natives—'

'You don't need to go on, Miss Boyd, I get the picture for myself.'

'I don't much like being shouted at either but his wife is such a gentle charming lady that I just put up with it.'

'You feel that you have had enough?'

'Yes.'

'We do expect a high standard from our staff at Drumoaks but I can assure you that there will be no shouting.' She smiled then frowned. 'This is rather difficult, I had all but decided on one of the other applicants, a local girl whom I may say has excellent references but I am going to offer you the position, Miss Boyd, for the simple reason that your training as a tablemaid may come in useful. Beatrice carries out this duty with her usual efficiency but there are times when she could do with some assistance when there are guests. You wouldn't object to that?'

'I'd be more than happy to oblige.'

'You are paid weekly?'

'Yes.'

'Then one week's notice is all that is legally required, but perhaps you would prefer that to be two weeks?'

'I would, please.'

'We will match your present wage and in six months if you prove to be satisfactory, this will be reviewed.'

'Thank you, Mrs Harrison.' Better and better, Agnes thought.

'It would be more suitable and give you a chance to settle in if you were to come in on the Sunday ready to begin your duties on the Monday.'

'That would be no problem, Mrs Harrison.'

She smiled. 'Now do you have any questions?'

'No, I don't think so.'

'Oh, mustn't forget your expenses,' she said handing Agnes a sealed envelope.

Agnes breathed a sigh of relief. She hadn't wanted to ask for them and was glad it hadn't proved necessary.

Mrs Harrison got up. 'Come along and I'll introduce you to Mrs Tomlinson, our cook. You'll be glad of a cup of tea and something to eat then Madge can – have you met Madge?'

'Yes, she showed me in.'

'Nice girl, you'll get on with her I'm sure. After you've eaten and if you have time before your bus, Madge will show you the bedroom you will be occupying. Regarding your duties we'll decide those when you arrive.'

Another bewildering journey took Agnes to the kitchen premises.

'I'm beginning to think I'll need a map to find my way around.'

Mrs Harrison laughed. 'Difficult to begin with but you'll master it in no time.'

Mrs Tomlinson was elderly, a stout and pleasant-faced woman. After wiping her floury hands on her overall she extended a large hand with thick short fingers. For a moment Agnes's eyes went beyond her to the extremely well-fitted, modern kitchen.

'Mrs Tomlinson, this is Agnes Boyd, our new housemaid.'

'Welcome, lass, you'll be the one from Dundee?'

'Yes.'

'Give Agnes something to eat, will you? And get Madge to show her where she will be sleeping.'

'I'll do that. Sit down, Agnes.'

The lovely warm smell coming from the ovens made Agnes realise just how hungry she was.

'What a beautiful kitchen, Mrs Tomlinson.'

'You expected an old-fashioned kitchen?'

'I suppose I did, I mean parts of the house look ancient.'

'Most of the big houses are modernising the kitchens and I have to say this is a pleasure to work in. Mind you, at the start I was against change, made me nervous, you see, but now I wonder how I managed before. Hungry are you?'

'Starving.'

'Bacon, egg and fried bread?'

'Sounds wonderful.'

'The pan's still hot, it won't take me long.'

True to her word Agnes was soon tucking in.

'Enjoyin' that?' Mrs Tomlinson asked unnecessarily.

'I'll say I am.'

'Like a lass who enjoys her food, can't be doin' with those that just pick at it. I'll have a cup with you. Can't stand too long with these varicose veins of mine. I'll talk while you eat and tell you somethin' about the family. I take it you'd like to hear about them?'

Agnes nodded, her mouth too full to speak.

'A scullery maid I was when I first came to Drumoaks. The old master and mistress were a fine couple, did a lot for the people hereabout and they were sorely missed when they went, God rest their souls.' She paused to drink her tea and perhaps to think back to those days. After putting down the cup she wiped her mouth. 'The two sons, Mr Adrian and Mr Gerald, were a pair of rascals. The tricks those two got up to – and many a dressing-down they got. The gentry can be real hard on their own. Spare the rod and spoil the child is how they see it.' She smiled. 'They used to sneak down to the kitchen here and stand and eat whatever they were given and in a wee while tears gave way to smiles.'

'Did they go to the local school?'

'You've a lot to learn about the gentry, lass. The boys had a tutor then boarding school and university. Both clever lads but Mr Gerald, he's the younger, was by far the brightest. Such a tragedy—' She shook her head.

Agnes placed her knife and fork together on the empty plate and waited for Mrs Tomlinson to go on and when she didn't Agnes prodded her. 'What kind of tragedy, Mrs Tomlinson?'

'Terrible, terrible thing. There'd been a storm, you see, not unusual but this was a very bad one and Mr Adrian and Mr Gerald went out to see the extent of the damage for themselves. The grounds and gardens are lovely around Drumoaks, Agnes, a sight to gladden the eyes—'

Agnes wished she would keep to the point but tried to hide her impatience the best she could.

'The accident I was tellin' you about that—'

'Yes.'

'Mr Adrian saw it happen, yelled a warnin' to his brother but it was too late. You see, lass, a tree slackened by the storm came crashing down pinning Mr Gerald by the legs.'

Agnes shuddered. 'How awful!'

'A nightmare for poor Mr Adrian as well. What a state he was in, he couldn't move the weight from his brother and had to run to the house for help. By the time they got the lad free they thought he was gone, but there was a flicker of life and being a strong, healthy laddie he pulled through. A big, handsome lad who'll never walk again. Bitter too he is and difficult.'

'Who could blame him?'

'Aye, as you say, who could blame him?' Mrs Tomlinson, after filling up Agnes's cup, took up the story again. 'Now for the rest of the family. There's the master's wife, a proper lady and very involved in charities and good works. They have two bairns. Master Mark is seven and his sister, Mary, is five. With this new nanny I don't see much of them. Pity, I like the wee ones coming in and getting a biscuit but Miss Reynolds doesn't approve.'

'Perhaps she's got orders from above,' Agnes suggested.

'I doubt that, I doubt it very much. The master would mind when he liked to come in and get a tasty bite. Are you all right for time?'

'Yes, if I'm at the gate by five I'll get the bus.'

'You've a while then. Miss Gertrude comes between her brothers.

Should have been a laddie that one, daft about horses. She's no oil painting but I will say this, she looks well sitting on a horse.'

'All easy to get on with, are they?'

'I've no complaints. Keep out of Mr Gerald's way would be my advice. He gets into terrible rages about little or nothing.'

Agnes got up and began to collect her dishes meaning to take them over to the sink.

'No, lass, leave them and here's Madge.'

'Thank you for a lovely meal, Mrs Tomlinson.' She grinned. 'If for nothing else I'm looking forward to the food here.'

Mrs Tomlinson looked pleased. 'Fine to see food you've cooked being appreciated. Bye, lass, we'll look forward to you coming.'

'She's a gem, isn't she?' Madge said as they climbed to where the servants slept.

'She certainly is. The only fly in the ointment seems to be Beatrice.'

'She's terribly efficient, I'm a bit scared of her.'

'Don't be and you certainly won't be when I start.'

Madge looked impressed. 'Why, do you think you'll be able to stand up to her?'

'No bother, I've met that type before – face up to them and they soon stop their nonsense.'

'I'm glad you're comin'. Beatrice is worse than usual today and I can tell you why that is.'

'Go on then.'

'She was desperate for her friend to get the job and she very nearly did.'

'So I believe.' Agnes kept her face straight. 'She saw me and there was never any question but that I would get the job.'

'Are you terribly efficient too? I'm not.'

'I'm no great shakes but I muddle through. To be honest I have some experience as tablemaid and that clinched it for me. Heavens! Is this mine?' Agnes asked as Madge flung open the door letting her see right into the room.

Madge nodded happily. 'We're terribly lucky. You see the mistress did an inspection of the servants' quarters and she was horrified at what she saw and had the painters in to freshen up the rooms. We got new furniture too.'

'The room I have in Kerne House is pretty good but nothing like this.'

'I wasn't used to much at home, Agnes,' Madge said delighting Agnes with her honesty.

'That makes two of us.' Agnes went right in and had a good look round. The walls were cream-painted and the curtains were heavy flowered cotton with plenty of fullness. Patterned linoleum was on the floor and there was a rug beside the single bed and that was covered with a peach-coloured bedspread. A small dressing-table, a single wardrobe and two chairs completed the furnishings.

'When do you have to leave?'

With a well-practised flick of the wrist Agnes looked at Molly's watch.

'Just as well you asked, it's time I got my skates on.'

'I'm saving up for one of them.'

'One of what?'

'A watch.'

'This isn't mine, I borrowed it. Like you, I'd better start saving for one as well.'

Back in Kerne House, Molly was given the news first. 'I got the job, Molly, I start a week on Monday.'

Molly's face fell. 'Funny, you know, I didn't realise how much I like you, it's only now when you're leavin'.'

'Start looking around for something better yourself.'

'I could, you know, but I don't think I will. This place isn't bad and I might make a bad move.' She paused and looked searchingly at Agnes. 'Are you sure you're makin' a good one?'

'Time will tell.' Reluctantly she removed the watch from her wrist. 'Thanks, Molly, it was good of you letting me have it.'

Molly took it and placed it back in its box.

'Gift, was it?'

'Yes, from my mother for my eighteenth. My uncle got it for her.'

'He a jeweller?'

'Not exactly, well I suppose I could tell you. He isn't a jeweller, Agnes, but he does deal in jewellery and other things too.'

'Got a stall in the market you mean?'

'I do not,' she said indignantly. 'My uncle is a pawnbroker and he makes a very good livin'.'

'I bet he does.'

'What do you mean by that?'

'A lot of sharks.'

'They are not,' she said heatedly.

'Molly, I should know, folk where I used to live were regulars at the pawnbrokers.'

'My uncle gives a – a—'

'A service.'

'Yes, a service, and he says folk wouldn't manage without him.'

Agnes shook her head. 'Have you ever heard of a poor pawnbroker?'

'I only know one.'

'I've known folk, Molly, hand over something good, worth a lot of money but they are so desperate for the money that they accept the little they are offered hoping to reclaim whatever it is later, only they never do. Your uncle and his kind make a mint.' Agnes grinned. 'Maybe your watch came from some poor soul.'

'Mebbe it did but it didn't stop you borrowin' it.'

'I didn't know where it came from then but you're right. I would have borrowed it just the same.'

'And if I got you one cheap you'd take it.'

'Too true.'

'Well, I wouldn't.' Molly's colour was up. 'Are we fightin''?'

'No, just a friendly argument.'

'Well mind this, I don't like folk miscallin' my family.'

'I wásn't. I was just wishin' one of my stupid uncles had the brains to be a pawnbroker.'

Molly looked uncertain and Agnes gave her a hug. 'You've been a good friend to me, Molly, and I'm going to miss you.'

'Will you?' she said wistfully.

'Old Templeton will be glad to see the back of me.' But there Agnes was wrong.

'May I ask where you are going?' she asked, her brows drawn together in an angry frown.

'Drumoaks, it's an estate just outside Kirriemuir.'

'As a tablemaid?'

'No, a housemaid.'

'Isn't that a backward step?'

'Could be but I think I'm doing the right thing.'

'Before going the length of finding yourself another job surely you could have given some indication that you were dissatisfied. You could have come to me to talk the matter over.'

'You know, Miss Templeton, that never occurred to me.' Something in Agnes's voice made her look up sharply but Agnes's face showed nothing. She was enjoying herself. 'After all you never seemed pleased with my work.'

'Admittedly you were very careless at the start but you improved thanks to the training you got here.' She glared at Agnes. 'Just be sure that for the remainder of your time at Kerne House you fulfil your duties.'

On the whole Kerne House held happy memories for Agnes. Saying goodbye to Mrs Robertson, Molly and Gloria proved to be more difficult than she expected. Particularly when on her last day Mrs Robertson handed her a small packet.

'That's with our best wishes, Agnes, lass, and the gardeners chipped in too.'

'For me?' Agnes was taken aback.

'Open it, Molly said as they all drew nearer.

Agnes opened the package then gasped. Her face paled then flushed as she took out the wristwatch, not new, the metal was slightly tarnished, but a watch.

'I – I just don't know what to say—'

'That makes a change,' Mrs Robertson chuckled. 'Fancy our Agnes bein' tongue-tied.'

'It's the best, the very best gift I've had in my whole life,' she said, fighting back the tears.

'It was to be a nice warm scarf,' Mrs Robertson said, 'but Molly knew that you would like a watch and she knew where she could get a good one cheap. I'm tellin' you that just in case you think we've come into a bit of money.'

Agnes looked gratefully at Molly then put the watch on her wrist and could hardly take her eyes off it.

'Put some fancy biscuits on a plate, Gloria, and you, Molly, make a good cup of tea, none of your dishwater.'

'Strong tea is bad for you,' but she ladled in three heaped caddy spoons of tea before adding the boiling water.

'Agnes, I can't stand it a moment longer. Give me that watch, it's goin' back in the box till night or there won't be a stroke of work done.'

★ ★ ★

They were in the bedroom, Agnes was doing her packing.

'You won't forget us will you?'

'How could I with a watch to remind me?' She grinned cheekily. 'Three cheers for the pawnbrokers, especially your uncle. I take back all I said.'

'You are the limit, Agnes Boyd, and I nearly forgot to tell you I saw Tommy Kingsley and I told him you were leaving Kerne House.'

Agnes waited. Her face showed no change but her heart was hammering.

'What had he to say to that?'

'Nothin' much, just that he hoped it would all work out for you. Funny thing to say, why couldn't he have just wished you all the best or somethin'? In a way,' she said thoughtfully, 'you and Tommy are two of a kind.'

'In what way?'

'Neither of you comes out with what you're thinkin', you never say it straight.'

'Maybe that's because we don't know what we mean ourselves.'

'There you go again,' Molly said exasperatedly.

'When you see him again tell him it is all going to work out for me, that I'll make sure it does.'

'If I can remember all that,' she said doubtfully.

After giving in her notice Agnes never set eyes on either the master or mistress before she left Kerne House. Mrs Taylor was confined to her room with a feverish cold and the master had business in London requiring his attention.

One week after Agnes's departure from Kerne House Rachel's letter arrived. Miss Templeton had a forwarding address and to be fair to her she had every intention of redirecting it. But something claimed her attention and she put the letter in the drawer with receipted accounts meaning to deal with it later on in the day, but it completely slipped her memory.

Guilt at not attending her sister's wedding still bothered Agnes and she wrote two short notes, one before she got the position at Drumoaks and the other after being successful. With some impatience she awaited a reply and eventually one came. It was a happy letter, a bride clearly bursting with happiness and painting a picture, a very nearly perfect picture, of married bliss. As she said herself it wasn't many who praised their mother-in-law but Sam's mother was a gem. The wedding itself barely got a mention. It had been little more than the signing of names but it put the gold band on her finger and that was all she cared about. As a postscript and very much an afterthought, she hoped that Agnes had made a good move and wouldn't regret leaving such a nice place as Kerne House.

Was it envy Agnes was feeling? Perhaps just for a little it was. For the majority married bliss didn't last long. Hardship, unemployment, unwanted pregnancies saw to that. Meg could be the exception, she was getting a decent start and Sam was nice, dull but nice. Dull in her eyes but not in Meg's. Into her mind and unbidden came Tommy Kingsley, not the laughing lad she had gone off with on the back of his bike, but Tommy with his face showing only contempt for someone like her. Yet all she was doing was making sure she didn't end up like her mother. Admittedly what Tommy was offering was far above what she had been used to, it should be enough for her, but it wasn't. Something inside her would not let her be satisfied. She had to aim higher.

Chapter Twenty-One

Wildly her eyes were seeking a way of escape but he was blocking the narrow path with his big, powerful body. What could she do? For a start, she told herself, she could stop panicking and letting him see that she was afraid. It was that strange knowing smile that was making her uneasy, unnerving her. She forced herself to be calm and repeated firmly, 'Mr Meldrum, you are blocking the path and I wish to get past.'

'Such a tease you are, my dear.' He wagged a finger as though to a naughty child.

Fear was quickly giving way to anger. 'Mr Meldrum,' she said icily, 'let me through at once.'

They were about a foot apart and she stepped to the side. It meant going nearer to the shrubs, thick in this area and menacing in the grey light, but she thought it her only chance of getting away. Turning back would plunge her into more of the thick growth and take her further away from the house. This was probably his idea of fun, scaring the maids and feeling safe to do so since they would be too afraid of losing their job to complain.

She made her move but he was quicker. An arm stopped her flight then both arms went round her and he drew her close.

'Relax, my dear Rachel, and let us enjoy this little while together.'

She felt the roughness of his coat as his sleeve brushed her face, then the prickly moustache as his mouth sought hers. She struggled, was fighting desperately to free herself but her strength was nothing against his. All she was doing was exhausting herself. With brutal hardness his mouth was on hers almost suffocating her and she tasted blood as he forced her lips apart. In those moments Rachel knew and understood what was meant by complete and hopeless despair. She made one last desperate bid for freedom then allowed her body to go limp. She felt his hold on her ease as he fingers fumbled with buttons and she took her chance. Her right foot was free and with all the pent-up fury of a caged animal she kicked out at his legs with her sturdy shoes. The sharp, unexpected, agonising pain made him throw her from him as he clutched at his leg.

'You bitch, you'll suffer for that, by God, you will,' he snarled but Rachel barely heard. Already she was running, the branches tearing at her clothes as she slithered, lost her balance, regained it and ran on only stopping when she reached the servants' entrance. As she tore up the back stairs her breath was coming in painful gasps. She reached her room without anyone seeing her, shut the door, put her back to it and slithered to the floor. Shaken and bruised she sat there for a long time then slowly got to her feet and went to look in the mirror. The eyes looking back were wild in a chalk-white face with traces of blood around her mouth and streaked down one side of her face. Her clothes were muddied where she'd fallen, her stockings ruined and a button was missing from her coat with another hanging by a thread.

A bath, she must have a bath, though she wasn't entitled to one. Janet would complain bitterly if there wasn't enough water. She liked a lot and she liked to soak in it but Rachel was uncaring, her need was greater.

It certainly helped and after it she gave her teeth a vigorous brushing to wash away the traces of that horrible mouth on hers. The memory of it made her almost throw up.

Of one thing she was certain and that was that she was in no fit state to assist Janet with the serving of the evening meal to the family. It wasn't far from the truth to say she was unwell and her white face would bear witness to that. Mrs Anderson was the one to approach but she couldn't bring herself to do that. She glanced at the clock. Hetty might be on her own. Dressed in a clean blouse and skirt she went along to the room shared by Janet and Hetty and knocked.

'Come in.'

Relieved to see that Hetty was on her own, Rachel opened her mouth to explain but the words wouldn't come and instead she burst into tears.

Hetty was full of concern and put her arm round Rachel's shoulder. 'What is it, Rachel, what is the matter?'

'I don't want Janet—' she managed to get out between sobs.

'She could be here any time. You get back to your room and I'm goin' along to the kitchen to make tea. You badly need a cup.'

Rachel smiled weakly as Hetty arrived with a tin tray on which was a chipped brown teapot and three cups. Two had some milk in the bottom and the extra cup held sugar and a spoon.

'No one about,' she said, spooning a liberal amount of sugar into Rachel's cup. 'Best thing for shock and that is obviously what you've had.'

'Thank you, I—'

'Not a word until you get that down you.'

The sweet tea did help but most of all it was Hetty's presence.

'Feelin' a bit better?' she asked kindly.

'Yes, I am.'

'Right,' she said, sitting herself firmly in the chair. 'I'm gettin' to the bottom of this and it's your Auntie Hetty talking so no fobbin' me off with half-truths.'

'Hetty, I want to tell you, you are the only one I can tell.' Haltingly she related all that had happened.

'The swine, I hope you crippled him.' She paused and said quietly, 'He didn't—'

'No, Hetty, he didn't harm me.' She knew what Hetty meant. 'Having you beside me is letting me remember things that didn't make sense. Things he was saying, Hetty. He more or less suggested that I was just teasing, that I – that I wanted him,' she said incredulously.

'Proper conceit of himself that one.'

'I know, Hetty, but he seemed genuinely to believe – wait, I can remember his words or near enough.' She took a deep, shaky breath. 'He said a little bird told him that his advances wouldn't be unwelcome.'

'Rachel, no one would say a thing like that.'

'I know, but why should he say it?'

'Dear knows and it wouldn't be Janet that's for sure. Better just put it all out of your mind and be thankful it wasn't any worse.'

'I know but I can't face him tonight.'

'Of course not, I'll say you're not feelin' well.'

'It means you helping Janet.'

She made a face. 'She'll just have to put up with me, in any case all I'll get to do is collect the dirty dishes and even I can do that.' She got up and turned at the door. 'Keep to your room and I'll get Mrs Morton to prepare a tray.'

'I won't be hungry, Hetty.'

''Course you will. Any leftovers I'll see to them, nothing wasted when I'm around.'

★ ★ ★

'Seemed well enough earlier on. What's the matter with her?' Janet said sharply.

'She's not feelin' well, that's all, and she's as white as a ghost.'

'That's me landed with you then?'

'You do most of it anyway.'

'How true.'

The table was set, everything in place when Mrs Maud Meldrum, looking flushed and not a bit like herself, came into the dining-room and over to where Janet and Hetty were standing.

'Janet, don't take the cups through to the dining-room, we'll have coffee served at the table this evening.'

'Yes, Mrs Meldrum.'

'I wonder why,' Janet said thoughtfully once the door had closed.

'Looked a bit on edge,' Hetty answered.

'Nothing unusual about that,' Janet said with unconcealed contempt. 'She's as nervous as a kitten.'

'Kittens can scratch.'

'Whatever that is supposed to mean.'

'Still waters run deep.'

'Good heavens! What's got into you?'

Hetty grinned. 'Not sure I know but anyway it means less work.'

'But I enjoy serving coffee in the drawing-room.'

'It'll be only for one night.'

'But why?'

'None of our business.'

Janet glowered. 'Once the dessert plates are cleared you can go. I'll see to the rest myself.'

'Good, that'll let me get a tray up to Rachel.'

'If she's as ill as you suggest she won't be interested in food.'

'Then I'll eat it.'

'No wonder you're fat.'

At the usual time the family came into the dining-room and sat down in their usual places. Betsy and Brian were having a good-natured argument. The old lady smiled to them as she sat bolt upright in her chair. Henry Meldrum had a bad-tempered scowl on his face and glared across at the young couple who studiously ignored him. With her back as straight as her mother's, Maud Meldrum spoke clearly.

'You may begin serving, Janet.'

Startled looks went to the old lady who always gave the orders but her face was expressionless. The meal was served in near silence. After dessert Hetty removed the plates. It was the signal to get up but Mrs Craig had to make the first move and she showed no sign of getting up.

'Coffee for this evening is to be served at the table,' Maud announced quietly. 'Janet, pour the coffee, then you and Hetty just go. I'll ring when you are required.'

'Very good, m'am.' Janet finished pouring and put down the coffee pot. She gave a quick glance to Henry Meldrum but he wasn't looking her way. The door gave a click leaving the family alone.

'Mother, why are we having coffee here?' Betsy demanded, 'and are you all right, Grandmother?'

'I'm perfectly well, thank you, Betsy.'

'Why the change of routine?' Henry Meldrum asked irritably as he added more sugar to his coffee.

'All in good time, Henry.' There was colour in the usually sallow cheeks and about her an air of suppressed excitement. Mrs Craig kept her eyes on her daughter and a little smile hovered round her lips.

'Brian, sugar if you please.'

'Sorry, Betsy, thought you'd had it.'

Maud lifted the cup to her lips then put it carefully down on the saucer having only wet her lips.

'The change in routine, Henry, is because I have something to say and I prefer to say it in front of you all, here in the dining-room where we are unlikely to be interrupted.' Her eyes went to her husband. 'Henry, I am divorcing you and I want you out of Duncairn House, my mother's home, by tomorrow morning at the latest.'

There was a shocked gasp. All were looking at this timid woman as though they couldn't believe the words had come from her.

'What – I—' Henry Meldrum blustered. 'Is this some sort of joke, Maud?'

'Since you always complain that I have no sense of humour you can be assured I mean every word.'

'This is ridiculous nonsense. You can't without—'

'Proof?'

'That is something you do not have,' he said, but some of the bluster had gone and a new wariness was in his expression.

'Does the name Miriam Brownlow mean anything to you?'

He smiled showing more confidence. 'A friend, no more than that, my dear. You are just letting your imagination run away with you, old girl.'

'A friend with a husband conveniently abroad and no children to complicate matters.'

'An acquaintance whom I see from time to time and always in other people's company.'

'Not good enough, Henry.' She gave a half laugh and moistened her lips. The hands in her lap were clenched but no one saw them. 'I've had you watched and the solicitor has in keeping all the evidence required.'

'I don't believe you.'

'That is your privilege.' She paused. 'Even without it, there is always Janet.'

That brought a look of shocked surprise to his handsome face, then he recovered. 'A maid, an ignorant servant, Maud, my dear. Give me credit for some sense and knowing you if you'd had the least suspicion of anything of that nature she would have been dismissed.'

'Wrong, Henry,' his mother-in-law said acidly. 'Why on earth should we get rid of Janet? She is a first-rate servant and those aren't so easily come by these days.'

Henry Meldrum made a last appeal to his wife. 'All this drama, my dear, is so unlike you. This could have been settled between us and any little problems ironed out. It still isn't too late to do that.'

'Oh, but it is, Henry. All those years you've humiliated me and I was fool enough to give you yet another chance. Don't waste your breath trying to get me to change my mind, there is no chance of that. I am divorcing you and our only contact from now onwards will be through my solicitor.'

'If that is the way you want it, very well.' He got up, pushed back his cup and spilled coffee on the white tablecloth leaving an ugly brown stain. 'Come along, Brian, we are not spending another night here.'

'You were told to go, it did not apply to Brian.' Maud smiled to her stepson who was looking bewildered. 'This is your home, Brian, and you are welcome to remain at Duncairn House for as long as you wish.'

'My son goes with me.'

Betsy had a restraining hand on him. 'Don't go, Brian.'

'Brian has no intention of going, have you Brian?' The faded eyes of Mrs Craig met his.

'He does as I say. There is a good job waiting for him in London.' He looked at his son. 'Time you saw a bit of life, began to enjoy yourself instead of being stuck in this dreary place.'

That was too much for the mistress of Duncairn House. 'You wanted Duncairn House, it was the perfect background to impress your business colleagues. Nice to be able to boast of an estate in the country especially when those same guests were entertained at my expense,' Mrs Craig said witheringly.

'Dad, I am not going with you,' Brian said quietly and firmly. 'London holds no attraction for me. I have never had any intention of going.'

'Rather live on the old woman's charity, would you?'

Brian flushed. The normally placid young man had a temper and Betsy was pleased to see it. 'You forget, sir, that I am almost twenty-one and Mother's money comes to me then. I don't need charity and it wouldn't be charity I'd be offered. My stepmother and my adopted grandmother have shown me nothing but kindness.'

'And me? What about me?' Betsy said huffed.

'Need someone to fight with, don't I?' They grinned at each other.

'That money you talk of should be mine not yours.'

'No, Mother meant it for me and in case I blew the lot when I became twenty-one she left it so that I wouldn't get my hands on the rest until I'm twenty-five.'

'Sensible woman your mother, Brian.' Mrs Craig nodded approvingly. 'Tell you what you could do.'

He smiled.

'Help your father pack and hasten his departure from Duncairn House. This'll be a happier place without him.'

Defeated, Henry Meldrum, in his haste to be gone from the room, knocked his damaged leg against the chair and winced with pain as he limped to the door. As if remembering the cause of his damaged leg he turned, and Betsy cringed under that look of loathing.

'You've a lot to answer for, you little—'

'No bad language in this house if you please, Mr Meldrum.' The old lady turned to her daughter. 'Quite an interesting evening, my dear. You can ring for the maids to clear up then assist me to my room.'

Maud gave a pull at the bell that would bring Janet and Hetty then went to assist her mother. A smile passed between them and the quiet words were for Maud's ears alone.

'Well done, Maud, I couldn't have done better myself.'

All next day rumours and counterrumours went round the servants' quarters. Everyone knew that something momentous had happened, that it concerned Henry Meldrum, but no one knew what. Curious faces, smilingly satisfied faces but only one glum face and that belonged to Janet. She went about her work in her usual competent fashion but made no contribution to the conversation.

'He's gone and three cheers for that,' Hetty said gleefully with a special glance to Rachel.

'How can you be so sure?' Rachel asked.

'Because I do out his room, don't I? He didn't sleep in his bed last night and everythin' has gone, wardrobe cleared out and the drawers emptied.' They were in the kitchen drinking tea with work temporarily forgotten.

Mrs Morton sat in a chair with her feet up on a box ready for a gossip.

'Your young man was tellin' me, Hetty, he saw Mr Meldrum loading up his car and gettin' in it and drivin' off like the wind.'

'What do you mean my young man?' Hetty said going pink in the face.

'Stupid we may be but blind we are not. That's a fine laddie with his eye on you and you could do a lot worse.'

'Mr Meldrum is away for good then?' Rachel asked hopefully.

'Seems like it. You feelin' better now?'

'Much better.'

'Mrs Anderson told me to strip the bed and to put everything in the wash.'

'Hope you opened the window, Hetty,' Mrs Morton said.

'Wide as it would go.'

The door opened, Janet came in and there was an uncomfortable silence. The silence continued as Janet went to get a tin of polish from the cupboard. All the time she kept her face averted and went out again without a word.

'Poor Janet, she's been cryin', should I go after her?'

'No, let her be, Hetty,' Mrs Morton said sharply, 'The lass has feelings and mebbe she was genuinely fond of him. There's no accounting for taste if I've got the right expression.'

Rachel slipped away and along to Janet's room, knocked and put her head round the door. 'Wondered if you'd be here.'

'Well, I am.'

'Would you like me to bring you a cup of tea, Janet?'

She gave an odd little laugh. 'If you think it would help.'

'I'm sure it will. I won't be long.'

Chapter Twenty-Two

Finding her way about Drumoaks wasn't as difficult as it first appeared and Agnes soon had it mastered. Heating such a large house was a problem and many of the passageways and corridors were icy cold during the winter months. Comfort was important to the family at Drumoaks and it had taken a great deal of thought and care to marry the old with the new but it had been done. The drawing-room and smaller sitting-room showed how to achieve comfort without losing its old-fashioned charm. Having dealt with their own creature comforts the master and mistress undertook a tour of the servants' quarters and were appalled by what they saw. Perhaps because of it and the guilt they felt, the upgrading went further than could reasonably have been expected.

Agnes kept congratulating herself on attaining such a desirable job, few in her position had such comfort. If there was a jarring note it came from Beatrice. She wasn't openly hostile but had an unpleasant way of examining the work done by Agnes and finding fault. Polishing was an example, she never got the desired shine.

'A bit more elbow grease, Agnes.'

'You got promotion to housekeeper or something?' Agnes snapped.

'Mrs Harrison is fully occupied and as the senior—'

'Don't give me that, you are only a tablemaid, Beatrice, and I was one myself at Kerne House.'

'So I believe and that strikes me as being very peculiar.'

'For your information I am not losing out financially and I am to be helping out in the dining-room on occasions.'

'That I find hard to believe and it is the first I've heard of it.' She began to move away.

'Suit yourself and before you go let me tell you this. It wasn't my fault that Mrs Harrison chose me rather than your friend.'

'It was a pity but I agree it wasn't your fault.'

'Then stop picking on me. If you do have the authority to boss me and Madge then just make sure it's fair.'

Beatrice took off her spectacles and there were dark violet shadows beneath her eyes. She had good features and a clear complexion and without the ugly steel frames she was a good-looking girl and Agnes said so.

'Why on earth do you wear those things, you look far better without them?'

'Why do people wear spectacles? Don't be so stupid, Agnes, do you think I would wear them if I didn't need to?'

'What I meant was, get yourself a decent pair. I've seen some really nice ones.'

Beatrice looked uncertain then came back to stand beside Agnes. She had the superior height and Agnes, sure that she had gone too far, waited for the storm.

'Maybe I have been hard on you.'

'No question about it you have and that applies to Madge too. She's scared stiff of you.'

'She's just plain silly.'

'No, Beatrice, she isn't. She's shy and nervous, we can't all be the same and what's more she's nice.'

Beatrice wasn't paying attention to what Agnes was saying. 'You think I should get other spectacles?'

'If you can afford it, of course.'

'I don't spend much, I have a bit saved.'

'Meaning you don't go out?'

'Hardly ever.' She bit her lip and Agnes could see the struggle she was having.

'If you want a second opinion—'

'You would come with me?'

'Of course. Any outing would be welcome, I'm a stranger remember.'

'You know Mr Bannerman?'

'Been introduced, yes.'

'Most Thursdays he takes the car into Perth and if I asked him he would give us a lift.'

'Great! I've never been in Perth.'

'You'll like it, it's a good shopping centre.'

'Could this mean we are friends?' she grinned.

'Just as long as you remember I'm the boss.'

'You'll keep reminding me, I'm sure.'

Beatrice walked away but she was smiling.

'She's all right, Madge, honest she is.'

Madge didn't look convinced.

'Know her real problem?'

Madge shook her head.

'Loneliness and she's doesn't want anyone to know it.'

'That's sad I suppose. Fancy you getting that out of her.' She paused. 'Know what Mrs T said?'

'No, but you're going to tell me.'

'She said, there's a lass who knows what she wants and like as not she'll get it.'

'Did she now? Well all I say is I hope she's right.'

'What do you want, Agnes?'

'I'm not sure I know but of one thing I am certain and that is I won't always be a maid.'

'Neither will I, I want to get married and I expect I will.'

'I'm sure of it too,' Agnes said with a smile. She spoke her thoughts out loud. 'One day I'll have a lovely house with maids to do the work and I'll be free to read books or do anything I want.'

'I was bein' serious and you are bein' funny.'

'Madge, I was never more serious in my life.'

'I never know whether you are kiddin' or not.'

November was mild, indeed much of it was warmer than October. Agnes had become an aunt, Meg had given birth to a son and straightaway Agnes had bought a rattle and teething rings which had made a hole in her savings. The wedding gift had never materialised but it wasn't forgotten. One day when funds permitted she would buy Meg and Sam something really good and they would know then that it had been worth waiting for.

By December winter had set in and Agnes and Beatrice made that visit to Perth. Mr Bannerman was to allow them three hours to do what they wanted then he would pick them up at the North Inch.

The optician was horrified. 'When did you get these?'

'I can't remember,' Beatrice mumbled, 'but it was a long time ago.'

'Were they meant for you in the first place?'

Beatrice blushed crimson. 'No, they were my sister's but she wouldn't wear them and since I could see better with them—' she swallowed. 'My mother said there was no use them going to waste.'

'Have you been suffering from headaches?'

Beatrice looked surprised. 'Yes, she admitted, 'they've got worse these last few months.'

'I'm not surprised,' he said drily. 'You could have permanently damaged your eyes, young woman.'

'I haven't though, have I?' she said anxiously.

'No, but you must stop wearing these,' he fingered the offending spectacles with distaste then smiled. He was fiftyish, stout and with greying hair. 'Why do you want to hide a bonny face behind those ugly steel frames?'

Beatrice dropped her eyes in embarrassment.

'Told her the same myself,' Agnes said.

'Good for you. Now, miss, I'm going to give you a pair of spectacles to wear until your own are ready.'

'Thank you very much but how much extra—'

'There will be no charge for these provided you bring them back in good condition.'

'I'll take very great care of them.'

'And these, my dear girl,' he said handing over the old ones, 'if you'll take my advice you'll put them where they belong in the nearest bin.'

'Better let her put them in yours.'

He smiled. 'I'll drop you a postcard when your spectacles are ready for collection,' he said, putting the old ones in his bin and wishing them both good day.

They were outside and walking towards the shops. 'Have you been troubled with headaches?'

'Off and on. An aspirin used to help but it isn't much good now.'

'Fancy you being stupid enough to wear specs meant for someone else.'

'Maybe it seems that way to you, Agnes,' Beatrice said quietly, 'but my parents were poor, and I do mean poor. My eyesight was always weak and those did help.'

'Is your home hereabout?'

'I used to live quite near but both my parents are dead, my father before I was at school and my mother,' her voice wobbled, 'nearly two years ago.'

'And what about your sister?'

'Elsie is very good with children and the family she was with were going to America and took her with them.'

'All right for some.' She paused to look at a shop window. 'Don't run away with the idea that you are the only one. Believe me, I know all there is to know about poverty.'

'Are you bitter about it?'

'Sometimes, but what's the point?' Agnes shrugged and decided to change the subject. 'What is Christmas like at Drumoaks?'

'Very good. There's a big tree, holly and the usual Christmas trimmings and Mrs T does us proud. The family eat first but we get the same meal except, of course, for the wine but Mr Bannerman and Mrs Harrison get together and buy a couple of bottles.' She laughed. 'Two sips and our Madge is at the giggly stage. Things don't get hilarious until the master and mistress have been to the kitchen to wish us all a Happy Christmas.'

'Just that – no more?'

'No presents if that is what you mean, but don't look so glum,' she said as Agnes's face fell, 'we get an extra week's wages and that to me is better than a box of hankies.'

'Couldn't agree more,' Agnes said cheering up instantly. She smiled to herself as she caught Beatrice looking into shop windows not so much to see the goods on display but to admire herself. The tortoiseshell frames suited her face.

'How long have we, Agnes?'

Agnes consulted her watch. 'Just over half an hour.'

'Time for tea and a bun, my treat.'

'No, I'll pay my own.'

'You will not and that is an order.'

Christmas went by and the last day sof December gave way to a cold, damp, depressing January. Stripped of their leaves the trees appeared black and all around was the dirty yellow tangle of old bracken. Until then there had been only flurries of snow but those born in the country could smell snow in the air and forecast a heavy and prolonged fall. Used to harsh conditions they were always well prepared. Emergency food was stocked up as well as a good supply of fuel. It was all hands on deck with the stable-boy, gardeners and odd-jobmen chopping up wood for the fires and piling up the logs in the cellars.

'You wanted to see me, Mrs Harrison?'

'Yes, Agnes, come in and sit down.'

Agnes sat with her hands folded in her lap.

'From time to time I change duties round and with winter upon us there is a need for more fires – even to those rooms that are seldom used dampness can spread very quickly. The library, as you know, is heated for most of the day, it has to be. There is a valuable collection of books and a degree of heat is necessary to keep them in good condition. That duty I am giving to you; you will see to the fire in the library.'

'Before or after the bed-making?'

'Before I think,' she said thoughtfully. 'Once you have cleared up the dishes in the breakfast-room and tidied up there go along and clean out the fire. Do remember, but I'm sure you will, to put a newspaper over the ashes to keep the dust from flying. Then you will lay the fire and light it.'

'When do I begin, Mrs Harrison?'

'Tomorrow morning.'

Wearing a dark blue overall over her dress, Agnes got down on her hands and knees and raked and cleaned out the grey ash using a small shovel to transfer it to the pail. That done she covered the pail with a double page of newspaper and used the rest rolled up to set the fire. Thin sticks of firewood went on next in criss-cross fashion then small pieces of coal. In Kerne House it hadn't been allowed but here a half firelighter was used to hasten the blaze. Satisfied with her handiwork Agnes put a match to the paper, watched as the small flame caught the firelighter and the sticks began to burn. She would have to wait until it got a good hold before adding more coal. Since her overall was soiled anyway, Agnes wiped her hands on it taking away the worst of the dirt. Coming in she had only taken a quick look round but now she took the time to study it. Books, hundreds of them, lined every wall and over at the window was a handsome desk with a leather-seated chair under it. On the desk was a crystal inkstand and a marble oblong-shaped dish holding an assortment of pens with some spare nibs.

Fascinated, Agnes wandered over to look at the books, some were protected by glass but others were on open shelves. So engrossed was she in examining the titles that she failed to hear the tap, tap of crutches. The angry bark made her nearly jump out of her skin and she swung round guiltily.

'What the devil do you think you are doing?' he bawled.

'N-nothing.'

'Nothing? Poking about where you have no right to be and you have the impudence to say – nothing.'

This could only be Mr Gerald Patterson. She knew of him but hadn't seen him and that was because he had been in hospital undergoing treatment. That he was blazingly angry was obvious and what was also obvious was that she had no right to be where she was. She began to move away.

'Don't you dare move. You'll stay where you are.'

Agnes watched his painful journey from the doorway to the desk and wondered how he was going to get himself into the chair. She longed to bring it out for him but dare not. Was it just bad temper or were those lines of pain? Putting one crutch against the desk he manoeuvred the chair to the desired position then managed to swing himself into it. For a moment his eyes closed and when he opened them she was looking into dark blue eyes that were almost black. His hair was crinkly and was a rich nut brown and without the scowl Gerald Patterson would be a handsome man.

'I am waiting for an explanation.'

'Before I give you one do you mind if I see to the fire or it will go out.'

'Be quick about it.'

Her hands were shaking but she managed to coax it back to life with a few more dry sticks. Soon it was burning well and she got off her knees.

'Over here.'

She swallowed nervously. 'I'm very sorry, sir.'

'I want to know what you touched with your filthy hands.'

'Nothing.'

'That I do not believe, not for a moment.'

Crippled or not Agnes wasn't standing for that. 'When I said I touched nothing that is exactly what I meant.'

'You mean you didn't touch anything.'

'That is what I said.'

'No you didn't.'

'All I did was look. I've never been in here before and I've never seen so many books.'

There are public libraries with many more, but what would someone like yourself do with books?'

'Read them same as you,' she shot back, 'or maybe you think I can't read.'

'Hardly, since everyone is entitled to an education of sorts these days.'

'Since I'm getting the sack let me tell you something.'

'If you've more to say, for God's sake sit down.'

Agnes sat. 'You and your kind don't know you're living.'

'That's true for me anyway. With two bloody useless legs life has very little meaning.'

The anger drained out of Agnes.

'I'm sorry, you've plenty to be bitter about.'

He smiled and it was a nice smile. 'One of my passions was trees, I had a great love of them and it was one of them that did this to me.'

'I heard about it, sir, and if I can borrow your language it was a bloody awful thing to happen.'

'I apologise for my bad language.'

'No need, I was brought up on that word.'

She saw he was trying to hide his amusement. 'What is your name?'

'Agnes Boyd.'

'New here are you?'

'Been here since November.'

'You've lasted that long.'

Those last few minutes and she was beginning to think her job might be safe after all, but not now. 'You've lasted that long,' was what he'd said and all there was to add was – but it won't be for much longer.

Without waiting for permission Agnes got up, added more coal to the fire, picked up the pail of ashes and let herself out of the library.

Chapter Twenty-Three

Janet gulped down some of the tea then put the cup back on the tray. Her apologetic laugh rang out before she buried her face in her hands.

Rachel longed to give comfort but stopped herself. It would be unwelcome. Better to do nothing and stay silent and if Janet should indicate that she wanted to be left alone then she would get up and go. Janet didn't.

In a little while he dried her eyes and balled the handkerchief in her hands. 'Sorry, I feel all kinds of a fool.'

'Would you rather I went?'

'Not unless you want to go.'

'I don't.'

'Thanks. I need to talk, get things sorted out in my own mind.'

'Take your time, I'm a good listener and if you need the assurance nothing goes further than this room.'

'I know that.' She shook her head sadly. 'You should be gloating after the way I've treated you.'

'It's all right,' Rachel said awkwardly.

'Getting involved with a married man, you would never have done that and I suppose I'm getting what I deserve.'

Rachel didn't know how to answer that. 'We all make mistakes, Janet,' she said quietly.

'You never liked him?'

'No, I didn't.' She thought of what she had gone through with Henry Meldrum and only just managed not to shiver.

'If you'd really known him you would have liked him. Henry could be absolutely charming, Rachel. If I'm to be honest my head was turned with all the posh places he used to take me. I was terribly nervous at times particularly at the beginning, but Henry was so good, letting me know in a quiet way what was acceptable and what was not.'

'Didn't you feel guilty about Mrs Meldrum?' Rachel was forced to ask.

'He said I had no reason to be, that we were hurting no one and, Rachel, it's awfully easy to believe something you want to believe.'

'I know it is.'

'He said he wasn't cheating on his wife.'

'What did he call it then?'

She shrugged. 'His wife was so dull, he said. He'd thought of leaving her but couldn't bring himself to do it. Laughable in the light of what has happened.'

'From what I gather, Janet, Duncairn House was the attraction and poor Mrs Meldrum didn't realise that until it was too late.'

Janet didn't look convinced. 'I think you've got that bit wrong. A little of country life was enough for Henry, he was all for the bright lights, although he did admit to me that it was rather nice to boast of an estate in the country.'

'But he didn't own it,' Rachel said indignantly. 'Duncairn House wasn't his, it belongs to Mrs Craig.'

'Of course, everyone knew that,' Janet said impatiently, 'but in time it would have gone to her daughter. Maud Meldrum and Betsy are her only relatives.'

Wrong, Janet, Rachel said silently, her other granddaughter is sitting here talking to you. It set her off to wondering how long she could keep up this pretence yet with each passing day it was becoming more and more difficult. Her grandmother liked her but liked her as a servant girl with a pleasant voice. Even if her grandmother accepted her as Amelia's daughter there was Aunt Maud and there was Betsy and she could hardly expect a welcome from either, most certainly not from Betsy. Coming to Duncairn House had been a mistake, a foolish, impulsive action on her part. What a mess she had made of her life. Thinking back with the benefit of hindsight she saw Peggy with a reluctant stepdaughter and herself with a reluctant stepmother. They had both been at fault and her poor da caught up in the middle. It was too late for regrets, her father would never forgive her for what she had done. He knew where she was, that she had chosen her grandmother and Duncairn House and he had washed his hands of her.

'I'm sorry, Janet, you were saying—'

'He promised to take me to London, show me the sights and he would have done too, Henry kept his promises. You know this, I was to arrange my holidays to suit.' Her voice broke. 'I could have forgiven him a lot,

Rachel, if only he hadn't gone off like that without a word to me.'

'Maybe he didn't get the chance.'

'He had the chance all right, we had our own way of communicating,' Janet said bitterly.

They were both silent, everything seemed to have been said. Janet drank the rest of the lukewarm tea then cradled the cup in her hand.

'Better to hand in my notice rather than await my marching orders.'

'Don't do anything hasty, Janet.'

'Mrs Meldrum will want me out of Duncairn House.'

'That's possible and natural in the circumstances but Mrs Craig may or rather will have the final say and I rather think she'll want to hang on to you.'

'You really think so?' There was a glimmer of hope on Janet's face.

'You are very efficient and would be difficult to replace.'

'You could take over and do the job just as well.'

'No, I couldn't, and I'm going to tell you something no one else knows. That first breakfast tray—'

'Now you're making me feel rotten. I deliberately made it difficult for you.'

'Wouldn't have made any difference. I don't have steady hands and to make matters worse the spout of the teapot was turned towards the toast.'

Janet gave a scream of tearful laughter. 'Soggy toast, oh heavens, you didn't offer her that?'

'I apologised for it and offered to get fresh but she was very nice about it, said to put it in the fire and say nothing to Mrs Morton.'

Janet looked amazed and perhaps envious. 'No one else would have got away with that, she must really like you.'

'She likes me to read to her, Janet, but not to take up her breakfast, she made that clear.'

'You've just been the tonic I need.'

'Good, I'll get on my way then and, Janet, let me say one thing more before I go. Forget Henry Meldrum, he isn't worth a single tear so put him right out of your mind.'

'Better fish in the sea?'

'Much better.'

'Rachel, you don't go out much do you?'

'Not a great deal, why?'

'Fancy us going out together?'

'Yes, I do.'

'There's a dance advertised, a local hop.'

'I think I've forgotten how to dance.'

'No one forgets how to dance.'

'What do I wear?'

'Any old thing, no one dresses up and speaking of clothes that blue skirt and blouse you've been wearing I really do admire. Where did you buy them?'

'I didn't. The lady who taught me to sew gave them to me as a parting gift.'

'Lucky you.' Her face fell at the mention of the parting gift making her remember her own difficult position. 'You do think I have a chance of being kept on?'

'Personally I do, but I don't want to raise your hopes. I could be wrong.'

'I know,' she said glumly.

'It could be that nothing will be said and things will just go back to normal.'

'I need a friend,' she said abruptly.

'So do I.' It was true, Rachel thought, she had no one really close. Every day she had expected, hoped to get a letter from Kerne House but there had been nothing. Writing again would be pointless, she had done all she could. The next move would have to come from Agnes. Even though she had all but given up hope there was an aching longing inside her that one day they would meet again.

The village hall was well filled, the band was too loud but there was plenty of laughter. Three chairs were put together to hold the coats. Rachel and Janet added theirs.

'That's nice,' Janet said admiring the brightly coloured cotton skirt.

'Made it myself from a remnant I got at the sales.'

'Wish I could sew, takes me all my time to sew on a button.'

'When I've time I'll run up something for you but nothing complicated I'm not that good. I like what you're wearing.' The slightly flared primrose yellow dress with its square shaped neckline and stiffened belt set off her figure and looked fresh and attrractive.

'Henry bought it for me,' she said a little defiantly. 'It should be nice, it cost enough. I bet in my place you would have thrown it out.'

'Janet, there is no answer to that since I wouldn't have accepted it in the first place.'

'You and I are very different. It belongs to me, I like it, I wear it.'

'Fair enough.'

'I'm not broken-hearted, just terribly hurt at the way he treated me.'

'Then you weren't in love with him.'

'I was in love with what he could give me and I enjoyed being with him. There now I've shocked you.'

'That's what you are trying to do and I think we should drop the subject.'

'You could be right at that. Don't turn now but a couple of very presentable fellows have just come in and I think we are getting the once-over.'

The band struck up a quickstep.

'May I have this dance?' the taller of them asked Rachel while the other smiled to Janet.

Rachel smiled, bit her lip, went into his arms and just hoped that her feet obeyed the music.

'Been here before?'

'No, my first time.'

'What do you think of it?'

'Noisy but nice,' she smiled and he laughed.

'Live around here, do you?'

'I work at Duncairn House, I'm a maid.'

'Your friend too?'

'Yes. Are you local?'

'Born and bred these parts.'

'You asked my occupation, may I ask yours?'

'I work at Braelands, that's a farm.'

'You're a farmhand then?'

'You could say that.'

It didn't at the time, only later the peculiarity of the words struck her. He was either a farmhand or he wasn't; it would seem he wasn't.

'I'm Ian Thompson.'

'I'm Rachel Donaldson.'

She supposed him a good dancer, putting in all the twirly bits and after a few apologies when she'd stood on his toes, she was getting the hang of it.

★ ★ ★

'Fun wasn't it? Glad I persuaded you to go, aren't you?' Janet said as they began setting the table in the dining-room.

'Yes, I enjoyed myself.'

'Your fellow seems nice, quite good-looking too.'

Rachel nodded agreement. He was pleasant-looking in a boyish way, not like – she closed her eyes. Why had she to compare him with Peter McGregor. It angered her that he kept intruding in her thoughts.

'Bobby said they only intended popping in for half an hour or so but changed their minds when they saw us. Incidentally, in case he didn't tell you, Ian Thompson's father farms Braelands, one of the biggest here about.'

'Oh, dear, he said he was on the farm and I put him down to be a farmhand.'

'A bit well-spoken for a farmhand.'

'I don't know, Janet, you could say that about us.'

'Two superior maids,' she grinned. 'Asked you out again, has he?'

'Yes. He has to deliver some produce in Perth, then it's the first house of the pictures. What about you?'

'Bobby's a mechanic, his dad owns the garage opposite the school and he's taking me for a spin on my day off.'

'Sorry it's just the van, my brother has the car,' Ian apologised. He was dressed in dark trousers with a tweed jacket with leather patches on the elbow. Peter had leather patches on the elbows too and she wondered if it was to reduce wear or just for appearance.

'I don't mind.'

'I'll say this for it, it is dependable, it has to be to get us to the market in all weathers. The back is filthy but my sister cleaned out the two front seats so there is no danger of getting your clothes soiled.'

Rachel climbed in, it was clean and comfortable too.

'There's a tartan rug on the back seat and if it gets cold coming back you can wrap it round your legs.'

'Ian, I'm not a hothouse plant.'

'No, I didn't think you were, but the temperature is going to plummet. I've had it from a reliable source,' he paused, 'my father.'

'Farmers are good at predicting the weather or so it's said.'

'My dad's pretty good.'

He kept up a good speed but he was careful. 'Mind if I ask how old you are?'

'Eighteen in April. I might not be so keen to answer that question in a few years' time.'

'Women are funny like that. I'm twenty.'

Ian delivered the produce and got back in the van. 'Thought we would have high tea at the Grosvenor then go to the pictures if you'd like that.'

'Sounds lovely. What's on?'

'Never thought of looking to see but if we don't like it we can come out.'

'What a shocking waste of money.'

'It won't ruin me.' He took his hand off the steering wheel and went into his pocket to bring out two tickets which he put in Rachel's lap before returning his hand to the wheel.

'Keep the eighteenth of February free, that's three weeks tomorrow.'

'What for?'

'You've got the tickets in your hand, the Farmers' Ball.' He smiled and glanced sideways at her.

Rachel read it and gasped as her eye caught the corner and the price of the ticket.

'You'll come, won't you?'

'I'd be thrilled to but I don't think I can. I mean it will be very grand and nothing in my wardrobe would be remotely suitable.'

'Nonsense, you'd look lovely in rags.'

She laughed. 'Oh, I could do better than that.'

'Then it's a date?'

'Thank you very much.' It was true she didn't have an evening gown but she did have money in her Post Office savings account. Yes, she would treat herself even if it meant blowing the lot. Suddenly Rachel felt carefree. This was an occasion and she wanted to look her best.

As the date of the Farmers' Ball drew near, Rachel was filled with nervous excitement. Janet could have been of assistance, helped her choose something suitable, but they were seldom free at the same time. Nothing else for it, she would just have to choose carefully and hope she got a helpful shop assistant.

The small amount of money payable on demand was insufficient and Rachel sent off the necessary form leaving just enough in her account to keep it open. The gown might not take it all and she would be able to put some back.

The February day was bitter when Rachel, the money making a bulge in her purse, took the bus into Perth. She knew the Fair City by this time and where to find the best shops. Browsing was what she intended doing at the start and she stopped at one window. It was its stark simplicity that attracted her. No fussy window-dressing detracted from the beautiful black velvet gown displayed. It was for someone older and sophisticated but it was the sheer magnetism of that window that kept her glued. Almost without thinking, she went in, her feet making no sound on the carpet. There were two curtained cubicles and the air was faintly but pleasantly perfumed. Voices drifted from one of the cubicles and a girl came from the back and walked towards her. Her lips curled as she took in Rachel's shabby coat and Rachel wished herself a thousand miles away.

'Did you want something?' she drawled.

'A – an evening dress. I'd like to see what you have, please.'

'We don't go in for the cheaper models.'

That angered Rachel as it was no doubt intended to do. Her nervousness vanished, she wouldn't buy anything but she would put this insolent madam in her place.

'Perhaps you would be good enough to show me what you do have.'

The shoulders shrugged and the girl went away returning a few minutes later with two gowns over her arm.

'Just go into the cubicle.' She went ahead and laid the gowns over the back of a chair. Then she closed the curtain and left Rachel to it. One of the gowns was in a sweetie pink, a colour she disliked. A pale pink, yes, but not that shade. The other would have suited a mature woman, it was in a coffee colour with a matching bolero. The girl drew back the curtain.

'Neither of these appeals to me, I'm afraid.'

'You can't tell until you've tried them on.'

'I don't need to try them on, I don't like either.'

'If it is the colour that is bothering you try them on for style.'

Rachel swithered, maybe she was being awkward. She removed her skirt and blouse and allowed the gown to be slipped over her head.

'That shade of pink suits you very well. Your sort of gown I would say and it is one of our less expensive models.' The drawl was more pronounced as was the look of boredom.

'I don't agree, I don't think it suits me at all.'

'Try the other then.'

'No, thank you, if that is all you can show me I won't trouble you further.'

The curtain was gently pulled aside.

'Miss Brown, go and see to the stock at the back, I'll look after this young lady.'

Rachel bit her lip. 'I'm sorry I don't care for either of these.'

'Of course you don't, they are completely unsuitable.' Mrs McMaster who owned the shop was a small woman, plainly but fashionably dressed and Rachel knew instinctively that here was someone who would rather lose a sale than have a customer leave with something that did not suit her. 'Just excuse me, I shan't be long.'

The voices drifted through the half-open door and Rachel could not but hear.

'What on earth were you thinking about? These, as you very well know, are not part of my stock just what I inherited with the shop and they'll be got rid of at the next sale.'

'By the look of her she can't afford our prices.'

'That is not for you to decide. My regret is that I was persuaded to take you on but unless your manner improves, young woman, it will be the parting of the ways for you and me.'

She was back. 'Try these, my dear. You are so lucky to have such a nice slim figure and with that lovely colouring you could wear almost any shade.' She held up the peacock blue. 'Very simple and that is the secret of good style.'

'A friend of mine, a dressmaker, once told me that,' Rachel said shyly.

'She spoke good sense. I can't tell you the number of times I've wished for a pair of scissors to snip off those unnecessary bits and bows. There now, what do you think of that?'

Looking at herself, Rachel felt a tingle of excitement. The gown was lovely and could have been made for her. 'It's beautiful but before you go to any more trouble I'd better tell you how much I can afford to spend.'

The gowns cost more, a lot more, but there was something about this girl that she liked and she was still seething at her assistant.

'We'll manage to keep within your budget,' she smiled.

'Meaning I can afford this one?' Rachel asked.

'Yes, but one does not decide as quickly as all that on something as important as an evening gown. May I ask if this is a special occasion?'

Rachel felt a flush of colour rise in her face. 'I've been invited to the Farmers' Ball.'

'My dear, how perfectly splendid, it is the occasion of the year. Slip out of that and we'll try the turquoise.'

'I can't decide, they are both – both perfect. Which do you think? I'd value your opinion.'

'Not yet, my dear. I want you to try on one more then I'll give it.'

'What a lovely and unusual shade,' Rachel exclaimed when the gown was brought to her.

'Isn't it? It's called tangerine and what I, myself, would call a deep orange with just a hint of red. Not many can get away with that colour but it's an eye-catcher.'

As Rachel slipped it on, Mrs McMaster added, 'One or two of my regular customers were very taken with the shade but it wasn't right on them. It needs black hair like yours to set it off.'

Rachel looked at herself, turning this way and that. Mrs McMaster nodded.

'Your gown, my dear, don't you agree?'

'Oh, I do, I really do,' Rachel said with a sigh of happiness.

Mrs McMaster opened the curtain and called to her assistant, 'Miss Brown, come here, please.'

She came hurrying. 'You wanted me, Mrs McMaster?'

'Yes. The tangerine gown has always been your favourite?'

The girl swallowed and nodded.

'Unfortunately you have neither the figure nor the colouring to carry it off whereas it is quite perfect on this young lady. And this very lucky lady is going to the Farmers' Ball.' She smiled at Rachel. 'A few of my regulars will be wearing my creations but I can assure you that none will outshine you. On you go, Miss Brown, you can get on with your work now.'

Rachel felt sorry for the girl and it showed on her face. 'She deserved it, my dear, she was appallingly rude to you and I will not have my customers treated like that.'

Back into her own clothes Rachel approached the glass counter.

'Don't be tempted to wear a necklace of any kind no matter what anyone says. You have a lovely, long, graceful neck, let it be shown. A sandal with a small heel would suit best.' She was chatting as she carefully inserted tissue paper between the folds then gently lowered the gown into the dress box. While Rachel was getting out her money the woman disappeared and came back with a fine shawl. 'That has been lying about and is soiled and I can't sell soiled goods. A careful wash and it will come up like new.'

'I don't know what to say, you've been so kind.' Rachel was taken aback at this show of generosity.

'Caught me in a good mood.'

'Thank you very much indeed.'

'I hope you have an unforgettable evening.'

Flushed with her successful shopping expedition Rachel headed for the bus. A cup of tea would have been welcome but she wasn't going to spend a penny more. Only when she was on the bus did it hit her. She had cleaned out her savings on a gown that would perhaps only be worn on the one occasion. She was all sorts of a fool, she thought ruefully, yet even if she could take it back she wouldn't.

'Rachel, it's fantastic, gorgeous, beautiful and must have cost you the earth. On the never-never, is it?' The two were in Rachel's room.

'No, it's paid for, a lot more than I intended spending, but there it is, I need my head examined.'

'Need it examined if you let a creation like that slip by you,' Janet said openly envious.

Hetty came in and Rachel did a twirl for her benefit. 'You look like a princess,' there was awe in her voice.

As the lady had said, after a careful wash the shawl came up like new. She threw it around her shoulders. 'There, that's me ready for the Ball.'

'Need something over it.'

'I'd rather freeze than put on my old coat.'

'You are welcome to my cloak.'

'You mean it, Janet?'

'Yes, I rather like to think of it being at the Ball. Mind, I would have preferred if I had been inside it.' They all laughed.

'Rachel, I've got pearls – they belonged to my grandmother. I don't think they are real but they look nice.'

'Sweet of you, Hetty, but the lady in the shop made me promise I wouldn't wear jewellery of any kind.

'Probably got a point,' Janet nodded.

★ ★ ★

It was here, the longed for night of the Farmers' Ball, with the weather dry and blustery. Janet and Hetty were engaged in the dining-room but Rachel was glad to be alone. Excitement had given her petal-smooth skin a rosy glow and her hair shampooed the previous evening was the length she preferred – neither short nor long. Black springy curls framed her face and her blue eyes were shining like twin stars as she stared at herself in the mirror.

She wasn't vain but she knew she looked beautiful. The colour was right and the cut of the gown emphasised the long slenderness of her body. It was a young dress full of youthful promise yet with a subtle elegance. She thought how kind everyone had been, all so anxious to give something of theirs. Janet, her cloak and evening bag both very much appreciated, Hetty, with her pearls and Mrs Morton her amber beads. The jewellery she had gently but firmly declined but in a way that gave no offence.

Always sparing with make-up, sometimes she wore none at all, tonight she gave her face a dusting of powder and added colour to her lips.

Mrs Morton had requested that she pop into the kitchen before she left and half an hour before Ian was due she went along.

'A fair picture you are, lass. The lads won't be able to take their eyes off you.'

'I'm going with a partner.'

'I know that, lass, but some of them toffs is right persistent.'

'I'll do then?'

'You'll do. See and have a lovely time and if you were my daughter I would be tellin' you to mind yoursel'. I'll get them to leave a light on for you comin' in.'

'Thank you and I promise to be as quiet as a mouse.'

Time she went downstairs, then Rachel had an uncomfortable thought. She'd forgotten to tell Ian to come to the side door, but surely he would. He would remember she was a servant in the house. The knock came, she heard Hetty opening the door to him.

'Rachel ready?'

'Yes, I am,' Rachel smiled. 'Hetty, this is Ian, or should I have said Ian this is Hetty.' Ian shook hands and Hetty went beetroot red.

'Have a good time,' she said, waiting until they were well away from the door before closing it.

Taking Rachel's arm, Ian hurried her through the blustery, dry night to where the car was parked. Once she was comfortably settled he closed the door and went round to the driver's side.

The roads were narrow, it was grey-dark and Ian concentrated on his driving saying little until they reached the Grosvenor Hotel. All but a small part of it had been given over to those attending the Farmers' Ball. An attempt had been made to organise the parking with white lines indicating the space allotted to each car. This had been largely ignored by the first arrivals who had more or less abandoned their vehicles.

'Typical,' Ian fumed.

'What's typical?'

'Farmers, they don't obey any rules except their own.'

'Does that apply to your father?' she teased.

'It would if he was here. If I park where I am I'm blocking two cars from getting out – oh, what the blazes, if *I* don't someone else will.' He switched off and went round to open the door for Rachel and she carefully lifted the skirt of her gown lest her heel caught in it. The wind whipped around them but it was a short step to the entrance where the uniformed attendant had the glass door open. There was warmth and people congregating and greeting each other noisily. Most of the women had fur coats or fur jackets over their gowns and the men were in evening or Highland dress. A few smiled her way and gave a word of greeting to Ian.

'Ian, where do I leave my cape?'

'Over there, you'll have to join the queue.' A girl behind the counter was taking coats and handing over tickets.

'Don't lose your tickets, ladies, you'll need them to reclaim your belongings.'

Rachel put it carefully in the evening bag she had borrowed from Janet and turned to find Ian at her back.

'Nothing to wear! Heavens, you look ravishing.'

'You like it then?' she said shyly. His open admiration was embarrassing her.

'I'll say I do. Come to that I like what's inside it even better.' His arm went round her waist as he led her into a very large room with huge crystal chandeliers that glittered and sparkled as the dancers circled the floor. There was a mixture of old and young as Ian had said there would be. Some of the older women were heavily jewelled and wore gowns that were fashionable and no doubt very expensive, Rachel thought. There were others for whom fashion was unimportant and it looked as though the same gown came out of its mothballs year after year.

The band had just finished playing an old-fashioned waltz, a favourite of the older generation.

'Have to cater for all tastes,' Ian apologised.

'Nothing wrong with an old-fashioned waltz.'

He made a face. 'How are you with an eightsome reel?'

'I won't disgrace you,' she laughed.

'You couldn't,' he smiled. 'I much prefer modern dancing but I don't mind getting up for a reel.' The band at that moment struck up a quickstep and Ian immediately led her on to the floor. She was still nervous about the extra twirly bits he put in but she was managing to follow him though it meant concentrating.

After three dances in succession they sat down. 'Why do you keep putting in those complicated steps?' she complained. 'It must be obvious to you that I'm not in your class when it comes to dancing.'

'Rubbish. You have natural rhythm, you just have to learn to let yourself go.' They were chatting happily when someone drew near and they both looked up.

'Ian, do you mind if I borrow your partner for this dance, that is, of course, if the lady is willing?'

Rachel felt herself flush then go pale as she looked into the face of Peter McGregor.

Chapter Twenty-Four

'You'll have to leave that, Agnes,' Mrs Harrison said as she came into the kitchen, 'you're wanted in the library.'

'Wanted in the library?' Agnes repeated in dismay.

'Yes, on you go,' she said, and gave a smile as though to reassure Agnes, but then she wasn't to know that this was the summons she had been dreading.

She dried her hands, smoothed down her skirt and went along, not hurrying, she needed the time to pull herself together. If only she hadn't let her tongue run away with her but it was too late for regrets. Her outspokenness was to cost her her job. She swallowed the lump in her throat and wondered even at this late hour if an apology would do any good. She doubted it but it was worth a try. She took a deep breath and knocked at the door.

'Come in.'

She did and closed the door behind her. Gerald Patterson looked up briefly then went on with his writing. After a few moments he put down his pen. 'What are you doing standing there? Come over here.'

She went to stand in front of the desk. 'Mr Gerald, sir.'

'Yes.'

'I – I just wanted you to know how very sorry I am for the way I spoke to you, I don't know what got into me.' She paused and swallowed. 'Please don't sack me, sir, please give me another chance.' She was grovelling and if it meant saving her job she would do any amount of it.

'Don't sack me!' he said with heavy emphasis on the words. 'For someone anxious to better herself that was a shockingly bad expression. Much better if you had said, "Please don't terminate my employment" or even "Please don't dispense with my services".'

Agnes flushed angrily. The rotten so-and-so was making fun of her. With difficulty she bit back the words she longed to say and instead lowered her eyes to the carpet and picked at the thick pile with her toe.

'When I am addressing someone I expect that person to look at me.'

Reluctantly she raised her head.

'I did not call you here to terminate your employment, someone else would have done that.'

'You didn't?' Agnes felt dizzy with relief and let out a huge sigh.

He laughed, a real laugh that was full of amusement and chased away the lines of pain and suffering. 'Nothing was further from my mind. What I wanted was to find out if your declared interest in books was genuine or not.'

'It's genuine all right.'

'Did you work hard at school?'

'No,' she answered truthfully.

'And why was that? Before you answer, bring over a chair for yourself.'

She did and was glad to be off her legs. Her hands, she never quite knew what to do with them and she had been standing with them behind her back. Now she put them in her lap and locked her fingers. 'The answer to your question, sir, is it seemed like a waste of time and,' she looked over at the fireplace she cleaned every morning, 'not much learning is required to clean out the ashes.'

'Perhaps not but learning is never wasted.'

'I appreciate that now but I didn't then.'

'Given the opportunity what would you have done with your life?'

'I'm clever.'

'And modest.'

'Well, I'm only saying what my teacher said,' she defended herself. 'She said I had a good brain but I was too lazy to use it.'

'And was she right?'

'No, she wasn't. My ma, I mean my mother, said too much learning just makes you discontented.' She stopped.

He nodded. 'Go on.'

'My best friend was staying on at school then going on to college, only she didn't because her da married again and the money went on his new wife.' Why on earth was she telling him all this and why didn't he stop her.

'You must have been distressed for your friend?'

'Should have been, I know, but I wasn't. I wanted to be a teacher too and her not getting to be one made us the same again.'

Gerald Patterson was having great difficulty in hiding his amusement.

It wasn't just amusement, the girl fascinated him. How refreshing to hear someone being so honest. Many would have felt the same but quite unable to admit to it.

'May I ask what you should be doing at this moment?'

'You took me away from my job helping in the kitchen, after that I was supposed to clean the silver.'

'Boring, repetitive jobs?'

'Yes and no to that. I do my thinking then.'

'Let me give you something to think about.' He paused to look at her. 'I have selected some reading matter for you.'

She beamed. 'That is very good of you, sir.'

'You won't hoodwink me, my girl. I'll know if you have read them, for I mean to question you on them.'

Agnes gave a broad grin, she couldn't help it.

'What is so funny?'

'You, you sound like a schoolmaster.'

A look of great sadness crossed his face. 'A schoolmaster is precisely what I would have been had it not been for these—'

'Bloody, useless legs,' Agnes finished for him, then appalled, clapped her hand over her mouth.

The roar of laughter could have been heard through the whole of Drumoaks and indeed it had been heard by Gerald's unmarried sister, Gertrude, who knocked first then poked her head in.

'What is going on, Gerald? I haven't heard you laugh like that in a very long time.'

'Never had very much to laugh about. Come in if you want.'

Agnes got up hastily. 'Excuse me, sir, I'd better get back to work.'

'Yes, perhaps you had. Here, take these and read them.'

Gertrude was frowning. 'Is that wise, Gerald?'

'She'll take good care of them.'

Gertrude sat down with her feet slightly apart in her sensible brogue shoes and studied her younger brother. 'Do you mind telling me what is going on?'

'Nothing is going on, my dear Gertrude, and if you will forgive the crudeness, my accident saw to that.'

She winced. 'Of course you are bored, I know you are, but if you weren't so rude to people they would come and see you. You can be horribly rude when you choose.'

'Their sympathy I can do without and the way they avoid looking at my legs makes me sick.' He looked down at them. 'Covered with trousers they look perfectly ordinary, wouldn't you say?' The peevishness disappeared and he gave a sudden grin. 'That red-haired piece referred to them as my bloody useless legs.'

'Only repeating what she heard you say I have no doubt. That red-haired piece as you call her should not be encouraged. She is after all only a maid in this house and you would do well to remember that.'

'Not your ordinary maid, Gertrude, not by a long way.' He gave her a sidelong look and a smile. It wasn't difficult to win over his sister and he wasn't above using his disability to get what he wanted. 'Do something for me, will you?' he asked.

The face that her brother Adrian sometimes described as 'horsey' softened. 'You've only to ask.'

'Her name is Agnes Boyd and she's intelligent. Her speech isn't too bad when she remembers and she wants to make something of herself.'

'Is that what she told you?'

'More or less. Given the chance she'll get on I'm sure of it.'

'She may feel that way just now.'

'What do you mean by that?'

'She'll get married, have a family and that will be that.'

'Not Agnes, not that redhead, she won't throw herself away on some ignorant lout. She interests me, Gertrude, and God knows I need something in my life.'

Better than anyone Gertrude knew her brother, knew too how close he had been to taking his own life. 'What have you in mind?' she said carefully.

'Perhaps a couple of hours' tuition here in the library. You know how that could be arranged?'

She was thoughtful. She didn't approve but where was the harm in it. The girl would be bored in no time and Gerald didn't tolerate fools gladly. It would burn itself out but meantime it would keep him happily occupied.

'Well?'

'I was thinking. If you're serious I'll have a word with Mrs Harrison, make out that you have plans for rearranging the books, or something of the sort.'

'Brilliant, that should do it.'

'If it goes on for long, Mrs Harrison can ask one of the others to do an extra hour or so.'

'Thanks, Gertrude.' He suddenly looked depressed and she glanced at him worriedly. He had such swings of mood.

'Yes, I think I am very much in favour of it after all. It would be a start. Tutoring here at Drumoaks could be a worthwhile career, Gerald, you have excellent qualifications and students wouldn't be in short supply. What you need is your confidence back and this little maid may be the answer.'

Mrs Harrison was none too happy, in fact she was very displeased. Agnes Boyd was a maid and maids were engaged to do household tasks not play around with books. This sort of preferential treatment could go to the girl's head, give her ideas above her station and cause discontent among the others. She pursed her lips and drew in her brows, but an order was an order and had to be obeyed. She had no say in the matter.

'Agnes, finish what you are doing and then come along to my room,' she said severely.

'Yes, Mrs Harrison.' The tone didn't sound too promising but she couldn't recall doing anything dreadful and she wasn't unduly worried.

The housekeeper was looking out of the window when Agnes entered. Taking her time she turned round to face Agnes.

'I have had a most peculiar request concerning you. It appears that Mr Gerald is once again taking an interest in things and wishes to catalogue the books in the library and apparently you are to do the fetching and carrying.'

Agnes could feel Mrs Harrison's displeasure and hid her excitement as best she could. She waited for the housekeeper to go on.

'You are required in the library at ten o'clock tomorrow morning. See that you do your usual duties before that time, and should your work fall behind I shall expect you to work extra in the evening.'

'Yes, Mrs Harrison.'

'That is all, you may go.'

Risking a reprimand Agnes went quickly to her own room and once there gave in to her excitement and hugged herself. Mr Gerald was going to help her, she just knew he was. It was happening, slowly but surely her dreams were coming true. She was to be given the right books to read and questioned on them. She was privileged indeed and Agnes couldn't help smiling at the thought of scruffy Agnes Boyd, formerly of Spinner's Lane, being taught by Mr Gerald who, but for his accident, would have been teaching the toffs in one of those posh schools. For a moment she felt a rush of compassion mixed with guilt that she should benefit from another's misfortunes. But that, she told herself, was life.

A moderate show of interest was all that Gerald expected from Agnes and he was deeply touched to see her genuine eagerness to learn. Daniel Defoe's *Robinson Crusoe* had delighted her as had John Buchan's *The Thirty-nine Steps*. Now as a complete change he had given her *Far From the Madding Crowd*.

'What did you think of Thomas Hardy, Agnes?' Gerald asked as they sat together in the library.

'Well, he must be a good writer,' she grinned. 'I mean I didn't know the first thing about country life but after reading that I think I do now.'

She saw him nod approvingly and relaxed. It was so very important for Agnes to please this gentleman who was giving her so much of his time.

'Did you study it as you were reading?'

'No, I read it quickly to see how it was going to end then I went back and read it properly.'

'Good girl.' He put his elbows on the desk. 'What is your opinion of Bathsheba?'

'In the beginning I thought her too concerned with her appearance.'

'Too vain?'

'Yes. Always wanting to make a good impression but I think by the end she was a stronger character.'

'Go on,' he said smiling encouragingly.

'Pretty rotten joke to send that valentine to that farmer whats-his-name?'

'Boldwood?'

'Yes, him.'

'Why was it cruel, Agnes? Lots of people send valentines, after all it is only a light-hearted piece of nonsense. Haven't you given or received one?'

She looked scornful. 'Folk where I come from have more to do with their money. Anyway it was a mistake. Boldwood took it seriously and once he discovered who it was from he set about courting her believing she felt the same way about him.'

'Was Bathsheba in love with anyone?'

'Mostly herself, I would say, but she was very taken with Troy or maybe it was the uniform.'

'Would Troy have appealed to you?' he asked with a mischievious grin.

'Absolutely not, I can see through that kind. Mind you, a bit of flirting might be fun but when it comes to marriage—' she stopped and flushed.

'Don't be embarrassed, go on.'

She hesitated then decided it would be better just to carry on and say what she was going to. 'Liking and respect are more important than love, more lasting too, but of course if you're lucky enough to get all three,' she broke off and looked at the ceiling.

'Improbable but certainly not impossible, Agnes, if we are to believe all we read.' A spasm of pain crossed his face and Agnes wondered if he were in actual pain or it was something he was remembering. 'The fire is going down, see to it.'

'Sorry, I should have noticed,' she said getting hastily to her feet. She used the poker to clear the ashes then added a log and placed coal around it. All this she managed without dirtying her hands. Once she had used a paper bag for her hand but now there was a large mitt for the purpose. She came back to sit opposite him and waited with her hands folded in her lap.

'You enjoy reading?'

'I love it.'

'Books are one of the greatest joys in life as you are just beginning to find out.' He paused and frowned as if in thought. 'You've read *Emma* and you've read *Pride and Prejudice* so I think we'll give Jane Austen a rest. How about Charles Dickens?'

'I've read *David Copperfield*.'

'So you have. Go and get down *Great Expectations*. It is a wonderful novel, Agnes, but after that we turn our attention to history. No use being well-read if you have no knowledge of what went on in this great country of ours to make it what it is today.'

She couldn't let that pass. 'That sort of depends on your position in this country,' she said tartly and he raised an eyebrow.

'My dear girl, I was not thinking of material things but rather of the wars and the bravery of our fathers who gave their lives that we should know freedom.'

'I suppose if you put it that way.'

★ ★ ★

As the weeks went by and spring brightened the lawns with masses of large, golden-trumpeted daffodils, Agnes was to be seen poring over books. Sometimes she thought her head would burst with all this learning and occasionally she would suffer the lashing of his tongue if she was slow to grasp his meaning. That had bewildered her, made her angry too at the unfairness of it, but she kept quiet. In bed at night she fought tiredness to read and study the work he gave her, sometimes dozing off with the light still burning and having to get up later to turn it off. Did he forget, or perhaps he didn't know, that she still had to get through her chores?

Not that she would ever complain, she was too grateful for what he was doing for her. The highlight of her day was when he would tell her to stop what she was doing and they would have a discussion on a particular book, politics or whatever he had in mind. Politics had them at loggerheads. There would be heated arguments and sometimes Agnes would forget herself sufficiently to bring in a few choice adjectives. Far from angering him it had the opposite effect and Gerald Patterson was reduced to helpless laughter.

Beatrice and Madge at first accepted the explanation that Agnes was helping to reorganise the books in the library but as the weeks turned into months curiosity got the better of them and they all but demanded to know what was going on.

'Nothing is going on, you two, but it's confidential and just you remember that.' She stopped and wondered what to say but knew too that nothing short of the truth would satisfy.

'We wouldn't say a word, would we, Beatrice?'

'Of course not and Agnes knows that.'

'All right I'll tell you but no laughing. It's just that I showed an interest in the books in the library and it went on from there. Mr Gerald was going to be a schoolmaster so he knows how to teach. He, well, he sets me passages to read then questions me on them.'

'Better you than me,' Beatrice said feelingly. 'I had enough of school when I was there.'

'Me too.' Madge looked puzzled. 'What are you goin' to do with all that learnin', that's what I'd like to know?'

'I'm not sure myself, Madge, but at least I have the satisfaction of knowing things I never knew before.'

'I suppose there's that to it.'

As for Gerald Patterson, he was a changed man. Everyone noticed it but only his sister understood it. She was both pleased and disturbed. Gerald seemed to be obsessed with the girl and it worried her. Adrian and Olive knew nothing of it and she wondered what they would say if they did know. Blame her for encouraging it and try to talk sense into Gerald.

Gertrude wasn't the only one who worried. Gerald did a good deal of it himself. What had been intended as a way of helping to put in the day had become a necessary part of his life. Saturdays and Sundays when he didn't see her were just days to be got through. Strange that he should find her presence disturbing when he had thought never to be interested in a woman again. No longer did he see or think of her as a servant at Drumoaks; he saw her now as a young, attractive woman whom he could engage in conversation and get a lively response.

Looking at her bowed head he wondered what it would feel like to bring his fingers through that thick auburn hair. Her mouth fascinated him, so set and determined one moment then in the next turned up in the sweetest smile that churned at his insides and was the cause of those cruel, sarcastic remarks he hurled at her. She took it in silence but he would see the hurt in those brown eyes and hate himself.

His nightmare was that she would leave him, leave Drumoaks. Gertrude had warned him that it was to be expected, that girls of her class married young and started families almost immediately. What could he do about it? Nothing. There was nothing he could do. Or was there?

What was going on in his mind was impossible, laughable, yet it stayed with him.

He waited another month before plucking up courage. His hands under the desk were sweating and he wiped them on his trouser legs.

'Agnes, do you find the life at Drumoaks quiet for you?'

'I love it,' she said simply.

'You would miss all this if it were to stop?'

She looked away from him, the pain was a hard lump in her throat as she thought of these precious hours coming to an end and her return to full-time domestic duties. Yet she had known they couldn't go on.

'Yes, I would,' she said quietly and managing to steady her voice, 'you have been very good to me, sir, and very patient and I'll always be grateful to you.'

'You have been a joy to teach.'

There is something you will never know, Gerald Patterson, Agnes thought, and it would be embarrassing for both of us if you did, but I'm going to miss you as much as the lessons.

'I'm glad about that.' She had to get out before she made a fool of herself. 'Excuse me, sir, I'd like to go now if you don't mind.' Her voice was wobbling and she got up almost knocking the chair over in her haste to be gone.

'Sit down at once,' he bawled at her and when she didn't, he said quietly, 'Sit down, Agnes, and tell me what has upset you.'

'Nothing.'

'Agnes Boyd doesn't get into a state like this about nothing. Out with it, girl.'

She bit her lip. 'I'm just being foolish and yes, you're right, it isn't like me but these hours in the library have come to mean a great deal to me. Of course I knew they would have to come to an end but it was springing it on me like that.'

'Springing what on you?'

'That this is the end of the lessons.'

'I didn't say that, you went off on that tack on your own.' He was silent for a long time, then he spoke softly, so softly that she barely heard him. 'As far as I'm concerned, Agnes, these lessons can go on for a lifetime.'

'I don't understand.'

'Don't you? Have you no inkling?'

She shook her head.

'Agnes Boyd, I am asking you to marry me.'

She stared at him, then the swift colour came to her face flooding it.

'I am not in the mood for jokes.'

'This is no joke, I am being completely serious.'

'Would you mind repeating the question?'

'I was proposing marriage to you, Agnes.'

'You want me to be your wife?'

'That is what it usually means. Do you want time to consider?'

Her eyes widening in shock but thankful that her brain was functioning properly, Agnes wasn't prepared to risk delaying her answer but in the moments before accepting, Tommy Kingsley's words came back to her. 'You'll always be working class, Agnes, and those with breeding will make use of you for as long as it suits them.' He could very easily be right, she wasn't denying that, but wasn't she doing the same thing? She was using Gerald Patterson to get what she wanted.

Her mouth widened into a huge smile. 'I don't need time to consider, the answer is yes, please, sir.'

'Gerald. You'll have to get used to calling me that.'

'Take a bit of doing.'

'You'll manage.' He paused. 'How old are you, Agnes?'

'Eighteen going on nineteen.'

'I'm thirty-two. Does that seem very old to you?'

'Not for a man, but I'd be old if I were thirty-two.'

'You'll never be old, Agnes, in years perhaps but not in any other way.'

'I'm not sure if that is a compliment or not, sir, I mean, Gerald. Sounds as though I'll never grow up.'

He laughed then grew sober. 'You have to understand, Agnes, that this can never be a proper marriage,' he said slowly and keeping his eyes on her. 'You do know what I mean?'

'Yes,' she said gently and feeling an overwhelming compassion for him.

'No children – ever—'

'Truthfully, that wouldn't worry me. There were seven of us at home and at times it was sheer hell. That's not to say I don't like kids, as a matter of fact I do, but I don't need any of my own.'

He nodded, well pleased. He knew that Agnes could be relied on to tell the truth. 'I don't see a great deal of my nephew and niece but then they are usually with their nanny.'

She didn't say anything. She could see that there was something else he wanted to say and at last the difficult words came out.

'You would be getting a cripple for a husband and as you know as well as anyone I can be the very devil to get on with. As Gertrude could tell you it was my appalling behaviour that chased away more than one person from Drumoaks.'

'You shouldn't let that bother you. True friends wouldn't have let a few tantrums drive them away.'

'Tantrums? Is that how you would refer to them?'

She grinned. 'Never do get the right word, do I? But it's near enough.'

'You could put up with that?'

'Yes, but I would try very hard to make sure that you had no cause to fly off the handle.' She frowned. 'No, I take that back, a good burst of temper doesn't do any harm, does a lot of good actually. My parents go at it hammer and tongs, it clears the air and they are reasonably pleasant to each other until the next time.'

'What are your parents going to say about this?'

'It has nothing to do with them, it is my life and I knew a long time ago that I had to break away.'

'Why?' he asked gently.

'Because they would always hold me back. They won't change and the person I have become, largely through you, they wouldn't want to know.'

'You would make a complete break?'

'In the sense that we wouldn't see each other but I would like to go on sending them a little money.'

'How on earth have you managed that on the pittance you get?'

She grinned mischievously, 'You do admit it is a pittance?'

'The going rate I am informed.'

'Every little helps is what my mother would say.'

'We'll have to improve on that, give them a monthly allowance to cover their rent, heating and the like.'

She shook her head. 'Very nice of you, but that isn't the way to do it. What seems a very little to you is a great deal to them and it would be squandered. Saving is something they don't understand. The best way to help them is to pay the rent directly to the rent office.'

'In case they spend the money unwisely?'

'They would, no doubt about it. My mother would decide that something was more important than paying the rent and they would quickly get into arrears. I know them, Gerald.'

'Very well, my dear, we'll work that one out later.'

'Seems to me that I'm getting a lot out of this marriage and you very little.'

'I am getting a refreshingly honest, spirited girl of eighteen going on nineteen and you a man of thirty-two and a cripple at that.'

'I'm not afraid of the word cripple and you shouldn't be either. Apart from—'

'My bloody, useless legs.'

'Yes, apart from those legs you have everything. Brains, good looks, a privileged background and a beautiful home and that can't be bad.'

'Can't it, Agnes? What if I told you I would give up everything if I could throw away my crutches and walk?'

'I'd believe you and I wish with all my heart that it could be.' And if it could we wouldn't be talking like this, she added silently.

'To seal our engagement and forthcoming marriage and since I can't come round to you—'

She got up feeling suddenly shy and went round to stand beside him.

'Don't be afraid of me, Agnes.' Taking her face between his hands, he pressed his lips to hers. The sensation surprised her, she hadn't expected to feel anything, certainly not the little thrill that went through her as their lips met for that first kiss. Yet she shouldn't have been surprised, for hadn't she been drawn to him these last few weeks and on occasions disturbingly so.

Had it been the same for him? she wondered and decided it couldn't have been. Not once had the word love been mentioned and she would do well to remember that. Liking and respect were all she could expect and her own feelings she would keep well hidden. But did she know her own feelings? Tommy Kingsley was always there, unbidden his image would rise up, but now he must be banished for ever.

'The wedding as soon as possible, Agnes, no reason for delay.'

'What about the master and mistress and Miss Gertrude? They are going to be shocked.'

'Let them be shocked.' He frowned deeply and drummed his fingers on the desk. 'There is so much to talk about and this isn't the best place for it.'

'May I say something?'

'Of course.'

'Let me carry on with my duties as normal—'

'No, at least no longer than the next few hours. Tell you what – bring afternoon tea for two to my room about three thirty and that is to be your very last duty as housemaid. I'll see that Gertrude tells Mrs Harrison to engage another maid in your place.'

Gerald Patterson made his slow way to his own sitting-room and once there rang the bell for Bannerman, his manservant, who filled so many roles in his master's life. He came very quickly.

'Bannerman, do you know if Miss Gertrude is in the house or in those damned stables?'

'In the house. I saw her a few minutes ago.'

'Good! Tell her to come in, that I want to see her at once.'

* * *

'What's so urgent?'

'You are the first to congratulate me on my forthcoming marriage.'

She knew, of course, but she had to ask. 'To whom, dear brother?'

'How many women of marriageable age do I see?'

'Your fault. A few of them would be very happy to come and visit.'

'I've asked Agnes to marry me.'

She whitened.

'You must have guessed?'

'I suppose I just hoped against hope that I was wrong. You've actually proposed?'

'Yes, and been accepted.'

'I see.'

'Like the others will do, you are going to put forward every objection you can think of.'

'I can think of plenty.'

'Forget the objections and think of my happiness.'

'That is what I am thinking of. Gerald, you are rushing into something without giving it careful consideration. You have nothing, absolutely nothing in common and I doubt if she would ever be accepted by your own circle of friends.'

'My steadily declining circle of friends.'

'And we know whose fault that is.'

'Come on, Gertrude, you can't deny that I'm a changed man since Agnes entered my life.'

'I don't deny it and I'm grateful to the girl, but marriage – apart from your own position have you given a thought to how difficult it would be for her?'

'She'll cope, she's a quick learner.' He paused. 'Gertrude, Agnes is nobody's fool, she knows what is ahead but in a way I'm giving her what she wants. She's desperate to make a break with her old life and her family won't be a problem, she has made that clear.'

'That's something, I suppose.' She gave a deep sigh. 'All right, Gerald, if you are determined to go through with it I'll do what I can to help.'

'Thanks.'

'For a start her belongings will have to be transferred to one of the guest rooms and no more contact with the servants. See that she understands that, Gerald, and to ease matters, Mrs Harrison will need to know the circumstances.'

'I can leave that to you – and the marriage – I want that to take place as soon as it can be arranged.'

'Is she getting an engagement ring, or is that unnecessary?'

'She'll want one, I imagine. Get the jeweller to send up a tray. And clothes, Gertrude, organise that too will you, and have everything charged to my account.'

'Fashion as you know isn't my scene but I must just enjoy this. She is a pretty little thing and get that horrified look off your face. I'm not going to choose for her.' She grinned displaying large perfect teeth. The same features on a man would have been handsome but on a woman they were too heavy.

Gertrude was with her brother when Agnes arrived with a tray and it was she who opened the door.

'Want to join us, Gertrude?'

'No, I won't, thanks.'

He looked at her pointedly and Gertrude got the message.

'Gerald has just told me the news, Agnes. May I be the first to wish you every happiness.'

'You can't be pleased,' Agnes burst out, 'you don't have to pretend.'

Gerald frowned, but Gertrude smiled. 'Directness is something I admire and I propose to be equally direct. You are perfectly correct in thinking that I am against this marriage. It is no disrespect to you as a person but to the difference in your background. The way ahead, my dear, will not be easy.'

'You forget, Gertrude,' Gerald said irritably, 'that there will be very little socialising, if any at all. We'll be marooned on our own little island, won't we, Agnes?'

It was said in a jocular way but a little shiver went through her at Gerald's words. He was making it sound like a prison, a comfortable prison, but a prison nonetheless, then she ridiculed herself for such fanciful thoughts.

'Miss Gertrude – Miss Patterson – I'll do my best to make your brother happy.'

'I'm sure you'll do that, Agnes, and since you are about to become family you had better address me as Gertrude.'

'Thank you.'

'This tea is going to be stewed.'

'I'm just going, Gerald, but a word to Agnes before I do. Your clothes are being moved to one of the guest rooms and from now on there will be no contact with the servants. I'm sure you will appreciate the wisdom of that.'

Agnes was dismayed. She hadn't given any thought to it. So much had happened in such a short space of time that she was bewildered. The thought of losing the friendship of Beatrice and Madge upset her but Gertrude had spelt it out and she had to agree.

'Yes, I understand,' she said quietly.

'You'll need clothes. I'll bring the car round to the front tomorrow morning. Be ready at nine thirty.' She nodded to them both and left.

'Your first ordeal over and it wasn't too bad was it?'

She smiled. 'I've a feeling the others won't be so understanding.'

It was a masculine room they were in with no frills. The deep leather chairs looked comfortable in their shabbiness. Gerald occupied a wide, high-backed chair recommended by the surgeon as being the easiest to get in and out of. There was a wheelchair in the corner. He saw her eyeing it.

'My transport,' he said with a trace of bitterness, 'crutches can be damned tiring.'

'So I imagine. Gerald, do I have to be tactful all the time?'

'No.'

She took a deep breath. 'If you had been badly wounded in a war or some conflict would you have been ashamed to get yourself about in a wheelchair?'

He drank some tea and she thought he wasn't going to answer, but he had been considering his answer. 'No,' he said, 'no, I wouldn't.'

'Then what is so different about your situation? You had an accident, no one's fault, just an act of God.'

'I doubt if the Almighty would take the blame,' but he was laughing.

'Then use the blasted thing to get about.'

'Such language from my wife-to-be.'

'A lifetime of lessons was what you promised,' she said gently.

The silence was comfortable as they ate the sandwiches and Agnes poured second cups. When they had finished she lifted the tray and put it nearer the door meaning to remove it later.

'Agnes, someone will collect that later.'

'But—'

'Leave it, you are no longer a servant.'

She got up and wandered round the room knowing that his eyes were following her.

'You have a nice figure, Agnes, and in the right clothes you are going to be a very attractive young woman.'

She had no answer to that but her heightened colour showed that she was pleased. Most of the pictures were of country scenes but one was of a group of cricketers. She looked at it closely.

'That's you in the front?'

'Yes.' He reached for his crutches then changed his mind. 'Bring that damned thing over.'

She looked at him uncomprehending then her mouth stretched in a smile. Carefully she manoeuvred the wheelchair into the position he wanted, then with her heart in her mouth watched as he swung himself into the wheelchair. The perspiration was beaded on his brow and seeing it Agnes's quick temper got the better of her. 'Is it beneath you to ask for help?'

'I prefer to manage on my own,' he said stiffly.

'Then you are bloody stupid and I'm not apologising for the language, you use it often enough yourself.'

'From a gentleman it is acceptable.'

'Since I'm no lady—' she stopped and for a split second she was hearing Tommy Kingsley's words again. "A lady is born a lady and you'll always be working class like me".'

'You didn't hear what I said; you were miles away.'

'Sorry.'

'I said it is possible to be a lady without being ladylike.'

'There's hope for me then.'

He brought the wheelchair close to her and studied the picture.

'I was a good cricketer.'

'A good-looking lot especially that one in the front row,' she teased.

'I made captain for a couple of seasons.'

'Which means you weren't just good you were very good.'

'I loved the game,' he said wistfully.

'Do you ever go to watch?'

He shook his head.

'Then you should. You can look back on what you did and enjoy watching others play.'

'Maybe I will at that.'

'You can explain the game to me if women are allowed anywhere near, that is.'

'A few go to see to the tea.'

'Oh, that's typical, and speaking of tea I hate to bring up the subject of food but I'm starving. I've had nothing since breakfast apart from those tiny sandwiches with you.'

'You poor girl and I do apologise. For myself I seldom bother with lunch but you must learn to order for yourself.' He saw her face. 'I usually dine with the family but we'll have our meal together in the breakfast room – you'd rather that, wouldn't you?'

'Yes, Gerald, I would. Incidentally, which room am I getting?'

'I think Gertrude said the second guest room but pop into each until you see your own belongings.'

'Gerald, would you mind if I – if I went away for a bit.'

'Went away for a bit?' he said puzzled.

'No, what I meant was I'd like to go to my room for a while.'

'Of course, heavens, girl, you don't have to ask permission for everything. Do what you want to do. In any case you'll want out of that outfit and into something of your own.'

'Yes,' she answered but she knew that the maid's outfit was better than what she had in her wardrobe.

'Seven o'clock in the breakfast room.'

No one was about as she hurried to her new bedroom. Her duties had never included cleaning out the guest rooms so it was something of a shock when she opened the door. It was hers all right, she recognised a few of her things on the dressing-table. Slowly she went in and closed the door. She judged it to be three times the size of her old room with a double bed. The furniture was heavy and old-fashioned but looked what it was – top quality. Lined curtains in a leafy design were draped at the double window and there was a watercolour on one wall. She should have been delighted and impressed but she was neither. Her old room she had come to love; this was too big, she felt lost in it. If only she had been allowed to make the transfer herself, this was like being catapulted into a new life without being permitted a single backward glance.

Who, Agnes wondered, had taken her clothes from the wardrobe and emptied the drawers of her possessions? Beatrice? Madge? She thought not. More than likely it had been Mrs Harrison and she must have been given some explanation. The kitchen must be buzzing with gossip and soon they would all know and of one thing she was sure, it would not go down well. The servant classes did not like it when one of their own moved up in the world. It made them uncomfortable and resentful. Agnes Boyd, a nobody, to wed the master's brother. In her mind's eye she could see it all. The wise nod of the head, then the shaking of it as they reminded each other that the poor soul was a cripple and that Agnes wouldn't have her sorrows to seek. Not much of a catch really when you thought about it and as everyone knew he had a filthy temper.

Opening the wardrobe door she saw her few garments hanging up, lost in the vast space. One of the drawers, long and deep, was enough to hold her underwear and the rest. Deciding what to wear at night wasn't a problem. It would have to be her green accordian-pleated skirt and a pink-and-blue-striped blouse, her only white one was badly soiled at the neck. That was the worst of being an impulsive buyer, nothing ever matched up. Rachel used to laugh and say that her taste was all in her mouth.

The skirt could have done with a press, the pleats didn't stay the way they should for very long. Remembering four squares of chocolate in her coat pocket she went to see if they had survived the change over. They had and she sat down and ate them.

A good soak in plenty of water, she would enjoy that and the bathroom was right next door. Going through she saw a pink towelling robe hanging on the back of the door and took it with her into the bedroom. Better than wearing her petticoat to get from bedroom to bathroom. Taking off her clothes she slipped into it, a size smaller would have fitted better but tightening the belt would keep it up over her ankles. Back in the bathroom she turned on the water and looked about her. There was scented soap, a large tablet for the bath and a smaller one for the wash-hand basin. On the glass shelf were various bottles and a tin of talcum powder.

Lying back in the scented bath water, Agnes had her first experience of luxury and she was loving it. This was sheer bliss and best of all was the thought that she wouldn't have to clean up after herself.

Gerald's lips quirked into a smile as Agnes came into the breakfast-room. She smelt like a dream and looked like God-knows-what he thought. The girl had no dress sense, those colours screamed at one another and with that hair—

'That smells good,' she said appreciatively.

'Just arrived. I thought you would prefer to serve us yourself.'

'Thank you, I would.' That was thoughtful of him, she thought. For Gerald it wouldn't be awkward, people of his class could carry off anything, even dining with a maid. But for her it would have been acutely embarrassing. Beatrice would be in the dining-room serving the family and it would have fallen to Madge to serve them. Poor Madge would have got herself into such a state of nerves that she would probably have dropped the serving dish on the floor, or worse, over one of them.

'A sherry first, I think.'

'I don't care for sherry, thank you.'

'Have you ever tasted it?'

'No.'

'Then how do you know you won't like it?' He smiled. 'Just take tiny sips.'

'Is that to make it last out?'

'No, that is the correct way to drink it.'

Agnes took tiny sips.

'All right?'

'Nothing to write home about.'

'In time you'll acquire a taste for it and I had better tell you now that my brother and his wife wish to meet you.'

'Not for a while, I hope.'

'Thursday evening actually. We'll all dine together.'

He saw her shocked dismay and was irritated by it. 'For God's sake, Agnes, we have established that you have above average intelligence—'

'I'm blessed with brains not social graces.'

'Then we need to concentrate on your weaknesses. Adrian and Olive are not going to eat you, and speaking of eating, when are you to serve us?'

'Sorry.' She concentrated on the food. The main dish was tender chicken breasts with small roast potatoes and a selection of vegetables. A place had been set at either end of the table but Agnes had altered this, removing the place mat and cutlery to be next to Gerald. He nodded his approval.

'Is your head buzzing or can you take more?'

'Not much more. I'm in a kind of daze but I'll do my best.'

'You know the Laurels, of course, though I don't imagine you have been inside it.'

'It looks lovely and no I haven't been in it.'

'There is, of course, plenty of rooms at Drumoaks but it might be nice to start our married life a bit apart from the family.'

She brightened visibly. 'Gerald, what a lovely idea. I would love that, but only if it suits you.'

'Makes little difference to me. Bannerman will come too, he sees to my needs.'

Should she say it or should she keep quiet meantime? She decided to risk it. 'As your wife, shouldn't I be looking after you?'

He put down his knife and fork and subjected her to a cold stare. 'As I said, Bannerman comes with us and that is an end to it.'

They were silent during the dessert course. Madge knocked and brought in the coffee but studiously avoided looking at Agnes. Instead she looked at Gerald. 'Shall I pour, sir?'

'No, just leave it.'

'Very good, sir.' The door closed quietly.

Agnes hardly touched her coffee.

'Is the coffee not to your liking?'

'I prefer tea but no doubt in time I'll acquire a taste for this stuff.'

She hadn't meant to say that but she was tired, her head ached, and she longed for this day to end. 'Sorry, what was that about the Laurels?'

'Until about four or five years ago the house was occupied by an uncle of mine, an unsociable fellow who preferred his own company.'

'What happened to him?'

'He died. Since his death the house hasn't been lived in but it has been kept aired. Some redecorating will be required but that should be all.'

'May I see round it?' she asked eagerly, her tiredness temporarily forgotten.

'Yes, I'll get the keys for you and you can have a good look round. The wedding now, we'll discuss that then we'll call it a day. Naturally it will be very quiet, just immediate family and the ceremony here at Drumoaks.' He paused. 'Robert McLean, our local minister, will officiate.'

Agnes had seen his name on the board outside the church but she had never entered it. According to Mrs Tomlinson there had been a time when all the domestic staff were forced to attend the service but that rule had been relaxed. Only Mr Bannerman and Mrs Harrison put in an occasional appearance.

'Will you have a best man?'

'Michael, a friend from my schooldays, will undertake that duty.'

'May I have a friend from my schooldays to be my bridesmaid?'

'You told me you didn't want family,' he reminded her.

'Neither I do, but I said a schoolfriend. Trouble is, I don't know how to find her, we've lost touch.'

'Write to her family and get your letter forwarded.'

'I'll write to her father.'

The long, long day came to an end and Agnes lay in the strange bed in the darkness, staring up at the ceiling where the moonlight threw a pattern of branches. Through sheer exhaustion sleep claimed her and when she awoke at her usual time of six thirty her fuddled brain took some time to adjust. When it did she snuggled down again. Seven thirty, even eight o'clock would be time enough to get up.

She remembered her appointment with Gertrude and as she came down the front steps of Drumoaks a twist of excitement squeezed at her stomach and brought a flush to her cheeks. For this outing she wore a badly fitting checked costume, a bargain that had turned out to be not a bargain at all but a bad buy. Nevertheless, good money had gone on it and it had to be worn. She hurried the remaining steps, Gertrude was at the wheel with the passenger door wide open.

Good mornings were said and Agnes got in.

'Give that door a sharp pull.'

Agnes did and it clicked shut. After a noisy gear change the car shot off. Agnes sat well back in her seat and looking out at the passing scenery wondered what she could find to say.

''fraid I'm not sociable while I'm driving. With so many fools on the road these days one has to concentrate on one's driving.'

Agnes had a great urge to answer with, yes, one does, doesn't one.

'Yes.'

'Need to get Bannerman to teach you to drive, could come in useful.'

Almost swooning at the thought of herself at the wheel she managed to croak, 'Is it difficult?'

'Nothing to it.' After that exchange she lapsed into a silence that lasted until they were in Perth town centre. 'There is a lane next to McNeil's where I can park unless someone has beaten me to it.'

Agnes knew of McNeil's – who hadn't heard of the store that catered for the country folk of Angus and Perthshire? Leaving the car Agnes had almost to run to keep up with Gertrude's long strides. Her eyes darted to the windows where country tweeds and tartans filled two of them and the latest fashions were displayed in the others. The vulgarity of a price ticket was nowhere to be seen.

The heavy glass door was open and Gerald's sister strode purposefully in with Agnes following. In her shabby but well-cut tweed costume and flat sensible shoes heads turned to watch her. Agnes was seeing at first hand that it wasn't clothes that made a lady, it was that indefinable something called breeding.

Following Gertrude's tall figure Agnes was vaguely aware of the walls mirrored to reflect the pale gold carpet. Black leather chairs with gold studs were placed here and there for the convenience of the customers. Huge chandeliers added their brilliance to the scene. On they went through the departments showing exquisite lingerie, some of it plain wicked to Agnes's eyes. She only knew sensible knickers and plain petticoats. In passing, she glimpsed handmade leather shoes, belts, handbags and a heavenly perfume wafting over from the cosmetics counter. Gertrude stopped to look at a cashmere twin-set.

'May I help madam?'

'Tell Miss Inglis it's Miss Patterson.'

Miss Inglis must have been within earshot and wearing a welcoming smile she came forward.

'Good morning, Miss Patterson.'

'Good morning.' Gertrude turned to Agnes. 'This is Miss Boyd, she requires a number of outfits all to be charged to Mr Gerald's account.'

'Certainly.'

'A complete wardrobe from the skin out, you understand?'

'I do. Shall we start with a lightweight suit now that summer is approaching, two or three afternoon dresses, skirts and blouses—' Gertrude tiring of the flow had moved away then came back.

'That cream suit,' she pointed to the stand, 'You would suit that, Agnes, and get the accessories to go with it.'

Miss Inglis checked on the size. 'Yes, this should be your size, if not it can be altered to fit.' She beckoned to a young assistant.

'Take the young lady into a cubicle.'

Agnes had hoped to be left alone but no such luck, the girl in her attractive shop outfit was here to stay. Agnes took off her jacket and handed it over. Next she unbuttoned her blouse, stepped out of her skirt and handed both to the girl. Standing in her petticoat before the full-length mirror, Agnes felt self-conscious. It was her best and fresh on that morning but it was cheap and awful and clung unbecomingly. Spending money on what wouldn't be seen seemed to her like a criminal waste of money. She had gone for the very cheapest. Sometimes she didn't wear a petticoat at all.

Miss Inglis came in, took one look and despatched the assistant to the lingerie department. A kindly woman, she saw Agnes's embarrassment and said quietly.

'The undergarments must be of the correct length, yours is on the short side.'

Two slips arrived, both white, one in very fine cotton, the other in silk. She was left alone to make the change and chose the cotton slip.

All agreed that the cream two-piece suited Agnes and she agreed wholeheartedly. All it needed was a slight adjustment to the sleeve and could be done in the workroom right away.

Time flew as Agnes tried on garment after garment and she was amazed at Gertrude's ability to select outfits that suited her and as though she knew what Agnes was thinking, she looked amused.

'Agnes, I am large and clumsy and as a result I wear what I am comfortable in. You have the advantage of being small-made and neat and a joy to dress.'

'That is the nicest compliment anyone has ever paid me, do you know that?'

Gertrude smiled, then as Agnes was about to take off the pale green linen suit stopped her. 'Keep it on, Agnes. What should she wear over it, Miss Inglis?'

'The boxy jacket is very fashionable and the camel shade would look well with that shade of green.'

Agnes put it on. 'It's beautiful, Gertrude,' she said, digging her hands into the deep pockets.'

'Good, now it's my turn. I'm rather fond of that colour myself.'

'I have it in two shades of camel. Shall I send both jumpers on?'

'You might as well.' She turned swiftly. 'Agnes, you don't need to bother with those old clothes.'

'I want them,' she said stubbornly.

'I'll have them parcelled up.'

'Thank you.' She avoided Gertrude's eye. Her ma would be glad of them.

On the way out, Gertrude stopped at the handbags. She looked at several.

'Which one do you like, Agnes?'

'The crocodile one,' she said without hesitation and thinking it was for Gertrude herself.

'A good choice.' She spoke to the assistant. 'Charge that to Miss Patterson, Drumoaks. There you are, Agnes, my gift to you.'

'Oh, I didn't, I thought it was for yourself.'

'I've more than I'll ever need.'

'Thank you very much. It is very, very good of you to spend all this time on me. I really do appreciate it.'

Gerald was in the library where she had expected him to be. She had taken off her coat and given herself a quick freshen up.

'How did it go?'

'Gerald, I'm speechless and you are going to be the same when you get the bill in.'

'Bad as that is it?' His eyes softened as he looked at her. 'You look lovely in green, suits your colouring. Turn round slowly.' She obliged, 'Never noticed before,' he said with a mischievous gleam in his eyes, 'but you go in and out at all the right places.'

'I should hope so too and for your information the lady in McNeil's said with a few more inches I could have been a model.'

'I prefer my women slim and petite.'

The smile left Agnes's face, she was remembering what Gertrude had said in the car coming back.

'Agnes, money is not important.'

'It is if you haven't got any.' Agnes couldn't let that pass.

'Yes, well, I suppose that is true but I was about to tell you that I am not just doing this for you but for Gerald too. Most men like to see an attractive, well-dressed woman and Gerald falls into that category.' A look of great sadness crossed her face. 'Before his accident Gerald had everything. He had looks, charm, he was gifted academically and a good sportsman.'

'I know that, Gertrude, and I have no doubt he had a string of female admirers.' She tried to say it flippantly but a catch in her voice gave her away.

'He was engaged to a very lovely girl.'

Agnes moistened her lips. 'What happened?'

'Myra broke it off. She couldn't bear the thought of being married and tied to a cripple.'

'Precious little love there.'

'As you say, precious little'

'How did Gerald take it? Badly I suppose?'

'Once it was broken off he never spoke of it and neither did we.'

'That was a mistake I would have thought. Better surely to have spoken of it rather than let it fester.'

Gertrude looked at her in some surprise. 'Go on, you were going to say something else.'

'Only that if you'd all had a go at the Myra female, said what you thought of her, Gerald might have realised he wasn't missing much.'

'Lot of sense in that little head of yours.'

Agnes grinned. She was beginning to enjoy talking to Gertrude.

'Result of a deprived childhood. Brings out the fighter in you, or as you lot would say, brings out the fighter in one.'

'Oh, dear,' Gertrude said then bellowed with laughter.

'Come over here, Agnes, I have something to show you.'

She went over and watched him take from the drawer a velvet pad on which was a selection of engagement rings that winked and sparkled in the light.

'Take your time then choose the one you want.'

'I'm going to wake up any minute. I like that one,' she pointed.

'Give me your hand.' Agnes had never given much thought to her hands apart from keeping her fingernails clean and short. She put out her left hand and Gerald, after slipping it on, shook his head. 'The stones are too big, you need to have long slim fingers to show that to advantage.'

'Meaning mine are stumpy? You do know how to boost a girl's confidence,' she said pulling back her hand and taking off the ring.

'Short and fat then?' He was laughing at her.

'You wouldn't have lily white hands either if you'd cleaned out as many mucky grates as I have,' she answered, glaring at him.

'For someone as outspoken as yourself you are quick to take offence.'

'All right, you choose then.'

'This one.' The ring had three small diamonds and she had to admit it looked much better on her hand.

'You don't have to take that one but it suits your hand. How is the fit?'

'Needs a little pressure to get it over the knuckle but I prefer it that way.'

'Yes, better be firm and now to the wedding ring and the choice of it I leave entirely to you.'

Mindful of her short, fat fingers – it still rankled even though she knew he was teasing – she ignored the broad gold band and chose one that was narrower.

'Fine, that's that done.'

'Don't I get to wear the engagement ring?'

'Yes, of course, here it is, I wasn't thinking.'

She admired it on her finger. 'Thank you, Gerald,' she said softly and giving in to impulse kissed his cheek. If only he had taken the initiative then and kissed her properly but he hadn't. Maybe he didn't want to, perhaps she didn't appeal to him that way. She went back to her chair hiding her hurt.

Gerald wondered too why he had let the moment go. Heaven knew he desired her but that kiss on his cheek had been no more than a thank you, what else could it have been? he asked himself. Agnes was young and fresh, kind-hearted too, but it was only to escape the kind of life she knew and hated that she had agreed to tie herself to a cripple. What kind of marriage would it be? How long would it last?

He broke the silence. 'Remember we are dining on Thursday with Adrian and Olive. Gertrude will be there, of course.'

Agnes felt her mouth go dry.

'Wear something nice. Gertrude will advise you, she tells me you have some lovely clothes.'

'Yes, I do.'

'You'll be the prettiest there.'

'Gerald, don't treat me like a child. I don't want to disgrace you but acting the lady doesn't exactly come easy to me.'

'Just be yourself.'

'That's the daftest thing you've ever said.'

'Agnes, no matter how we come into this life we all have difficulties to overcome.'

'I know and I'm just being stupid.'

'You'll manage very well and now run along and do whatever you want.'

'Can't, I haven't any money. I didn't get my wages.'

'I don't believe what I'm hearing.'

'You don't understand. I want to get my hair done for Thursday and I need money for that and my fare into Perth.'

'Lord! I don't keep money on me. Ask Gertrude to get some for you. That is something I'll have to see to, opening an account for you once we're married.'

Gertrude was coming away from the stables and Agnes hurried to meet her. She looked well in her jodhpurs and smiled at Agnes. 'Hello, where are you off to?'

'Get my hair done.'

Gertrude had hers cropped short. It was light brown, thick, healthy-looking hair and Agnes wondered how she would look with it longer. 'Of course, you'll want to look your best for Thursday.'

'I hate to mention this after all that has been spent on me but I've no money. I didn't get my wages or I wouldn't have asked,' Agnes said desperately.

'Don't keep much myself, just charge it up. Did you ask Gerald? Come to think of it, he isn't likely to have any. Come back with me.'

In her room she emptied her purse. Agnes counted four pounds twelve shillings and sixpence.

'That won't be enough?' Gertrude said.

'It's more than enough, I'll just take -'

'Take it all for goodness sake and remember you can charge it up in McNeil's.'

'For my hair you mean?'

'They have a first-class hairdressing department.'

'I'm not known. I can't charge it up.'

Gertrude frowned then brightened. 'Get hold of Miss Inglis, better still I'll give you a note for her, that'll clear the way. In time you'll get your own account there. Sorry I can't take you in myself, but see if Bannerman is free.'

'If it's all the same to you I'd rather go by bus.'

Gertrude shrugged her shoulders. 'Up to you.'

Agnes enjoyed her day, enjoyed having money in her purse. After some thought she wore her fine tweed suit with a cream silk blouse, on her feet leather small-heeled shoes and carried Gertrude's gift, her crocodile-skin handbag. It might be the last time she would be able to do this, so she was going to make it a day to remember. First she treated herself to coffee – almost she'd weakened and had tea – but coffee was what they drank at Drumoaks other than in the afternoon. With cake thick with cream the coffee went down rather well. A second cake was a temptation but she resisted it and for the first time in her life she left a tip, a threepenny piece under the plate. She sailed out with her head high and made for McNeil's. To Agnes's surprised delight Miss Inglis recognised her and after reading the note she gave Agnes a printed card signed by herself with the instructions to allow the bearer, Miss Agnes Boyd, to purchase goods or services as required and the same to be charged to Mr Gerald Patterson of Drumoaks.

Thursday, the dreaded day, had arrived and all too soon for Agnes it was time to get herself ready. Applying the make-up she had bought in Perth, she was careful to keep it light. She had a good skin but it got shiny when she was excited and using the tips of her fingers she smeared on a little foundation then a dusting of powder. Lipstick next then in her own language a good squirt of perfume behind her ears and at her wrists.

Stepping into the turquoise silk dress, feeling the folds of the soft material about her legs, Agnes forgot her apprehension for the moment and revelled in the unaccustomed luxury. What would Rachel think of her now?

The high heels gave her the height she longed for and glancing at her watch – her parting gift from Kerne House – she went along to Gerald's room for his approval. She knocked and entered.

Sitting in his chair, he looked very handsome in his dinner jacket and his eyes lit up when he saw her.

'Enchanting, my dear Agnes,' he said and she blushed to the roots of her hair. 'You'll have to get used to compliments, my dear.'

'Not many have come my way up to now,' she said with some of the old sparkle. 'Do you like my hair?'

'Lovely. Get rid of that though.'

'What?'

'That watch.'

'No, I like it, it was my parting gift from Kerne House.'

'Get rid of it, it spoils your outfit.'

Reluctantly Agnes took it off and put it on the side table, she would collect it tomorrow.

'Agnes, I'll buy you a watch.'

She nodded. Gerald couldn't be expected to know how much the watch meant to her and she knew in her heart of hearts that no matter how much he paid for one it could never give her the thrill of owning that first timepiece.

'Are you ready then?'

'Yes.' As ready as I'll ever be, she thought. She watched him as he reached for his crutches.

Together they went along to the drawing-room and Agnes kept turning the ring on her finger and forcing herself to be calm. Her hands felt clammy and she worried about the handshake. Taking a handkerchief out of the small pouch she carried, she wiped them.

'Give a small knock then open the door. It isn't usual,' he said seeing her expression, 'but this is a special occasion.'

They were both in and she closed the door just as Adrian Patterson got to his feet. He was broad-shouldered, of slightly above average height with brown hair just beginning to recede. Like Gerald he wore a dinner jacket. Olive Patterson watched her brother-in-law until he was safely seated. From the chair he said.

'Adrian, Olive, this is my fianceé, Agnes.'

Just then Gertrude breezed in. 'Sorry I'm late, folks, I got tied up.'

'With a horse I expect,' her brother Adrian said.

She gave him a withering look then smiled as he crossed to Agnes and extended a hand. He said nothing but his piercingly blue eyes seemed to go right through her.

'How do you do, sir?'

Olive gave a small titter. 'Now that you are to be family, dear, you'll have to learn to call my husband Adrian. That right, Adrian?'

'Yes, yes, of course.'

Agnes was looking uncertain, she hadn't been offered a seat then she was and she was grateful.

'Come and sit beside me on the sofa, Agnes,' Olive said kindly. She was a plump woman in a flame-coloured dress.

'Thank you.'

'May I say how charming you look.'

'I take quite a lot of the credit for that,' Gertrude said as she drew her chair closer to Gerald's. 'And no wisecracks, Adrian, if you please.'

'Nothing was further from my mind and isn't it time we drank a toast to Gerald and Agnes?'

'You do the honours then,' his wife said.

Suitable words had been said and they were all holding a glass of champagne. Agnes felt her face stiff with having to keep a smile there and she was just congratulating herself that things were going better than she had expected when a little of the champagne went down the wrong way and Agnes spluttered into her handkerchief which she had fortunately taken out of her pouch.

'I'm sorry,' she said with an agonised look in Gerald's direction but he wasn't looking.

'Don't worry,' Olive said putting her own glass down, 'I've done that myself. Much overrated, I don't like it.'

Gertrude laughed. 'Olive used to check that no one was looking then pour hers into the nearest plant.'

'No wonder we have such a healthy lot of plants at Drumoaks,' Gerald said.

'That was when I was young and silly, but enough of this, isn't that the dinner gong I hear?'

Afterwards Agnes could never have said what she ate but from all accounts it was an excellent meal. It was served by Beatrice who looked at Agnes as though she had never seen her before. Back in the drawing-room where the coffee was served Beatrice handed a cup to Agnes. 'Thank you, Beatrice,' she said and smiled and was rewarded with what was very like a wink. The conversation had drifted to people she didn't know and Agnes was glad to sink into her own thoughts. Soon the staff would be settling down to their meal in the kitchen, tucking in and chatting and Agnes had a few moments of envy. It was all such a strain thinking before she spoke and watching her manners. Come to think about it, it was more exhausting than a day's work in the kitchen.

It was after breakfast the next morning and she'd left Gerald reading the newspapers. The May sunshine was streaming through the windows and she decided to have a walk in the grounds. Crossing the hall she came face to face with Beatrice.

'Hello!'

'Can't speak, not allowed,' she muttered.

'That's ridiculous, of course you can speak to me. Anyway I'm speaking to you.'

'Never got the chance to wish you all the best but I do.'

'Thanks.'

'There's a letter for you in that pile on the hall table,' she said as she began flicking a duster around.

Agnes found her letter, saw that it had a Dundee postmark and her heart began to thud. She put it in her pocket and on an impulse she took off the watch, her parting gift, and handed it to Beatrice.

'Tell Madge she can stop saving up for one, she can have mine.'

'She'll be thrilled. Somebody's coming,' she said agitatedly. 'I'm going or I'll be out of a job.'

'Not if I have any say in the matter.' But she didn't object to Beatrice scurrying away, she was anxious to be on her own to read the letter. There was an old summer house in a state of disrepair and Gerald had said that it wasn't worth the money to restore, and very shortly it would be removed and that part of the garden tidied up. No one would be there and she made for it. Rain had seeped through and damaged much of the interior but the cane chair looked reasonably clean and she sat down. With a shaking hand she opened the envelope and drew out – her own letter. The feeling of disappointment was so great that she could have wept. Then as she opened it out she saw that there was an address at the foot of the page. Nothing else, just the address but it was all Agnes wanted. Duncairn House, Hillend, Perthshire, she read it out aloud. Heavens! They weren't all that many miles apart.

Going back to the house she went in search of Gerald and found him in the library.

'Come for a lesson?' he joked.

'No, I have not. You can further my education some other time. Right now I have something important to tell you. I've got Rachel's address.'

'Good, you'll be able to write to her then.'

'She's at Duncairn House, the address is Hillend, Perthshire.'

He raised an eyebrow. 'Not so far away. If I recall correctly it belongs to the Craig family.'

'Do you know them?'

'Not personally.'

'I'm not going to write, Gerald, I'm going to see Rachel and surprise her. You won't know anything about buses but I'll find out.'

'Your days of travelling by bus are over, Agnes,' Gerald said firmly.

'Who says so?'

'I do.'

'I'll travel by bus if I want, we aren't married yet,' she said stubbornly and added silently, and after that too.

'Just listen to me will you? Since you are not writing to your friend you cannot know for sure that she will be there. What I suggest is that Bannerman drives you there, you will ascertain if your friend is available and if she is then tell him when to return for you. Should she not be there Bannerman will drive you back here. Now doesn't that make sense?'

She smiled sheepishly. 'Yes, it does and thanks.'

Chapter Twenty-Five

'Hello, Dr McGregor,' Ian turned and smiled at Rachel and she got to her feet. The unexpectedness of seeing Peter had brought a tell-tale flush to her cheeks and her breathing had become fluttery. In casual clothes Peter was handsome, in formal dress even more so. She wished that she could be as relaxed as he appeared.

'May I say how very lovely you look, Rachel,' Peter said softly as he led her on to the dance floor.

'Thank you,' she murmured.

As she went into his arms the strains of the waltz filled the room. She liked the way he held her, firm but without the pressure Ian seemed to find necessary. Soon her breathing became normal and her nervousness vanished. Her feet were obeying the music, Peter was easy to follow, no silly little extra steps, and she gave herself up to the sheer enjoyment of being in his arms. As more couples took to the floor, the lights were dimmed to a romantic glow and Rachel willed the music to go on for ever. The touch of his lips on her brow sent her heart fluttering wildly and she closed her eyes. All too soon the music died away and stopped, the lights went on and was it her imagination or did she hear an echo of her own sigh?

Other eyes had followed them. Other eyes had seen that tender moment and Betsy was almost trembling with rage. How dare that girl be here. Had she known she would have declined to dance with Clive and hung on to Peter, but she had wanted Peter to see that she was desirable to other men. She wanted to make him jealous, instead of which she had sent him straight into the arms of that hateful creature. In fact he must have made a beeline for her. Just as infuriating was Clive asking about the stunning girl in the tangerine gown. Betsy had pretended not to hear.

She wanted to weep. Her own peach-coloured gown had been bought especially for the occasion and everyone had said how lovely she looked. In the mirror she had smiled happily at her reflection, enchanted at what she saw. Peter, she thought, couldn't fail to see that she was a beautiful, desirable woman and tonight she wanted a lot more than the usual peck on the cheek. If necessary, and she hoped it wouldn't be, she'd take the initiative. Now all that was ruined. Peter seemed obsessed with that servant girl and something would have to be done about it. It was just too humiliating. Destroying the letters hadn't been enough.

Her eyes narrowed. That tangerine gown, she knew it, had wanted it for herself but had had to agree with her mother and the woman in the shop that it just wasn't her. Where did a servant girl get the money to buy a model gown? There was something here that needed investigating.

Betsy left Clive abruptly and made her way to where Peter and Rachel were smiling into each other's eyes as though they were in a world of their own. The voice startled them and they drew apart.

'Come along, Peter, have you forgotten that we are going into supper with Marie and Angus?' Betsy said sharply.

'No, I hadn't.' She saw by his quick frown that she had annoyed him. 'Just let me take—' He turned but Rachel had already slipped away leaving him with only a glimpse of the tangerine gown before it was lost to sight.

'What's the matter, Betsy?' Marie asked as they joined the queue and Peter and Angus were in conversation.

'Nothing,' Betsy said shortly.

'Sorry, you seemed a bit upset that's all.'

'If I am it is because of this queue, I hate waiting like this.'

'We're moving quite quickly, I thought.' Betsy was a spoilt little madam and something had most certainly displeased her but she wasn't going to be the one to humour her, Peter could do that. The foursome hadn't been her idea.

Rachel had left her bag on the chair. She lifted it and sat down. Her feelings were mixed. She couldn't deny to herself that she was in love with Peter but she couldn't understand him and Betsy had been furious.

Her thoughts were interrupted as Ian returned after having danced with the petite and pretty daughter of a neighbouring farmer. He was still smiling.

'Stella's wee but boy can she dance,' then as an afterthought. 'Didn't know that you and the good doctor were acquainted,' he said as he sat down.

'Dr McGregor visits Mrs Craig.'

'Seems interested in the granddaughter, he's here with her.'

'Come on, Ian,' someone shouted, 'grub is up and you're not usually so slow.'

'Just coming,' he shouted back. He held Rachel's hand as they joined the group. There was a lot of laughter and hilarity among people very much at ease with one another. Most were farming people or with farming interests. 'I apologise for that rowdy lot.'

'No need, they are just enjoying themselves.'

'And you, are you enjoying it?'

'Very much indeed,' she said smiling into his face.

On the long white-clothed tables were every imaginable delicacy and on another were liquid refreshments of every kind.

'Some spread, wouldn't you agree?' Ian said as though he'd had a hand in its preparation.

'Never seen anything like it,' she said truthfully as Ian began to introduce her to his friends. Stella had joined the group and Rachel couldn't fail to see the way she looked at Ian, a wistful look that told its own story. The girl was in love with Ian but there was no resentment or jealousy in the smile she gave Rachel.

'I love your gown, everybody is remarking on it,' she said shyly.

'Thank you, it was kind of you to say so and may I say how very sweet and charming you look.'

Ian came and put an arm round each of them. 'Come on, girls, get a plate and help yourself.'

After the supper Ian did his duty dances and Rachel found herself much in demand. On the crowded dance floor she saw Peter and Betsy and flashed him a smile to let him see how much she was enjoying herself. Strangely enough he didn't appear all that happy himself.

She had the last dance with Ian. She knew that he didn't drink much but she had the uncomfortable feeling that he'd had more than usual. His cheek touching hers she could hardly object to that, but his murmured endearments made her increasingly uneasy. On the occasions she had been out with him he had behaved as she would have wished, a kiss after a pleasant evening. She hoped that what was ahead was no more than that. Unfair to Ian she knew it was, after all she owed the evening to him, but the truth was she couldn't help thinking of Peter and his arms were the only arms she wanted around her.

Car doors banged, good nights were shouted across the car park. Ian carefully tucked her gown in to be free of the door then went round to the driver's side.

'Thank you, Ian, for a very enjoyable evening, it has been lovely.'

One hand came off the steering wheel to pat her knee. 'Save it for later, then you can tell me just how much you enjoyed it.' He gave a secret, satisfied smile.

'Why later?' But she had the sinking feeling that she knew what he was leading up to.

'Perfect little spot and it's not far off the road.'

'No, Ian,' she said sharply. 'I don't want that.'

'Stop kidding yourself, of course you do.'

'I meant what I said. It's been a lovely evening, Ian, don't spoil it, please. I want back to Duncairn House, straight back to Duncairn House.'

'Know how to lead a fellow on, don't you?'

'That is just not true and if you got that impression I am very sorry.'

She could sense his anger but was not prepared for his words.

'Bit high and mighty for a servant girl, aren't you? They don't usually put up much resistance, but could be you're just playing hard to get.'

'Stop the car this instant,' she said icily, 'I'll walk the rest of the way.'

'Shut up and don't be so ridiculous.' They had been going slowly but now his foot went down hard and she clung desperately to the seat as the car screeched round corners on the narrow, twisting road.

Believing it would only make him worse Rachel didn't shout to him to slow down but she was terrified that some other vehicle could be coming towards them. Thankfully they met no one and with a squeal of brakes he brought the car to a standstill then dropped his head on the steering wheel.

'Ian,' she said uncertainly.

His head came up and he gave her a sheepish, apologetic look. 'I'm sorry, I don't know what got into me.'

'It's all right,' she said shakily as she opened the door and got out, 'but please do be careful on your way home.'

'Is this the end for us, Rachel?'

'I think it has to be, Ian, and I'm genuinely sorry if I – if I—'

He shook his head. 'You didn't lead me on, that was just wishful thinking on my part. I'm sorry I spoilt the evening for you.'

'It was a wonderful, an unforgettable evening and thank you again.'

She could hardly tell him that it had been unforgettable for those precious minutes she had been in another's arms.

'Still friends?'

'Of course.'

'Goodnight then.'

'Goodnight, Ian.'

He drove off after she was inside. Not wishing to disturb anybody, Rachel went quickly and quietly to her own room glad of the light that had been left on for her benefit. Stepping out of the gown she wondered if there would ever be another occasion to wear it. Sighing, she put it on a coat-hanger and hung it on the outside of the wardrobe where it would remain until the morning.

Routine set in dulling the pain but the ache remained. One day followed the next, the fourteenth of April, her eighteenth birthday passed without notice. No one cared, no one sent her a card. Her own fault, a hint to Janet and Hetty and there would have been some kind of celebration but Rachel hadn't wished it. She was in no mood to celebrate.

The sky had darkened as she was returning from the village and hearing the growl of thunder she quickened her pace. As the firt spots of rain fell on her face she wished that she'd had the sense to bring a raincoat or an umbrella but then when she left the weather had seemed settled. It was getting heavier with a flash of lightning followed by a roll of thunder. She looked about her for some place to shelter but there was nothing. Only the trees but she knew that to shelter there was dangerous in case lightning struck. With only a cotton dress, cardigan and flimsy sandals she was going to get well and truly soaked. At first she didn't hear the call, only the swishing of tyres warned her of an approaching car. She drew further into the side until it would pass.

'Rachel!'

This time she heard her name, saw the passenger door being opened and only then did she see that the driver was Peter.

'In you get, quickly.'

She needed no second bidding. 'Thank you very much for stopping. I didn't expect this kind of weather when I left.'

'So it would appear.' He was just beginning to get up speed when the heavens opened and sheets of rain came down. 'My windscreen wipers won't take this, Rachel, we'll have to pull in until it passes.' Inching along he got the car to where it would not be a hazard to oncoming traffic.

'Can't remember seeing rain like this before.'

'It doesn't happen often, thank goodness.' They were both silent for a few moments then he said, 'Did you enjoy the dance?'

'Yes, I did, very much.'

'Ian Thompson the steady boyfriend?'

'No, he isn't,' she said curtly, 'he's a friend that's all.'

'I'm really disappointed in you, Rachel.'

'And why should that be so?'

'Not replying to my letters. I sent a second in case the first had gone astray. You see I gave you the benefit of the doubt.'

'Peter, I did not receive either of your letters.'

'But you must have.'

'I assure you I did not. If I had I would have replied.'

'That is what I thought. Can't understand it,' he said sounding puzzled. 'My writing is shockingly bad but letters usually arrive at their destination.'

Her heart was singing. 'What – what were you writing about?'

'Can't you guess?'

'I'd rather you told me.'

'Very well. I wanted to see you again and you can't begin to know how disappointed I was. Surely you expected me to get in touch?'

She was smiling now. 'I must admit I hoped to hear from you and when I didn't—' she shrugged.

'You gave up on me. Oh, Rachel! Rachel!'

The smile left her face as she remembered Betsy. 'What about Betsy?'

'What about her?'

'I think she is in love with you and I know it's generally believed—'

'She's just a kid,' he exploded, 'and there is absolutely—' he seemed lost for words. 'Look Rachel, I get roped in to escort her to various functions – family pressure, but that stops now and would have stopped before this if I'd had an inkling of what was being said.'

'Peter, I think Betsy's in love with you. I'm sure she is.'

'Stuff and nonsense, if anything she is just using me to give Brian Meldrum a hard time. The poor lad is besotted with her.' He turned to smile into her eyes. 'Satisfied now?'

'Yes.'

'From now on I'm calling at Duncairn House and demanding to see you and if I'm not admitted then I'll stay put in the car until you come out.'

'You are Mrs Craig's blue-eyed boy', Rachel said mischievously, 'she wouldn't do that to you.'

Neither knew how it happened but in that cramped space she was in his arms, his lips on hers in a kiss that left them both breathless. He kept hold of her hand. 'By a stroke of bad luck I'm to be in Birmingham next week, a medical conference and impossible to get out of since I made such a fuss about wanting to attend.'

'You must go, of course you must.'

'The minute I get back we'll be together.'

'Provided I can arrange the time off. Incidentally it's stopped raining or hadn't you noticed?'

'What a pity. Not often I bless a storm but this one I do,' he said as he started up the engine. He drove to the gates of Duncairn House, kissed her lightly on the lips and waited until she was well up the drive before moving away.

Was it possible to be exhausted with happiness? She thought it must be. All she wanted was to throw herself on the bed and go over each detail of the time she had been with Peter but such a luxury would have to wait. After changing out of her damp clothes into her serviceable dress Rachel went along to her grandmother. She would have had her rest and be ready for a chapter of her book. Just recently the old lady had seemed confused, dwelling in the past she called it. Amelia's name was never mentioned yet Rachel felt sure that it was of her younger daughter she was thinking.

'Your voice, certain movements of your head and I'm reminded of someone—' she shook her head and seemed perplexed and there and then Rachel decided the time had come to reveal her identity but first she wanted to tell Peter.

Leaving her grandmother's room she saw Mrs Anderson hurrying over to her.

'Rachel, you have a visitor.'

'A visitor for me?' she said sounding her surprise.

'Yes, a very charming young lady. I've shown her into the morning-room.'

What was Mrs Anderson thinking of, the morning-room was for family guests.

'Come along, you don't want to keep her waiting.' Mystified, Rachel followed her along the passageway and pushed open the door. A girl got up from the chair and gave a squeal of delight.

'Agnes! Agnes! Oh, Agnes! I don't believe this,' she cried as the two friends hugged one another. Becoming aware of Mrs Anderson still hovering, Rachel broke away. 'Agnes is my school friend, my best friend, and we haven't seen each other for ages and ages.'

'Mrs Anderson, would you do me a great favour?' Agnes said in her recently acquired cultured voice.'

'You want some time together, of course I understand, and Rachel is excused her duties.' She smiled as though bestowing a great favour.

'How very kind of you. I have a car waiting, just let me run down and tell the driver—'

'Not at all. Hetty or one of the others can go down and give him your message.'

'An hour, is that asking too much?'

'No, that will be all right.'

'Agnes, you besom,' Rachel said as they both dissolved into helpless laughter, 'come on up to my room, no one will interrupt us there.'

Once inside Rachel's room and the door shut she took a long look at Agnes and shook her head. 'You look absolutely marvellous, hair, clothes, everything and what is this?' she said pouncing on Agnes's left hand and admiring the ring. 'An engagement ring, it's beautiful. This is you getting married,' she said softly.

'Yes. Oh, God, I've so much to tell you,' she said sounding like the old Agnes. 'Where to begin, yes I know where to begin, how could you leave without a word to me? I was hurt and angry.'

'Agnes, I wrote to you, wrote two letters as a matter of fact and I was hurt at not getting a reply.'

'Honestly, Rachel, I didn't get either.'

'The first I sent to Spinner's Lane.'

'Must have been after they moved house. The whole shooting match was knocked down. Ma's in a corporation house.'

'Does she like it?'

'Not much.'

'The other I sent to Kerne House.'

'Moved from there to Drumoaks in Kirriemuir. With the hope of hearing from you I left my new address. Tell you, I could murder that lot.'

'How did you get this address?'

'Your da, I wrote to him.'

'And he told you?' Agnes saw the look of pain.

'Just returned my own letter with this address on it.'

'I wish I could turn the clock back, Agnes.'

'Sorry you took off like that?'

'Yes, I am. I don't regret leaving Dundee, only the way I did it.'

'You could put that right.'

'Not so easy, there are complications – but enough about me.'

'I'm someone to talk about getting in touch. I never go near my family but then if you remember I made up my mind about that a long time ago.'

'Do you miss them?'

'In all honesty, no, just Meg, I miss her. Oh, better tell you, Sam, the man in her life, made an honest woman of her and they dote on the wee lad. Really happy they are.'

'I'm glad and now before I burst with curiosity, tell me about the man in your life and this wonderful new Agnes. Chauffeur-driven cars and the like.'

'We'll skip Kerne House, it served its purpose and from there I got a job at Drumoaks.' A born storyteller, Agnes embroidered on her first meeting in the library and had Rachel in stitches. Then her eyes widened as Agnes told her friend everything.

'Sounds like a fairy tale, younger son falls in love with the maid who blossoms into the lovely creature with me here. What is he like?'

'Gerald is thirty-two, very intelligent, nice-looking and by this time you must be wondering what on earth he sees in me?'

'He saw someone very special,' Rachel said softly then added, 'You are in love with him, aren't you?'

'You are remembering what I said, that respect and liking were enough?' She paused. 'I do love him, Rachel, I don't know when it happened, but I do. But I'm confused too, about love, I mean. There was an ordinary working bloke I thought I was in love with but he wasn't good enough for me or so I thought.'

'You got over him?'

'That's just it, I'm not sure.'

'Meet him again and you probably wouldn't give him a second look.'

'You could be right at that.'

'What does your fiancé do?'

'Gerald helps his brother to run the estate. He was to be a schoolmaster at one of those posh schools but he had this accident. Bloody tree fell on his legs and he'll never walk again.'

'Poor, poor man.'

'He gets frustrated and has a filthy temper and I'm the only one who can help him. That's because I don't give him sympathy, to my way of thinking he's had too much of it already.'

Poor Agnes, Rachel thought, life wasn't going to be a bed of roses.

'The girl he was to marry threw him over, couldn't bear the thought of being married to a cripple.'

'Well rid of her then and I hope he appreciates the treasure he's got in you.'

'Oh, Rachel, you can't know the relief it is to be able to talk freely and you are the only one with whom I can do that.' She giggled. 'Please note the "with whom". I'm hot on that. All this is a far cry from Spinner's Lane, isn't it?' There were tears in the brown eyes. 'I owe Gerald such a lot, he's made me the person I am and I want to be worthy of him.'

'You will be, Agnes,' Rachel said gently, then added, 'What about Gerald's family?'

'Not exactly thrilled, you wouldn't expect them to be, would you? But they are quite pleasant and I like his unmarried sister, Gertrude.'

'In time they will all love you.'

'No, that won't happen, I'll never quite fit but enough of that. Now I'm coming to the important bit. I want you to be my bridesmaid, Rachel.'

'Agnes, I'd love to be your bridesmaid and I'm very honoured.'

'Needless to say it will be very quiet, immediate family only, and no one from mine of course, but that is the way I want it.' She paused. 'That was why I was so desperate to find you. You were the only one I wanted with me.'

'I'm so glad we've found each other and we're never going to lose touch again,' Rachel said firmly. 'Is Gerald's brother to be best man?'

'No, an old school chum and immediately he said that I said I wanted my school chum too.'

'You like his sister and that's important. What is she like?'

'Gertrude? Very county if you know what I mean, tweeds, pearls and flat-heeled shoes. Mad about horses and Adrian, her brother, says she looks like one.'

'Beastly man.'

'Water off a duck's back, that lot can insult each other but it doesn't seem to bother them. Us now, we'd fly off the handle.'

'I most certainly would if someone told me I looked like a horse.'

'No danger of that, even in that maid's outfit you look terrific. Like my ma said you could wear a dishcloth and look marvellous.'

'Same old Agnes under all that finery.'

'Before I forget, when is your day off?'

'Tuesday.'

'Could you manage to get yourself to Perth?'

'No problem.'

'Meet you about eleven o'clock outside McNeil's.'

'Window shopping, I hope, I can't stretch to their prices.'

'All goes on Gerald's account and don't start objecting, it is the bride's privilege. Honestly, Rachel, he's terribly generous and he'll want us to get something very special. That said I must be careful to see that you don't outshine me.'

'Not a chance.'

'Unfortunately there is every chance. And now tell me about you, there must be someone in your life.'

It was too soon to talk about Peter. 'There is someone, Agnes, but there is a lot to tell you and there just isn't the time. I hate to say it, but the hour is up and I don't want Mrs Anderson to think I am taking advantage.'

'No, right enough, she's been very decent.'

'Only because you impressed her,' Rachel said getting up from the bed and smoothing the cover.

At the door they hugged each other. 'Until Tuesday,' Agnes said.

'Until Tuesday,' Rachel smiled and watched her friend hurry down the drive.

At Drumoaks the June sunlight streamed through the open windows and the air was scented with the flowers which had been picked that morning to grace the window-sills and tops of furniture. The joining together of Agnes and Gerald was to take place at two thirty and Bannerman had been despatched to Duncairn House in the morning to pick up Rachel.

She sat in the back of the car with her carefully wrapped parcel. The problem of a gift had at last been solved. She had chosen book ends, plain but good looking. Not exciting but she rather thought that Agnes would like them.

How was Agnes feeling, she wondered? Was she apprehensive now that the big day was here? Rachel just wished that there had been an opportunity to meet Gerald but there had been no time. The journey was completed in silence and then Rachel got her first look at Drumoaks. She couldn't but be impressed; it was very big and very grand. Much grander than Duncairn House, but to her mind not so attractive. There was a brooding look about it and her first impression was of a very old family house with its own dark secrets.

As Bannerman opened the door for her Agnes came flying down the steps to greet her. 'I told Gerald that I want you all to myself for the first hour at least.' She was trying to appear cool and calm but Rachel knew that she was far from that, that her nerves were taut as violin strings.

'For you,' Rachel said handing her the parcel.

'You shouldn't, you know. I seem to have everything, but thank you very much. Do you mind if I take you up to the bedroom? I always feel more relaxed there.'

'So do I.'

Inside the bedroom Agnes tore off the wrapping.

'Not very exciting,' Rachel apologised.

'It's perfect, quite perfect and very special because it is from you.'

Rachel looked at her worriedly, she didn't seem able to keep still.

A maid arrived with coffee. 'Thanks, Madge.' They smiled at each other then the girl went out.

'Awful, isn't it? She's my friend and she's not allowed to talk to me.'

'It's a difficult situation, but you'll get used to it, Agnes.'

'I'll have to, won't I? You pour the coffee, Rachel, I'm sure to spill it.'

'Yes, of course,' she said going over to the tray, 'but listen, Agnes, you were never the nervous type so calm down and just be yourself. Take a deep breath and say to yourself: this is my day and I'm going to enjoy every moment of it.'

'Some hope, I'll be glad when it's all over and if you drink up that coffee we'll go down to the sitting-room, they should all be there now.'

Rachel put down her unfinished coffee and got up. Agnes's

nervousness was affecting her too and she was glad to be going downstairs and getting the introductions over.

When they entered Adrian Patterson stood up but Agnes drew Rachel over to where Gerald sat.

'Gerald, this is Rachel.'

He held out his hand and Rachel felt its firm grip. 'You must excuse me for not getting up but may I say how delighted I am, how delighted we all are, to meet a friend of Agnes's.'

'Thank you, Mr Patterson, I'm very pleased to be here,' she said quietly.

'Gerald will do.'

I like him, she thought, and felt a wave of compassion for this man confined to a wheelchair or crutches.

'My brother, Adrian, the head of the household and his wife, Olive.'

Rachel smiled and shook hands. 'My sister, Gertrude.' A tall woman had got off her seat and gone over to Rachel. Keen eyes looked into hers then nodded as though satisfied.

'Welcome to Drumoaks.'

'Thank you.' A door banged, there were voices then a head popped round the door.

'Ah, this is where you all are.'

'Mike, come in,' Gerald called. 'I think this is what you call a full house now. Bride, groom, best man and bridesmaid all present and correct.'

It was said in a jocular fashion but Rachel had the impression that Gerald was almost as keyed up as Agnes.

'Like me, Agnes wanted her school friend to be present. Let me introduce you. Mike, this is Agnes's friend, Rachel Donaldson. Rachel, this is Michael Fairweather.' Another firm handshake.

He wasn't very tall with broad shoulders, his hair was dark and his complexion sallow, an ordinary-looking man except for the intensity of his grey eyes.

'Touch and go whether Mike would manage. A happy event is expected any time now but we are hoping Daphne will oblige by waiting another few hours.'

There followed a murmur of voices. 'Daphne looked positively blooming last time I saw her,' Olive smiled, 'but we do understand and you must just dash off after the ceremony.'

A light refreshment was served at midday then they separated. Agnes and Rachel went upstairs. 'So far so good,' she breathed.

'Gerald is charming, Agnes, and so are the others.'

'They took to you, that was easy to see. You can have a room to yourself to change or share mine.'

'Share yours, of course, silly question I would have thought.'

'Thought you would say that so had both our outfits spread out on the bed.'

Rachel thought back to when they were in McNeil's. Agnes suited green, it was her favourite colour but Miss Inglis had looked worried. She had the responsibility that both girls chose wisely.

In the end Agnes decided on a dress in eggshell blue, plain but stylish, with a bolero embroidered in a darker blue. Rachel let Agnes choose for her. And her choice was a dress in salmon pink with long sleeves that ended in a broad cuff secured by pearl buttons. It had a scooped-out neckline that showed Rachel's long, graceful neck.

'Put that away,' Agnes ordered as Rachel took out the thin chain she intended wearing round her neck. 'Your gift from Gerald,' she said, handing Rachel a long, narrow, velvet-covered case. Taken aback Rachel opened it and gasped. She didn't have to be told that she was looking at real pearls.

'I couldn't, Agnes, it is far too much.'

'It is not and you can. Turn round and I'll fasten them for you.'

Rachel stood admiring herself in the mirror then turned to the bride. A small smile played round her mouth as she looked at the lovely auburn-haired girl and just for a moment her thoughts went back to the child in the heavy clumsy boots and the ill-fitting hand-me-down clothes.

'What are you thinking about?'

'You, Agnes,' she said softly. 'Gerald won't be able to take his eyes off his beautiful bride.'

'I still expect to waken up and find it all a dream.'

'It's real, Agnes.'

'I'm scared, Rachel,' she whispered. 'I've just discovered the truth that I'm acting a part and I'm wondering how long I can keep up the performance.'

'It's not an act, this is the real you.'

She grimaced. 'The real Agnes is just under the surface, the Agnes

Boyd of Spinner's Lane. No,' she said as Rachel made to speak. 'That boy I told you about, he said – he said – that a lady was born that I'd always be working class. He was right, Rachel, he said they would accept me only for as long as I was of use to them.'

'He's wrong, so very, very wrong and I think he sounds horrible. Thank goodness you had nothing more to do with him. I bet he just said it because you wouldn't have him.'

'The family are accepting this marriage without too much show of opposition because I am relieving them of a burden.'

'What on earth do you mean?'

'Gerald has terrible bouts of depression and an explosive temper and there have been times, Gertrude told me, when the family has been at its wits' end. He has a manservant, Bannerman.'

'He drove me here?'

'Yes, and as you would see he is getting on a bit. Up to now he's looked after Gerald and drives him here and there. Later on Gertrude wants me to take lessons and learn to drive. To put it bluntly I am really a future replacement for Bannerman.'

'What absolute nonsense. If that was all he wanted he would have employed another manservant.'

Agnes managed a smile. 'He likes me, he likes being with me but that is a far cry from being in love with me.'

'I have a feeling that everything will work out for you.'

'Of course it will, just pre-wedding nerves. Ready?'

'Yes.'

'Then we'll get ourselves downstairs.'

'One minute, you didn't let me see your watch.'

'My gift from Gerald,' she said, holding her arm up to show the tiny wristwatch encrusted with diamonds.

'It's beautiful, you must be thrilled.'

Agnes smiled. 'I am but I'll let you into a secret. My first watch was a cheap little thing, from a pawnbroker's actually and was my gift from Kerne House when I left. Nothing but nothing could ever give me the same thrill again.'

Agnes opened the door to the knock. 'We're just coming, Gertrude, come in and give us the once-over before we go down.'

Gertrude nodded approvingly, 'Very nice, both of you.'

'That goes for you too, Gertrude,' Agnes said unsuccessfully hiding her surprise. The change was quite startling. In her lovat green soft wool suit and her small-heeled court hoes she didn't look the same person.

'Thank you,' she said gruffly, 'I do occasionally make the effort and this is one.' She smiled at them both. 'Since you two were such close friends you must keep in touch, but I expect we will see you occasionally at Drumoaks.'

'The Laurels, Gertrude,' Agnes reminded her.

'Dear me, yes, I almost forgot, but the invitation still stands.'

Gertrude led the way down the broad stair with its thick carpet and shiny brass rods keeping it in place. Not so long ago it had been Agnes's job to polish those same rods.

They were all there in the drawing-room. Gerald in his wheelchair, the minister having a few words with him then he spoke to Agnes and smiled at Rachel.

It was over, they were man and wife. No photographer was there to take photographs of the bride and bridegroom. It had been Gerald's wish and though saddened, Agnes had tried to understand. The cake had come from a leading Perth baker and bride and groom, their hands together on the knife, cut through it. Beatrice, solemn-faced, cut up the cake into dainty pieces and handed them round. Drinks were poured, the bridegroom made a short but fitting speech and everyone shook hands with Gerald and gave a peck to the bride's cheek.

Rachel managed a few words with Gerald. 'Thank you very much indeed, Gerald, for the lovely pearls. I shall always treasure them.'

'My pleasure to see them on such a lovely young woman.'

She would have had to be blind not to see the admiration in his eyes and she knew that this was a man who had appealed to women and who had probably flirted outrageously.

'Thank you.' Agnes had returned and he took her hand in his. 'Agnes, I was about to tell your charming friend that she will be a welcome visitor in our home.'

'Rachel knows that, I told her,' Agnes said shortly.

No one could have faulted the meal but Agnes found that she had no appetite. The demon jealousy had raised its ugly head and that sick, humiliating feeling attacked her again making her want to cry out her frustration. For heaven's sake, Rachel was just a maid, a nobody and she had thought to impress her. She should have known better, there was no envy in Rachel's heart only a genuine wish for her friend's happiness.

By rights, in such company, Rachel should have been paralysed with fright as she herself had been, but instead here she was, completely at ease and chatting away as if she were their equal. Yet she wasn't trying to impress, she was just being herself.

Everyone had gone home. After driving Rachel back to Duncairn House, Bannerman returned to drive the newly weds to the Laurels which had undergone a thorough cleaning. The decorators had been in and everything looked bright and fresh. Curtains had been cleaned and some replaced.

'Don't you want to change anything, Agnes?' Gerald had asked her.

'Not at the moment, everything looks fine to me.'

'In time you'll want to make your own mark but if you're happy as things are there is no rush.'

She looked about her, the house was as big as Kerne House and she was the mistress. Her dream had been realised, she had arrived but instead of being deliriously happy she felt flat and deep down she knew the reason for it. Rachel. Gerald was looking at her and it was though he were reading her mind.

'We all thought your friend quite charming, a delightful girl.'

'So I gathered.'

'If I may say so a strange relationship.'

'Why?'

'Because, my dear, although you like and admire Rachel, you also resent her. I'm recalling what you told me and at the time I admired you for your honesty. There is a lot about you that I admire, Agnes.'

'Do you, Gerald?' She swallowed painfully. 'Do you feel married? I know I don't.'

He didn't answer the question, just gave her a funny look. 'Did I hear Bannerman come in?'

'Yes. What do you want him for?'

'To help me into something more comfortable.'

'Why can't I do that?'

'Certainly not, that is what Bannerman is here for.'

'You use him as an extra crutch, you don't need him.'

She saw that she had angered him and was holding in his temper with difficulty.

'I am not going to answer that in case I say more than I want.'

Agnes had less control over her temper. 'Fine thing, Bannerman has the bedroom next to yours and mine is upstairs. How do you think I feel about that?'

'I told you that this could never be a proper marriage and you accepted it.'

'In the physical sense, I knew that, but what is wrong in sharing a room? God knows they are all big enough to take two beds.'

'This conversation is distasteful to me.'

'You didn't need to marry me. You could have engaged me as your companion,' she said, and burst into tears.

'A companion, how quaint,' he said trying to hide his amusement. 'Incidentally, Agnes, would you have accepted?'

'You never know, I might have,' she said rubbing at her eyes with a tiny, sodden handkerchief.

'Take mine,' Gerald said, taking a clean, unfolded handkerchief out of his pocket, 'and mop up for heaven's sake or folk will think I'm ill-treating you.'

'I'm not the weeping type and you're the only one who makes me this way I'll have you know.'

'Then I'm more than distressed that it should be I who reduces you to tears.'

'So you should be,' but she was half laughing now.

'As to your reply to my question—'

'What question was that that, I've forgotten?'

'Whether or not you would have agreed to be my – er – companion and your unsatisfactory answer. A refusal was a possibility and I couldn't risk that, hence my offer of a more permanent position.'

'You always manage to put me in the wrong but I'm sorry for the waterworks. I don't know what is the matter with me.'

'I do. Today has been a strain for both of us but it's over and after a night's sleep you'll waken up your old self again.'

Her old self – would she ever be that again? She very much doubted it. The suddenness of having all this responsibility thrust on her was terrifying and she was so afraid of making a fool of herself. Where was the old Agnes Boyd? she asked herself angrily, she was being pathetic.

Gertrude had bent backwards to be helpful insisting that she be present during the interviews for the position of cook/housekeeper and she had been in wholehearted agreement that Mrs Yuill was the most suitable. The woman was forty-five, had excellent references and before her husband's death they had both been employed in a large house, he as head gardener and she as cook. Since then Mrs Yuill had held only temporary jobs and the Laurels would suit her very well. As at Drumoaks extra domestic staff would come from the village, those employed full-time arriving at eight o'clock and the others for the number of hours required. The Laurels was to have one live-in maid and sixteen-year-old Brenda Black had been chosen. She was fair-haired and nondescript and assured them breathlessly that she wasn't afraid of hard work.

Mrs Harrison undertook the job of organising everything at the Laurels to make it ready for Mr Gerald and his bride.

Agnes had got up to wander over to the window then came back and sat on the arm of the chair beside Gerald. Better to say what she had to say now. 'Mind if we get one or two things settled?'

'Not at all.'

'Gerald, I do need some guidance.' She took a deep breath. 'Regarding the bedroom arrangements you've made that clear enough.'

He nodded.

'Now I want your promise that you'll back me up if there are any domestic difficulties.'

'Do you anticipate any?'

'I want to be prepared.'

'Anything you can't handle yourself see Gertrude, or Olive for that matter.'

'No, I don't want to do that.'

'Then you must deal with it yourself.' He paused. 'You will be quite a lot on your own since I'm now involved more in running the estate.'

'Why does Adrian have to be in London so often?'

'Didn't I tell you? Olive lost her father and since she is his only child Adrian has to protect her interests.'

She was biting her lip.

'Something else troubling you? Better deal with it now, Agnes, so out with it.'

'If you must know I'm scared of being laughed at.'

'Who would want to laugh at you?'

'Gerald, until a very short time ago I was a maid at Drumoaks and here I am at nineteen years of age and mistress of the Laurels. The new staff if they don't already know, very soon will.'

'Is that all that is bothering you? Where is Agnes, my brave, spirited girl?'

'She's well and truly lost.'

'No, she's just hiding.' He looked at her kindly and his voice was so gentle that the tears threatened to overflow but she blinked them back. 'Make it a challenge, Agnes, and remember that you are my wife and that is all the authority you need. Start as you mean to finish. Let them know straight away, my dear, that you are mistress and what you say goes and if you have reason to believe that you are not getting their respect then to use your own expression – sack them.'

'Rachel would carry it off better than me.'

'Stop always comparing yourself unfavourably with your friend. You are very different, so cease thinking of yourself as inferior to Rachel.'

'Crazy, isn't it? She's just a maid and I'm Mrs Gerald Patterson.'

He laughed. 'That's the spirit but don't let it go to your head.'

'Ta – thanks, I mean, for the words of wisdom, they've done me good.'

'It's made me thirsty, so pour me a drink if you will, then ring for Bannerman.'

She did so. 'I'll go up and change.'

'Do that then come down and talk to me.'

He watched her leave the room, her shoulders drooping a little, and he felt a rush of guilt. She was young and attractive and for how long would she be content with the life he offered her? There was so much loving in Agnes and she was offering herself to him. It was only his pride that was getting in the way and she was sensible enough to know that a satisfying relationship was possible for them. A crippled body, a crippled mind, was that how he appeared? Was he capable of love, he wondered, or had being jilted made him feel a lesser person and soured him for ever? If only Myra had waited, had let him be the one to break off their engagement. Surely she must have known he would.

Upstairs in the large, lonely room that was to be hers, Agnes looked about her. Dreary would have been her own description – it was essentially a masculine room apart from her own clutter on the dressing-table. There was her make-up, two bottles of perfume, a jewellery box and silver-backed hairbrushes, a gift from Adrian and Olive's children and one from which she got a great deal of pleasure.

There had been that one time when their nanny had been called away and she had been unexpectedly asked to keep an eye on the children. A lucky day though she hadn't thought so at the time. In the garden two pairs of eyes were regarding her unsmilingly.

'Couple of smilers, aren't you?' she mumbled to herself but their sharp ears had caught the words and it set them giggling. Agnes was very much at home with children and apart from speech and manners she didn't imagine these two any different from her own sisters and brothers.

'Want me to tell you a story?'

'Only if we haven't heard it before,' Mark said.

'All my stories are home-made so you can't possibly have heard them.' She sat down between them on the rug spread out on the grass. Stories that had delighted the Boyd children were now amusing Mark and Mary and the return of Nanny was greeted with dismay as she bade her charges to hurry themselves up and return with her to the house.

Olive, tired of hearing from her offspring about the stories, made a point of thanking Agnes personally.

'You obviously know what children like. Where do you get your material?'

'Material?' Agnes repeated, puzzled.

'Your children's stories, where do you get them?'

'Out of my head.'

'You mean you make them up?'

'As I go along.' She grinned. 'If their eyes get like saucers I'm doing all right.'

'My two were certainly impressed. Maybe you should start writing them down, Agnes.'

'What for?'

'Perhaps they are good enough to be published. Show them to Gerald and get his opinion.'

'He would laugh his head off.'

Changing into her green polka-dot dress she began to think seriously about Olive's suggestion. With Gerald occupied for some of the day she could use the time to write down a few of her stories. She wouldn't ask his opinion, she didn't want to be patronised. Perhaps he wouldn't be patronising but she wouldn't risk it. This was something she could do on her own and if, as she supposed likely, her efforts were returned with 'Thanks but no thanks', no one else would know. It would mean writing them out clearly then finding someone to type them. As for publishers she would get them from children's books.

The thought had cheered her, it was something to look forward to. Pleased with her appearance in the mirror she patted her hair into place and went down to join her husband, but this time she held her shoulders back.

Chapter Twenty-Six

Time off was a problem for a busy doctor but it made their time together all the more precious and their love was blossoming.

In the small tearoom where they had become regulars Rachel and Peter were in their usual table tucked away in a corner and far enough away to carry on a conversation without being overhead.

He was looking at her thoughtfully as she poured the tea. 'Rachel, now that you have met my parents and visited my home, don't you think you should tell me about yours?'

She replaced the teapot and nodded her head. 'My mind was made up to tell you everything before I told – before I told someone else.'

He looked puzzled but remained silent.

To prepare herself Rachel took a few sips of the tea then put down her cup and began. 'Peter, did you know that Mrs Craig had a younger daughter by the name of Amelia?'

'Now you mention it I vaguely remember something about a younger daughter running off with some chap.'

'That chap was my father, is my father.'

'That means,' he said slowly and incredulously, 'that you are—'

'Mrs Craig's granddaughter. It's a long and not very happy story but let me begin at the beginning.'

Peter didn't interrupt, time seemed to stand still for them and only when the tearoom was about to close did he lead her out to the car where she finished telling her story.

'I'm not proud of my own part in this, Peter. I blamed my stepmother but looking back I was just as much at fault.'

'It is high time those hurts were healed, my darling.'

'But difficult after all this time.'

'True.' He drew her into his arms cursing the awkwardness of the front seats. 'Of one thing I am very glad.'

'What would that be?'

He grinned wickedly, 'That I proposed to you believing you to be a humble maid.'

She stroked his face and there was a tightness in her throat as she said unsteadily, 'Peter, I am so lucky to have you, you make me feel safe where before I used to feel so alone.'

His arms tightened round her and his voice was husky. 'We'll be together for always, my darling, I love you very, very much.'

'And I love you too, more than I can say.'

With great reluctance he consulted his watch and cursed under his breath. 'If time would just occasionally stand still but alas it won't. These split hours are the very devil,' he said, moving back to start up the car. 'I'll just have time to drop you at Duncairn House before getting myself to the surgery.'

'Will there be many waiting, do you think?' she asked.

'Too many. Half of them don't really need me, just think they do.'

'Reassurance?'

'That and a wee chat,' he laughed. 'Mind you, a friendly neighbour could do as much good, probably more. Of one thing I can assure you, my precious, nothing but nothing is going to spoil Thursday afternoon for us. We go for that ring and I refuse to accept that anything is an emergency.'

'That'll be right, Peter McGregor, and I don't think. With you, your patients will always come first and I wouldn't want you any different.'

'Bless you.'

Happiness was brimming over and her eyes were shining as she let herself in at the servants' door then hurried along the passage. She was late but perhaps no one would notice.

'Rachel!' Hetty was hurrying after her and looking agitated. 'I've been lookin' all over for you.'

'I know I'm late but not by very much. Is something the matter?'

'You're wanted in the sittin'-room, urgent like.'

A terrible fear gripped her. 'Mrs Craig—'

'No, she's fine. Go on, Rachel, don't keep them waitin' any longer.'

Curious rather than worried Rachel went along to the sitting-room, knocked on the door and when told to come in did so. Once inside the room the smile died on her lips and her happiness took a plunge. Rachel had the strongest feeling that something dreadful had happened and that in some way she was to be held responsible. Her grandmother's face was a stern mask as she sat in her chair with her back rod-straight. Sitting close by, Maud Meldrum dropped her eyes rather than meet Rachel's. Betsy, her colour high, was on her feet and going round the back of Rachel. Opening the door she called for Mrs Anderson and the housekeeper came quickly.

'Do be seated, Mrs Anderson,' Betsy said.

Rachel began to tremble without knowing why. 'What is it? What is the matter?' she asked and wishing that she too could sit down.

'You are about to find out though I imagine by the state you look to be in that you've guessed.' She took a deep breath. 'Perhaps you could explain how a brooch of mine came to be in your room. This brooch,' she said, displaying it in her mind.

Rachel was pale with shock but there was growing anger. 'I have never seen it before.'

'That won't do, I'm afraid. Unfortunately for you my memory is good and I recall wearing it when I went into the drawing-room but I didn't have it when I came out. The clasp is faulty and so positive was I that it had fallen off that I went back to check. You were coming out and it was your startled, guilty look that stayed with me.'

Rachel shook her head in bewilderment, made to speak, but Betsy silenced her.

'So sure was I of your guilt that I asked Mrs Anderson to accompany me to your room. Mrs Anderson,' she looked over to the woman, 'you saw this brooch in the girl's room?'

'Yes, Miss Betsy.'

Rachel's eyes were smouldering with anger. 'How dare you search my room when I wasn't present. You had no right to do such a thing.'

'The girl is right there, Betsy, you had no business to do that,' Mrs Craig said.

That hurt, that really hurt, to hear her grandmother call her girl rather than use her name. It meant she had been found guilty without a chance to defend herself.

'Are you denying that it was in your room?' Betsy said haughtily.

'If Mrs Anderson said she saw the brooch in my room then I'm sure she did, but since I didn't put it there someone else did.'

'A likely story,' Betsy sneered, 'and I wonder where you got your other treasures.' She opened a drawer and placed the articles for all to see. 'Such expensive jewellery for a maid to possess. Real pearls no less and what I recognise to be a very valuable brooch.'

Rachel had stopped shaking and a cold anger was urging her on.

'You are perfectly correct, the pearls are real and the brooch is valuable.'

'Where did they come from?'

'That has nothing to do with you.'

'Meaning you can't answer the question.'

'Betsy, I don't think—' her mother started then looked at Rachel. 'Perhaps it would be better and put an end to this unpleasant scene if you were to – if you were to—' she foundered to a stop.

'Very well, Mrs Meldrum,' Rachel said with icy coldness. 'You can decide whether I am a thief or your daughter a liar.'

'How dare you—'

'Be quiet, Betsy,' her grandmother thundered.

'I know nothing about your brooch or perhaps I have my suspicions,' she said looking her cousin full in the face and seeing it change to a dull red. 'The pearls were a gift for being bridesmaid to a friend of mine. As for the brooch,' the voice that had been steady began to shake, 'be kind enough to give it to Mrs Craig.'

Now decidedly uneasy, Betsy handed it to her grandmother.

For a long, long time the old lady kept her eyes on the brooch and then in a voice hoarse with emotion she said.

'Where did you get this?'

'From my mother.'

'Your – mother?' The dropping of a pin could have been heard.

'Yes. My mother was your daughter, Amelia.'

Maud gave a funny little cry and signalled for Mrs Anderson to leave. The housekeeper went quickly and quietly. Betsy was backing to the door, looking terrified and desperate to escape but no one tried to stop her.

'Amelia's daughter,' Mrs Craig shook her head from side to side. 'I should have known—'

Rachel felt the sudden pain take her breath away as she saw her grandmother, that proud, unbending woman, struggling with the tears that filled her eyes then rolled unchecked down the worn cheeks. 'There was something about you, your voice, movements of the head that brought back memories.'

Maud who had been silent all this time now spoke.

'My sister was small and fair and you are so dark.'

'I take after my father,' Rachel said shortly.

'Then he must have been a very handsome man,' her grandmother had recovered a little and spoke in her usual voice.

'You wouldn't know, would you? You couldn't bring yourself to meet a common working man.'

'Bitterness doesn't become the young, my dear.'

'My father was – is a proud man. He wanted to do the right and honourable thing and ask for your daughter's hand in marriage but he didn't get beyond the gate of your Dundee home.'

'Maud, I'd like to be alone with Rachel if you please, and you can tell Betsy and Mrs Anderson that I will deal with them later.'

'Very well,' she got up reluctantly and before leaving looked pleadingly at Rachel. 'It is a lot to ask, I know, Rachel, but try not to hate Betsy. At heart she is a good girl.'

Rachel nodded.

Left alone, her grandmother patted the chair beside her and Rachel, after only the briefest hesitation, went to sit beside her.

'You have a lot of explaining to do, Rachel.'

'So have you and I'd like to hear you first,' Rachel said unsmilingly.

'Very well,' her grandmother said tiredly, 'but it was all such a long time ago.' She sighed but Rachel wasn't helping her. 'Amelia, your mother, was an adorable child and badly spoilt. She was your grandfather's favourite and he didn't hide it. Doing what she did almost broke his heart and he never got over it, my dear.'

'Couldn't he have found it in his heart to forgive her?'

'No, she had done the unforgiveable.'

'And you, Grandmother—' she managed the word this time and was rewarded by a smile and a nod of the head— 'could you find no forgiveness in your heart?'

'My dear, I was caught in the middle and oh, yes, I was prepared to forgive. I wanted my daughter back but my first loyalty had to be to my husband. In these modern times that may sound strange but I am part of a bygone age when a wife obeyed her husband. What I did do, however, was make sure that Amelia was safe and well. Forgive me, but I am not going to tell you how I went about that.'

'Did you know about me?'

'Yes, I knew that Amelia had a daughter and then much later—' her voice broke.

'You heard of her death?'

'Yes, that was a dreadful time. Your grandfather was in a terrible state and it brought on a stroke leaving him paralysed and his memory gone. I sat by him almost constantly until he died.'

Rachel pictured the scene and felt a lump in her throat. Impulsively she reached out and took her grandmother's paper-dry hands in hers.

'We've all suffered, each one of us, and it makes me want to cry to think how little it would have taken to avoid the heartache. My mother missed you, missed her family, I knew that though she said very little.'

'Thank you, my dear.'

'Leaving me your address showed that she wanted me to get in touch. She had my father's promise that he would give it to me when I was old enough to understand.'

'That was good of him, he could have destroyed it and who could have blamed him?'

'He wouldn't have done that, my father is an honourable man.'

The old eyes were pleading. 'Tell me a little about them. Was she happy, my little Amelia?'

'Very happy,' Rachel said softly, 'they adored one another. I was nine when she died but I have only happy memories of those years.'

'The brooch, tell me about it.'

'It was in a little rosewood box, the brooch and a few other pieces. My father said the brooch was valuable, that it had been an eighteenth birthday gift and that I must take great care of it.'

'He said that?'

It wasn't altogether true, she tried to recall his words and knew there had been reluctance to hand over the box with her grandmother's address but why add to the pain? 'Something like that but though he didn't say so I knew that he would have preferred to have me go on believing my grandparents dead. I didn't want to get in touch, didn't think I ever would.'

'What was it that made you change your mind?'

'Let me tell you it in my own way. With the help of a very dear neighbour, we managed quite well, or so I thought. I was too young to understand how deeply my mother's death had affected him and how lonely he was. You see, I thought my company should have been enough for him.'

'My poor child, let me guess, your father eventually found someone else and you resented her.'

'At the time I didn't recognise it as jealousy. You see Peggy was so different from my mother and I couldn't understand what he saw in her. Neither of us made much effort to get on together and in a rebellious mood I decided to leave home without telling anyone.'

'Like mother, like daughter,' she said softly, too softly for Rachel to hear.

'I wanted to hurt my father the way he had hurt me.'

'Yet all he did was take another wife.'

'No, he broke his promise to me and that I could not forgive. I wanted to go to college and the money was there until Peggy arrived on the scene and she wanted this and that and my father seemed unable to say no to her.'

'Poor you, what did you do?'

'Served as a dressmaker's assistant until the business closed and it was then that I made up my mind to see what my mother's people were like.'

'But I don't understand why—'

Rachel smiled. 'Grandmother, I was brought up in a tenement and seeing Duncairn House for the first time terrified me. I couldn't bring myself to go up to the front door and introduce myself as Amelia's daughter.'

'You could have written to me.'

'No, I wasn't prepared to do that in case you tore the letter up.'

'As if I would have done such a thing,' she said indignantly.

'I wasn't to know that, was I?' She smiled as she remembered that day. 'What really happened, Grandmother, was that I found myself at the back door with another girl. Someone, it was Mrs Anderson actually, waved to me to come along quickly and I found that I was being interviewed for the job of maid.'

Her grandmother was wiping the tears of laughter from her eyes. 'My dear, this gets better by the minute but do go on.'

'I was about to tell Mrs Anderson of her mistake when the thought struck me that it was the ideal way to find out about my family without them knowing who I was. If I liked you I was to tell you my true identity and if I didn't then I would stay until I found another position.'

'What was your verdict on us?'

'I grew to love you, Grandmother, though I thought you very intimidating at first. This you will find hard to believe but I had decided this very day to tell you but I wanted Peter to know first.'

'Peter?'

'Peter McGregor,' she said shyly, 'we are engaged to be married.'

Mrs Craig beamed. 'My dear, I couldn't be more delighted. I'm very fond of Peter – oh, dear me, I am just beginning to understand, not that there can be any excuse for that appalling exhibition, but jealousy is a dreadful disease. It makes even good people do something completely out of character. Poor, silly Betsy imagining that Peter was interested in her. Maud, another silly girl, was almost as much to blame, encouraging it the way she did. There was no spark, anyone could have seen that. Peter, kind lad that he is, was only acting as escort because of the family pressure.'

'You won't be too hard on Betsy, we all make mistakes.'

'Not of that magnitude, she made you out to be a thief.'

It had been horrible and she was still a bit shaken. 'Did you believe it of me?'

'Not for a single moment, but to remain quiet is to find out more and I was curious as to the reason behind it. For the moment let us forget it. I must see to an engagement party for you and Peter and try in some way to make up for all those wasted years.'

'I should be hard at it in the sewing-room, do you realise that?' Rachel said tongue in cheek.

'To think that my granddaughter – words fail me. This very night you will remove yourself to one of the guest rooms.'

'No hurry.'

'Oh, but there is. My poor Amelia loved pretty clothes and her daughter, I am sure, is the same.'

'My father saw that she got them,' Rachel said proudly, 'and she was very good with a needle.'

'Good with embroidery, I remember, and no doubt she had the talent to pick up dressmaking.' She was silent for a long time, just gazing ahead and Rachel was becoming alarmed.

'Grandmother—'

'It's all right, child, I was just coming to a decision. Go and see your father, my dear, make your peace with him and if it isn't too late for an old woman's apologies, he has them.'

'Peter said that too.'

'Then go together; that way it will be easier for you.'

'Yes, I feel I want to go. I've missed him.'

'No doubt he's missed you too and for all you know your stepmother as well. She, like you, has had time to think and realise that there were faults on both sides.

'You look tired,' Rachel said anxiously.

'I am rather but before I go and rest will you promise me something, my dear?'

'You know I will.'

'Forgive my selfishness but let me have you with me for a while before Peter takes you away. What I'm asking is a longish engagement if Peter will agree to that.'

Rachel laughed. 'Depends what you mean by longish.'

'Six months at the very least.'

'It'll probably take that to find a suitable house in Perth. Peter wants to live near his surgery.' Her grandmother's eyes were almost closing though she was trying hard to hide the fact. 'Let me help you to your room.'

After Rachel saw her grandmother settled, she went along to her own room. She had a desperate need to be alone and think back on all that had happened on this momentous day but as soon as she turned the knob she knew that someone was there. Betsy was sitting on the bed her eyes red and swollen.

'What are you doing here, Betsy? Haven't you done me enough harm?' she said harshly, hardening herself against Betsy's distress.

'I'm very ashamed, Rachel, and I don't expect you to forgive me but I want you to know that I'm very, very sorry, not only for the brooch.' She paused and said through her tears, 'I destroyed two letters, I knew they were from Peter I recognised his writing.' She couldn't bear to admit that she'd opened them. 'I was so jealous of you and thinking of you as a maid made it worse. I knew how fond Grandmother was of Peter and I wanted to please her and my mother,' she gestured hopelessly and bowed her head.

'Love isn't made to order, Betsy.'

'No, and if I'm honest, I wanted Peter but I'm not sure if I loved him. Oh, it's all such a horrible mess and Grandmother is going to hate me. She'll send me away, I know she will.'

'No, she won't. You'll get a severe scolding and you deserve it but it won't be more than that.'

She looked genuinely surprised as if just making a discovery. 'If I was to be sent away the person I would most miss would be Brian. Now, isn't that strange?'

'I don't find it in the least strange nor would anyone else.'

'I've always liked him but I looked on him as a brother, he sort of is, but without us being blood related. My stepfather, that awful toad, wanted a match between us so that he could get his hands on Duncairn House, but my mother surprised us all by giving him his walking ticket.' She dropped her eyes in confusion. 'That was another awful thing I did to you. The way his eyes followed you around I knew that he was interested and I gave him a hint that you might be—'

'Attracted to him. Yes, that fits in with what happened.'

'Was he very objectionable?'

'To me he was, but he got rather more than he expected. I gave him an almighty kick on the leg that almost crippled him.'

She was smiling. 'Good for you and I remember now that he was limping and sending me filthy looks.'

'Which again you deserved.'

'I know. I wish we could start again,' she said wistfully.

'Then why don't we? We are cousins and we can be friends.'

'I'd like that very much.'

'Right now, I'm going to throw you out. I need to be on my own to get used to all that has happened.'

She got off the bed. 'I'm just going.' She began to giggle.

'What is so funny?'

'Dinner tonight. I can't wait to see Janet's face when she sees you at the table.'

'You know, I hadn't given any thought to that though I rather think Mrs Anderson may have told her and Hetty. Wonder what I'll wear,' and in the moment she said it she knew that it just had to be the skirt and blouse from Miss Reid. The newness had long gone from both garments but they had kept their shape and somehow it was fitting that she should wear them on this very special evening.

'You'll need lots of new clothes and you must let me help you choose them. I really would love to do that.'

'And so you shall but – out—'

She gave Rachel a broad smile then went out.

Chapter Twenty-Seven

Rachel found she was shivering in spite of the warmth of the September day. 'Peter, I'm scared,' she said in a small voice.

'No, you aren't. Apprehensive perhaps but no more than that.'

Whatever it was her stomach was churning with nerves and with each mile bringing her nearer to Dundee it was getting worse.

Peter took his eyes off the road for a moment to give her a quick smile. 'Relax, my darling, your father will be relieved and happy to have his daughter back and that could well apply to your stepmother.'

'I don't think I could have done it on my own, Peter, I need you with me.'

'You need never do anything on your own again. Blast! Did you see that idiot overtaking on that hill? He could have involved more than himself in an accident.'

She hadn't, she had been too busy with her own thoughts. Peter had slowed down but now he increased his speed and with it being a Sunday traffic was light. Rachel had enjoyed two shopping sprees with Betsy who had gone out of her way to be as helpful as possible. The outfit she wore had been Betsy's choice and Peter's eyes had widened in appreciation. It was a pale blue button-through dress with a matching blazer-style jacket with embroidery on the pockets. The price had shocked Rachel but Betsy had dismissed it as nothing. She had been ordered by her grandmother to spare no expense and that Rachel was to get anything she wanted.

They were going through Inchture and Longforgan where the first touches of orange and brown were tinting the leaves but Rachel barely noticed, she was reliving the day when she had turned her back on Dundee for an uncertain future. Never in her wildest dreams had she imagined herself working as a maid in her grandmother's house. The thought made her smile.

'What brought the smile on?'

'Just thoughts. You know, Peter, no matter how many regrets I have at the manner of my leaving home, I can only feel glad that I did. You see, my darling, if I hadn't I wouldn't have met you.'

'Don't you believe it, it was written in the stars that we would meet, and pay attention, will you? You are supposed to be giving me directions.'

'Sorry! Sorry! Carry on for a bit yet but keep your speed down.' Very soon they were in the west end of Dundee and on to Blackness Road. 'Nearly there, Peter,' she said with a tremor in her voice. 'Blackford Street is the next on your left and twenty-three is about halfway along.'

Peter stopped just outside the close and Rachel got out and waited for him to lock the car door. She didn't look about her, she didn't want to be recognised.

Seeing her strained look, Peter gave her arm a reassuring squeeze then together they went up the stone stairs. The paintwork in the close and on the stairway was drab, some of it peeling, but the brass plate with the name G. M. DONALDSON had been polished.

Mutely she looked at Peter, she couldn't bring herself to knock, and it was he who gave a sharp rap on the door. When she heard the heavy footsteps Rachel unconsciously stepped back. The door opened.

In that split second when father and daughter looked at one another, her first thought was that he hadn't changed. It was much more likely that he would see a change in her.

'Da,' she said nervously.

He didn't utter a word, just held out his arms and she went into them. His woollen cardigan smelled faintly of the tobacco she remembered so well and she held her face into it fighting back the tears. They remained like that until Peggy's voice reached them.

'Geordie, who is it?' They heard her hurrying feet.

Peter was standing on the door mat and Rachel held out her hand to bring him in. He smiled at her and closed the door behind him. They were all together in the narrow lobby. Peggy's mouth fell open, then like Geordie she held out her arms. Never one to do things by halves she promptly burst into tears and it was Rachel who was comforting her.

'Sorry, lad, you're being ignored and we're making an exhibition of ourselves and what am I thinking of having you standing here in the lobby, come away into the kitchen.' He was nervous not pausing for breath and went on, 'Away and put the kettle on, Peggy.'

'Da, this is Peter, Peter McGregor, my fiancé. We – we're engaged to be married,' she said breathlessly.

'That it was something of the sort crossed my mind,' he smiled and held out his hand to Peter then shouted to Peggy hovering at the scullery door. 'Come and be introduced before you put that kettle on.'

'I'm happy to meet you, Mrs Donaldson,' Peter said with his ready smile.

'Me too – I mean I'm pleased to meet you,' she said flustered then looked at Rachel. 'You won't mind sitting in the kitchen, will you, the front room is cold without a fire?'

'As I well remember,' Rachel smiled. 'The kitchen was always homely and still is.' It was nerves of course but Rachel started to giggle and once started she couldn't stop.

'How about sharing the joke?' her da said and shaking his head at Peter.

'Just remembering something – you wouldn't see the joke but Peggy would.'

'Me! How would I see it?'

'That time when the old range came out and I arrived from school to find you covered from head to foot in grey dust.'

'Oh, I mind, and the mess, will I ever forget it! Yon,' she said looking at Peter, 'was the nearest we've been to a divorce.'

'You're right there and now, woman, that kettle won't boil in your hands.'

'Forgot what I was doing, I'm that excited.'

'I'll leave you two to chat and I'll give Peggy a hand.' Rachel went into the tiny scullery and it could have been yesterday she had been there, nothing had changed.

'There's only gingerbread, bought needless to say, and Abernethy biscuits,' she said apologetically. 'And it being Sunday—'

'Peggy, that will do very nicely.' She closed the door and her stepmother turned after bringing the cake tin down from the shelf. Keeping her voice down, Rachel said, 'I'm older now with a bit more sense and I'm sorry for what I did. Was Da very upset?'

'Nearly out of his mind and he wasn't the only one. Believe it or not I was in a state mysel'. You did wrong, no doubt about that, but I was a lot to blame.'

'Most of it was my fault. Looking back I suppose it was jealousy.'

'Daft when you think about it, it was jealousy that was the matter with me too.'

'We'll begin again. I'd like that if you would.'

'I'd like it fine,' she beamed. Her voice dropped. 'That's a fine lad. You've landed on your feet and he's doin' all right for himsel' too.'

Rachel shook her head. 'You're just the same old Peggy.'

'What does he do? I want to hear all about him.'

'I'll tell da and you together. Are you going to infuse that tea or am I?'

'You do it and I'll set the things on the tray.'

The tray was on the table, the tea poured and the cups handed round and when everyone had something to eat Rachel exchanged a smile with Peter.

'There's such a lot to tell you I scarcely know where to begin.'

'Is it to be a long or short engagement?'

'It all depends on how long it takes to get a suitable house, Mrs Donaldson.'

'Make that Peggy seein' as you'll soon be family. And if you don't mind me askin', what do you do?'

'Peter is a doctor,' Rachel said, not hiding the pride in her voice.

Peggy looked suitably impressed which she was.

'Where will you be living?' George asked.

'Perth and as near to the surgery as possible. It's more convenient that way and saves a lot of time in useless travel.'

'A bonny place, it's years since I was there,' Peggy said wistfully.

'It is very pleasant and once Rachel and I are settled in our home you both must come and spend a few days with us.'

'That would be grand, wouldn't it, Geordie?'

'Da,' Rachel swallowed, 'there's so much I have to tell you but first let me say how very sorry I am for all the worry I caused you.'

He nodded. 'I would have been more worried if I hadn't known where you were.' He paused. 'I guessed where you had gone and Mary confirmed it.'

They were all silent and Peggy reached over for the plate of gingerbread.

'Another piece of gingerbread, Peter?'

'Yes, please, I enjoyed it.' He took a piece and avoided Rachel's eye. She knew that gingerbread was not a favourite with him.

'It wasn't quite as you thought, Da. I worked in my grandmother's house as a maid.'

He almost dropped his cup. 'You what?'

'I fell for her first in her little frilly apron and white cap,' Peter teased. 'Sorry, darling, you go on with your story and believe me it is some story.'

Rachel did her best to relate all that had happened since she left Dundee.

'I became very fond of my grandmother, Da, and once she explained I could see how difficult it was for her. One day I'll tell you that part but there isn't the time just now.' She paused and looked at him pleadingly. 'She said that she hopes you will accept the apologies of an old woman and let bygones be bygones.

He didn't say anything, just nodded.

'Da, I didn't have the courage to come here myself, it was Peter and Grandmother who insisted that I did.'

'And a good job too,' Peggy said as she caught Rachel's left hand. 'Let me see your ring.'

Obediently Rachel showed off her ring with its three diamonds.

'Lovely, just lovely,' she breathed. 'I like the diamonds squint like that instead of straight across. Is it to be a big wedding?'

'Nothing has been arranged as yet, but I want, I mean I hope – Da, you will give me away, won't you?'

Peggy answered for him. 'Of course he will. He's your da, isn't he?'

'Da?'

'I take it it'll be in the Craigs' place, Duncairn House?'

'Yes, Grandmother would like it there and Peter's parents live nearby.'

'I don't know, lass, I'd feel like a fish out of water.'

'If I may say something, sir, that is complete nonsense. You and Peggy would be made most welcome. Indeed it would be a very great disappointment to us all if you weren't to be present.'

'Da, I don't just want you there, I need you.'

Peggy had disappeared and when she came back she had two gift boxes in her hand. 'You want them, Geordie?'

'No, you carry on.'

'Your da forgot your birthday once and he said it would never happen again. We knew you'd come back one day. Here,' she said putting them in Rachel's lap, 'open them and see if they are to your likin'.'

It took a supreme effort to hold back the tears as she undid the wrappings. In one box on cotton wool was a silver bracelet and in the other a fine silver chain.

'Oh, Da, I love them,' she said going over to hug him. 'I'll treasure them always.'

'Can't take all the credit,' he said gruffly, 'Peggy did the choosing.'

'Chose well, didn't I?' she said smugly.

'You did, Peggy.' Life was full of surprises, Rachel thought. A few years ago she would not have thought this possible.

She carefully closed the boxes. 'How is Mrs Rodgers? Do you ever see her?'

'Slowing down but otherwise just the same Mary,' her da said.

'That family of hers have taken a thought to themselves and not before time. She's havin' a wee holiday with the one that's gone to live in Tayport.'

'I want Peter to meet her, we'll have to arrange something.'

Her da nodded and turned to Peter. 'How well do you know Dundee?'

'The town centre, that's about all. At one time my father knew it quite well and was horrified to read that the Pillars was to be demolished.'

'Tell your father from me that I and many like me fought tooth and nail to save the Pillars.'

'Miss them dreadfully, Peter, I mean that was the meeting place; all Dundonians used it to shelter under and now there is just a big draughty square,' Peggy said as she collected the cups and saucers and put them on the tray.

'Tell you, Peter, lad, I despair. Progress is what they call it but to me it is criminal. In years to come the folk will have only anger for those responsible for destroying what should have been their heritage.'

'That's Geordie on his soap box.' Peggy winked at Rachel.

'Did I not read somewhere that Dundee received high praise for its building programme?'

'Oh, aye, that was said – see if I mind—' His voice was heavy with sarcasm. 'A paragon of civil excellence and a fine example to other municipalities.'

'Ah, come on, Geordie, be fair, yon corporation houses are a great improvement on the tenements, I wouldn't mind one mysel'.'

'Here we go,' George said but he was smiling, 'but before I get off the topic you two young ones mark my words. In twenty years, could even be less, it'll no' be the Dundee we know. Rumours are that there are plans to wipe out the Overgate and other places I cannae bear to mention.'

'Geordie, there are places in the Overgate not fit to live in, crawlin' with vermin and bairns brought up in that.'

'No reason to raze it to the ground, all it needs is a bit of cleaning up.'

Peter looked at his watch then at Rachel and she nodded.

'We'll have to tear ourselves away,' she said.

'You'll come back, though,' Peggy said anxiously, 'and let me know and I'll have a meal ready.'

'That is very kind of you, Peggy,' Peter smiled, 'but next time we come we'll take you out for a meal.'

Peggy beamed. What a lot she would have to tell her friends.

George lumbered to his feet. 'You've got the road now. How did you come?'

'Peter's car is at the end of the close.'

'Fine to have your own transport but then you being a doctor you need it.'

They all trooped down the stairs and George and Peggy, both in carpet slippers, saw them off and waved until the car was out of sight. A few people were about and Peggy smiled broadly to them making sure that they knew that the occupants of the car had been visiting them.

'Peter, you'll never know how worried I was and there was no need.'

'No need at all,' he said changing gear.

'You did like them?' she said anxiously.

'Very much. Your father is a fine man and a real character too and his happiness at having you back was a joy to see. Peggy is a character too and for the short time I was with them I would say that is a good marriage. They are well suited.'

'I would never have admitted this to myself before but I know what you say is true. It brings back too what my father once said to me. He told me that he loved my mother very much, would have done anything for her but that he was more comfortable with Peggy.'

'He could be himself.'

She smiled. 'With my mother he had to watch his ps and qs. Young as I was I do remember how particular she was, whereas Peggy—'

'Muddles along.'

'That's about it.'

Chapter Twenty-Eight

Owing to circumstances beyond their control the friends rarely saw each other but they corresponded regularly and it was the latest letter that had Agnes feeling depressed. Happiness leaped off the pages as Rachel brought her up to date with events. Her writing was small and neat yet there were pages and pages of it and as Agnes read through the letter she could understand why. Such an amazing tale of events were unfolding that she had to go back and back again to read them. Amidst it all Peter's name cropped up on almost every page. Agnes, she had written, I didn't think it possible to love like this. Peter is my whole world and the days when I don't see him, thankfully there aren't many, are grey and empty. To me it is nothing short of a miracle that he can love me in the same way.

'It was very obvious the girl was of good family, Agnes,' Gerald said infuriatingly, as she read out passages to him. Gertrude, when she heard, said something similar.

That night she wept into her pillow. She was neither fish nor fowl, didn't belong with anyone. Once out of sheer loneliness she had risked Gerald's wrath and gone in search of Beatrice and Madge but the get-together hadn't been a success. Each in their own way had tried but it was soon obvious that they had nothing now in common.

The bitterness welled up inside her as she faced the truth. What she most wanted was out of her reach. She wanted Gerald to love her, to want her as she wanted him but he had no such feeling for her.

As her mother would have said, she had made her bed and she must lie on it and it was true that she had gone into this sham marriage with her eyes wide open. Her dream had materialised, she had everything she had ever wanted, a lovely home, beautiful clothes, jewellery, her position as Gerald's wife and Gerald was a fascinating and intelligent man.

When had she first realised that she loved Gerald? It had happened slowly but the first stirrings of desire had become a longing in her that was becoming too strong and the strain was making her irritable and bad-tempered.

To fill in her day Agnes had begun to write down her children's stories and had quite a selection ready to be typed. A typist in Perth was prepared to do them and rather than post them Agnes decided to deliver them herself. It would also give her the chance to visit a bookseller's and take a note of the address of a suitable publisher.

'Gerald, I am not asking permission to go into Perth. I am telling you that I am taking the bus in.'

'What do you want in Perth?'

She could so easily tell him but she was blowed if she would. She didn't want to. 'Nothing in particular, just a look around.'

'Don't you have enough clothes?'

'I have more than enough of everything, Gerald, except –' she stopped.

'Go on, I'd like to hear the rest – except what?'

'Except freedom.'

'Do I keep you locked up?'

'Don't be ridiculous, of course not.'

'You are meeting someone, aren't you?' he said accusingly.

She stared at him. 'Who on earth would I be meeting?'

'You tell me.'

'There is no one, Gerald,' she said wearily, 'and if you want a detailed account of my intentions I am taking the bus into Perth town centre, having a look at the shop windows, having afternoon tea somewhere and getting the bus back.'

'Sounds like a waste of time and I don't like you using the bus.'

'As regards my driving lessons I'm either a slow learner or Bannerman is a poor instructor. My own opinion is that he isn't keen for me to learn in case I take over from him.'

'Nonsense, there's no danger of that. You'll get a small car for your own use and Bannerman will continue as before.'

'Then let him know that.'

'I may do just that and as there is nothing urgent about your visit to Perth wait until Gertrude is free to take you in.'

'No, my mind is made up, I'm going to get the bus.'

'Then go,' he said coldly.

She sat well forward in the bus taking her into Perth and now that her anger had cooled she was regretting all the fuss. She could have delayed it but on the other hand why should she?

The day was bright and sunny but there was a cold wind and Agnes was glad that she had decided to wear her camel jacket over a tweed skirt. In them she felt both comfortable and smart. Her first call was to the office where the typist seemed to know exactly what was needed and a date was arranged for the work to be collected. Browsing round the bookshop was pleasurable and she spent some time studying the children's section. In her notepad she copied down the addresses of a couple of publishers then left the shop. The rest of the afternoon was hers to do as she wished.

When she had no money, window shopping had been enjoyable but now that she could afford to buy what she wanted it ceased to interest her. She was just considering taking an earlier bus home when she heard someone call her name. She swung round and found herself face to face with Tommy Kingsley.

'What are you—' they both began then broke off and laughed.

'Hardly recognised you, Agnes, you look absolutely marvellous,' he said, admiration in his eyes. 'What are you doing in Perth?'

'Having a look around, nothing special. What about you?'

'Saw a good second-hand van advertised and thought I'd take a look at it.'

'Was it any good?'

'Just what I was looking for but didn't let them know that,' he winked and touched the side of his nose. 'No flies on yours truly.'

'Kidded on that you had others to look at and got the price down.'

'Same old Agnes, quick on the uptake. You got time for tea or something?'

'Yes.' It would put in a little time, she thought.

They began walking until they came to a tearoom advertising afternoon teas with home-made scones and pastries. 'This do?'

'Yes, fine.'

They were shown to a table and their order taken. While he spoke to the waitress she studied him. She didn't like his loud-checked suit but perhaps the old Agnes Boyd would have thought it smart. The tea came and she poured, handing him his cup.

'Ta.' She had put milk in but it wasn't enough and he lifted the milk jug and added so much that it slopped into the saucer but he didn't seem to notice.

She buttered a scone. 'Business thriving, is it?'

'Sure is. New houses going up our way and that means families and families need butcher meat. Coining it in, Agnes. You and me could have done all right.'

She smiled. 'Are you married, Tommy?'

'About to be but then I might change my mind.'

'Can't be all that keen on her then, can you?'

He shrugged. 'Had a few but come to think about it you were the only one I really fancied. You're married,' he said looking at her left hand.

'Yes.'

'Seem to remember you were aiming high. Got what you wanted, did you?'

'I'm happily married if that is what you mean,' she said coldly.

'You fancied me just as much as I fancied you.'

'You're letting your imagination run away with you.'

'I'm not and you know it. He paused. 'Easy for you to get into Perth is it?'

'It means a couple of buses but I get a run in occasionally .'

'With your husband?'

'No, my sister-in-law.' Then she couldn't resist showing off. 'Actually,' she said with studied carelessness, 'I'm learning to drive and then I'm getting my own car.'

'Good for you. Must be a catch though. All that money, is he old or crippled or something?'

He saw her face go pale.

'Touched on the truth, did I?' There was a hard look on his face. 'You and me were meant to be together, and why not? Shouldn't be difficult to arrange something, nobody would be any the wiser, I would see to that.'

He didn't know that she was too angry to answer and took her silence as encouraging. 'Life is too short, so why deny ourselves some pleasure?'

She got up. 'Thank you for the tea and as to the rest you are quite mistaken. I am very happily married and now I must get home. Goodbye, Tommy, and good luck.'

She almost ran from the tearoom. How could she ever have imagined herself in love with Tommy Kingsley? He was brash, ill-mannered and full of himself. Had he always been like that and was the change in herself? The change was in herself, it must be. She was Mrs Gerald Patterson. Gerald had moulded the new Agnes and it was the way she wanted to be. She glanced at her watch and hurried to catch her bus.

On the way home she had the strangest feeling that something was wrong. She tried to shrug it off but the uneasiness persisted and all she wanted was to reach Drumoaks. The local bus was just leaving but stopped for her. Getting off just short of the gate she all but ran the rest of the way and as she reached the drive she saw Gertrude on the steps and the uneasiness gave way to panic.

Gertrude made to speak but Agnes tore past her and into the house. Gerald, something had happened to Gerald. Oh, please God, don't let there be anything wrong, she prayed. She burst into the sitting-room and he was sitting in his chair. The relief was so great that she threw herself on him, her arms going round his neck. 'I thought something awful had happened to you.' She was shaking and he held her close to him. It was the first time she had been in his arms and held close and the feeling was of coming home at last, of feeling safe.

'My darling,' he loosened her hold but held on to both her hands, 'you must be brave, there is bad news. 'A car mounted the pavement and your brother-in-law Sam was killed outright and your sister is—'

'Meg, what about Meg?' she whispered.

'She's badly hurt—'

'Where is she? I must go.'

'The infirmary, D.R.I. Bannerman is ready to take you there and Gertrude got the maid to pack a case for you, overnight things.'

She nodded too choked to speak and looked dazed as he picked up a bundle of notes. 'Put that in your bag.'

'I have money in my bag.'

'Take it,' he said putting it in her hand, 'you don't know what you'll need.'

She had a sudden thought. 'How did you get the news?'

'From the police. Your parents gave them this address.' He broke off and she saw his despair. 'If only I could be of assistance, I feel so damned useless.'

Just then Gertrude came in with the case in her hand and gently took Agnes's arm. 'Bannerman is waiting in the car.'

'Thank you, you're all very kind,' she whispered.

'Agnes?' It was Gerald. 'Stay for as long as you are needed and Bannerman is at your service, he'll do whatever you require of him.'

Her lips quivered but she managed to give him a smile before going with Gertrude to the car. She got in the front seat and Gertrude put the case in the back.

Since her marriage Bannerman had been addressing her as m'am but that was forgotten. 'Try not to worry too much, Agnes,' he said, but even as he said it he recognised the uselessness of the words.

'Do you know how to get to Dundee Royal Infirmary?'

'Yes and I'll get you there as quickly as I can.'

It was in record time that they drove up the steep hill and in through the gates of the hospital.

'I'll let you out here and I'll find a parking place then wait for you just inside the entrance.'

'You don't need to, Bannerman, I can quite easily take my case and you can get back.'

'No, I'll wait and take whatever message there is to Mr Gerald.'

She looked about her not knowing where to go and when a nurse appeared she asked directions. A porter was nearby and offered his services.

'I'm going that way, I'll take the lady.'

Agnes smiled gratefully and hurried along with him. The smell of disinfectant was getting stronger as they went through a maze of corridors.

'This is it.'

She didn't need to be told. Two people sat on a bench in the passageway outside the ward. 'Thank you,' she said to the porter's departing figure.

'Got here at last then!' The woman raised her eyes to Agnes but the man didn't.

'I came as soon as I got the message, Ma.' She swallowed painfully. 'How is – how is Meg?'

Her mother's face was grey but she was very composed. 'She's not goin' to make it but she's been askin' for you.'

Hearing the voices a nurse came through the door. 'Excuse me,' there was the rustle of a starched uniform, 'are you the patient's sister?'

'Yes, she's Agnes,' her mother answered for her.

'If you would just come this way, please. She's very weak but keeps asking for you.'

Dear God, this isn't happening, not Meg. You can't take Meg. It took her a moment or two to realise that the figure in the bed surrounded by a curtain was her sister. Her head was heavily bandaged to the eyebrows and one hand lay outside on the cover. Agnes took it gently in hers. 'Meg, it's me, it's Agnes.'

Her eyes opened and her lips moved.

'Don't talk, don't tire yourself.'

'Must. Sam's gone – won't say – but I know—' The voice was a thin whisper but Agnes could feel the urgency. Her fingers clutched at Agnes. 'Ronnie – want you – take him. Not Ma, promise not Ma. Look after my baby—'

'Yes, Meg, don't worry, please don't worry.'

'No! No!' she was getting agitated. 'Promise, say it, promise.'

It was like when they were children, Agnes thought. Cross my heart and hope to die. And Meg was dying. She would have to promise and if it was a promise it would have to be kept.

'Agnes, please—'

'I promise to look after Ronnie—'

'Like he was yours.'

'As if he were my own child,' Agnes said and as she heard her own voice she wondered how that could be managed. Gerald would never – couldn't be expected – she thrust the thought aside and bent over to hear what were to be Meg's last words.

'Thank you from me and Sam.' There was the ghost of a smile, a long drawn-out sigh, and Agnes knew that her sister had gone to join her husband.

'Nurse!'

She came quickly, looked at the bed and silently drew Agnes away.

'She's gone?'

There was sympathy and understanding in the soft brown eyes. 'Yes.'

Mrs Boyd looked from one to the other. 'It's over.' It was a statement not a question. 'Mebbe she's better where she is.'

'Come into the office, I'll get a cup of tea brought to you and the doctor will be along directly.'

She saw them seated in the small office then left.

'Where's Da?'

'In the pub. No use lookin' like that,' she said harshly, 'he took it bad and he needs a drink. 'Greetin' like a bairn he was, she was his favourite.'

'Meg was everybody's favourite, Ma,' Agnes said unsteadily.

'Funny like how the good are always taken first.'

There were no tears but Agnes guessed her mother had gone beyond them. Tea was brought to them but neither of them touched it and after about ten minutes with the doctor they walked together along the corridor.

'Good thing wee Ronnie was with Sam's ma or we might have lost him too. Her havin' the shop she won't be able to look after the wee soul but I'll take Meg's bairn.'

'Meg made me promise that I'd take Ronnie.'

'That won't come to pass,' she said dismissively. 'I'm havin' him, he'll be best with me.'

'I won't break my promise to Meg, Ma.'

'You don't want him, he wouldn't fit in with your life.'

In the midst of her grief Agnes felt outraged. 'You have no right to say that.'

'I know you too well, lass. You'll always put yourself and your ambitions first and that fancy family you're married into won't want anything to do with Meg's bairn.'

Agnes swallowed the hurt knowing that some of it was true, but she felt a flash of anger. 'My husband, part of that fancy family as you call them, happens to pay your rent and a bit besides or would you rather forget that?'

'No, it's a help I grant you that, and to ease your conscience about the bairn you could pay towards his upkeep.'

'I'm taking Ronnie.' Agnes's defiant look was met with a small grim smile.

'Huh! Time will tell.'

They were in the main corridor and Agnes saw Bannerman in conversation with one of the porters. He was seated and had a cup of tea in his hand which he put down when he saw Agnes and got to his feet.

'Do you want a run home, Ma?'

'No, ta, I'll need to get hold of your da.'

'Do you know where he'll be?'

'I'll find him, if he's no' in the first pub he'll be in the second.' About to move away she stopped. 'Needin' a bed for the night are you?'

'No, I'll go and see Sam's mother in Barnhill.'

She nodded. 'To tell her about Meg, yes, you'd best do that.' She gave a strangled cry. 'Give the bairn a hug from me.'

The animosity between them was forgotten as Agnes put her arms round her mother. 'I'm not takin' it in, Agnes, I know it's happened but I'm not believin' it.'

'It's the same for me, Ma. I want to waken up and find it all a nightmare.'

'Makes you wonder if there is a God in heaven.' She paused and there was a pleading look on her face. 'The arrangements, Agnes – your da wouldn't know where to begin.'

'I'll see to everything, help Sam's mother as much as I can.'

'Mebbe I haven't been fair to you, you're no' a bad lass at heart.'

Agnes watched her mother walk away, her shoes were down-at-heel but then she and Agnes didn't have the same size of foot. Agnes occasionally sent off a parcel of her clothes, some seldom worn. She had such a lot, and she liked to think that the Boyd family were better turned out than they used to be. The herringbone coat looked well on her mother and on the whole Agnes thought that she was taking more interest in her appearance.

Once her mother had gone Bannerman came over. 'Are you all right, lass?'

'My sister is dead but thanks to you I saw her – saw her before the end.'

'Life can be cruel, lass, but it must have been His will. There is a reason for everything though I'll grant you it's not easy to understand.'

She hadn't known that Bannerman was a religious man and she wasn't sure that she agreed with what he said. Where was the sense of taking Meg and Sam and leaving a three-year-old orphan? She wanted a good cry but the tears refused to come. Her mind kept going back to Spinner's Lane and to the poverty and harshness they had endured and to their dreams of a better life. Both Meg and she had managed it but in her sister's case it had been for such a short time. A cruelly short time. Was it any wonder, she asked herself, that Meg had used her dying breath to try and secure a better life, a better future for her son? Agnes couldn't blame her but her head ached abominably as she tried to picture the scene when she arrived at the Laurels with a three-year-old boy.

Times like these brought out the best in people, Agnes thought.

Bannerman couldn't have been kinder as he settled her into the front passenger seat. He seemed to sense that she didn't want to talk and he remained quiet throughout the journey to Barnhill.

Agnes closed her eyes and imagined herself talking to Meg.

'Meg, you and Sam up there have nothing to worry about. I gave you my word that I'd look after Ronnie and you know me well enough to know I'll keep that promise. It won't be easy but whatever the cost to me and my marriage Ronnie stays with me.'

'Agnes, I'll need directions now,' Bannerman said apologetically as they approached Barnhill.

'Yes, of course,' she said looking about her. 'Straight on to the garage at the corner then left and it's the shop at the far end.'

The car drew up outside the shop door and in the window was a handwritten notice stating that owing to a family bereavement the shop would be closed until further notice. Agnes read it and mentally adjusted it to double bereavement. The house door was separate from the shop and Agnes knocked. It was opened almost immediately by Sam's mother. They had only met once briefly since the marriage and after Agnes left Kerne House but Mrs Robson knew her immediately. Mutely she beckoned for her to come in but Agnes had turned to Bannerman who was behind her with her case.

'Mrs Robson, would it be convenient for me to stay the night with you?'

'I'll be glad of your company, lass, and if the gentleman would like a cup of tea he's very welcome.' There were black smudges under her eyes and a weariness about her but the smile was warm.

'That's kind of you but I'll have to get back.'

'You'll tell my husband—' she hesitated and they were both aware as they looked at each other that Mrs Robson didn't know of the death of her daughter-in-law.

'I'll do that.'

She nodded, aware that she was nearer breaking down now than she had been in the infirmary. 'Tell – tell my husband that I'll phone him when – when I have news for him.'

Bannerman got back into the driving seat and Agnes went inside with Mrs Robson. It was a small comfortably shabby room with a brightly burning fire that made Agnes realise that she was cold. The day had been coolish but the evenings could be chilly with autumn giving way to winter and the first early frost appearing. She shivered.

'Take that chair and get yourself a heat. I'll make a cup of tea.'

The tears that wouldn't come before came now in painful racking sobs and Agnes found herself held against a warm soft body.

'Meg – she's dead.'

'I know, lass, I knew as soon as I saw your face.' They clung together, their tears mingling and the comfort she hadn't been able to get from her own mother she got from Sam's.

The harsh sobs had ceased and Agnes was crying quietly now. 'Where is Ronnie?' she managed to ask.

'Through the wall and sound to the world. Poor bairn to be robbed of both parents in the space of a day.' Her eyes filled and she turned away.

Agnes had taken off her camel jacket and put out her hands to the heat. The door to the scullery was open and Mrs Robson busied herself making tea then cutting bread to make a few sandwiches with meat paste. With one hand she pulled out a small table and set it before the fire then put down the plate of sandwiches. She finished setting the table then sat down.

'Come on now, lass, you must eat something.'

'I couldn't.'

'You'll eat to please me and I'll try and get something down me too.'

Agnes lifted a sandwich and began eating it surprised that she could then she remembered that she'd had nothing since that scone in the tearoom with Tommy Kingsley. It seemed like another life.

'I was with Meg when she died,' then added unsteadily, 'she wanted me to have Ronnie, Mrs Robson, made me promise that I would bring him up.'

'That would have pleased Sam too, he had a great admiration for you, Agnes, and it would be better for the bairn to be with young people.' She stopped and looked at Agnes thoughtfully. 'A promise is difficult to break and not something you would do lightly I know, but if it is to cause trouble in your own marriage then I'll take the bairn. He'll be fine with me, I'm no stranger to him and we get on well.'

'You have the shop.'

'It won't be easy but where there is a will there is a way.'

'No, Mrs Robson,' Agnes said quietly but firmly, 'Ronnie is my responsibility and I couldn't live with myself if I broke my promise to Meg.'

She nodded. 'I'll miss him,' she said simply.

'I know that but I'll write and let you know how he is getting on and once I feel he has settled I'll bring him to see you.'

'You're a good lass, just like your sister was.'

'She was happy with Sam I know that.'

'They hadn't long but they were happy the pair of them and doted on their bairn. Maybe fate had a hand in it because by rights he would have been with them but I was baking when they came in and by his way of it he wanted to help me.'

'My mother wanted Ronnie,' Agnes said abruptly, 'but Meg didn't want her to have him.'

'Meg was right,' she said carefully, 'with a handicapped daughter your mother has enough to do.'

The fire was down, almost out, but the room was warm. Agnes yawned and she had difficulty keeping her eyes open.

'Time we were both in bed, Agnes. It's just a fold-down bed I have in the front room but I think you'll be comfortable enough.'

'Thank you, I'm sure I shall.'

'Do you want a peep at Ronnie?'

'Better not in case it disturbs him.'

'I doubt that but you'll see him in the morning.'

It was a well-attended funeral. The double tragedy had left everybody stunned and all wanted to pay their respects. Close relatives returned to the house where helpful neighbours had tea and sandwiches ready. Ronnie was with other neighbours who kept him until evening. Agnes undressed the sleeping boy, put on his pyjamas and tucked him into his small bed which had been brought down from his own house.

From a call box Agnes made two phone calls, one to tell Gerald the funeral arrangements and the other once it was all over. Gerald's concern and sympathy flowed across the line and almost she blurted out that she would be bringing Meg's little son but she held back.

'Everyone here is concerned about you, dearest, and I'm missing you very much.'

'Thank you,' she whispered.

'Bannerman will come for you and bring you home.'

Bring her home! It had a lovely sound. Until a short time ago the Laurels had been a beautiful house in which she was fortunate to live but now it was truly home. All she wanted was to be there with Gerald.

Ronnie was a sturdy little boy with light brown curly hair and big baby blue eyes wet with tears.

'Don't want to go.'

'A wee holiday with your Auntie Agnes, of course you do.'

Agnes, usually at ease with children, was too upset and worried as to the kind of reception they would get at the Laurels. Her nephew's clothes and toys were packed in two cases and put beside Agnes's own case.

'Grannie come too?'

'And who would look after the shop, tell me that, my wee man?'

His lips quivered. 'I want my mummy and daddy.'

'That's the car, Agnes,' Mrs Robson said as she moved the curtain the better to see.

'Come on, Ronnie, and see the car.' She took his hand. He turned round.

'Kiss,' he said to his grandmother.

She kissed him and held him close to her. Agnes could see how much the parting was costing her but she was smiling bravely.

'You'll be a good boy?'

He nodded and then they were on the pavement.

'This is Ronnie, Bannerman,' Agnes said, 'he's coming to the Laurels with us.'

'Hello, Ronnie, would you like to sit in the driver's seat before we go?'

The tears about to begin were forgotten in the excitement of sitting in the front and pretending to drive. Agnes smiled her appreciation to Bannerman. She was amazed at just how good he was with the child answering his questions at length and taking them seriously.

'The lad has an enquiring mind, m'am.'

'So I'm discovering.'

Just before they reached the Laurels Ronnie's eyes flickered then closed. His breathing was regular, his head resting in the crook of Agnes's arm as the car stopped beside the house.

'Leave him on the seat, I'll carry him in once I get the cases inside.'

'Thank you.'

Gently extricating herself and leaving the sleeping child comfortable, Agnes went indoors. Gerald was in his usual chair and had heard the car stopping. As she entered he held out his arms and she went into them feeling that she had truly come home. For those precious moments she had forgotten about Ronnie, then just as she was bracing herself to tell him Bannerman came in with the sleeping child in his arms.

Quickly Agnes moved away from Gerald.

'On the sofa, please, Bannerman, he'll be all right there,' she said as she arranged a cushion for the child's head.

'The cases, m'am?'

'Put them in my room and thank you for – for everything.'

'Glad to be of service.' He left and closed the door.

She swallowed nervously. 'Meg's little boy.'

'Poor little mite, we must all try and keep him amused and happy for the time he is to be here.'

For the time he was to be at the Laurels – Agnes breathed a little easier – it was a reprieve saving her saying anything for the time being. She put her jacket on the back of the chair and sat on the sofa beside Ronnie.

Gerald, the practical, was arranging things. 'A small bed will have to be brought down from Drumoaks but Brenda can see to all that. You look exhausted, my dear,' he said with concern in his voice. 'It must have been a dreadful ordeal.'

'It was, Gerald, I wouldn't like to live through that again.'

'A little brandy might help, Agnes.'

'No, I'm all right, really I am, and Ronnie had better sleep with me for a few nights. He knows that something is wrong and I'm going to be the one who has to tell him and I don't know how I am going to do it.'

'How old is—?' He nodded to the sleeping form.

'Ronnie is three and a half and I had better get him upstairs.'

'He's too heavy for you.'

'No, he isn't. You forget, Gerald, that I had to carry my little sisters and brothers around.'

He ignored the shake of her head and rang for attention. Brenda came running. 'You wanted me, m'am?' she said when she saw Agnes. Her eyes widened when she saw the child.

'Get my bed prepared and open up the cases. You'll find pyjamas on the top, I think.' She picked up the child who whimpered then settled again, smiled to Gerald and went through the door which Brenda had opened.

'He's lovely, m'am,' Brenda said as between them they undressed the child and got him into his pyjamas. 'If you want I'll keep an eye on him, I like kiddies,' she added shyly.

'You stay with him until I come up. I'm going to have an early night.'

'If you'll pardon me saying so, m'am, you look done in.'

'That's the way I feel.'

'You're too tired to talk, my dear. What you need is a good night's unbroken sleep and drink this, I insist you do.' Gerald had poured a little brandy in a glass and obediently she drank some and made a face.

'Get it over, the taste isn't as bad as all that,' he smiled.

Wakening up in the big strange bed, Ronnie looked about him with frightened eyes and his screams for his mummy and daddy could be heard through the house. Brenda was in tears as she came into the bedroom and it was a battle to get him washed and his clothes on but at last Agnes's soothing words reassured him. She would have her breakfast in the kitchen with him, Agnes decided, as she dragged an unwilling boy with her.

Brenda had gone ahead to warm Mrs Yuill, the cook-housekeeper, of their arrival and she was ready with a welcoming smile.

'Hello, little love, what would you like for breakfast?'

He scowled and went behind Agnes.

'Brenda, did you see a little boy a minute ago?'

'Yes, but I don't see him now.' She made a great show of looking all over the kitchen and was rewarded by a laughing little face peeping out.

They were both so good with him and it was a huge relief to Agnes who was becoming more worried by the minute. They stayed in the kitchen until Gerald had some time with his morning papers, then with Ronnie's hand in hers they went through to the sitting-room. Gerald was sitting in his chair with his crutches by his side.

'Good morning, Ronnie,' he smiled.

'Say good morning to – to – Uncle Gerald.'

He mumbled something after a little persuasion but his eyes were on the crutches.

'Come over beside me, Ronnie.'

Agnes was surprised when he obeyed but it was the crutches that he was interested in.

'What are those for?'

'To help me walk.'

'I can walk and I can run fast.'

'I'm sure you can.'

'Why can't you walk?'

'Because I had an accident and hurt my legs.'

For a while he looked at Gerald's legs then went down on his knees.

Agnes's heart was in her mouth. Gerald, she knew, couldn't bear anyone to touch his legs. Should she say something or would it make matters worse? She waited and watched. The little arms went round one leg and he placed his cheek against it.

'Poor leg, all better soon.' He did the same with the other leg then got to his feet.

'Thank you, Ronnie, it's a nice thought.'

'What's that?' he said pointing to the wheelchair in the corner.

'That is my special chair to get me to places.'

'It's got wheels.' Something must have reminded him of his parents and his lips quivered. 'When is Mummy and Daddy coming for me?'

Agnes looked at Gerald helplessly and his arm brought Ronnie closer.

'Ronnie, I know that you are a clever boy and a brave one too.'

The little head nodded in full agreement.

'Do you know about heaven, Ronnie?'

'Mummy told me, it's where the angels live.'

'That's right and that is where your mummy and daddy are.'

His little arm shot up. 'Way, way up in the sky?'

'Yes.'

He looked uncertain. 'How will they get down?'

It wasn't a question he had been anticipating and as their eyes met she saw the pity in his.

'Your mummy and daddy are happy with the angels and they want you to be happy too. Shall I whisper something, it's a secret and not even Aunt Agnes knows?'

'Tell me! Tell me!'

'I know a place where there are lots of toys.'

'Where?'

'Not far away but Aunt Agnes will take you.'

'She doesn't know, it's a secret.'

Gerald laughed. 'Good for you! Agnes, this is a bright little fellow.'

Agnes smiled, happy that things were going so well. 'Uncle Gerald will have to tell me, won't he?'

'Drumoaks. There's plenty in the attics and some of Mark's toys must be up there too.'

'One for you, Agnes,' Gerald said picking a letter out of the bundle. They were sitting together in the breakfast room. After four weeks Ronnie was settling in well, only at night was he tearful and those times were getting less frequent. Brenda considered herself nursery maid and another girl had been taken on to help with the kitchen work. All in all life at the Laurels was cheerful with childish laughter ringing out.

Rachel and she corresponded regularly and she expected it to be a letter from her friend but the typed address showed that it wasn't. Trying not to raise her hopes but with growing excitement, nevertheless, she tore it open then closed her eyes postponing the moment when she would know its contents.

She wasn't aware that Gerald had raised his eyes and was watching her.

The writing blurred then cleared, the colour rushed to her cheeks and her eyes were sparkling.

'My! My! You must have got good news.'

'Read it,' she said giving it to him then watching his expression as he read it.

He was beaming. 'Many, many congratulations, my dear, this is perfectly splendid. We now have a budding authoress within the family.'

'In a very small way,' she said shyness overcoming her. It was a new and welcome experience this feeling that she had done something worthwhile.

'I heard about the stories you told Mark and Mary but—'

'It was Olive who suggested I try and get them published,' she interrupted. 'That day I wanted to go to Perth – would she ever forget that day – 'it was to take them to be typed.'

'Why did you keep it from me?' he sounded hurt.

'I didn't expect them to be any good and if they weren't I didn't want anyone to know.'

'The publisher obviously likes them and wants more. Children's stories are in great demand, Agnes, and who knows your name may be well-known one day.'

She smiled at that. 'Do you know what I am really, really pleased about?'

'Not until you tell me.'

'Well, I'm the cuckoo in the nest, no don't deny it, I am.'

'I deny it most strongly and I am going to tell you something, my girl, so put that ridiculous idea out of your head. When you were away do you want to know what Adrian said?'

'If you think I can stand it.'

'He said I miss that wife of yours about the place, she sort of grows on you.'

'He said that? You're not making it up?'

'Why on earth should I do that? You belong, Agnes, and now I feel I have to ask this. How long is Ronnie to be here? I only ask because we are all becoming very attached to him and the child seems very contented. The longer it goes on the more difficult the separation.'

'Would you miss him, Gerald?'

'The child has come to mean a great deal to me and yes to your question, I would miss him very much.'

She went over to kneel by his chair. 'I should have told you before but I couldn't, I was so afraid.' She swallowed. 'Before Meg died she made me promise to look after Ronnie. She was dying, Gerald, I had to give her my promise.'

'Of course you did,' he said his fingers going through her hair. 'Tell me though what you would have done if I hadn't wanted the child, refused to have him?'

'I didn't know what I was going to do, only that I wouldn't break my promise to Meg.'

'I would have expected no less from you but now I can put your mind at rest. Ronnie will be ours and that means legally. He shall have my name,' he said smiling, 'added on to his own.'

'Ronald Robson Patterson. Sounds all right. Thank you, Gerald, you are very good to me.'

'I think we are good for each other and I've asked Bannerman to remove himself to Drumoaks and just to come here when he is required.'

She blushed. 'That means—'

'That means we will be sharing a room if you are still agreeable.'

'Perfectly agreeable,' she said demurely.

'Oh, God! that woman is never away.'

'Language, darling, remember there is a child in the house.'

Agnes knew to whom he was referring but went to the window just the same. Gertrude gave her a wave.

'Where is my little friend?' she said coming in without ceremony.

'You'll see him in a few minutes, meantime we have news for you, in fact you are the first to know,' Gerald said.

She raised her well-shaped eyebrows. 'Come on then, has Agnes had more of her stories accepted?'

'Better than that,' Agnes laughed, 'but as a matter of fact I have and Gerald is to get me a typewriter so that I can learn to type.'

'We are adopting Ronnie, Gertrude, and I want everything legalised as quickly as possible.'

Gertrude sat down heavily. 'I can't tell you how pleased I am, that little rascal is a heart-stealer. This has been a happier house since he came.'

'I couldn't agree more,' her brother said, 'and my temper has improved which must be a great relief to everyone.'

No one disputed that.

'Have to see about getting him his own pony although Mary raises no objections to sharing Brownie.'

'Thought that would be your first priority.'

'The younger the better and he's keen which is more than the other two were at that age. Excuse me, you two, and I'll go and find him.'

'Ronnie?'

'What?'

'Aunt Agnes is going to be your mama and I am going to be your papa. Papa and Mama are much easier to say, aren't they?'

He was giving the matter some thought then smiled brightly. 'Auntie Ger – trude Mama too?'

'Heaven forbid.'

'Gerald!' Then she began to giggle. 'Come here, rascal, and I'll explain.'

He ran to her. 'Auntie Gertrude is still Auntie Gertrude but I am going to be your mama and—'

He turned a beaming face to Gerald. 'You my papa. Mama, Papa, that's funny.'

'It isn't funny, that's what I called my mummy and daddy when I was little.'

Mummy and daddy had disturbed his memory but the tears didn't come. Agnes had kept her word and Sam's mother received an occasional letter which judging by her replies were greatly appreciated. In a month or two she would take him to see his paternal grandmother but it would be much later before she took him to see her own family in Dundee. She felt no guilt. It happened in some families that they got on better apart. Their rent continued to be paid and a few pounds sent periodically but not once had there been a letter of thanks.

As Christmas approached the weather deteriorated and a thin coating of snow lay around the Laurels but inside was warmth and laughter. An excited Ronnie was helping or more truthfully hindering Bannerman as he began decorating the drawing-room with holly from the gardens and tinsel and decorations from the attics at Drumoaks. Agnes, helped by Brenda, was busy with the Christmas tree and Agnes was anxious that everything should be right. It was Gerald's suggestion that the family Christmas lunch should be at the Laurels and the kitchen was busy with the preparations. Mark and Mary were frequent visitors to the Laurels and very often took their little cousin back with them to Drumoaks. Sometimes Agnes was afraid that such happiness couldn't last and confessed her fears to Gerald.

'None of us knows what life holds for us, Agnes, but we must just enjoy each day as it comes. Once my spirits were so low that I didn't know how I would get through the long endless days, then you came along and suddenly life became precious and each day valued.'

'You taught me how destructive envy could be and now I envy no one, I have all that I could ever want. A loving husband, a darling son and a supportive family.'

'Five pages of news from Rachel,' Agnes laughed as she waved the sheets towards Gerald.

'She must have a lot to tell you.'

'She has. They've managed to get a house near Peter's surgery, a big old-fashioned house that needs a lot done to it, and the wedding is arranged for July. Are you listening?'

'Of course I am, I'm reading and listening at the same time.'

'That's impossible.'

'No, it isn't, my brain accepts the important facts and ignores the trivia.'

'I'll tell Rachel what you said.'

'You wouldn't be so mean.'

He laughed and put aside the paper. 'You now have my undivided attention.'

'Glad to hear it,' she said with mock severity. 'The wedding is to be at the village church and the reception at Duncairn House.'

'The old lady, Mrs Craig, making a splash of it, is she?'

'Obviously, Rachel doesn't say that but I imagine there will be a fair number there. Our invitation will come in due course but she would like Ronnie to be a pageboy.'

Gerald looked horrified. 'My son is not wearing a velvet suit.'

'Who said anything about a velvet suit?'

'Well, isn't that the usual attire?'

'I wouldn't know, but Peter and his best man are to be in Highland dress.'

'Wearing the kilt, now that's different! Ronnie is a sturdy wee lad, he'll suit the kilt. You can see to that, Agnes, get him measured for one, the full outfit and it has to be the Stewart tartan.'

'Why the Stewart?'

'My mother belonged to the clan Stewart and Adrian and I always wore their tartan.' A look of sadness crossed his face. 'Believe it or not, I used to have the legs for the kilt though I say it myself.'

'I know, dear,' Agnes said gently. 'Gertrude showed me some family albums and snapshots and if you promise not to let it go to your head, I thought you were by far the most handsome.'

He grinned. 'Limited competition in our family but enough of that. You, my dearest, must get something extra special for this wedding. I want everyone to see what a sweet, charming and beautiful wife I have.'

'You'll have me blushing. I've been called lots of things and sweet, charming and beautiful weren't included.'

There was to be no battle, Gerald was to attend the wedding and hopefully it was the gradual return to a social life after the painful years of hiding himself away.

Chapter Twenty-Nine

The village church was packed and well-wishers crowded round the gate, all anxious to get a good look at the bride. Tall and regal with a froth of white net over her satin gown Rachel looked breathtakingly beautiful and felt unbelievably calm. Not so her father, she could feel him shaking and she gave his arm a reassuring squeeze as they entered the porch. There they were met by the bridesmaid looking pretty as a picture in pale apricot. Little Ronnie Patterson, cute in his Stewart tartan kilt and green jacket, looked on solemnly as Betsy dealt with the bride's train.

The joining together of the popular young doctor and Mrs Craig's newly-found granddaughter was an occasion few were prepared to miss.

It was over. They were man and wife. In the grounds of Duncairn House and in the hot July sun everyone was happy to be outdoors and strolling around, chatting and admiring the gardens before going in to drink to the young couple's happiness and enjoy the magnificence of the meal that awaited them.

On the church steps the photographer had taken pictures of the bridal party then a family group. Peter's parents had taken charge of Peggy until George was free to do so and now Peggy stood with her husband looking flushed and proud. For this very special occasion she wore a shocking pink suit with matching wide-brimmed hat decorated with a large feather pointing like an arrow.

Tired of being arranged this way and that Ronnie was glad to be released from his duties and made a beeline to where his papa and mama were. Gerald was in his wheelchair with his crutches leaning against it and he greeted his son with a broad smile.

'Papa, I had my photo tooked and tooked and tooked,' he said excitedly as he jumped up and down.

'Taken,' Gerald corrected him as Agnes went into helpless laughter. She wore her favourite colour, lime green. The silk dress was plain but beautifully cut and made her look taller as well as showing her nicely rounded figure to advantage.

Rachel's eyes roved the grounds for Agnes and Gerald. 'There they are, Peter. I don't want to upset Gerald but I would so like a photograph of them.'

'He'll oblige, I'm sure, the way he looks at his wife he'll want to please her.'

'They are in love,' she said softly, 'just like us.'

'Impossible. No one could be as much in love as we are,' he said smugly.

As she looked at her husband Rachel's eyes were like stars. 'No one,' she agreed.

Agnes was openly admiring. 'Rachel, you make a beautiful bride, everyone is raving about you.'

'May I add my piece,' Gerald said in his clear diction, 'and say that I agree with every word my wife says.'

'Thank you,' Rachel blushed, lowered her eyes then raised them. 'Peter and I would love to have a photograph of you both for our wedding album.'

'Me too,' Ronnie said outraged at being left out.

'No show without Punch,' his papa laughed.

Agnes looked at him her expression showing that it was entirely up to Gerald.

'Not in this contraption,' he said firmly as the photographer took a step forward. 'I'll take my crutches, Agnes, if you please.'

Once he was ready, Agnes stood beside her husband with Ronnie in front and as the camera clicked they were smiling happily. It was a photograph that was to take pride of place at the Laurels.

While Peter and Gerald were talking, Rachel and Agnes had a few minutes together.

'Do you ever think back to our schooldays, Rachel?'

'Strangely enough just this morning I thought of that day in the playground when we became friends. Such a lot has happened to us and the best of all was falling in love.'

'Especially that,' Agnes agreed and her eyes went to Gerald who at that moment looked over and smiled to her.

Peter was moving away. 'Time we were going in, darling, your grandmother is trying to attract our attention.'

'A royal command, Peter,' Rachel said mischievously as they took their leave of Agnes and Gerald.

Mrs Craig looked well in her coffee-coloured lace dress and beside her was a gentleman. She took her granddaughter's hand. 'Rachel, my dear, this gentleman will introduce himself. He would like a word with you, and you, Peter, can look after me.'

He didn't move, just looked into her face. 'So you are Amelia's daughter,' he said softly. He had a nice smile, his hair was thick and pure white which probably made him look older than he was, Rachel thought.

'You knew my mother?'

'Very well. Indeed had your father not come on the scene we would most likely have been married.'

'Oh, dear, were you very heartbroken?' It was difficult to know what to say.

'Upset and worried like everyone else but not brokenhearted. You see, my dear, Amelia and I were childhood sweethearts and both families expected us to marry.' He smiled. 'When your father came on the scene Amelia fell in love just as I did with the lady who is now my wife.'

'Thank you for telling me, Mr—?'

'Charles Adamson. Your grandmother thought I should tell you.'

'I'm so glad you did.'

'I mustn't keep you any longer as I'm sure your husband is impatient to have you back with him.'

'What was all that about?' Peter asked as the guests began to move towards the house.

'Tell you later,' she whispered as they followed the old lady into Duncairn House to begin the celebrations.

Life stretched before them full of hope and promise and with so much love how could they go wrong?